MRS A'S [illegible] GENTLEMEN

DAWOOD ALI McCALLUM

For Muriel
Wishing you a very happy Birthday!
Dawood Ali McCallum
Sept 2020

hachette
INDIA

First published in 2019 by Hachette India
(Registered name: Hachette Book Publishing India Pvt. Ltd)
An Hachette UK company
www.hachetteindia.com

1

ISBN 978-93-88322-89-8

Hachette Book Publishing India Pvt. Ltd
4th & 5th Floors, Corporate Centre
Plot No. 94, Sector 44, Gurugram – 122003, India

Typeset in Dante MT Std 11/13.9
by Manmohan Kumar, Delhi

Printed and bound in India
by Manipal Technologies Limited, Manipal

Dedicated
to the town of Swindon,
a place that welcomes, embraces, adopts, adapts and survives.
To my mother, Kathleen McCallum,
a Swindonian in the time this story is set,
who reflects these values in great abundance.
And to Prita Maitra,
without whom
not one word of this story would have been told.

EXHIBIT

MEMORANDUM

From: Editor, *Gaumont British News*
To: Censorship Division, Ministry of Information
Date: 22 August 1943

FOR APPROVAL

Music: 'The Yanks are Coming'
Images: American troops lining the side of arriving ship, waving and smiling. Tanks, etc. being unloaded. ENSURE NO INSIGNIA OR SIGNS ENABLE THE ENEMY TO IDENTIFY UNITS, VESSEL OR DISEMBARKATION POINT

Voice-over: Yes, they're coming all right, and plenty more to follow!

CUT to Images: Empire and Dominion troops disembarking. SEE ABOVE

Voice-over: From the wide prairies and big open spaces of the West they come, and from the exotic East too! (Music: Elgar – *Pomp and Circumstance*) India send her troops to ~~join in~~ the build-up as preparations for the attack on Fortress Europe continue apace. REPLACE 'JOIN IN' WITH 'SUPPORT'

Images: Indian civilians, looking around them. Serious faces.

Voice-over: And it's not just soldiers and airmen. Say hello to the Boffins! Scientists, engineers, technicians, the brightest and the best they have to offer are coming to ~~Britain's aid~~. REPLACE WITH 'SERVE THEIR KING EMPEROR'

Image: Cheering dock workers waving caps. Handshakes. Thumbs up. ~~Arms around shoulders~~. Smiles. ??

Voice-over: And they can be sure of a warm welcome in ~~dear old Blighty!~~ REPLACE WITH 'THE MOTHER COUNTRY'

APPROVED FOR DISTRIBUTION, SUBJECT TO THE ABOVE.

RS, MoI 23/8/43

'Mr Rosario? Mr Ray?'

As the newsreel camera was being packed away, two figures walked cautiously down the gangway from the ship. The voice that had called their names had barely been raised above the conversational yet it cut through the fuss and bustle of disembarkation as effectively as a bellow. Well-modulated, overweeningly confident. It was a voice that they had both heard a thousand times back home in India. The pretence of exaggerated indifference. The voice of assured authority. The voice with a yawn in it.

The speaker matched the voice. Tall, thin and with a long face capable of only three expressions: faintly amused, vaguely disappointed or studiously bored. 'Ah, there you are. Not the "First of the Few", more the "Last of the Lot". The name's Dawlish,' he drawled, raising his hat but not offering his hand. 'India Office. You two are presumably well acquainted after weeks at sea, what? No? Gosh, you surprise me. Well, Mr Rosario, of the Bombay, Baroda and Central India Railway. Mr Ray, of the Presidency College, Calcutta. Welcome to England.'

'It's doctor, in actuality,' said the smaller and younger of the two new arrivals, looking down and removing his spectacles to clean them on his handkerchief. 'Dr Ray.'

'Really?' said Dawlish, raising a doubtful eyebrow. 'Well done, you. Now, there's things that need to be done before we can send you on your way. Customs. Immigration. Tedious stuff, but there we are. Landing chits all properly filled out? Good. No one's got any contraband I suppose? No? Oh, well. That's a shame! Ha! Right, let me have your papers. Dump your bags and hang on here a tick while I see if I can pull a few strings and get you through the Services channel. I've got railway warrants for each of you – afraid both are for "Mr"s, Dr Ray, but never mind…'

As Dawlish strode off the two men studied each other. Rosario, the older and taller of the two, looked warily at his companion: so young, earnest and seemingly brimming with confidence. The younger man reached out a hand. 'Akaash,' he said with a smile. After a brief pause, the two tentatively shook hands. 'Rosario,' said the older man with the briefest of nods. 'You didn't want to be part of that circus either?'

'The filming? No.'

'Nor me.' They looked at one another. 'A doctor?' Rosario asked doubtfully.

'Of philosophy. Mathematics, really. But it's a PhD. Thus, a Doctor of Philosophy,' the young Bengali replied.

'I know what a PhD is,' Rosario assured him. 'It means you're not a proper doctor.'

Akaash Ray bristled. 'I suppose that depends how you define proper. For a mathematician, proper has a whole range of meanings. There are proper subsets for example, but I assume you neither knew nor meant that. Then there's proper fractions… Maybe you're using the term "proper" to mean real or genuine? In which case, I have to correct you. I am a proper doctor. I even have a very beautiful piece of parchment to affirm the fact. If you narrow the term to its colloquial use to describe a medical practitioner, then no, I'm not, in your limited and inaccurate terms, a proper type of that doctor.' He looked around. 'It's certainly not Bombay, is it?'

'No,' agreed Vincent Rosario, irritably. 'It certainly isn't.'

Their journey had been a steady progression from technicolour to monochrome. There had been times in the North Atlantic when it had been impossible to tell where grey sea became grey sky. Now, a transition arrival at Southampton on a dull autumn morning completed, drizzle hung like damp gauze in the air and the sea, oil-slicked and torpid, heaved itself against the harbour wall with a greasy slap and a tired sigh.

The two men glanced out across the harbour as the destroyer which had shadowed them from Gibraltar sounded three cheery klaxon blasts and hauled off for Portsmouth. There was both fond farewell and self-congratulation in the rising cadence: another convoy escorted home without loss. They returned their gaze to the buildings and activity around them, the cranes and warehouses, the hoses and ropes criss-crossing the puddled dock, the barrels and tea chests stacked and shrouded in stained tarpaulin. The damp morning air reeked of oil, salt, paint and fish and echoed to hammering, the whump of sacks in net slings dropping onto awaiting trucks, shouted instructions, an alerting curse and the crash of wood against stone. Overhead, like white slashes against the grey, gulls screaming like souls in torment jinked, swooped and dived around bovine barrage balloons slowly turning on their mooring cables to each shift of the freshening morning breeze.

'So, what do you do?' Akaash asked.

'I'm a railwayman,' said Vincent Rosario. 'A proper one. And I don't need a piece of paper to prove it.'

Akaash looked the older man up and down. 'Well, you wouldn't, would you?' he sneered.

There was an uncomfortable silence, broken only when another disembarking passenger approached. Taller than both Akaash and Vincent, the new arrival was bearded and expensively dressed. His hands were thrust into the pockets of a tweed overcoat and he wore a paisley patterned silk scarf and brown trilby hat. 'Did I hear someone say railwayman?'

Vincent and Akaash turned to the beaming man. They had both seen him from the ship – he had been one of the first to disembark, and was only too happy to pose, posture and perform for the camera. In fact, his generosity with cigarettes and general bonhomie led to a late script change and the (Ministry of Information approved) addition of the line, 'Although this cheery chappie seems to be making himself pretty much at home already!'

'Khan, Gwalior State Railway,' he boomed. 'Don't suppose you've seen a fellow called Lockyer around anywhere?' His voice was deep, enriched by an expensive education. 'Bugger was meant to be meeting me.'

Dawlish returned with permission to clear them through the Services channel. He studied the third man with a lazy eyebrow raised. 'And this is?'

The Gwalior man introduced himself once more. Dawlish frowned, his attention seemingly fully engaged for the first time. 'Not one of the Gwalior Mansoor Khans by any chance?'

The tall man chuckled and thrust out his hand. 'Younger son of a younger son, so a mere rude mechanical, but that's me. I'm impressed.'

'Breeding will out,' the Englishman purred. 'Dawlish. Roddie. I was in Ujjain. '36 to '38.'

'A pleasure, Roddie. Surprised we didn't bump into each other. Call me Billy. Everyone does. Don't suppose you can help a chap out here at all? The Maharajah's man Lockyer was meant to meet me but…'

'I'll do what I can. Where are you headed?'

'Swindon. On loan to the Great Western Railway, no less.'

'As are these fellows. I tell you, lack of coordination will be the death of us! I suppose HH forgot to mention your coming to the Res?'

'Don't think so. The Residency was immensely helpful…'

'Excuse me,' said Vincent. 'Our papers?'

'Yes, yes,' sighed Dawlish peevishly. 'Here you are.'

Vincent took the papers impatiently thrust towards him and glanced through them. Dawlish looked at him askance. 'They're all there, I assure you.'

'I check everything,' Vincent replied, scrutinising the stamps and signatures.

'Good for you. Once you've satisfied yourself, take your bags over to the customs shed and join the line nearest to the dockside. No *saaman*, Billy?'

Billy Khan jerked his head back, indicating a porter standing a respectful distance away with four suitcases and a hat box stacked on a sack truck.

'Want me to sneak you through the Services channel too?'

'Decent of you, old man, but no need. I think someone's clearing me as we speak. Just need to sort out onward transport.'

'There'll be someone at the station who can handle that for you.'

Billy smiled as they watched Akaash and Vincent drag their bags towards customs. 'Interesting pair,' he observed. Taking out a gold cigarette case, he flicked it open and offered a cigarette to Dawlish.

'Turkish?'

'Balkan. There's an Armenian in Bombay who can still get them. Lord knows how.'

'Best not to ask.'

'Absolutely.'

They lit their cigarettes, drew on them contemplatively and exhaled. 'That really is fine tobacco. You must give me his details. So, the Anglo,' mused Dawlish. 'What do you reckon? Semi or Demi?'

Billy Khan sniffed. 'Oh, at a guess, I'd say Demi. Yes, definitely Demi. You?'

Dawlish nodded. 'You have to feel for them. Neither fish nor fowl. Salt of the earth, most of them. Couldn't run the railways without them, that's for sure. And their women can be very fetching. Blue gums, you know? If only they weren't so bloody…'

'Absolutely. Say no more.'

'And the Bengali? Dr, supposedly, Ray?'

'Brahmin would be my bet. Mind you, they all say they are. What are they here for?'

'No idea, old chap. Here to help the war effort, apparently.'

Billy Khan frowned. 'The best we breed, and all that? Things must be bad.'

Dawlish raised a significant eyebrow. 'Keep an eye on them for me, would you? Especially the Bengali. I need to get back to town.'

'Am I my brother's keeper, as I think you fellows ask?'

'Are they your brothers, as I think you fellows say? Just try to make sure they don't actually make things even worse, there's a good chap. We'll speak again.'

2

'I tell you it is just not physically possible to get that number of trains across that number of points in that amount of time. It simply can't be done,' insisted the Head of Movements. Teeth gritted and face contorted with anger, he flung the sheet of statistics contemptuously on to the table.

'And I'm telling you for the umpteenth time it is,' the Chief Mechanical Engineer chairing the meeting replied, exasperation exaggerating his rich, west country accent of extended vowels and over-emphasised consonants.

These meetings and this tetchy exchange were a depressingly frequent occurrence in the board room of the mighty Swindon Works. This morning the mood was particularly sour. Ten pale and ageing men in baggy suits sat on either side of a long table, at the head of which sat Hartshorne, the Chief Mechanical Engineer and senior company man. His secretary, Miss Jennings – the only woman in the room – was at his side to take the minutes. Most of the men were smoking cigarettes. Those that weren't sucked on pipes, mostly unlit. A hazy fug hung over the table on which well-filled ashtrays smouldered like bomb craters. All the windows, criss-crossed with brown tape, remained firmly closed.

'With respect, Chief,' snapped back the Head of Movements, his tone anything but respectful, 'I'm speaking from over twenty years of experience of not building engines but managing train movement. Something of which, again with respect, great engineer though we all know you are, you have no experience. And I say again, it can't be done.'

'By you.'

'By anyone. It simply isn't possible.'

'Care to put a bet on that? Because we're going to put that refrain of yours to the test. Tomorrow morning I'll be introducing you to a Mr Vincent Rosario from the Bombay, Baroda and Central India Railway.'

There was a groan. Hands thrown up in disgust. Shaken heads and a murmur of dissent. 'And he's supposed to be able to do what?' the Head of Movements asked with a sneer.

'The impossible, according to you,' said Hartshorne airily. 'As Movements Manager at Victoria Terminus in Bombay, this chap gets more trains in, unloaded, reloaded and out over a complex web of junctions quicker and safer than anyone else, anywhere else in the empire. As far as we know, faster than anyone else anywhere in the world. I'm told he's got a particular flair for shifting personnel and materiel from harbours and docks,' he added, with a raised eyebrow and a significant look unfortunately lost on the Head of Movements, who was fully absorbed in sighing and staring at the ceiling.

Hartshorne took out a pair of half-moon spectacles, unfolded them and carefully curled the temple tips around his ears. He held out his hand to his secretary, who passed him a thin folder. In the voice he usually reserved for reading the lesson at Christchurch on Sunday morning, Hartshorne read out from the folder the statistics on the throughput and turnaround times of BBCI trains during morning and evening rush hours.

The tonnage of goods unloaded in Bombay docks. The mean and median number of hours for their post-customs clearance transportation. He put the folder down and looked around. 'Do I need to remind you of our current performance figures? I thought not. This man Rosario is here to help us achieve something like what he seems to have been able to do in Bombay. We all know tens of thousands of American troops are arriving at OUR docks in South Wales every week, being transported on OUR passenger trains to holding camps in OUR region. Yet more ships are offloading hundreds of thousands of tons of their equipment and munitions that OUR freight trains need to move. And when the invasion happens, perhaps a million men – Americans, Canadians and our own lads – and all the materiel a great army requires will need to be shifted in an impossibly short amount of time to ports, docks and harbours all over OUR region. All while we continue to run a full passenger and freight service whilst being bombed by enemy aircraft. What we are going to have to do is far beyond anything we or any other railway company has ever done before. And every single day this man manages to achieve far nearer to what we need to than any of you have ever done. So I'm bringing him here to show you how to do the impossible.'

There was an unhappy silence. Then a bald, short man sitting towards the bottom of the table said, 'Bombay's one thing. The GWR network is quite another.'

'He has the same engines, same rolling stock, same points and crossings, same signalling equipment, same permanent way,' recited Hartshorne, counting the similarities off on the fingers of his left hand. 'He also has more extreme weather, more difficult terrain, far higher passenger numbers and much tighter frequencies.'

'But he knows nothing of how we do things here! There's a combined knowledge around this table of well over two centuries. He's come from the other side of the world and he thinks he's going to get to tell us how to do our jobs? Jobs we've done all our lives?'

'From the other side of the world…just like the Americans, who, at this very moment, are unloading their own engines at Cardiff Docks and threatening to run them over our tracks if we can't do better. Would you prefer to see that happen?'

'The government would never allow that!'

'Care for another bet on that?'

There was a mumbling around the table as several conversations sparked up about special circumstances, unique challenges, sacrosanct practices. The importance of maintaining standards. There being a proper way of doing things. Miss Jennings looked up from her note-taking but no one seemed inclined to speak on the record.

'But he's an…an Indian!' a grey-haired pipe smoker with a strong Welsh accent spluttered above the muttering. 'A native!'

'Anglo-Indian, apparently, Mr Dadge,' Hartshorne corrected him. 'From several generations of railwaymen, just like your good self.'

'Well, I'm sorry but I think that distinction will be lost on the men. We're meant to be telling his lot what to do, not the other way around! My lads will never take orders from a coloured man. Or a half-caste. No self-respecting Englishman would.'

'A Welshman might,' murmured the Head of Movements under his breath, prompting a couple of smirks from those nearest him and a baleful glare from Dadge. 'No offence, Taffy. Just kidding,'

'They won't need to,' said Hartshorne, not hearing, or choosing not to hear, the exchange. 'He isn't here to give orders. He's here to study, learn, suggest and advise. He's to have free run of the place – except obviously the out-of-bounds parts handed over to the War Office – and full access to all files, registers and stats. On his arrival, Mr Rosario will be appointed GWR Chief Traffic Control Advisor. And he'll make suggestions and he'll give you advice. And you will be very well advised to accept and act on both. Because if anyone chooses not to do so I will want to know why immediately.'

'Do we have any choice at all about this? Is there really no alternative?'

'I thought you'd ask that, so I checked. And, yes, the Ministry of War Transport does have an alternative.'

'Which is?'

'To bring in the Movements Team from the London, Midland and Scottish Railway to replace the lot of you.'

Cries of disgust greeted this announcement.

'Jesus Christ! Better a wog than the bloody LMS!' declared Dadge. 'Sorry, Miss Jennings,' he mumbled contritely as Hartshorne's secretary treated him to an icy stare. 'Forgive my blasphemy. Forgot there was a lady present.'

Hartshorne leaned over and rested his hand lightly on Miss Jennings' arm. 'I think we'll minute that last comment as "the meeting looks forward to Mr Rosario's arrival and wishes him well in his new role".'

'Hopefully there's no more of these "advisors" on their way?' asked the Head of Movements.

Hartshorne smiled. 'One or two more. But they will have nothing to do with you, so you just make sure this Mr Rosario gets everything he needs and let me worry about the others. Any other business? Thought not. Tomorrow, then.'

The disgruntled Movements men stood to a scraping of chairs on the wooden floor. Hartshorne took off his spectacles and folded them away. 'What's next, Miss Jennings?'

'Elsie Coggins, Mr Hartshorne.'

'Again?' He sighed and rubbed his eyes with the heels of his palms. 'Is she represented this time?'

Miss Jennings nodded. 'By young Cynthia. Although her father said he'll come over if you'd prefer.'

'No, I'm sure young Cynthia will do fine. There's no need to call Abbot all the way over from the Carriage and Wagon side. There's only one way this will end… I don't suppose we could have a cup of our special tea before they arrive?' he asked tentatively.

Miss Jennings frowned. 'They'll already be in your office. And it is only 9 a.m.'

'You're a hard woman, Miss Jennings.'

'Hard but fair, Mr Hartshorne,' she said with a tight smile as she gathered up the files that lay on the table in front of them both. 'Just like you.'

At the dockside railway station in Southampton, sappers, miners and engineers from across northern India rubbed uncomfortable shoulders with retiring colonial administrators returning with broken health. Resentful widows grumbled to cashed-in box-wallahs. The offspring of the Heaven-born, destined for good boarding schools, were honing their arrogance on the hungover squaddies and matelots heading inland on leave. Three women in capes led a crocodile of small children, paired up, neatly labelled and holding hands, through the crowd. Tired people, flushed and troubled people and many who looked, just like their surroundings, worn out and somewhat ground down.

Akaash looked around at the stonework station. Even the posters were grey: he saw one with a monochrome image of a booted foot driving a spade into soil, proclaiming 'Dig for Victory', and another with a head-and-shoulders photograph of the prime minister in a hat and coat, chin thrust out resolutely against a background of a flight of Hurricane fighters and advancing tanks with the words 'Let us go forward together' in Times New Roman typeface superimposed. He was struck again that so few of those entering the station with him appeared at all interested or even aware of others around them. They seemed unwilling to engage with anyone or anything but themselves and their immediate requirements. How placid, anaemic, damp and really rather small everything appeared. He paused, feeling homesick and suddenly somewhat intimidated by what might await them. He glanced across at Vincent and wondered if he was feeling the same thing.

'You gonna stand there all bleedin' day?' asked a grizzled porter struggling with Billy Khan's luggage. Of Billy himself and Dawlish there had been no sign since they'd left the customs shed. Akaash looked around, surprised to find there were several other people behind the porter who had also come to a sullen and resentful halt, waiting silently for him to move on.

'Sorry,' he mumbled and moved forward, wondering why they didn't just squeeze on past him if they were in such a hurry.

'I should think so,' grumbled the porter. 'These people haven't spent weeks dodging U-boats and dive-bombers to gawp at a bleeding railway station, mate, even if you have.' He looked around for support and approval but met only blank stares. 'Acts like he's never seen one before. Arsehole,' he added, under his breath.

A man in his fifties with a salt-and-pepper walrus moustache and thick white eyebrows under a black bowler hat approached them. He carried a battered attaché case and had a newspaper tucked under his arm. Akaash had spotted him earlier, striding up and down the lines of arriving passengers, stopping hopefully beside every vaguely foreign-looking individual.

'Destination Swindon?' he asked, as he raised his hat politely. On confirmation he sighed with relief and shook hands vigorously with both of them. 'Now, there's meant to be three of you? Khan, Rosario and Ray?'

'I'm Rosario,' said Vincent. 'Khan's luggage is on the sack-truck behind us and this is… Ray.'

'Excellent! I'm Mr Keenan, Deployment Supervisor, Great Western Railway. We'll just wait for Mr Khan and then we can be on our way…'

Billy Khan arrived a couple of minutes later, smiling and waving a ticket. Dawlish was nowhere around. They followed Keenan in silence onto the platform, beside which stood a black 4-6-0 engine at the head of a train of a half-dozen brown carriages out of the steamed-up and grubby windows of which pale, tired faces gazed. Behind the carriages stretched a long assortment of freight wagons, each proclaiming their owner's name and business in faded lettering. Vincent wandered along the platform, jotting down notes in a small book he took out of his jacket pocket until Keenan frowned and shook his head. 'Wouldn't be seen doing that if I were you. People might think you're one of them fifth columnists.' Vincent had no idea what that meant; some sort of undesirable trainspotter, he assumed. He looked around and indeed several people were watching him with evident suspicion. With a shrug, he put his notebook away. Billy had headed off in the opposite direction, towards the engine. He was staring at it intently. 'King Class,' he muttered, almost to himself, as the others caught up with him.

Keenan nodded, smiling proudly. 'No. 6021… *King Richard II.*'

'Not a very lucky king, if I recall my schoolboy Shakespeare. Swindon-built?'

'Naturally.' Keenan looked along the platform, frowning at the motley collection of carriages and wagons. 'Not seeing any of this at its best, I'm afraid. Those carriages are crying out for a refit and a lick of paint. This beauty should be in gleaming GWR company colours, not wartime black. Looks long overdue for a full Shop A strip down and rebuild too. But that's what Make Do and Mend is all about, I suppose…'

Billy frowned. 'Those driving wheels? Standard size?'

'Well spotted!' said Keenan, clearly impressed. 'Two and a half inches smaller on the diameter. Allows a bigger boiler in this loading gauge and thus greater tractive power, although I've never been convinced personally. But then, what do I know? We'd better get on board…'

'Was any of that even English?' Akaash whispered to Vincent as they climbed into the first of the carriages and eased their way along the corridor in search of an unoccupied compartment.

'If you're a railwayman, yes,' Vincent assured him with a superior smile, although he too hadn't followed much of the conversation. The guard blew a sharp double blast on his whistle and raised the green flag he'd had tucked under his arm. Doors slammed along the length of the train, the engine sounded two throaty blasts and the first great whump of steam announced their imminent departure.

They found an empty compartment, once plush but now with threadbare seats that reeked of stale cigarette smoke and damp upholstery.

'This is first class?' said Vincent uncertainly.

'I've got GWR rail warrants for all of us,' Keenan told him, misunderstanding his disappointment for concern about their right to occupy the compartment. He flung his attaché case up onto the luggage rack and slumped into a seat by the window with a contented sigh. 'We'll have to up sticks if any paying first-class ticket holders get on. Otherwise, it's all ours.'

Billy offered his ticket to Keenan. 'That's me! I'm a paying first-class ticket holder. Just bought it.'

Keenan sighed. 'You want us to move?'

'Good Lord, no! I was just saying…'

'Shouldn't have wasted your money, Mr Khan. Still, never mind. At least no one will be kicking you out. Right. All tickety boo?' With that, he spread his newspaper out carefully on the seat opposite him. He then put his feet up on the paper, tilted his bowler hat forward over his eyes, crossed his arms and promptly went to sleep.

Three silent women sat in the Chief Mechanical Engineer's office awaiting the conclusion of his acrimonious meeting with Movements. The oldest, Mrs Deakes, was a frequent visitor. She was in her early fifties, the widow of a GWR draughtsman who had been a contemporary of Hartshorne and had perished at The Somme. Her grey hair was pulled back in a tight bun; her face – with just a hint of powder – stern. She sat upright, knees together, hands resting on a Manila file on her lap, staring straight ahead. She wore a white blouse, black skirt and sensible shoes. Charged with special responsibility for the sudden influx of large numbers of female employees, Mrs Deakes was – sometimes several times a day – calling on the Chief Mechanical Engineer to raise issues of welfare, suggest adjustments to procedures and in general to promote the efficient use and best interests of this new and, to Hartshorne, wearisome group of workers. Hartshorne regarded their meetings with wary gratitude. A confirmed bachelor, he found women in general, and those in his Works in particular, a source of constant mystification. The memory of Mrs Deakes's euphemism-rich attempt to explain to him the labour deployment implications of menstrual cycles would remain with them both for a long time to come. In Hartshorne's world, machines were central, men necessary (although he dreamed of a day when that might not be true) and women, with the sole exception of Miss Jennings, creatures to be avoided if at all possible. In the present circumstances, they were a temporary intrusion into his empire – to be tolerated, managed and, as soon as possible, politely dispensed with.

And in any list of all the women in the world he would most wish to be rid of, Elsie Coggins would feature above all others.

Elsie sat now in the middle, like a prisoner escorted to court: Mrs Deakes on her left and her Union representative on her right. Elsie had wounded truculence down to a 'T'. Although unspeaking, she couldn't resist offering up the occasional, hard-done-by sigh, a resigned shake of the head or a disgruntled tut. She sat with her arms folded, her face a picture of resentful victimhood. Like her Union representative, she wore the steel-capped boots, overalls and headscarf of the women employed in the Sheds and Shops of the Works. She was secretive about her age, and looking at her it was hard to tell if she was in early middle age but had led a tough life or a much older woman, well-preserved. There was certainly a knowing world-weariness about her; she appeared as both an angry victim and a belligerent fighter. Indeed, it was that final trait that had once again led to this appearance before the Chief Mechanical Engineer.

On Elsie's right sat Cynthia Abbot. In her early twenties, Cyn Abbot was not only granddaughter, daughter, niece, cousin and sister of Swindon GWR men but also the newest, youngest and only female Shop Steward in the Works. She was no more fond of Elsie Coggins than was Mrs Deakes, but knew her responsibility as a National Union of Railwaymen official to a member in trouble as well as her duty to her class. She was also keenly aware that she too was on trial today at this, her first Disciplinary. Her dad, a convenor on the Carriage and Wagon side, had quietly suggested he handle this for her and when she'd refused, had offered to come along just to give her moral support. She'd declined, telling him that the Engines side looked after its own. She's been rather proud of that. Secretly, so had he. Later, dewy-eyed over a second pint of Arkells 3X, he'd shared the tale, boasting of his little girl as a true trade unionist and a proper socialist.

Elsie, sensing that the thoughts of the other two women were wandering and that she might not be the centre of everyone's attention, took out a grubby handkerchief, loudly blew her nose and needlessly dabbed at the corners of her eyes. Mrs Deakes sighed and glanced at the ceiling. Cyn leaned over and patted Elsie's knee encouragingly. Elsie reached out and took Cyn's hand. Chin trembling, she nodded bravely, took a shuddering breath and gave a resolute smile.

There was nothing wrong with the heating in the carriage – except any ability to regulate it. The temperature in the compartment steadily rose as the three new arrivals and the dozing Keenan left the soot-stained and war-damaged warehouses and long rows of red-brick terraced houses of Southampton. Condensation formed on the window, obscuring the view of the countryside through which they passed. The warmth and the rhythm of the train worked on Akaash Ray and Billy Khan, and before long the former was nodding off and the latter snoring deeply. Vincent Rosario stepped out into the corridor, careful to close the sliding door quietly behind him so as not to disturb his dozing fellow passengers. He lit a cigarette, took out his notebook, checked his watch and noted down the time, duration and his best guess at the cause for the delay every time the train jolted to a stop on the journey up through halts and country stations to Newbury and on to Didcot. The excitement he had felt when arriving at Southampton returned as the double time of the train's wheels over the tracks signalled that they had crossed the points on to the London-to-Bristol main line. He returned to the compartment to find Keenan awake and full of apologies.

'Must have dozed off. Early start! Anyone peckish?'

He stood, retrieved his attaché case and took out two square packages wrapped in brown paper that had clearly been used several times before. He opened them both and offered around the limp white-bread sandwiches within. 'These look like cheese. Processed. Those are paste. Fish, I think. Probably not what you're used to at home, but they'll fill a gap.'

They helped themselves. Keenan said there should have been a tea trolley in first class 'But well, that's the war for you. Still, not to worry,' he added, through a mouthful of cheese sandwich. 'We should be in Swindon before too long and we can get a cuppa there.'

'We're all going to Swindon?' asked Akaash.

'That's what I was told,' said Keenan.

Akaash frowned. 'I'd assumed I was heading for Oxford or Cambridge. I was told I'd be joining a world-leading institution in need of my special skills.'

'You will be,' Billy assured him, as Vincent rolled his eyes and reached for another sandwich. 'God's Wonderful Railway! And Swindon is the biggest railway workshop in the world, isn't that right, Mr Keenan?'

'The biggest and the best, Mr Khan!' Keenan said with a proud nod. 'Over 300 acres. 14,000 workers. Huge. It's a world leader, all right.'

'You work there?' asked Akaash, clearly unconvinced.

'Man and boy! I was apprenticed Inside – that's what we call it, the Swindon Works, 'Inside' – before I was called up for the last lot. Got my job back after the armistice but couldn't cope in the Foundry and the Machine Shops any more. Not after the trenches. Sounded too much like the whiz-bangs. So now I'm what you'd probably call an office-wallah! Collar and tie. Bowler hat. Proper gent!'

'Do you know what we'll be doing?'

'No idea.'

'I don't think we should be talking about it, anyway,' said Vincent. 'I was told it was strictly confidential. Only to be revealed when we arrive.'

'Me too,' mumbled Billy, through a mouthful of sandwich. 'I was just told we'll all return heroes!' He looked sceptically at the flaccid remains in his hand. 'You said this was cheese? Odd…'

'What about our living arrangements?' Vincent asked, shaking his head at the offer of the last paste sandwich. 'Accommodation?'

'Oh, that I do know about! You'll all be billeted together. We thought it would help you not to feel too homesick,' Keenan assured him, with a patronising, understanding nod.

Akaash and Billy shared a silent look and a slight smile. It was clear that was precisely what the reserved Anglo-Indian hadn't wanted to hear.

'Is it true all the jobs in the Works are now done by women?' Billy asked to break the strained silence.

'Well, not all. Management and specialist trades are of course still all done by men. Skilled railway work is supposed to be a reserved profession but thousands volunteered, and all the unskilled lads fit to fight have been called up. So all their places have been taken by women, and a few old codgers like me! Some of the machine operators are girls, too. Several thousand of them at the last count, so they say.'

Billy sighed happily. 'The greatest railway workshop in the world and full of thousands of beautiful women! I think I've died and gone to heaven.'

Keenan chuckled. 'I don't promise they're all beautiful. And most of them have husbands, boyfriends and fiancés fighting overseas, so they're spoken for. I can see we're going to have to keep our eye on you, Mr Khan! Bad as the bloody Yanks, pardon my French! I thought Mr Rosario here would be the ladies' man.'

Vincent bristled. 'What's that supposed to mean?'

Keenan put up his hands. 'No offence! I just meant a natty dresser like you. Good-looking chap… ah, Uffington White Horse,' he said, pointing out of the window to the low rolling hills in the distance. 'You can't see it now. Turfed over. Too much like a signpost for the Luftwaffe. But it's still there, as it has been for thousands of years – prehistoric shapes cut out of the chalky Downland. This is an ancient land, full of history and mystery. And in a few more minutes, Swindon Junction and that cup of tea!'

Miss Jennings entered the Chief Mechanical Engineer's office with a steaming cup of tea, which she placed on the blotter of his desk. She wished the formidable Mrs Deakes a good morning, ignored Elsie and treated Cyn to an encouraging wink and mouthed 'Good luck'. A minute later Hartshorne arrived and the three women stood up. He greeted them in much the same way as his secretary had and they all sat down.

As Mrs Deakes recited Elsie's latest offence – initial refusal to obey an instruction properly given, subsequent swearing, hair pulling and a bite to a restraining hand – Elsie buried her face in her handkerchief and wailed her muffled regrets. Hartshorne wondered how many of these hearings he'd sat through. He was a justice of the peace and chair of the local magistrates for the past three years, for goodness' sake! On the bench he'd listened to countless tales of brutality, greed, lust and wanton viciousness. He'd considered the just repercussions for all the trivial, petty meanness and blind stupidity of everyday life in a factory town after one drink too many or one thought too few, and never once doubted his judgement. Why then did he find these female squabbles so difficult to deal with?

Mrs Deakes summarised Elsie's employment record and dismal history of previous breaches of discipline: recurrent tardiness, disrespectful language, an unproven allegation of petty pilfering and, just the previous month, a similar tussle which had resulted in a docking of pay and a final warning. Dismissal, she concluded, was now the only and inevitable outcome.

'Anything you'd like to say, young Cynth…Miss Abbot?' Hartshorne asked, ignoring the sobbing Elsie.

Cynthia Abbot stood up. 'Thank you, Mr Hartshorne. Just two things. Elsie Coggins was one of the first to volunteer to come Inside when the men went. She's applied herself assiduously,' she continued, using the word her dad had advised her to get in as early as possible, 'and is a skilled rivet hotter and is well on her way to becoming a full riveter. She loves her work and even those foremen and supervisors who have criticised her behaviour on occasions have all said how good she is at her job.'

'When she can be bothered to turn up, keep her mouth shut and her hands to herself,' Mrs Deakes couldn't resist adding, earning her a cool look from Hartshorne.

'Elsie understands she has been very silly and promises not to ever do this again...'

'Like the last time,' Mrs Deakes muttered.

'And she'd like to volunteer to join the women working for the Indian gentleman everyone says is arriving soon.'

Hartshorne's eyebrows shot up and he stared at Mrs Deakes, who shrugged and shook her head. Was it totally impossible ever to keep anything secret in this place for more than five minutes, he wondered?

'And if you agree,' continued Cyn, 'Elsie says she is sure she can bring at least another eight workers with her. Maybe ten.'

Hartshorne frowned and took a sip of his tea. That would certainly solve a problem which so far had seemed intractable. But he would be sorry to miss the opportunity to see the back of this ghastly woman...

Seeing that he was about to go into one of the long, silent contemplations for which he was renowned, Mrs Deakes interjected, 'And your second point, Miss Abbot?'

Cyn took a folded slip of paper from her breast pocket. 'Thank you, Mrs Deakes. This is a medical slip from Dr Falk at the Medical Fund Hospital. She diagnoses Elsie as being...' Cyn stared at the note, looked confused and passed it across to Mrs Deakes with an apology.

Cyn couldn't quite hide the glimmer of triumph in her eyes as Mrs Deakes glanced at the paper then glared up at her.

'Well?' asked Hartshorne.

Mrs Deakes fumed. 'Oh, very well! Dr Falk diagnoses Elsie Coggins as displaying behaviour consistent with being perimenopausal.'

'It means her womb…' began Cyn.

'Aargh!' cried Hartshorne, putting his hands over his ears. 'Very well. One last chance, in view of the medical evidence, but only if, only if mark you, she can find twelve willing volunteers to join the… well, whatever.'

'And perhaps,' added Mrs Deakes with a sweet smile and a basilisk stare, 'Miss Abbot should go with them to keep an eye on things.'

'Excellent idea,' said Hartshorne before Cyn could protest. 'Right. Off you go. And er, Coggins. Um. Pull yourself together.'

Cyn paused next to Miss Jennings's desk in Hartshorne's outer office as the other two trooped out – Mrs Deakes striding off down the corridor in a foul mood and Elsie, without a word to Cyn, heading back to Shop A with a swagger to flaunt yet another victory over the system.

'Did you play the "ladies problems" card?' whispered Miss Jennings without looking up from her typing.

'I did! I even pretended I couldn't read "perimenopausal" and got Mrs Deakes to do it for me. You should have seen her face!'

'Serves the old bat right!'

'I've got to go with Elsie to work with the Indian gentleman though,' Cyn added.

Miss Jennings looked up at her. 'How do you feel about that?'

'Don't know really,' Cyn admitted. 'To be honest, I'm a bit bored with Shop L. It'll be a change, I s'pose.'

'But working for…' Miss Jennings let the thought just hang in the air.

'As long as they're decent railwaymen and good workers, they're no different from us,' Cyn declared. 'And should be treated that way. At least, that's what our dad says.'

'Sounds like you've done well today. Your dad will be pleased.'

'Thanks to you, Auntie Pat. I owe you.'

'Poor old Mr H! I'll make him one of his special cups of tea now. He must be in need of it. Tell your mum I send my love.'

In the front bedroom of No. 23 Ashton St, a two-up, two-down mid-terraced Victorian house in the shadow of the Railway Works, Sally Atkinson smoothed out a slight bump in the eiderdown on the double bed. Satisfied, she straightened up and looked around. She opened the window to give the room a final airing. Then, taking a soft yellow cloth from the pocket of her floral housecoat she quickly ran it over the bedside table, washstand and four-drawer cabinet, although she'd dusted the room thoroughly just an hour earlier. She checked the matching towel and flannel were folded neatly at the foot of the bed and was about to carry out a similar final check on the back bedroom when she heard a horribly familiar treble knock on the front door.

The tallyman.

She instinctively stepped back, as far from the net-draped window as possible, although there was no chance she could be seen as he was almost directly below her. Equally illogically, she held her breath. She could feel her heart racing and a sick churning in her stomach.

The knocking sounded through the house again, more urgent and impatient this time. If she stayed still, maybe he'd think she was out doing her chores? There was a pause. Maybe he would go away? Then a striking of a match. She caught the smell of freshly lit tobacco through the open window.

'I know you're in there, Mrs Atkinson. I saw you open the window,' he called up, his tone exasperated rather than angry. 'You want the whole street to hear your business?'

She ran down the stairs, holding back a sob, and opened the door. The tallyman looked at her, feeling not for the first time that he could think of several things she could do to help settle the debt. In fact, he found himself thinking about that more and more. If only she wasn't married to Derek bloody Atkinson, he might even have tried it on before now.

He licked his upper lip, then picked a bit of tobacco off his tongue as he looked at her. He looked up and down the street. 'Not going to ask me in?'

'I know I'm a bit behind…'

'Four weeks behind.'

'Well, I'm taking in lodgers. They're coming today. I'll sortit out.'

'I hope so,' he said, looking down at her cleavage. She shifted uncomfortably and tugged the neck of her housecoat up. He gave her a last, leering smile. 'Interest is building up. Every day. Must be hard, you being all alone here…'

'You'll get paid. Tomorrow. Come back tomorrow,' she said, shutting the door and slipping the bolt.

The tallyman laughed. 'Tomorrow then,' he said. 'Ta ta for now.'

The train with the three Indian gentlemen arrived at Swindon Junction later than Keenan had estimated. There was a further delay a few hundred yards east of the station, and a flustered Keenan forgot his promise of tea as he was anxious to get to their already overdue appointment at the Chief Mechanical Engineer's office as quickly as possible.

Finally arriving, they left their luggage at the station and were hurried through a long, poorly lit tunnel under the tracks and into the Works – a vast estate of industrial buildings that had grown over time. Workshops, engine sheds, stores, offices and warehouses, all constructed, repurposed, extended or converted over decades to meet changing requirements and accommodate advancing technology. Almost all were built in red brick, with grey stone arches, rows of latticed windows and huge wooden doors.

They half-ran after Keenan as he strode briskly through slabbed yards, where steam rose from vents on either side of them and soot-laden smoke dribbled down from chimneys high above. They skirted transversing bays where tracks ran across tracks. They went down dank, narrow passageways between towering blank walls and past a large turntable at which six sets of rails converged and on which a gleaming, reconditioned tank engine was slowly being revolved towards an awaiting shed. Everywhere, there was activity. The place echoed with the sounds of sawing wood, grinding metal and humming machinery. Chains hissed through creaking lifting gear, whistles sounded, sparks flew and beneath all this cacophony, the regular *whump-whump-whump* of the drop forge in the Foundry vibrating through the place like the heartbeat of some gigantic subterranean being.

Keenan had to shout to be heard over the clatter and crash of the place as he pointed out the purposes and designations of the various buildings they walked among – springsmiths, chainmakers, tube cleaners, turners, fitters, erectors and boiler mounters. 'Not much further now,' he bellowed encouragingly.

A moment later, turning yet another corner, he thrust out an arm to halt their progress and allow a four-wheeled truck piled high with scrap metal to cross their path. The truck was being dragged by a huge dray horse led by a slender young woman in the standard garb of overalls and heavy boots, her hair tied up in a floral-patterned scarf knotted at the forehead.

'Morning, Mr K,' she said brightly.

'Hello there, Mollie. Off to Concentration Yard with that lot?'

'That's right, Mr K,' she said, glancing at the new arrivals as she crossed in front of them. 'These the Indian gentlemen?'

'You shouldn't know anything about that, Mollie Bowen,' grumbled Keenan. 'Careless Talk Costs Lives.'

Mollie rolled her eyes and Billy treated her to a beaming smile. She looked him up and down appraisingly then grinned back. Brazen, thought Vincent with a disapproving sniff. Very promising, thought Billy, who stepped forward with a broad grin to pat the horse.

'I wouldn't if I were you,' Mollie warned. 'Not unless you want to lose a couple of fingers. He's got the 'ump good and proper this morning.'

Billy snatched his hand away. The girl looked back over her shoulder at him and gave him another smile as she continued on her way. Keenan sighed and shook his head.

The two-storey structure towards which they were being led was clearly built with pride and care and at some expense, unlike those which surrounded it. It was not merely to serve a function, but to celebrate, intimidate and impress. Dwarfed though it was by the vast noisy sheds stretching away on every side, the building looked like a Victorian manor house and exuded the quiet authority of a vicarage.

Bas-reliefs of early engines decorated its brickwork. It had fine, large windows, now taped over with a criss-cross pattern of parcel tape, and a slate-tiled roof topped with an elegant chimney. Once the heavy double door of the entrance closed behind them the surrounding industrial roar was muted and they entered a besuited world of hushed and worthy endeavour.

They hung their coats in the hallway and followed Keenan up a broad flight of stairs to the Chief Mechanical Engineer's waiting room. After a few minutes, Miss Jennings emerged, greeted them, had a brief, cheery exchange with Keenan and ushered them into a large panelled office. It was decorated with draughtsman's drawings of engines in dark wooden frames and dominated by a broad dark-wood desk, behind which sat a man in his fifties, smoking a pipe. He rose and shook hands with each of the new arrivals.

The Chief Mechanical Engineer had the short-back-and-sides haircut that the Indian men had noticed on every man they'd seen so far. His skin was pallid and he sported a neatly clipped little moustache. He was dressed in a somewhat crumpled three-piece suit with a pocket watch chain looped across his waistcoat, and looked like a man who did not waste time, words or thoughts on anything that would not advance the interests of his shareholders. Billy spoke up, saying his reputation was well known the world over. Hartshorne, with a puritan's distrust of flattery, regarded him silently for a long moment, and then awkwardly patted his shoulder.

'Thank you, Mr Keenan. That will be all for the moment,' he said.

Keenan touched a finger to his forehead. 'Fred,' he murmured in acknowledgement and, nodding encouragingly at the three new arrivals, left the room.

'Welcome, gentlemen,' said Hartshorne, standing with his hands behind his back and speaking in a formal tone. This was clearly a speech he'd given some thought to. 'Each of you has a vital role to play here over the next few months. It is no exaggeration to say that your contribution will be critical to the success of our great crusade to free Europe of the scourge of Nazism and restore peace and prosperity to the world. You all have very different jobs to do but each of those roles is vitally important, and we've been told you are each uniquely well-qualified to fulfil them. The best there is available, anywhere in the empire. That's what we asked for and I've no doubt that's what you are. Any questions? No?' He paused, and before they could say anything, continued, 'Good. Now, your status: you are not on official duty, and you haven't been conscripted – although your selection, transportation and allocation to us has been carried out by the relevant ministerial departments and your time here will of course be covered by the Official Secrets Act, 1911, which you will shortly be signing...'

'We already did that,' Vincent said. 'In Bombay. At least I did,' he added, looking around at the other two, who both nodded.

'Splendid,' said Hartshorne after a pause, clearly less than happy at being interrupted. 'Where was I? Oh, yes. You are from this moment servants of the Great Western Railway Company. Contracts of employment for each of you have been drawn up and my secretary has them ready for you to read and sign. Terms and conditions will be as for all other employees of the company. Pay and allowances have been agreed with the Remuneration Committee. Now, you must be tired from your journey so I suggest you go to the lodgings that have been arranged for you and settle in. You should also use today to register with the various offices necessary to get your ration cards and IDs. My secretary has prepared a list for you, and Mr Keenan can show you where you need to go. If you have any problems, one or the other of them will sort you out. Again, any questions?'

'What arrangements have been made to accommodate our different religious needs?' asked Akaash quickly.

'We've thought of all that,' Hartshorne assured them. 'Mr Khan can say his prayers as necessary...'

'Please don't go to any trouble...' said Billy.

'No trouble. And we've put aside a room for you to perform your ablutions,' he added, rolling the last word around his mouth as though savouring it.

'I'm really not that bothered…' Billy assured him with an irritated sideways glance at Akaash.

'No need to be embarrassed,' insisted Hartshorne. 'We may not be a big city but we're not country bumpkins. Why, we even had a chap working here who taught himself one of your languages! Miss Jennings!' he bellowed to his secretary. 'What was the Indian language that fellow Williams learned?'

'Sanskrit, Mr Hartshorne,' a disembodied female voice called back. 'I think it was called Sanskrit.'

'That's it! Sanskrit. Now, what do you think of that, eh? Don't you worry, we'll sort you out!'

He was interrupted by a long, deep, booming blast of sound which seemed to go on and on. He took out his pocket watch, checked the time, frowned and adjusted it slightly. 'The Works hooter,' he said with a wintry smile. 'From tomorrow morning your life will be dictated by that sound, just like everyone else in this town. That was the start of lunchtime. You will hear it several more times today. And tomorrow morning at 6.45, 7.20, 7.25 and 7.30, as on every working day. Arrive even one minute after the 7.30 hooter and you lose half an hour's pay. Be here at 7.25 tomorrow morning and I'll present you to your various managers and colleagues. And we'll make sure they know all about your special needs. Good day, gentlemen.'

'Was that really necessary?' asked Vincent as they left Hartshorne's office.

'Yeah, who appointed you God monitor?' grumbled Billy.

'It's important a man doesn't lose sight of his religion in a foreign land,' replied Akaash. 'And it's important they know we expect our culture to be respected.'

'*Our* culture?' said Vincent.

'In the future, you look after *your* cultural needs and leave the rest of us to take care of ours. Just because your religion is a big deal to you doesn't mean it has to be to the rest of us,' added Billy.

'I'm not in the least religious,' Akaash assured them airily. 'I'm a communist. Ergo, an atheist. I was simply making a point.'

'Ergo? What's that? Bengali?'

'Latin.'

'Is arsehole Latin?' asked Billy. 'No? Well, that's what you are. Do you think we're *ever* going to see a cup of tea?'

They did finally get their long-promised tea when they arrived at their lodgings. No. 23 Ashton St seemed to them indistinguishable from all the other red-brick, lace-curtained dwellings on the street, except perhaps for the two somewhat erratic rows of Brussels sprouts planted in the tiny patch of land beside the path to the front door. Keenan introduced them to their landlady, Mrs Sally Atkinson, proudly stressing the fact that Akaash was a doctor.

'Not a proper one,' Vincent muttered as she enthused about having a doctor staying under her roof.

Mrs Atkinson greeted them all nervously. She led them down the narrow hallway into the front room and offered them seats. Keenan and Vincent took the armchairs whilst Akaash and Billy sat side by side on the sofa.

'Kettle's on,' Sally Atkinson assured them, retreating to the kitchen. 'Make yourselves at home. I'll just be a moment.'

They looked around in uncomfortable silence. It was a neat, small 'kept for best' room with a loudly ticking clock over the mantelpiece of an empty fireplace. Black-and-white photographs were framed on the papered walls: a wedding group; a charabanc outing; some of the same faces in a church doorway; a younger Sally Atkinson cradling in her arms a baby lost in a long christening gown; and a studio photo, slightly tinted, of a soldier in a new uniform trying unsuccessfully to look martial. Lined up along the windowsill were a series of clay pots with cuttings of various plants, each identified with a name carefully written on a wooden stick.

'That's her hubby, Derek. He's a sergeant now. Got himself a medal. Regular hero, our Derek,' Keenan said, but there was something odd in his tone, and his constant good humour seemed to have temporarily deserted him.

'Cigarette?' asked Vincent, taking out a packet of Woodbines and offering him one. Billy quickly took out his cigarette case, flicked it open and thrust it towards Keenan.

'Spoilt for choice,' said Keenan, reaching for one of Billy's more exotic cigarettes. 'No disrespect, Mr Rosario, but yours are made just over the road.'

'Would you mind not smoking in here please?' said Akaash. 'I suffer from asthma.'

Billy shrugged and slipped his cigarette case back into his pocket, but not before Keenan had taken one and put it behind his ear. Vincent sighed heavily, laboriously taking the unlit cigarette from between his lips and replacing it in the packet. 'Happy now?' he asked.

'I couldn't help noticing the Chief Mechanical Engineer called you Mr Keenan but you called him Fred,' Vincent observed after a pregnant silence. 'I only mention it as I just want to make sure I understand how to address him.'

Keenan chuckled. 'Fred and I were apprenticed together. Started on the same day. But he was always a clever bugger. Done well for himself. Not that he doesn't deserve it. He should have been CME years ago. I know I should call him Mr Hartshorne like everyone else, but I like to remind him we went to the same school and come from the same streets. I respect him all right, make no mistake about that, and you should too. So he's Mr or Chief or the CME to you, like he is to everyone else.'

'Aren't you taking a bit of a risk?' wondered Akaash. 'Using his first name?'

Keenan shrugged. 'Not really. He's also my brother-in-law.'

Sally returned with a tray and Billy jumped up to help her. She pointed out a set of occasional tables and he placed them so that she could set down the tray and pour out the tea.

'Shall I be mother?' Billy asked, looking around the room proudly. Once they'd learned of his secondment to Swindon, the British Residency in Gwalior – after a flurry of huffy memos – had organised a rapid 'Working and Living in Britain' programme for him. The correct way to serve and enjoy afternoon tea, taught by the profoundly bored but rather fetching wife of the military advisor, had been his favourite. He'd enjoyed it so much he didn't bother telling her that traditional English tea had been a 4.30 p.m. ritual strictly observed in the Khan mansion throughout his childhood.

'Don't be silly,' chided Sally. 'You sit down and make yourself comfy. Be mother, indeed! Whatever next! Milk and sugar for everyone?' she asked, not waiting for a reply before ladling a heaped teaspoon of sugar into each cup and topping it up with milk from a slightly chipped commemorative coronation jug.

She handed round the cups and saucers and offered around a plate piled with four baked dry lumps.

'Rock cakes. I made them this morning. There's more in the oven. These should still be warm,' she said. 'No currants in them, I'm afraid. Can't get them, you see,' she continued, apologetically.

They each took one.

'Our Edie says the same,' said Keenan, taking a first bite. 'Mmm! Lovely. She thinks the government is hoarding them for Christmas.' He studied the half-eaten cake. 'Interesting colour…'

'Grated carrot for sweetener.'

'They're…delightful,' Billy assured her, enjoying himself immensely. 'May I possibly have another?'

Sally smiled, clearly relieved, and headed back to the kitchen to refill the plate. Akaash took the opportunity of her departure to pour his tea into the saucer and slurped noisily. Seeing the other three watching him he paused, the saucer an inch from his lips. 'What?'

Billy looked pained, nose wrinkled as though there was a bad smell in the room. 'Don't do that.'

Akaash pointedly, and even more noisily, drained the saucer. 'This is how I drink tea.'

'Well, stop it. It's embarrassing. You look like a bloody villager.'

'I am a villager. And proud of it. Who appointed you tea monitor?'

Sally returned, beaming, with more rock cakes. She had a kind face, which a smile lit up, Billy thought, and seemed so desperate to make them feel at home that she achieved precisely the opposite effect. She smoothed out her dress and fussed with her hair, said she hoped they'd be comfortable with her and if there was anything they needed they should just ask and if anything wasn't to their liking...

'Our rooms?' interrupted Vincent.

'Yes, of course. Sorry! You must be tired and keen to freshen up. There're just the two rooms, I'm afraid, so only one of you can have a room to himself...'

'That will be me,' said Vincent, looking at the other two as if expecting an argument.

'You two won't mind sharing, will you?' Keenan asked hopefully, looking at Billy and Akaash sitting now some distance from one another on the sofa.

'Not at all,' Billy assured him. 'It'll be like being back at school! Do we get bed tea?'

Keenan chuckled. 'You must've gone to a very different school to me! How about you, Dr Ray?'

'Do I pay less if I'm sharing?'

Again, Billy looked pained. Sally explained the charges for room and full board. She turned away from them, suddenly finding the need to shift the clock on the mantelpiece a half-inch to the left. 'It'll be two weeks in advance, I'm afraid,' she said quietly.

Akaash pointed out that they hadn't been paid yet. Billy sighed. He'd been brought up to find discussions about money dreadfully sordid. Taking out his wallet he offered up a selection of notes. 'Will that suffice?' he asked.

Sally's eyes widened as she saw how much he was holding out to her. 'That's far too much…' Keenan began but Sally snatched the money and thrust it inside her blouse. 'I meant a month in advance,' she said quickly. 'That will do fine.'

'Excellent,' said Billy, deciding that the brief glimpse of bra he had caught as she tucked the money away was worth every penny. 'You chaps can pay me back when you get your wages.'

'I can pay you now…' began Vincent.

'Now, your names,' Sally interrupted, keen not to have any further discussion about the money. 'Mr Khan and Dr Ray I can manage. But, Mr Rosario…' she said, pronouncing it Rose-aah-ree-oow, 'that's a bit of a mouthful. Can I just call you Mr Rose?'

Vincent gave an exasperated sigh. 'No, Mrs Atkinson, you cannot. I don't see why Rosario is any more difficult to say than Atkinson…'

'Well, Atkinson only has three syllables and Rosario has four, so by simple arithmetic it must be more difficult to say,' offered Akaash unhelpfully. 'Or at least involve proportionately more effort.'

Vincent glared at him. 'Well, as we're all going to be living together, must we be so formal? How does Vincent sound to you, Mrs Atkinson? That's my first name. No problems with that? Easy enough to say? Jolly good. And these two here are… oh dear! Akaash and Imtiaz, wasn't it? Hmm. Not so easy. A real mouthful, these foreign names.'

'Everyone calls me Billy. Anyone can manage Billy.'

'But Aaaaah-Caaash? Tricky. Perhaps we can call him Ash?'

Akaash shrugged. 'If I can call you Vin.'

'It's still Mr Rosario to you.'

'Then it's still Dr Ray to you.'

'Maybe Vin *kaka*?' suggested Billy, with a mischievous wink at a clearly confused Sally. 'More respectful. Him being that much older than us.'

'I'm not your uncle!' snapped Vincent.

'Sorry, Vin *dada*.'

'Or your damned brother! Mrs Atkinson, could you please show me to my room now? Thank you!'

Their rooms were comfortable, though small and overcrowded with furniture. Little bunches of dried lavender lay on the pillows, and the beds were heavy with blankets and shrouded in a thick eiderdown. A china chamber pot was discreetly thrust below the beds. Akaash and Vincent unpacked. Billy's more voluminous baggage remained in the left luggage store at the station, so he decided to go and try to organise its delivery. Keenan told him that the man who lived next door at No. 21 had a cart that could be used to bring the bags to the house if the station sack-truck wasn't available.

The afternoon was spent doing the rounds of the various offices with which they needed to register in order to legitimise their presence and ensure they could eat. Born, educated, apprenticed and employed in Gwalior State, this was all new to Billy, but it was depressingly familiar to the other two, both of whom were quietly surprised that such laborious registration seemed as much a part of life in Britain as it was in British India. The torches, gas masks and accompanying tin labelled 'Poisonous Gas Ointment No. 1' with which they were issued were a novelty to all three, but no one seemed to take the risk of a gas attack at this stage of the war terribly seriously. They were just told to carry the masks with them at all times and to read the leaflet inside its canvas holder to understand how to put them on.

They were next directed to the Food Office to be registered for ration cards, and came away with temporary documents. They then returned to the Works to complete the necessary paperwork to become employees of the Great Western Railway and be issued with an array of chits, cards and passes, stamped by various departments in the name of numerous agencies, and given individually numbered identity discs. They received a bored briefing on the various benefits employment brought with it: healthcare, education classes and the opportunity to join seemingly innumerable clubs and societies. Vincent and Billy became members of a range of associated organisations: the Medical Fund, the Railway Benevolent Institution and the Widows and Orphans Fund – having been assured these were appropriate for true railwaymen. Akaash declined membership of anything that would involve a deduction from his wages. Billy asked if there was a Works hockey team and on being told there was, mentioned that he'd been a pretty fair player back home. 'Ladies only', he was told, with a doubtful look. All three agreed to be rostered for fire-watching duties, which they understood to be something to do with putting out any incendiary bombs the Germans might drop on the roofs of the Works. It sounded profoundly risky to them, but they were airily assured that they'd be fully trained and properly equipped

They were taken around the huge, looming Mechanics Institute just outside the Works, where Akaash was near beside himself with joy to discover a lending library comprising tens of thousands of books, periodicals and papers for loan and reference. He immediately signed up as a member and promptly withdrew the maximum number of books that could be issued to him at one time. He then persuaded Vincent and Billy to register as well and, almost before the ink was dry on their newly issued reader's cards, snatched them from their hands and borrowed four more volumes.

Finally, there was a meeting with a Shop Steward of the NUR, which Billy and Akaash joined – Akaash as a matter of principle, enquiring too where he could join the Labour Party; Billy because the Shop Steward was female, fetching, and said her name was Cyn.

'As in original or deadly?' Vincent had quipped.

'As in short for Cynthia,' the Shop Steward had replied in a decidedly chilly tone. 'Funny, no one has ever said that before. Oh, yeah, I remember now. Loads have. Are you joining the Union or not?'

Vincent, dignity pricked, explained that as management, membership of any trade union would be inappropriate and he must therefore, with regret, decline.

'Good-looking girl, that,' mused Billy as he inspected his newly issued Union card.

'Really?' said Akaash.

'Didn't you think so? Very pretty nose, I thought. Pert.' For no particular reason he could think of, that made him chuckle to himself.

'I didn't see a woman, pretty or not.'

'No?'

'No. I saw a comrade. A sister in the struggle against capitalism and imperialism.'

'Really? Gosh! Poor old you!'

A long day that had started with their arrival at Southampton drew to a close with them returning to No. 23 Ashton St, loaded down with books. Akaash had slung his gas mask over his forearm so he could utilise the bag it came in to carry a particularly bulky work. When both Vincent and Billy lit cigarettes he pointedly donned his gas mask.

Vincent urged him to remove it. 'You look ridiculous.'

'I don't know,' said Billy. 'I think it's an improvement.'

A policeman on the corner of Farringdon Road beckoned them over, checked their papers, stared for a while at Akaash, who was struggling to see anything through the severely steamed up Perspex eyepieces of the mask, and asked if he was trying to be funny.

'Very slow learner, officer,' explained Billy. 'Bengali. Notoriously backward people. Still trying to get the hang of the thing.'

The officer smiled in a world-weary manner but grew a great deal more formal when he discovered the book that had replaced the gas mask in Akaash's holder was a German–English dictionary. He took out his notebook, pointedly jotted down their names and walked them to their new address where he watched them hand over their ration cards to their landlady.

Sally told them that they would eat in the back room at 6.30 p.m. Billy asked if it would be possible to have a bath first and Sally looked crestfallen. 'Bath nights are usually a Friday or Sunday,' she said, taking them out to the backyard to point out the tin bathtub hanging on a nail driven into the mortar of the brick wall. She explained that the bath would be placed in the kitchen and water would need to be boiled in saucepans on the cooker, and turns taken to bathe. She then brightened and said, 'There's always the public baths in Milton Road. Yes, that would be much better! Why, there's even a Turkish bath and steam room and everything there! Just like the Ritz hotel!'

She paused, then continued, eyes averted, 'Whilst we're out here…' and showed them to a narrow brick outhouse at the bottom of the long and narrow rear garden. It was a forbidding little structure with a plank door, on the back of which neat squares of torn-up sheets of newspaper hung threaded through a bent wire. They were shown in, one at a time. The interior, in permanent twilight, smelt of damp plaster and Jeyes Fluid. There was a wooden-seated toilet, its stained cistern high up on the wall behind it, operated with the pull of a rusting chain. They were told that this required a special technique – tug, hold for a count of two then suddenly release. Billy watched Sally show how it was done, thinking what an attractive woman she was and quite taken by the earnestness of the demonstration. He asked her to repeat the process – pretending to be interested in the potential causes of the faulty mechanism whilst surreptitiously admiring the sway of her breasts and the way the shape of her calf muscle changed as she reached up again – and then offered to fix the flush system.

'It's the parts,' she said, blushing slightly and running her fingers through her hair, aware of his scrutiny. 'Can't get them.'

'When you live next door to the greatest, um, engineererie in the world?' cried Billy, suspecting correctly that he'd just added to the English language. 'And, although I say so myself, you have a pretty decent engineer in the house now. Leave it to me: I'll have it right as rain in no time.'

'Do you have to keep showing off?' hissed Vincent. 'Always the big shot. And stop looking at her like that,' he whispered.

'Decency monitor?'

'No. Just decent.'

Akaash asked if they could have some water in the outhouse, perhaps in a small watering can or an old jug? Sally regarded him with a deeply concerned look on her face.

'You can wash your hands when you get back into the kitchen…'

Billy sniggered. 'I don't think it's his hands he's thinking about washing, Mrs A.'

Sally Atkinson put a hand to her mouth. Vincent glared at Billy. 'They can sort all that out for themselves, Mrs Atkinson. Just ignore them. Now, would it be acceptable if I hung up some family pictures in my room?'

Things got no easier over their evening meal, which Vincent referred to as dinner but Sally corrected to tea.

'It's a class thing,' Billy explained in a whisper as the three of them sat around the table neatly laid with an array of stainless-steel cutlery, waiting for their first course. 'The middle and upper classes call their midday meal "lunch" and their evening meal "dinner". They might also have a light meal mid-afternoon. If they do, that's tea. For the working class, dinner is the midday meal and tea the evening meal. Oh,' he added holding up two spoons, 'and this is a soup spoon and this one is for dessert, which, I'm reliably informed, the working class call pudding.'

He sat back, looking extremely pleased with himself.

'Do you really think I don't know the difference between a soup spoon and a dessertspoon?' asked Vincent.

'I didn't,' admitted Akaash. 'Nor can I see the point of the distinction. A spoon's a spoon.'

Vincent's look made it clear he wasn't at all surprised. 'How do you know so bloody much about it?' he asked Billy. 'I thought this was your first time here too.'

'Lessons before I left Gwalior. From the Resident's wife and a few of her friends,' he explained with a contented sigh. 'You have no idea how much they taught a simple, innocent young native like me.'

'You really are disgusting.'

Akaash took a handful of change out of his pocket. 'Did they explain this to you?' he asked, letting a cascade of coins fall onto the table. 'Because it makes no sense to me.'

'I thought you were some kind of mathematical whiz?'

'Maths is based on logic and structure. And believe me there's no logic or structure in this. Pounds, shillings and pence I understand. Although why it's abbreviated to LSD and not PSP escapes me. But the basic system is easy enough. Just like rupees, annas and paise, but based on multipliers of twenty and twelve rather than sixteen and four.' He spread out the money, finding the two smallest copper coins. 'This is a halfpenny,' he said, holding up the larger of the two. 'But this,' he said, indicating the smaller, 'whilst its worth is half of a halfpenny, it isn't a quarter penny – no, that would be far too sensible. It's a farthing. What does that even mean? And why is a two shilling piece called a florin? Why is there a coin worth two shillings and sixpence that's called a half-crown when there isn't a five-shilling coin called a crown? Why isn't there a five-shilling coin at all, irrespective of what it's called? And what on earth is a guinea?'

Billy tried to recall all he had been told of the origins and oddities of British currency until Sally brought three soup plates to the table. She placed them carefully before them and all three picked up their soup spoons. 'Cream of chicken,' she said.

Akaash put his spoon down. 'I'm a vegetarian,' he said quietly. 'I'm sorry, I thought they'd told you that. I don't eat meat.'

'It's not meat, Dr Ray,' she assured him, sounding like a mother talking to a particularly dim child. 'It's soup.'

'I don't eat anything that's made from meat or has meat in it.'

Sally put her hand to her mouth. 'Not *any* meat?'

'I'm afraid not.'

'How on earth do you survive?' she asked. 'No wonder you're so…'

'Daal. Rice. Vegetable curries.'

'I don't know how to make any of those,' she said, her eyes filling with tears. 'Excuse me a moment.'

'You're a strict Brahmin now?' Billy asked. 'I thought you said you were an atheist. Ergo.'

'I am indeed,' Akaash assured him. 'Religion is mere superstition the elites use to dissuade the disenfranchised from demanding what's rightfully theirs. I've foresworn meat until the British release Gandhiji.'

Vincent rolled his eyes.

'So this is like a protest? A hunger strike?' asked Billy, impressed.

'Absolutely,' said Akaash.

'Except you never actually go hungry,' pointed out Vincent. 'What an excellent form of civil disobedience: all you manage to do is upset someone who's trying to take care of you, piss off everyone around you and make no difference whatsoever to anything. Congratulations.'

'I'm sure everything will be fine,' Vincent reassured Sally when she returned, red-eyed. 'Daal is really just what…' – he looked around the table and sighed – 'we *Indians* call lentil soup.' He nodded dismissively at Akaash. 'I'm sure he's not going to starve to death if he just has whatever vegetables you've prepared for us tonight. Tomorrow you and I can work out a menu so his particular needs can be properly catered for.'

She nodded, with a tight smile. 'Thank you, Vincent,' she said. 'I'll give Dr Ray extra gravy with his veg. And the two of you can share his chop.'

A slow smile spread cross Vincent's face. 'That wouldn't happen to be a pork chop by any chance, would it?'

Sally nodded again, sensing further problems.

Vincent raised an eyebrow at Billy, who gave a slight shake of his head.

'And is there meat stock in the gravy, Mrs Atkinson? Perhaps it's best if *Dr* Ray has his veg dry tonight. And I suspect *Mr* Khan might prefer to polish off Dr Ray's soup and just have a few dry veg himself. You and I can share the pork chops between us.'

He beamed with malicious satisfaction at the two plates of limp greens and overboiled potatoes placed before Akaash and Billy, then glanced down at his own, dominated with two meaty chops swimming in a rich, dark brown gravy. 'So important we don't lose sight of our religion and our culture in this foreign land,' he sighed contentedly. 'Bon appétit, as the British say.'

As they ate in uncompanionable silence, each would have been surprised had they realised just how much reflection, discussion and paperwork their arrival had already prompted.

Just next door, in No. 21, Ernie Norris was counting out the money he'd received for fetching Billy's luggage from the station and wondering what other opportunities his new neighbours might open up. Eighty miles away in Whitehall, Dawlish, whom they had met at Southampton Docks, was sitting late at his desk in the India Office, finalising a report on his impressions of the new arrivals and taking the opportunity to reiterate the concerns over the whole initiative that he had previously put on record. He was particularly at pains to urge careful scrutiny of Akaash Ray and recommended Billy Khan's recruitment to achieve this objective. Hartshorne, sipping a final special cup of tea of the day, was dictating to Miss Jennings a memorandum to the Board of Directors assuring them, with just a twinge of conscience, that any early worries about the reception the Indian gentlemen would receive had so far proved unfounded. Mrs Deakes, tight-lipped, took pleasure in annotating both Elsie Coggins's and Cynthia Abbot's employment cards with their reallocation to work in Shop B. Keenan found himself overwhelmed with offers of free drinks as he was pumped for information about the new arrivals. Elsie Coggins celebrated her latest escape from dismissal in the same pub by complaining loudly about being made to work for 'one of them darkies'. Cynthia Abbot's father, the convenor, Carriage and Wagon side, nursing a pint of Mild in the same pub, looked pained at the term. 'You can call the Management one whatever you like,' he announced to the gathered drinkers, looking sternly at an unrepentant Elsie, 'but the other two are now Union men. No matter what the colour of their skin, you speak of them with respect in my hearing.' Turning away, he ignored the 'V' signs he knew Elsie was making behind his back.

The GWR Movements team, huddled around a corner table in the lounge bar, unanimously signed a petition to the chairman of the Board protesting the undermining of their professional status through the imposition of unwanted and unnecessary foreign advisors on their work. And the tallyman, hunched in the corner to which at intervals men crossed to settle up accounts, licked the stub of his pencil and noted in his book the need to revisit Sally Atkinson at No. 23 Ashton St to see if the addition of three rental incomes would enable her to catch up on her instalments. He hoped not. He was less than overjoyed at the improved prospect of the significant sums owing at that address being paid off. He was still hoping for the regrettable necessity of exerting some none-too-gentle pressure on the delectable Sally Atkinson.

9

Akaash was first down to breakfast as the 6.30 hooter sounded, followed shortly after by Vincent in a grey three-piece suit and a blue tie. Akaash, head buried in a book propped up against the sugar bowl, wore the clothes he had arrived in.

The table was prepared for three. 'You're not eating with us, Mrs Atkinson ?' Vincent asked.

'I've already had mine,' she said, although Vincent doubted that was true. She was full of apologies about the paucity of the meal on the table – a pot of tea, three slices of bread, a tiny cube of butter and watery strawberry jam. She assured them that now she had their ration cards she'd be able to do much better. In fact, as soon as she'd seen them off and washed up, she assured them both, she'd be off to the shops to stock up – particularly with vegetables, she concluded with a smile to Akaash, which he ignored.

'Mrs Atkinson,' Vincent began carefully. 'There are only the two bedrooms upstairs. I was just wondering where you…'

'Don't you worry your head about me,' she said, brushing his question aside. 'I make myself very comfortable. Snug as a bug in a rug. I only hope you all slept as soundly as I did.'

She poured out tea and as she leaned over Vincent's shoulder she confided in a quiet voice that, if he fancied it, she had *dripping*. Having no idea what she was talking about, he thanked her and declined.

'Well, let Mr Khan know,' she whispered.

'I will,' Vincent assured her, thinking that there were few things he was less likely to do.

'Did you hear the birds singing first thing this morning?' he asked Akaash.

'Above Khan's snoring? No.'

Vincent crossed his legs and leaned back, holding his cup and saucer on his lap. 'I think I might borrow a book about British birds from the Institute.'

Akaash gave a brief head wobble to acknowledge he'd heard.

'Funny how they sing so beautifully when they're such drab and dull-looking little things.'

Akaash sighed. 'You always this chatty in the morning? You're a one-man dawn chorus yourself.'

'I just think we got off on the wrong foot yesterday. What I said about your qualifications. And your… protest. I'm sorry.'

'Forget it.'

Vincent checked his watch. 'Where *is* Khan? We don't want to arrive late.'

'Getting dressed,' said Akaash, still not looking up. 'Said he wanted me out of the room before he got out of bed. Who'd have thought a big, ugly brute like him would be so prissy?'

'Any idea where they're putting you?' asked Vincent. 'I'm not asking you to give away any secrets. Just wondered.'

'Something to do with signalling is all I was told. Logistics. Movements. Communications. Want me to head up some new area.'

'Movements! That's my area too. Maybe we'll be working together.'

'Or maybe you'll be working for me.'

At that moment, Billy burst into the kitchen just as Sally was putting a replenished pot of tea on the table. To say he made an entrance would be an understatement. He was resplendent in lustrously polished knee-high boots, white jodhpurs and a hip-length woollen jacket with a wrap-over front, mandarin collar, and silver buttons bearing the Scindia crest. In his left hand he carried the hat box that had accompanied them from Southampton.

'Oh! Doesn't he look wonderful?' Sally sighed and promptly took out an old bed sheet to offer him as a giant napkin.

'No. He looks like an idiot,' Vincent said.

'Wait till I put my pagri on,' said Billy, waving away the sheet and opening the hat box. Carefully, as though he was handling a sacred relic, he lifted out a pre-tied, heavily starched deep blue turban. 'Then you'll get the full effect.'

Akaash finally looked up. 'I am not walking into the Works with him dressed like that. He looks like a…'

'I've already said that,' said Vincent.

'Up to you. I'm presenting a letter from His Highness and my credentials from the Durbar so I'm wearing uniform.'

'You have a uniform?'

'For formal occasions, of course. This is it.'

'I thought you were an engineer.'

'I am.'

'You look like a doorman at some posh brothel.'

'You'd know, would you?'

'Look,' said Vincent, 'much as I hate to agree with Comrade Stalin over there, I think he might have a point.'

'Why?' asked Billy huffily. 'Whatever happened to all that stuff about respecting our culture?'

Akaash shook his head and with an eloquent sigh returned to his reading.

'Well, think about it,' said Vincent. 'Today's not likely to be easy for any of us, is it? There's bound to be some, I don't know, resentment? Three foreigners marching in and telling these people how to do their jobs? Who likes that?'

Akaash gave a mirthless chuckle.

'I'm sorry, but I just don't see it,' said Billy stubbornly. 'They invited us to come here to help them. We're all in this together. Standing shoulder to shoulder against a common foe, and all that. Why should there be any…difficulties?'

'You really don't get it, do you?' said Akaash.

'No, I don't. Anyway, even if there are, putting on a bit of a show will help.'

'Impress the natives, you mean?'

'If you want to put it that way, yes.'

'You sure you're not British?'

Billy frowned. 'You two are the British. I'm from Gwalior.'

Akaash closed his book and opened his mouth to speak but Vincent threw up a hand. 'Don't! Don't even start!' He turned to Billy. 'I just think we don't want to draw too much attention to ourselves.'

'I think attention is going to be drawn no matter what,' Billy pointed out. 'We're three – well, two and a half – Indians walking through a town that hasn't seen a foreigner since they hanged a monkey 150 years ago thinking it was Napoleon.'

'Did that really happen?' asked Akaash, fascinated. 'Here in Swindon?'

'I don't know. It happened somewhere. Probably. I'm trying to make a point here.'

'You're determined to go dressed like that?' asked Vincent.

'Absolutely,' said Billy. 'And actually, if we're talking about who wears what, I think *he's* the one who needs to change,' he added, jerking his head towards Akaash.

'These are the English clothes I was issued with in Bombay. And I'm not spending good money on any more.'

'All finished?' asked Sally, coming in from the scullery, drying her hands on her apron. 'Lovely to hear the three of you sounding so much at home. Chattering away in your own lingo.'

The three of them looked at each other, confused.

'We were speaking English.'

'Oh.'

By the time they arrived at the Works to the sound of the 7.20 hooter, Billy was starting to think he might indeed have made a bit of a mistake. Throughout their short walk along the terraced streets of Swindon, as increasing numbers of men and women joined the flow of humanity heading towards the main gate, he attracted ever more cheers, jeers and wolf whistles. He was too stubborn to admit his error and in any case there was no time to go back to Ashton St and change. So he held his head high and acknowledged the greetings with as much dignity as he could summon. He shook hands with a few smirking well-wishers, patted the head of a small boy who stood transfixed and gaping, and returned the exaggerated salute of the watchman at the gate who threw his right hand up to his temple, palm out, stamping his right foot to the ground to much applause.

The catcalls continued into the Works and it was a relief to get to the Chief Mechanical Engineer's office, where Billy's appearance was met by little more than raised eyebrows, averted eyes and poorly hidden grins. They waited around a smiling Miss Jennings in the outer office for Hartshorne to finish what seemed – from what they could hear through the closed doors –

to be a difficult conversation. Billy, determined not to crease his uniform, declined the offered chair, and as the other two sat down he tugged his jacket straight, adjusted his pagri and cleared his throat. All three were more nervous than they cared to admit, and each was determined to show it as little as possible.

Hartshorne emerged from his office, closing the door quickly behind him, but not quickly enough for them to miss the shout of 'Over my dead body…'

'That would be too much to hope for,' he muttered to a sympathetic Miss Jennings, who indicated the three waiting men with a tilt of her head.

'Goodness!' said Hartshorne, looking Billy up and down as the other two stood. 'Right. All paperwork properly completed? Welcome to the Great Western Railway! I was going to introduce you to your new colleagues all at the same time but on second thoughts, I think we'll focus on Mr Rosario's role first. That's the one everyone seems to be getting most steamed up about. Miss Jennings? Can we rustle up some tea for our new employees? Mr Rosario, I'll be back for you in five minutes. Mr Khan…oh, never mind,' he said, returning to his office.

'Wonder what that's all about,' said Akaash, looking around the room. As the secretary had headed off to brew some tea, he took the opportunity to glance through the correspondence in her in-tray.

'I have a pretty good idea,' said Vincent. 'Do you really think you should be rummaging through Mr Hartshorne's mail?'

'Information is power,' said Akaash, unperturbed.

Vincent glanced over his shoulder at the document he was perusing. 'I'm sure the estimate for laundry costs for next month will be a huge help to the drive for home rule,' he sneered. They both quickly stepped back from the desk as Billy gave a warning cough on seeing the handle on Hartshorne's door turn.

Vincent was called in.

'Good luck,' said Billy, offering Vincent his hand.

Vincent glanced down, paused, then shook hands with him. As he withdrew his hand, he held it up and was pleased to see not a tremor of nerves. 'Thanks,' he said, 'but luck will have nothing to do with it.'

There were two other men in Hartshorne's office. They were introduced to Vincent as the Head of Movements and his deputy, Lapworth. Both regarded Vincent with little enthusiasm and neither reached out to shake the hand he offered. Vincent made no further effort to greet them beyond a brief nod. 'Chief…' began the Head of Movements, but Hartshorne spoke over him.

'We went through all this yesterday. There's nothing more to discuss. Mr Rosario is here to advise you. You will provide him with whatever he needs and you *will* take his advice.'

'This is ridiculous…'

Vincent cleared his throat. 'If I may, Mr Hartshorne?'

At a nod from Hartshorne he continued, 'I realise that I'm probably not welcome here. I expect you hate the very idea of me being here. I know I would if someone was brought in to advise me in Bombay on how to move my trains. You must be thinking that this man knows nothing about our railway. And you'd be right about how little I know. What can I know? Why, I've only made one trip!'

He took out his notebook and turned to the notes he had made during the journey the previous day. 'Let me tell you about it. We left Southampton Docks eight minutes after the scheduled departure time. During the journey we were held at signals nine times. The shortest stop was four minutes, the longest, eleven. Finally, we were held outside Swindon for seven minutes awaiting a platform when I could see clearly, just by looking out of the window, a platform was available. In total we were over an hour and eight minutes late, twenty-three minutes of which was spent sitting on the very stretch where your own *Cheltenham Flyer* set the world record back in 1932.'

He closed his notebook. 'Class of carriages bore no relation to the mix of ticket holders, resulting in massive overcrowding in third class whilst first-class compartments were virtually empty. Of the nine open freight wagons, three were empty and the others all had significant spare capacity. Finally, I found myself wondering why the train was timetabled to depart Southampton Docks before most passengers disembarking from the one liner scheduled to arrive that morning were able to clear customs and immigration?'

There were half-hearted references to special circumstances, liaison difficulties with the Southern Railway, exigencies of war and atypical conditions, but the wind had clearly been taken out of their sails. Hartshorne did a poor job of hiding his enjoyment.

'And you think you can do better, I suppose?' snapped the Head of Movements.

'I know I can. I do every day. My city would grind to a halt in a matter of hours if I didn't.'

'The question is, gentlemen, can you?' said Hartshorne. 'You know what's at stake. And what the alternatives are. This is your, *our*, last best chance.'

He asked them to wait outside whilst he had a final word with Vincent.

'You handled that well,' he said. 'I'm expecting great things of you, Mr Rosario. Don't let me down. And don't let anyone stand in your way. Movements are a bunch of London End moaning minnies long overdue for a wake-up call. Don't take on trust anything they say. They'll tell you they aren't really under my authority, but they are. They'll also tell you they're heading back up to Paddington and the General Manager's office any day now, but they're not.'

'Don't worry, sir,' Vincent assured him. 'I check everything. And I won't let you down.'

'Well, that went better than it might have,' said Hartshorne, rubbing his hands together as he and Vincent returned to the secretary's office and rejoined Billy and Akaash. 'Miss Jennings, ask the gentlemen from Movements to take Mr Rosario along to introduce him to his new colleagues, and perhaps Mr Keenan could take Mr Khan here on a tour of the Works? But tell him to avoid Shop B. I want to be there when we show him that. Dr Ray, your turn now! Come with me.'

In an office devoid of paper or activity, a few doors down from Hartshorne's office, sat two women dressed in the ubiquitous overalls with scarves wrapped around their heads. Hartshorne introduced them as Miss Grigg and Miss Fraser. Both stood, and the taller of the two offered her hand in a delicate gesture that made Akaash unsure if he was meant to shake it, kiss it or bow over it. 'Phyllida,' she said in a cut-glass accent. 'Phyl.'

'And I'm Joan,' said the second, with a little wave. 'I've read one of your papers!'

'These girls are both recent graduates of Oxford University,' Hartshorne announced with a hint of pride.

'Somerville,' said Phyl. 'Classics.'

'St. Hugh's,' said Joan. 'Modern languages.'

'Quite,' said Hartshorne, his west country accent suddenly significantly less pronounced. 'The three of you will be working together to sort out our signalling requirements.'

'So this is about coding? Cyphers and encryption – that sort of thing?' asked Akaash, pleased to have his assumptions confirmed. It may not be the groves of academe he'd envisaged, but this looked promising, at least as a first step.

'It is indeed,' confirmed Hartshorne. 'It's no secret we're going to be transporting vast numbers of troops and huge amounts of materiel over the coming months. If we're to do that successfully we need much more secure communications than we currently have. Our present methods are hopelessly outdated and almost certainly known to the Hun. Why, back in the '20s we had a delegation from the Deutsche Reichsbahn here and we even demonstrated it to them! I distinctly remember a lot of note-taking. You three are going to develop a completely new system. You'll report directly to me and no one else is to know what you're working on. If anyone asks what you're doing, you tell them you can't discuss it. If anyone asks twice, you're to come and tell me. Understood?'

'I don't actually know that much about modern codes,' confessed Akaash.

'Don't worry,' said Joan cheerily. 'Nor do we.'

'Well, the powers that be said you're the best match available for our requirements. The three of you are going to have to learn, and quickly. Everyone and anyone who understands codes has mysteriously disappeared. No one seems to know where they've gone or why, and I suspect it's best if none of us ask. But the result is that we've had to be rather…unorthodox in our approach. Hence, you three.'

He spoke the word 'unorthodox' with clear distaste.

'Well, I'll do my best. I'm sure I can come up with something. Especially with these bright young ladies to help me,' Akaash added in an attempt at gallantry.

The two women, clearly uncomfortable, looked away.

Hartshorne frowned. 'I think you might have got the wrong end of the stick here, Dr Ray. They're not here to be your assistants. You're here to be theirs. I'll let the three of you get to know each other. A lot depends on you all doing a good job.' He turned abruptly and strode out, shouting for his secretary.

'Right, now where's Mr Khan?'

'Just got back, Mr Hartshorne,' his secretary replied. 'He's in your office with Mr Keenan. How did it go with Dr Ray and the Debs?'

'I think I could have handled that better,' he admitted, not breaking his stride. 'Still, I'm sure they'll sort themselves out. Mr Khan! Did I say how grand you look? What do you think, Mr Keenan? The bee's knees! Miss Jennings! Get a photographer booked for this afternoon. How many engines do you look after on the Gwalior State Railway, Mr Khan?'

'Billy, please. And it's six.'

Hartshorne nodded. 'Do you know how many I'm responsible for?'

'Six hundred?'

Hartshorne laughed. 'A few more than that.'

'Six thousand?'

'Nearer. And how long have you been Gwalior's Chief Engineer?'

'Well, strictly speaking, I'm not. His Highness has the honorary title of Chief Engineer. I'm Deputy Chief Engineer and I've been that since '36. Before that I supervised the repair sheds and before that, I was studying.'

'Excellent! It's good to have all three of you Indian gentlemen with us but I've especially been looking forward to your arrival. The other two were found by the government. I specifically requested you.'

'Thank you sir. It's an honour to be here and I promise you I'll do my very best. Here, by the way are my certificates, accreditation from the Durbar and a letter from the Maharajah himself…'

Hartshorne took the proffered papers and to Billy's disappointment tossed them on his desk without looking at them.

'Well, perhaps you'll read them later? But I have to say now that I've been shown round a bit, I honestly can't see why you need someone like me. You've lots of engineers doing work far in advance of anything I can do. Our engines are years behind yours.'

Hartshorne laughed again. Keenan was also smiling broadly. 'Come with me.'

He led Billy and Keenan out of the office and across the yard to a pair of large wooden doors on which hung a sign painted in fine copperplate: 'Out of Bounds. Shop B'.

'Ready?' he asked, and without waiting for a reply nodded to Keenan, who pushed the huge doors open with a theatrical crash. Blackout sheeting on the glass roof of the cavernous shed kept the contents in the gloom, but as his eyes adjusted to the half-light, Billy made out a heavy steel structure supporting overhead cranes. His nose caught the tang of caustic soda, oil and rust. Dominating the shadowy space like hulking, dormant monsters stood a number of engines, lined up on two parallel tracks. His eyes widened.

'Six – no, eight – *Jiyajiraos*!'

Hartshorne slapped him on the shoulder. 'Now you know why you're here! Class 3300 Bulldogs. Just like your *Jiyajirao Scindia*. No one else still runs these, except the Gwalior State Railway. I think you're the man to get these beauties in running condition and keep them going as well as you seem to have been able to keep your *Jiyajirao* in service. I'm told she's never been out of action for anything other than routine maintenance since you took over in Gwalior.'

Billy was lost for words. He walked among the huge, rusting beasts, touching their cold metal, looking under their frames and climbing up into cabs. He felt like a child let loose in a giant's toyshop, albeit one where the toys had been roughly used and then sorely neglected for a very long time.

'These are all turn of the century?'

Hartshorne nodded. 'Oldest constructed 1899. The baby of the group is the one you're standing on now: 3443 *Birkenhead*. Built 1903. All made here. In this very shed, as it happens. And all withdrawn a decade or more ago. These have been rusting away in various sidings around the region awaiting scrapping. Do you think you can get them running again?'

Billy nodded.

'Good. Tell me what you need and if it's within my gift, you'll have it.'

Billy climbed down and looked around. He dropped to his hands and knees, careless of his fine clothes, and peered under the next engine. 'Do you have original drawings and patterns?'

'Drawings, yes. I've already taken them out for you. Patterns, no. All disposed of when the last of the Bulldogs was taken out of service. But cylinders, wheels and connecting rods are pretty much common across all designs. Patterns for any non-standard parts that you'll need will have to be recreated. I assume you can do that?'

Billy smiled confidently. 'I certainly can. I made quite a few in Gwalior. I could get them shipped over.'

'No time for that. We need to crack on.'

'I'll draw up a list of what craftsmen I'll need and I should be able to give you an estimate of materials, parts and timescales by the end of the week.'

'You'll be meeting your workforce immediately after lunch,' Hartshorne assured him. 'And you'll be making a start today. Why is that, Mr Keenan?'

''Cos there's a war on, Fred.'

'Exactly.'

'*Achcha…*' murmured Billy doubtfully. 'Can I cannibalise them?'

'Only as a last resort. I'd prefer you didn't. I want all of them in working order, even if it will take longer and cost more.'

'That one over there seems to have a tree growing out of its boiler.'

'A buddleia,' Keenan observed. 'Commonly known as a butterfly bush.'

Hartshorne rolled his eyes. 'I didn't say it was going to be easy. But I want the first pulling trains by the end of next month. Make a success of these and, who knows, I may be able to find a few more.'

'Can I ask a question?'

'Of course.'

'How did you know about *Jiyajirao*?'

'I've followed her progress since the day she was rolled out. She was one of the first of the 1899 Bulldogs. Originally 3332 *Avalon*. Sold to Gwalior State in 1924 and renamed in honour of your then Maharajah's late father.' He paused, hands thrust deep in pockets. 'She was the first engine I worked on as a new apprentice. *We* worked on,' he corrected himself, nodding at Keenan. 'Remember, Jim…Mr Keenan? Wasn't she the most wonderful thing either of us had ever seen? The very latest design. Raised Belpaire firebox. Mr Churchward's latest design of boiler. We knew even then, boys though we were, that these were something very, very special.'

'S'right,' Keenan nodded, dewy-eyed. 'A thing of beauty.'

'Remember, I sounded her whistle for the very first time?' Hartshorne said to Keenan, and then turned to Billy. 'I was the youngest apprentice working on her, you see,' he explained, his voice hoarse. 'A truly wonderful engine.'

'I feel that every day I see *Jiyajirao* get up steam,' Billy agreed. 'There's no finer sight. Or sound.' He paused, unsure whether he should raise what was on his mind. Oh, well, he thought. Now or never. 'You said that all these engines have spent more than ten years in sidings after being withdrawn. Why weren't they scrapped years ago?'

Keenan sniggered. 'I told you, Fred. This one's no fool.'

Hartshorne glared across at him and Keenan fell silent. 'Various reasons,' he replied, stony-faced. 'Problems with the paperwork. Scheduling difficulties. Fluctuating scrap-metal prices. Other priorities.'

'And the fact that they were the first engines you ever worked on…?' smiled Billy.

Keenan suddenly developed an exaggerated interest in the roofing high above them.

'I would take a very dim view of anyone suggesting that had anything to do with it. All that matters now is that we're desperate for working engines and haven't got the time, manpower or resources to build enough from scratch. Nor can the company justify diverting engineers more used to later models to learn how to sort these. Mr Keenan will be Superintendent for this Shop. He's as fond of these old Bulldogs as I am. Use him to get things done. He's not as daft as he makes out.' He took out his pocket watch. 'Right, you've got the rest of the morning to sort yourselves out before your workforce arrives. Remember: I want the first ready-to-pull trains by the end of next month. I suggest you get on with it. YBE, gentlemen, YBE.'

'Always, Fred. Always.'

'YBE?' asked Billy as Hartshorne strode off.

'Your Best Endeavours,' Keenan explained.

Meanwhile, the Head of Movements and his deputy Lapworth led Vincent to the Movements office, which was temporarily housed in a first-floor suite of rooms that had formerly been part of the draughtsman's office in the Carriage and Wagon side of the Works. The long walk from the Chief Mechanical Engineer's office passed in strained silence. As they left the Loco side behind them, the noise gradually decreased and changed from the metallic crash and screech to the more gentle sounds of carpentry and joinery. At one point the Head of Movements took out a packet of cigarettes and offered one to Lapworth, pointedly ignoring Vincent, who, equally pointedly, took out one of his own and lit up. On their arrival at the office, Vincent was struck by the clutter, apparent chaos and clear ill temper of the place. It was immediately obvious to him that the imposition of his unsought and unwelcome advisory role was just the latest in a long list of grievances the department nursed.

When the Head of Movements left Vincent and Lapworth, the latter became a little more forthcoming. Exactly as Hartshorne had predicted, he assured Vincent glumly that they shouldn't even be in Swindon. That they should be back at the Great Western's massive London terminus and headquarters at Paddington station. Although based in London End, Lapworth spoke with a marked west country burr. He also had a slight speech impediment: a sudden intake of breath before each statement, as though needing to take the words at a rush. 'This is all just temporary,' he insisted, 'because of the bombing. Once we get back up to Paddington, things will get back to normal.'

The underlying message was unspoken but still perfectly clear: don't make yourself too much of a nuisance. Don't make yourself at home. Because we're not going to be around here much longer and when we go, you won't be coming with us.

Lapworth introduced Vincent to the dozen men who made up the department. They were sitting around smoking and drinking tea, and whilst each nodded in his direction as their names were mentioned, none rose to greet him or made any effort to shake his hand. He nodded in return and did his best to ignore the clearly hostile stares.

'I suppose you'd better settle yourself over there,' sighed Lapworth, pointing to a narrow clerk's desk, stacked with papers that looked as though they'd been there for some time. No one made a move to clear away the clutter.

'I won't be needing a desk, thank you,' said Vincent. He pulled his notebook out of his pocket, opened it and placed it on the table in front of him. With elegant slowness he took out his fountain pen, unscrewed the top and began to write in silence. After a while, he looked up. 'Are all your papers and records in here?'

Lapworth looked around at his silent colleagues. No one seemed keen to answer. 'No,' he replied. 'A fair bit is still up at Paddington. But we brought down everything we need.'

'Thank you,' said Vincent, with exaggerated politeness, making a further note. He felt surprisingly calm and relaxed. After a lifetime of discreet sneers and studied slights there was something strangely reassuring about such blatant hostility. He closed his notebook, screwed the top back on his pen and looked around. 'I've seen everything I need to here. When's the next train to Paddington?'

Again, everyone looked at one another. Again, the silence.

'I assume you do have a copy of the main line timetable? This being the Movements department?'

'Why don't you just sod off back to where you came from?' a voice from the far side of the room called out.

Vincent smiled. 'When I've done what I was brought here to do.' He glanced up at the clock on the wall of the office, took out his watch, looked up again and said, 'By the way, that clock is three minutes slow. Now, the next train to Paddington?'

The office Akaash was to share with Phyl and Joan was furnished with three desks and chairs, a couple of tables and racks of narrow, empty shelves along two walls. In stark contrast to every other office, there was a remarkable lack of paper. Akaash could see no files or charts. An entire wall was given over to large windows and the room was awash with sunlight, which served to accentuate the vacuity and inactivity.

'We've sort of claimed these two desks,' said Phyl, pointing to the pair nearest the windows. 'First dibs. But if you'd prefer either we can always swap around.'

'I'm less concerned with where I sit,' replied Akaash sulkily, 'than with what we're meant to be doing.'

'Absolutely,' enthused Joan, 'us too!'

The three of them looked at one another. Joan was about the same height as Akaash; Phyl, a few inches taller. Both looked very fresh-faced, smelt of wholesome soap and expensive eau de cologne and seemed profoundly out of place in an office dressed in immaculate overalls and scarves. They'd hung up their gas masks on a hatstand by the door, so Akaash put his there too.

'Look, we realise it must seem a bit off,' said Phyl, pronouncing the last word as *orf*, 'for you to be told you're assisting us.' She seemed clearly uncomfortable. 'If we were back at college, you could well be supervising our theses! Well, if we were at college in India that is!' She gave a snorting half-laugh. Her elocution was BBC-perfect – the voice Akaash had always associated with blithely assumed authority, and duly loathed. 'But here we are,' she continued, 'in a world turned upside down. So in here, between the three of us, I propose we agree we're all in this together. Even if formally...'

'You're my bosses,' concluded Akaash.

Joan gave Phyl a hard stare. There was clearly little love lost between the two. 'You can get that idea out of your head right away, Dr Ray. I'm not your boss. Phyl's the queen bee. We're both her workers.'

'How many times do I have to say this, Joan?' asked Phyl exasperatedly. 'Only on paper. Let's just start again. Dr Ray, welcome!' Phyl said, shaking his hand once more. 'The three of us are all equal in here. Chums on a mission! Joan and I have been allocated to this work because we volunteered to do our bit. Someone thought our linguistic skills might complement your numerical abilities and we'd be more use in here than in the Women's Land Army.'

'And what languages do you have?' Akaash asked.

'French – obviously!' she said with another snort. 'German, Greek and Latin. Classical Greek, of course.'

'I can't see how that's going to be much use,' sighed Akaash. He turned to Joan. 'And you?'

'Hindi and Bengali.'

'What?' exclaimed Akaash amazed. 'Why did you study those?' he asked her in Bengali.

'Why not?' she replied in the same language. 'I was born in Cal and spent many happy years there.'

Akaash beamed his pleasure. Phyl was making it clear that she was feeling left out so they changed back into English. 'You said that you'd read one of my papers?'

'That's right. Read it first in Bengali. Didn't understand a word! Read it again in English. Still couldn't make head or tail of it!'

'You know why you're officially only an assistant?' she asked quietly in Bengali. 'Madam there says daddy would never allow her to work for an Indian.'

'And daddy has influence?' asked Akaash.

'By the bucket load! Number two in the Ministry of War Transport, no less. "One of the wheels of power, whilst I am one with the living creatures those wheels crush."'

'Tagore?'

'Of course! Back to English for horse-face?'

'What have you done so far?' he asked in English.

'Well, we've tried to read up a bit on codes and ciphers and all that,' Phyl explained. 'The librarian in the Mechanics Institute has been an absolute lifesaver! Got us all sorts of stuff…' She went to her desk, pulled open a drawer and took out two books. 'Kasiski's *Secret Writing,*' she said, holding up one and then the other, 'and Friedman's *Elements of Cryptanalysis.*' She tossed the books on to the desk. 'Loads of academic papers too but to be honest, they're probably more up your street than ours.'

'Neither of us can make out what they're all about,' admitted Joan cheerily, 'and it's not for want of trying. Or brains! Phyl's degree is an upper second,' she added sweetly.

'And Joan's is a first,' said Phyl through gritted teeth.

Billy and Keenan drew up their initial list of the parts that they agreed they'd need to get the best-preserved of their shed full of rusting Bulldogs into something approaching working order. They found their ideas on priorities and approaches matched and they worked together well despite their obvious differences of age, background and experience. Hartshorne's airy assurance that a lot of parts could be drawn straight from Stores proved over optimistic as the real drive for standardisation had come years after the Bulldogs had been built. The task would thus be more challenging, but Billy was looking forward to it all the more. He spent a happy hour poring over the dozens of sheets of plans and fading technical drawings, half-listening to Keenan cheerfully recalling anecdotes from his days working on their initial construction.

At the sound of the end of lunch hooter, thirty-six women and two elderly men gathered outside Shop B, chatting and smoking. Among them was the Shop Steward, Cyn, although Billy failed to spot her as he approached them. In the centre of the group, ignoring Cyn and holding forth to the cohort of not-so-willing volunteers she'd press-ganged into joining her as part of the deal made in Hartshorne's office the day before, stood Elsie Coggins, insisting obtusely that they shouldn't take any lip from the you-know-what, him being what he was and all.

The other employees at the Works had each been discreetly asked if they would have any concerns about taking orders from an Indian. Several of those initially nominated to the Shop B operations on the basis of the list of skills likely to be required had expressed just such reservations, some quite trenchantly, and they had been allowed to remain in their current roles. Their places were reallocated to less choosy workers or to those for whom, like Elsie, the alternative to a Shop B assignment was the sack and the dole. Thus, the group awaiting Billy had a minority for whom something different and the opportunity to extend their skills and experience appealed, and a majority for whom dismissal loomed large – a group whom Keenan cheerily characterised as 'the sick, the lame and the lazy'.

Inevitably, the matching of skills to the expertise required was not as exact as Billy or Keenan might have hoped. They did, however, have two immensely experienced hands – an inspector and a crane operator, the two elderly men. Enthusiasm, amusement, resentment and resignation were evident in the group's desultory and disjointed conversations, which all fell silent as the doors were unlocked and Billy and Keenan appeared. They all trooped into the huge shed.

Feeling an unusual flutter of nerves as he climbed onto the footplate of the engine nearest to the door, Billy prepared to speak to his new and somewhat intimidating workforce. He tugged straight his now creased and oil-stained jacket and adjusted his pagri. The women looked up expectantly, arms crossed. Keenan spoke quietly to the two elderly men and then eased his way through the crowd to stand below Billy. Conscious of the formality of the occasion, he doffed his bowler hat.

'Ladies and gentlemen,' Billy began. 'Thank you for coming today.'

'Like we had a choice,' muttered one of Elsie's cronies, prompting laughter, a glare from Keenan and a sympathetic wave of shushing. A cheery, 'Carry on, handsome!' followed.

'He is a bit of all right, isn't he?' another voice observed.

'Yeah, you wouldn't want to kick that out of bed on a cold night.'

'Looks like a cross between Rudolf Valentino and the Red Baron!'

'He can sneak into my tent.'

'Or climb into my cockpit!'

Billy coughed, cleared his throat and started again. He really wished he'd listened to Vincent and Akaash at the breakfast table. 'Welcome to Shop B and the start of our important work together. My name is, er, Mr Khan and I've been asked to help with the repairing and recommissioning of these engines, which – as you probably know – are 4-4-0 Bulldogs, a type of engine I…' He was about to lay out his experience and qualifications for this task at some length, but recalled what the Resident's wife had told him about the virtue of understatement. '… I know a little bit about,' he concluded somewhat lamely.

'Lovely voice,' someone sighed. 'Talks dead posh, don't 'e?'

'Shut up, Kath,' hissed Keenan. 'Give the poor bugger a chance.'

'Yeah, give him a chance,' echoed Cyn, catching Billy's eye and nodding supportively. 'He's got his Union card.'

'Well, that's not right for a start,' grumbled an outraged Elsie to her best friend Doreen. 'It's one thing that he's one of them, but 'e's not one of them who's one of us, I don't care what Arthur bloody Abbot has to say about it. 'E's Management.'

'Thank you, er, Miss Cyn,' said Billy, determined to struggle on. 'Together we're going to get every one of these engines fully functioning as soon as we can. As you can see as you look around, some are in better condition than others, but all can and will be fully renovated by us working together.'

'They look like a load of old scrap to me,' observed the first voice to speak.

'That's what they were, until very recently! All decommissioned and awaiting cutting up for scrap. But we're going to make them run again, as good as new! We're going to strip them down, scrub them up and…'

'And then will there be an erection?' asked someone cheekily, prompting a new wave of sniggering.

'Yes!' said Billy, disconcerted that his morale-boosting welcome speech clearly wasn't achieving the effect he had hoped. 'Hopefully many erections! It's a big job and it will be hard' – which prompted more sniggering – 'but we can do it if we all pull together. Any questions before we get started?'

'What grades and weekly rates apply to this work?' asked Cyn.

Billy had no idea what she was talking about and looked, bewildered, to Keenan.

'As agreed by the Remuneration Committee, young Cynthia, as per,' he replied stolidly.

'Well, that's all very well, Mr Keenan, but you and I both know that several of the jobs on your list are being filled by less-qualified workers. Will they get the rate for the job they're allocated to or continue to draw the pay for their substantive grade? And with this number of workers you'll need a Charge Hand as well as a Foreman and Supervisor. Who are they going to be?'

'I'll be Charge Hand,' said Elsie, glowering round to see if anyone felt inclined to challenge her claim.

'All right, Elsie,' said Keenan unenthusiastically. 'You're Charge Hand.'

Billy watched bemused. How had the British ever managed to capture and hang on to a vast empire when they seemed incapable of doing the simplest thing without making such a meal of it? It was probably conversations just like this that had led to the fall of Singapore, he concluded. He also thought that he should impose a bit of authority on the proceedings but was temporarily at a loss to know quite what to say or do. He caught Cyn's eye and she smiled encouragingly at him.

'Mr Keenan will allocate tasks,' he announced, 'and divide you up into teams. Our first task is to clean out the fireboxes, descale the boilers and scrape off as much rust as we can. Then we can really see how much more we have to do.'

'So there we are,' said Keenan, rubbing his hands together. 'Just like doing the housework! Clearing the ashes out of the grate, a bit of general scrubbing and cleaning. Just what you ladies like to do. 'Sept for you, Doreen. We all know what a tip your house is.'

'Cheeky bugger!' smiled Doreen, pleased to be picked on.

The three Indian gentlemen walked back together at the end of their first day, sharing information about their respective assignments. Smoke from a thousand coal fires hung in the still, damp air. Soot- stained brick, stone and tile. The air was tinged with a sulphurous, earthy reek, for every GWR employee had a coal allowance and many traded any excess with family and neighbours for allotment produce or stashed little comforts.

Vincent had made the journey up to Paddington, where he had been met by blank stares and unhelpful responses to his questions but still felt the journey was worthwhile as well as thoroughly enjoyable. He'd not really expected to gain much useful information. His trip was part research and part familiarisation, but mostly just bravado. He'd wanted to observe first-hand the traffic around the major junction at Reading and get a feel for platform allocation at the Paddington terminus. He'd also wanted to put the sullen and arrogant Movements department off balance and he was pretty sure he'd succeeded in all three objectives.

He was easily back before the end of the working day but rather than returning to the office he'd wandered around the Works, notebook in hand, watching and recording his impressions until he ended up in Shop B. Vincent and Billy were excited by the opportunities they anticipated in the months ahead and they spoke enthusiastically over one another, Billy explaining again about *Jiyajirao* and the Bulldogs and Vincent making initial comparisons with the BBCI.

They were joined by Akaash as they walked back to Ashton St. He had remained silent through their enthusiastic chat, but suddenly spoke. 'Should we even be doing this?' he wondered glumly. 'Should we even be here?'

The other two stopped and stared at him in amazement. 'Of course we should,' said Vincent. 'How can you even ask? The empire is under threat and we have a duty to do our bit.'

'And I'm under orders from my Maharajah,' added Billy. 'I have no choice about it. Not that I'd want to leave even if I could. I'm happy to be here. God's Wonderful Railway, eh, Vincent?'

'God's Wonderful Railway, indeed,' agreed Vincent. 'Although God and Movements seem to need a little help to get it running optimally.' No amount of resentment and ill will on the part of those he was meant to be advising could dampen his spirit. At last here was a challenge of a significance and complexity worthy of his ability.

'You're both happy to be here, helping our oppressors while they occupy our homeland and enslave and starve millions of our people?' asked Akaash.

'Well, they don't enslave and starve us in Gwalior State!' declared Billy proudly. 'They don't even occupy us. Never have. Never will.'

'How can you be so naive?' cried Akaash, turning to stare up at Billy. 'We're well-educated Indians, the elite of our nation, and that places a massive responsibility on each and every one of us.'

'There is no "our" nation. You're from Bengal, he's from Bombay and I'm from Gwalior. We're not part of British India, even if you are. Gwalior…'

'Is a backward, feudal state ruled by a bloodsucking British puppet from a family that have consistently betrayed their own people to keep themselves in wealth and luxury.'

Billy was aghast. He looked for a moment like he'd been slapped in the face. 'What did you just say?' he asked, his voice dangerously quiet.

'Your bloody *Jiyajirao* is named after the greatest traitor in our history since Mir Jafar,' sneered Akaash, taking his glasses off. 'This is the way they keep us at their mercy! Fighting among ourselves instead of kicking them out of our country. What are you going to do now? Hit me? You won't be the first. Or the biggest.'

Vincent eased himself between the two of them. He glanced around. Several others heading home from the Works had paused and were trying not to be too obvious about watching the developing argument.

'Can you both just calm down?' he urged. 'Impressive speech,' he said to Akaash as Billy strode furiously away. 'Unfortunately, he doesn't think your "us" and "we" includes him, and I suspect it doesn't include me either.'

'Well, he should know better,' grumbled Akaash, putting his glasses back on. 'You can't help what you are. But your loyalties can only ever be divided.'

'You really do have a way of making people like you, don't you?'

'You know,' continued Vincent, as they walked on in Billy's wake, 'I can't help wondering why this is suddenly such an issue for you. Didn't all of this occur to you before you ever left India? Seems a bit late now. You've taken the money and got your trip to England, yet now you whine. That doesn't sound so heroic to me.'

'Yeah,' chipped in Billy, turning to rejoin the debate. 'Why are you even here if you hate these people so much? What is it you're supposed to be doing anyway?'

'Writing out tables of numbers for a couple of graduates,' muttered Akaash. 'Me? A step away from full professor back home but here I'm just a glorified clerk. And they're not even scientists. Arts graduates! And women!' he added, the disgust clear in his voice.

Billy tried and failed to maintain his glower of disapproval. He started to smile, then guffawed.

Vincent shook his head. 'And you a doctor, too? Tragic. Sitting in a nice, warm office with two young women doing sums? The sacrifices some people have to make.'

The mood had improved a little by the time they opened the door to No. 23 and hung up coats and gas masks. Before they had left the house to walk to work that morning, their landlady – whom, following her seeming pleasure at Billy using the term, they all now called 'Mrs A' – had promised them a treat for tea. Billy and Akaash had glanced uncertainly at one another. She had caught the look and assured them that she wouldn't forget Dr Ray's *special needs* (over-pronouncing the words to emphasise the deeply troubling nature of those needs) and Billy's aversion to pork.

Sally now emerged from a steamy kitchen, drying her hands on her apron. 'Welcome back!' she said with a happy smile. 'Ready for tea? It's Bubble and Squeak.' She gave a nod to Akaash. 'No meat. And I promised you a treat…'

She looked over towards the table and they followed her glance. In pride of place was a glass jar filled with a bright yellow pulp with anonymous green and red lumps in it.

'Piccalilli!' she announced proudly. 'I had to go to three different grocers before I found it.'

She looked expectantly from one to another. Each looked at the table in silence and then at one another.

The smile faded from her face. Suddenly she looked extremely tired and very sad. Vincent stepped forward and picked up the jar. 'Piccalilli! Wonderful! Oh, thank you so much, Mrs A! You've no idea how much I've been pining for piccalilli! How about you two?' he added with a significant look.

'Oh, *piccalilli*! Sorry, Mrs A, I didn't hear you properly. All that noise in the Works. Lovely!' enthused Billy, sticking a finger in his left ear and exaggeratedly wiggling it about.

'Great,' muttered Akaash half-heartedly, prompting a glare from Vincent.

'I knew you'd be pleased!' sighed Sally in relief. 'Nothing like a little taste of home to make a person feel welcome. I'll get the kettle on and start tea. You make yourselves comfy.'

She hurried off back into the kitchen, humming happily.

'What, in the name of all that's holy, is piccalilli?' whispered Billy.

Vincent shrugged. 'No idea.' He unscrewed the lid, sniffed, frowned and passed the open jar to Akaash, who dipped a little finger into the contents and tasted it.

'Eech! I'm not sure what that's meant to taste like, but it can't be meant to taste like that. I think it might have gone off.'

'It's a taste of home,' Billy reminded him.

'Your home, maybe. Not mine. If this is a treat, what on earth is Bubble and Squeak going to be like?'

Bubble and Squeak turned out to be a bland mash of reheated potatoes and greens.

'I think I've seen some of these peas before,' said Billy as he disconsolately pushed the food around his plate with a fork.

'I think someone's *eaten* some of mine before,' said Akaash.

'Have some piccalilli with it,' said Vincent, who was slowly working his way through his portion.

'Very funny. It's all right for you. You probably eat like this at home,' said Akaash. 'Probably what makes him so grumpy all the time,' he added, turning to a still rather distant Billy.

Vincent laid aside his cutlery. 'No, Mr – sorry – Dr Know-it-all. I do not eat like this at home. These are leftovers from last night's meal. I've never eaten anything like it in my life. But Mrs A has made it for us and I'm sure if she could have got better, or done better, she would have. So I'm going to eat it if it kills me, because we're in her house and she's made it for us. And if you had any manners you would too.'

'Ooooh! I think someone's a bit sweet on Mrs A,' said Akaash with a smirk. 'Not thinking of cheating on the little woman back home, are we?'

'There is no little woman back home, if it's any of your business, which it's not. And no, I'm not "sweet" on her as you so pathetically put it. But if I was, that too wouldn't be any of your business and if I were to discuss it with you, which wouldn't happen in a dozen lifetimes, I'd talk about it like an adult, not a retarded twelve-year-old.'

Billy chuckled. He'd never been able to stay cross with anyone for long. 'You married, Akaash?'

Akaash shook his head. 'Too dark, too smart and too much to do. You?'

Billy wobbled his head.

'Define ambiguity. Oh, you just did. Was that a yes or a no?'

'It's a sort of. Promised, sort of. Distant relation in Lahore. There's an understanding. Probably get married when I return.'

'Pretty?'

'So they say. But then they're not likely to say anything else, are they? "I'm so glad you've agreed to marry your son to our daughter. By the way, she weighs twenty stone and has a face like the backside of a water buffalo."'

'Are either of you struggling to understand what these people are saying most of the time?' asked Akaash. 'My two female colleagues are clear enough, but Mr Keenan? Mrs A? Even the CME?'

Billy and Vincent both heaved a sigh of relief, each assuming and embarrassed by the thought that he alone was struggling.

'Is it the speed at which they speak?' wondered Billy. 'The way the words all run into one another?'

'They do seem to mumble a lot,' agreed Vincent.

'And add in or leave out sounds at a whim.'

'Enunciation,' concluded Billy, carefully enunciating every syllable. 'Or lack of it. That's the problem.'

They settled to clearing their plates. Vincent, having checked Sally was not likely to join them soon, tore a page from his notebook and laid it out on the table. He reached for the piccalilli jar and ladled two large dollops onto the paper. He held up the jar, studied it for a moment and took a third spoonful. Replacing the lid on the jar he carefully folded the paper around the yellow pickle, wrapped the package in his handkerchief and warily put it in his pocket.

'You have something to say?' he snapped at the grinning pair watching him.

Sally came in with their dessert. 'Semolina pudding,' she announced as she placed bowls of a milky, lukewarm paste before them. She glanced at the piccalilli jar, saw that it was half empty and beamed.

'You boys!' she tutted happily. 'I'll try to find you another jar tomorrow but I can't promise anything.'

She attributed their joint cry of 'No!' to their kind nature and good hearts. Imagine them being so caring that they'd be willing to go without their piccalilli just to save her queueing half the morning! With a tear in her eye she left them to enjoy their puddings, determined that, no matter what, piccalilli would be on the table every evening from then on.

'Does nothing taste of anything here?' mused Billy. He took a spoonful of the pudding, held it up and turned the spoon over. The pudding stayed adhered. 'Wonder if it would taste any better with piccalilli on it?'

All four of the residents at No. 23 had a considerable amount of adjusting to do. For the three Indians, there was an abiding sense of dislocation. Much was almost familiar, but not quite. The way people spoke, for example, or the way they obsessively queued on some occasions and shoved past one another on others. What was acceptable to say and what wasn't. Early misunderstandings and chilly receptions made it clear to all three that they had a lot to learn and were going to make quite a few mistakes along the way.

For Sally, accommodating three such unusual lodgers proved even more of a challenge than she'd anticipated. She'd thought, naively, that they would all be much more like one another. That what would do for one would do for all. She'd only the slightest idea of what Indians were like prior to their arrival, and that was based solely on the cinema and newsreels. She had never met an Indian, or indeed ever seen one except on the screen. The two that came most readily to mind were Mohammad Khan in the Gary Cooper film *The Lives of a Bengal Lancer* and Errol Flynn's enemy Surat Khan in *The Charge of the Light Brigade* – the first played by a Canadian, the second by an American. She hoped her Mr Khan did not turn out to be like either of them, she reflected with a smile to herself.

In the newsreels she could only recall three types of Indians ever featuring: bejewelled maharajahs, malnourished peasants and ungrateful revolutionaries. Well, she supposed Billy was a bit like the first lot, talking so posh, with all those lovely things in his trunks and cases: so much so that he'd have to find somewhere else to store half of it. So much money, too! She savoured the memory of the tallyman's resentful acceptance of Billy's cash that cleared her arrears. And he said he was going to fix the toilet cistern. That didn't sound like the kind of thing those Hollywood Khans would offer to do!

Akaash certainly looked half-starved, although that seemed to be mainly his own doing, and she'd heard and understood enough of their conversations to know he was like those troublemakers, always marching and complaining. But Billy and Akaash were so different from one another. She wasn't at all sure them sharing a room was such a good idea.

And Vincent? He was a complete novelty to her. He spoke with an Indian accent but didn't look like she thought Indians did. He was more Mediterranean. Like the Eyetie that used to have the barber's shop on Victoria Hill before the war. She guessed from his name that he'd probably got some European blood in him. Odd how, even in the short time they'd been with her, though nothing had been said, each seemed to feel himself superior to the other two. Funny lot. And all this no-meat/no-pork kerfuffle. Really! Fussy blighters.

She'd thought she could have a go at the lentil soup thing Vincent had mentioned – if she could get hold of the lentils. That Marguerite Patten from the Ministry of Food had a recipe for it, she recalled. But when she looked it up, it had bacon in it. Chicken stock too, so someone's got that wrong. Still, she was determined to try her best. They deserved that. So far away from home. And paying so well too. Word was that the Railway had to offer such generous terms as no one was willing to offer the three of them a place. Even then, hers had been the only offer made. Shame! Mind you, couldn't've worked better for her. It's an ill wind, as her Nan used to say.

She hoped the thought of the money would reconcile her Derek to the idea of foreigners in his house. He wasn't keen on foreigners, as her mother-in-law never failed to remind her. She had mentioned in her last letter to him that she might need to take in a lodger if she was ever going to pay off the tallyman. She hadn't told him she'd agreed to three. Or that they were, well, what they were. God knew what he'd say if he found out someone was sleeping in his bed and it certainly wasn't Goldilocks! Best leave well alone, she felt, for all concerned. They'll probably be long gone ages before Derek got his next leave or the boys came back for good. Then, it would all be past history, like it had never happened. Except that she wouldn't have that disgusting tallyman leering at her every Thursday afternoon when he came for his money. She was pretty sure, whatever Derek's views about her paying guests, he'd be very pleased to see she'd been able to settle his debts.

Now, what to make for dinner? Whatever it would be, she decided to sprinkle plenty of white pepper over it. It was something that until then she'd always put on the table in a wedding-present cruet set next to the salt but which no one ever used. Didn't bear thinking about how long that pepper had been hanging around. She couldn't remember ever actually buying it. Oh, well, hardly likely to have gone off, was it? And they all seemed to like their food messed about like that.

Food at No. 23 did steadily improve, at least in quantity now that Sally had four ration cards to work with. Each day started with a tea-and-toast breakfast, and jam sandwiches were lunch. Evening meals were invariably accompanied with a jar of piccalilli, which, much to his surprise and his fellow boarders' amusement, Vincent was starting to quite like.

Sally continued to struggle to accommodate Akaash's vegetarianism. Never having catered for anyone who didn't expect meat with his veg before and brought up on a country fare rich in animal products, she'd had to re-examine all sorts of assumptions: who'd ever have imagined, for example, that lard was made from pig fat? She'd always assumed that it was just, well, lard. She was not helped by Akaash's own lack of clarity about the boundaries of his atheist abstinence.

Akaash could, of course, have followed any number of communally prescribed diets which would have distinguished precisely what he could and couldn't eat, but he was determined not to adopt any dietary regime predicated on religious belief. So what should he eat, Akaash had wondered when embarking on his self-imposed protest. Meat was an easy, clear and obvious no. Fish? Well, the bloody things had eyes, bled and breathed so surely they were out too. Shame, really. He liked fish. Where should he stand on eggs? Milk? Butter? He wasn't at all sure.

The former he decided to forgo, but only after he discovered there was an active black market for eggs at the Works. (He'd already persuaded Billy to buy his rationed meat allowance off him.) He thought Gandhiji probably enjoyed milk and butter – good, natural, village products in any agrarian utopia. Also, he owed it to the cause to keep his strength up. So dairy products could stay. Shame Mrs A's milk puddings were all so horribly glutinous and tasteless, he reflected. Mind you, so was pretty much everything else she dished up.

Within days of their arrival, one of them found themselves at serious odds with the law.

It would have been easy, but far too glib, to characterise that arrest as evidence of blatant prejudice on the part of a deeply racist state. Akaash would certainly have done so. But even Vincent – for it was he who spent a night as a guest of the King in the cells at the Orange Grove police station in Bath Spa – would have admitted that he should probably have anticipated this might happen. An olive-skinned man enquiring about transportation in a funny accent? And jotting down everything he was told? Ministry of Information posters and public service shorts made by the GPO Film Unit chorused warnings to look out for possible enemy agents and the potentially disastrous repercussions of complacency. Britain may not have had a Gestapo, but it had something even more effective: a superficially polite but quietly bloody-minded citizenry keen to grass up any character who looked or sounded vaguely foreign and who seemed to be asking too many questions.

He hadn't even intended to visit Bath. He'd spent the day at Bristol Temple Meads station enquiring about the way in which the GWR had managed to shift several thousand American troops disembarking and entraining at Newport Docks over the past three weeks without the usual chaos ensuing. There were, he was convinced, important lessons to be learnt. He was on his way back to Swindon when the guard announced they'd be held at Bath for at least half an hour.

Keen not to waste the opportunity, Vincent decided to ask a few questions of the station staff. Unfortunately he was overheard by a retired solicitor from Chippenham, who was sufficiently concerned to mention it to a policeman directing traffic around bomb damage on Manvers St. A polite request to see his papers led to the discovery of a notebook full of details about troop movements, and Vincent was invited to come along to the police station.

Vincent found his arrest more embarrassing than frightening. No hands were laid on him. No angry crowd watched him being taken away. But it was very clear that 'invitation' disguised instruction. Whilst he'd been asked if he'd care to accompany the officer, it was perfectly evident it really didn't matter very much if he cared to or not. To the police station he was going. Once there, unable to satisfy the inspector of his authority to be asking people about troops and trains, he was told he'd remain until morning, when this would all be sorted out, one way or another.

Vincent would also have been the first to agree that there must be many worse places in the world to be banged up for the night. The cell was operating-room clean. Tiled walls scrubbed down with bleach and a blanket that had been freshly laundered. The arthritic custody sergeant handling nights that week was amiability itself. Having been garrisoned in India in the 1920s, mainly in Poona, he enjoyed recalling over mugs of tea boisterous nights on forty-eight-hour passes in Bombay. Next morning, after a quick phone call to Hartshorne's office, they returned his notebook, belt and shoelaces, offered him breakfast and then escorted him to the station. There, two constables saw him onto the 9.42 Up that would take him back to Swindon with some well-meant but firmly delivered advice to mind his step and carry better documentation in future.

The moment he got back to the Works he went straight to the Chief Mechanical Engineer's office. There, with Miss Jennings, he designed for himself a GWR warrant card and created a range of impressive certificates, authorities and permits. These were typed up on the GWR's best headed paper, signed by Hartshorne, stamped and witnessed, notarised and then stamped again just for good measure.

Hartshorne also proposed that someone from Movements accompany him in future. It was the enthusiasm with which the Head of Movements agreed to the suggestion that prompted Vincent's refusal. He was pretty sure any such escort would spy on and undermine his efforts far more than resolving any possible misunderstandings.

When he returned to No. 23 to change his clothes he was surprised by Sally's evident relief at seeing him. It hadn't occurred to him that she would have been worried. In truth he hadn't given her a thought, assuming that she would have ascribed his absence from the table for their evening meal to the difficulties of wartime travel.

He assured her he was fine and warned her that there were likely to be many more nights of very late arrivals or overnight absences over the coming weeks. He didn't mention the reason for his delayed return to her or to his fellow lodgers. He wasn't sure why, but he just felt he'd sooner keep it to himself. It hadn't been too onerous or even that unpleasant, just inconvenient. Most importantly, it was not germane to his assignment, of no relevance to them and thus unworthy of any further thought or discussion.

Billy and Akaash walked to the Works together each morning but tended to return to Ashton St separately. Akaash usually headed off as the hooter sounded to the reading room in the Mechanics Institute for an hour or so, arriving at No. 23 just before mealtime. After eating, invariably with a book propped up in front of him on the piccalilli jar, he'd disappear to the room he shared with

Billy to crawl into bed, usually fully clothed as he was feeling the cold, and read some more.

Billy spent his first few evenings writing letters home, sending assurances of safe arrival, kind welcome and interesting work. Thereafter, somewhat at a loss to know quite what to do with himself, he would wrap himself in his heaviest coat and with hands thrust deep into pockets, set out to explore his new home town. He dropped into pubs, stared at shop windows in darkness, called in at any shops still open and usually ended his walk at the Milton Road Baths or the Mechanics Institute.

He discovered early that there were in fact two quite distinct Swindons: the railway town, or New Town, in which he lived and worked and, looking down on this cramped, Victorian red-brick industrial settlement from the hill was the much older, less populous but far more prosperous Market Town with wider avenues, where the houses were much grander, set in large gardens and occupied by professionals and business people. As he strode up Escott Hill he could see the houses progressively getting bigger the higher he climbed.

There was a small corner shop a few streets away from his home that opened late to catch trade from workers on shifts or those fire-watching. Being newsagent, tobacconist and confectioner, it was a place that Billy often found excuses to visit. If nothing else, he'd buy a box of matches. He wondered how the shopkeeper, a woman in her sixties, ever managed to make a living. The store carried a varied stock of oddments, often items which someone had once asked for and which she'd carried ever since. The sweet jars stood in neat rows on the shelves, almost all empty. The glass cases on the counter were thinly stocked and, as he observed when chatting to her and another late customer arrived, most of her sales seemed to be on the promise of a settle-up at the end of the week. She didn't note down these debts. Carried them in her head, Billy assumed, or worked on trust.

'You know,' he observed to Vincent one evening as they both returned to No. 23 within minutes of one another, 'there's nothing like an English corner shop. What's the word? Like an example of something, typical…'

'Quintessential?' a yawning Vincent suggested.

'That's it! "A nation of shopkeepers!" Impossible to imagine another people doing it so well. Italians do barbershops, the French do restaurants. Here they do corner shops. It's so bloody English.'

Vincent's arrival and departure times matched no pattern as they were governed by the railway timetable rather than the hooter. Most days he was out of the house before the other two were up and returned long after they'd eaten. He soon became a familiar sight at Swindon station, stepping down from late trains. The workers on the night shift on the platform and the cleaner sweeping and mopping through the deserted buffet and ticket hall greeted him cheerily. A growing number of the young women waiting for the last train back to South Wales smiled and nodded to him as he walked past. After an evening of drunk custom in the alleyways behind Manchester Road, they found a dapper gent politely raising his hat as he passed them particularly appealing. Who first named him 'Boffin', quickly abbreviated to 'Bof', remained a mystery, but the nickname seemed appropriate to a quiet, studious man always busy scribbling down notes, and it stuck. He increasingly looked forward to and enjoyed his final arrival at Swindon each day, surprised at how quickly in this foreign land it had started to feel like returning home.

Despite his repeated pleading for her not to do so, Sally was always up in the mornings to make him a cup of tea and some toast no matter at what ungodly hour he departed. She invariably kept – plated up and covered by another dinner plate – an evening meal of whatever she had served Akaash and Billy hours earlier, ready to reheat over a pan of boiling water no matter how late he arrived.

Often falling asleep at the table and long past hunger, Vincent would silently work his way through the steaming meal, trying with ignore the tidemark of congealed gravy around the plate. And Sally, her responsibilities finally met for the day, except of course for this last little bit of washing up and preparing Vincent's sandwiches for another early start tomorrow, would watch him eat, and chat with him. Nothing serious. Nothing important. Just about everyday life, which Vincent found deeply comforting at the end of a long, weary and lonely day.

He knew she made up a bed on the sofa in the front room for herself each evening, quickly putting away pillow, sheets and blanket as soon as she heard Vincent stir. He was troubled by the thought that he had taken her bedroom. He raised it with her one late night.

'You know, it would make more sense if I slept on the sofa, given my comings and goings,' he said as he stood at the back door smoking a last cigarette whilst she washed up his plate.

'I started sleeping downstairs when I was on my own during the Blitz. We were lucky, but there were always sirens going off and warnings and all. It was just much easier. Now, I prefer it,' she assured him. 'Just became a habit, I s'pose.'

Billy, determined to sort out the temperamental cistern in the outside toilet at No. 23, set about sourcing the necessary tools from Shop B. He'd asked Keenan if it was permissible to do so and if it was, what the procedure would be. Unsurprisingly it involved more chits, requisitions, signatures, stamps and permits. Or, Keenan whispered with a conspiratorial glance around to check they could not be overheard, you can just slip it into your pocket and no one will be any the wiser. Billy, convinced his actions reflected on more than just his own reputation and honour, decided to follow the laborious rules. It was a decision he more than once regretted, as it meant that gathering even the few tools he thought he'd need and acquiring the necessary parts took longer than he would ever have imagined possible.

But then everything about the Swindon Works seemed surprisingly complex and breathtakingly bureaucratic to him. He was bemused rather than frustrated by this: he was willing to give them the benefit of the doubt about the effectiveness and necessity of all these rules and regulations, all this paperwork. After all, he was from a tiny operation by comparison, well-resourced and with short lines of command. This meant that he had the authority to decide more or less everything by himself, and had access to sufficient funds to implement his decisions. What few things he thought might be beyond his authority he referred to the Durbar where, given the ruler's known enthusiasm for his railway, they were invariably approved. He hadn't realised until arriving in Swindon what an incredible blessing that was.

Whatever reservations he had about the administrative aspects of the GWR, Billy was profoundly in awe of the engineering he witnessed all around him, and rejoiced in the facilities available in Shop B – two overhead cranes of a tonnage he could only dream of back in Gwalior, a bosh – which was a vast dipping tank of boiling caustic soda for degreasing and rust removal – and an eye-watering range of equipment, some so specialised that it had never occurred to him that a tool had been created solely for that task. He was used to having to design and make instruments for one-off jobs himself or make do with ingenuity and brute strength back home, and found the ready availability of virtually every tool or machine he could ever need a dizzying luxury.

Skills, however, were another matter – except for a few individuals.

His aged crane operator was astonishingly competent. A taciturn man who wheezed alarmingly, he was able to place huge loads with a remarkable lightness of touch and an accuracy of fractions of an inch. Keenan was a great help, extremely knowledgeable about everything to do with traditional methods of construction, maintenance and repair of GWR engines in general and Bulldogs in particular. Always good-humoured, always ready to offer sensible if unimaginative advice, yet willing to accept decisions Billy might make that diverged from the usual way of doing things and never seemingly the least resentful of or ever impatient with this rank outsider.

Cyn was keen to make a success of the work, eager to progress in her role in the Union as well as advance her technical knowledge. She was studying in the evenings at the local college, Keenan told Billy, and had ambitions eventually to qualify as a Mechanical Engineer. She was full of questions and Billy delighted in sharing tips with her and demonstrating techniques. In return she tried to help him navigate GWR's byzantine working processes. However, coming from a family in which all the men were employed Inside, and never having worked elsewhere, her explanations often concluded lamely with 'Well, that's just the way it's done'. Her main gift to him was her seeming unending supply of idioms and local expressions, which he absorbed like a sponge.

It was the rest of the Shop B team that were the problem.

Keenan had cheerily characterised them as the sick, the lame and the lazy but this was as unfair as it was inaccurate. Admittedly Shop B did seem to have more than its fair share of the chronically unwell and a worryingly high rate of absenteeism, but of those who did show up every day, only the gang Elsie had brought with her seemed determined to shirk whenever possible. Billy found the majority to be bright, ready to have a go at any task and generally enthusiastic and engaged. Unfortunately, they were also mostly poorly qualified for the roles they now held, with manual dexterity on a spectrum from somewhat inept to dangerously clumsy. In a poorly lit environment full of hot metal, moving parts, heavy machinery and corrosive liquids, it was little surprise that minor injuries abounded and near-fatalities were a frequent occurrence.

In the first few days these ranged from a hammer dropped from height that just missed a furious Elsie, who was convinced it had been deliberate, to a narrowly avoided tumble into the frothing bosh. Billy and Keenan agreed that if something wasn't done it could only be a matter of time before a serious injury occurred. To the plethora of Management/Union committees imposed upon him, Billy added a Safe Working Practices subgroup comprising himself, Keenan, Cyn, Dr Falk from the Medical Fund Hospital and the monosyllabic crane operator. Together they decided that the first thirty minutes of each day must focus on urgently needed instruction on how best to get the job done, if not without accident, at least with everyone still alive at the end of each shift. This would be followed by a fifteen-minute first-aid session from the doctor, who would also offer an informal surgery in Billy's office over the tea break every Thursday.

Reflecting on the first few days of his time in Swindon, Akaash concluded that he was falling short of all that he expected of himself. He knew that he was hardly the most sensitive or socially skilled person in the world, but he was not completely devoid of self-awareness. Indeed, he considered himself acutely attuned to the feelings of others and his impact upon them compared to the blithely unaware Billy who seemed to him congenitally incapable of picking up on hints and cues.

But this was about him, not Billy, he reminded himself sternly. Billy and all his type were destined for the dustbin of history. The future belonged to the workers, not latter-day aristos. And if he were to help shape that future, he, Akaash Ray, needed to up his game.

As was his wont, he mentally listed, categorised and prioritised his self-perceived failures to be thought through in turn. He found introspection came most easily when studying something else, so he picked up the first book that came to hand – the German–English dictionary he'd borrowed from the Mechanics Institute.

First and always most important was money. Was he absolutely satisfied he was spending as little of his weekly wages as possible? His only outings were to the Mechanics Institute reading rooms, which cost nothing. He did not accept offers of cups of tea, a slice of cake or even a biscuit. Anything which would create an obligation to repay a kindness at some point in the future represented the threat of a debt which he was not willing to incur.

He turned to the Ds. Debt: *Schuld*. He was all too well aware that this attitude was assumed to stem from some cultural narrow-mindedness that locals recalling tales of the Indian Mutiny – the First War of Independence, he corrected himself quickly – thought was about a fear of pollution. He was running the risk of being characterised as a bigot (*der frommler, der Eiferer* or *der bigotter mensch*). There must, he mused tangentially, be a fair range of bigotry in Germany to require three distinct terms. Worse still, they might assume he was a religious fanatic (*der religiöser fanatiker*). He'd thought that learning German would be pretty straightforward, and initial evidence supported that hypothesis. At the very least, it should be a lot more straightforward than attempting to master working-class English. Much more reassuringly logical.

He lay the dictionary aside and instead thumbed through *A History of Cryptography*. He suspected he had already earned himself a reputation for parsimony and, because all offers so far declined had been from his two female colleagues, probably misogyny too. He once more picked up the dictionary. *Misognie*, as he'd guessed. Much more of this and he'd be fluent.

Did he care? He hadn't come here to make friends. He did wonder, however, if he might be making a strategic error: perhaps if he engaged a little more freely with Phyl and Joan, and through them others too, he could find ways of raising some cash. Could he take on extra work in the evenings? Maybe Phyl or Joan had a younger sibling in need of some extra tutoring in mathematics? Even if they didn't, maybe they knew someone else who did? Could he teach an evening class at the Technical College? Both a bit beneath him, but needs must when the devil drives, as he had heard the locals say.

But the first step was to be a little more friendly, starting the next day.

Next on his list were his political responsibilities. Far from promoting the Quit India campaign in the UK as he'd confidently assured himself and his comrades he would, he was actually engaged in helping the British to win the war. Surely this must mean that he was actually strengthening, albeit currently not terribly effectively, their capacity and thus their determination to continue their grip on his homeland? In short, the exact opposite of what he was meant to be doing?

If so, this could not be allowed to continue. He had hoped to find like minds: Quakers, socialists and liberals with whom he could speak. People who supported the idea of home rule in India and perhaps could be persuaded to lobby for full independence. Influential people to whom he could explain what the everyday realities of imperialism felt like firsthand. Make them understand the scale of the famine. Persuade them its cause was not nature nor overpopulation but British actions and subsequent inaction. Convince them of its terrible impact on millions of ordinary people. He should be making connections. Talking to people who could change things – another reason to be more outgoing than he had so far. They ran a lecture series at the Mechanics Institute. He could perhaps speak there. Cyn had mentioned that he might like to talk to a branch meeting of the Union: that too could be a start.

But first and foremost, he had to start being less clever, less mean and…he picked up the dictionary once more. Yes, he liked the sound of that. *Freundlicher.*

In Shop B, whilst required parts were awaited, work proceeded on strip down, clean-up and renovation of all components that looked like they could be made to function once more. During these early days, before reconstruction started in earnest, Billy – now dressed in his informal outfit of tweed jacket, matching waistcoat and cap over khaki jodhpurs and boots – was everywhere. Explaining, demonstrating, encouraging. Always with an easygoing smile, raising his voice often over the racket in the shop but never in anger. No job was beneath him: he would pick up a mop or a broom as readily as a spanner or rivet hammer. There was no task he was unable or unwilling to show how he wanted done by doing it himself and patiently guiding repeated performances until he was satisfied the lesson had been adequately learnt. Then, with a cheery thumbs up and an affirming word or two, he'd be off to deal with the next struggling novice. This had the additional advantage of enabling him to personally assess the competence and willingness to learn of every one of the Shop B women, and in general he was impressed by how quickly they picked things up and amazed at how readily they took to their new roles. They were all, he assured them using a term he'd picked up from Cyn, 'bobby dazzlers'. Whatever they were, they were certainly something new and fascinating to him.

He had encountered very few English women in Gwalior. Those he had met at the Residency, and occasional guests of the Maharajah whom he'd formally welcome at the station, were of a decidedly different ilk. Languid, poised and, like their husbands, seemingly bred to drift above the practical, sullied realities of the everyday, looking upon the world with bored yet gorgeous indifference. A half-sigh and a slightly pained expression was more than sufficient to send dozens of bearers and servants scurrying off to resolve whatever had prompted such hinted ire. He had thus started with very low expectations of engagement, energy or even a willingness to get their hands dirty when he had learned his workforce would be extensively female, but had been delighted to be proven so wrong, so quickly. He even found refreshing the occasional, expletive-rich screaming matches among Elsie's cohort which sent Keenan's and Cyn's eyebrows simultaneously skyward.

As both competence and confidence grew among the workers and years of rust and dirt were stripped away from the engines, he could refine his assessment of the challenges ahead. The oldest of the eight Bulldogs was the 3334 *Eclipse*, built in November 1899. Four others were built the following year, and the remaining three in 1902 and 1903. Although they were much the same age, they varied greatly in condition. The 3368 *Sir Stafford*, 3370 *Tremayne* and 3443 *Birkenhead* had all been thoroughly stripped out and cleaned up prior to withdrawal, and then well greased and stored under cover. Billy assumed that these had been intended for resale as working engines rather than marked down for scrap, and thus had been better decommissioned. Apart from some surface rust, a few seized components and a declaration of undying love dated 1937 painstakingly scratched into the paintwork of the *Tremayne*'s boiler, these three locomotives were in good shape, and Billy thought they should be capable of being brought back into service relatively quickly.

The others had not been so effectively mothballed. Several were severely dilapidated, with battered panels, great gaping holes and smashed cabs. Two had had critical components totally removed. One seemed to have been set on fire at some point. There was a great deal of work to be done. But at least the first three could be rapidly overhauled and be up and running fairly quickly.

Billy told Keenan his opinion on the various locomotives. Keenan agreed with his analysis but looked doubtful about his conclusion. 'You want to give the CME three of these engines in the next few weeks?'

'You don't think that's possible?'

'I don't question your judgement on that, Mr Khan. I'm sure if you say it's possible then it is, but is it smart?'

Billy was mystified. 'I don't get you.'

'Well, the Chief only asked for one by the end of next month.'

'Yes! But we can give him at least two and possibly all three!'

'You ever hear of the story of the two bulls, Mr Khan?' asked Keenan, pushing the brim of his bowler hat up. 'This young bull sees a herd of cows at the top of a hill. "Let's run up that hill and put calves in a few of those cows!" says he to the older bull. "No," the older bull replies, "Let's walk up that hill and put calves in *all* of those cows."'

'Good story! Must remember that one. But I'm afraid I still don't see what you're getting at.'

'Well, it's in the nature of the young and keen to try to charge on, wanting to get on with things, but the more experienced of us know that sometimes you achieve more in the long run by taking it steady at the start.' Seeing Billy still seemed no wiser, he continued, 'Look, what I'm trying to say is, maybe we shouldn't be in too much of a rush right now when things are easy because we might just need an engine or two in reserve that we can roll out if we get into difficulties with some of these others. A little insurance scheme if you like.' He paused, then leaned forward and spoke more quietly. 'It's never a good idea to exceed a boss's demands: he won't thank you for it. It makes him look like he didn't know what he was talking about and leads him to demand a lot more the next time.'

Billy was genuinely stunned by such cynicism from a man who'd always seemed to him to epitomise goodwill and kind spirit. 'I thought Mr Hartshorne was boss, family and friend to you?'

'He is indeed. And I'd give him the shirt off my back. But first and foremost, he's the boss. And bosses need careful handling. All I'm saying is, meet his expectations, don't exceed them. Use what time that buys us to get the girls trained up properly. You know what the posters say: "Don't be a Squander Bug". We won't get this opportunity again.'

The next morning Akaash embarked upon his charm offensive. Joan was delighted that he wanted to discuss Calcutta and her childhood there with her in Bengali. Phyl was rather more distant, feeling left out of their shared experiences, but her icy manner thawed noticeably as Akaash suggested various ways in which they could move forward with their mission without the patronising, arrogant and somewhat petulant tone he'd previously adopted. They pooled their ideas and decided to experiment between themselves, creating some modified examples of classical codes to see how quickly they could break one another's efforts.

They were enjoying a cup of tea (fetched for the first time by Akaash) and some homemade biscuits Joan had brought in, when there was a knock on the door.

'Out of bounds!' shouted Phyl, but the door opened anyway and a large man in a trilby hat and raincoat sauntered in.

'Not to me, Missy,' he said, holding out a police warrant card as he took a cursory glance around the room. 'Inspector Curtis. Wiltshire Constabulary. Special Branch. Not exactly a hive of activity in here, is it?' He let his gaze fall and stay on Akaash. 'Dr Ray, I presume?'

'Does Mr Hartshorne know you're here?' asked Phyl, in her most imperious voice.

'Shouldn't think so, dearie,' said Curtis, not shifting his attention from Akaash, who sat in silence, very still, eyes down. 'I haven't come to talk to him. Or to you, Miss… Grigg, isn't it? So why don't you two ladies go and powder your noses and leave Dr Ray and I to speak, man to man? Close the door behind you on your way out.'

Phyl attempted a further protest but was ignored. Joan asked to see the warrant card properly but was met with a similar stony silence. Assuring the policeman that he hadn't heard the last of the matter, they left, determined to find the Chief Mechanical Engineer and complain about this blatant intrusion on their work. Curtis sat on the edge of Akaash's desk, took out a packet of cigarettes and offered him one. Akaash shook his head.

'Suit yourself,' said Curtis with a shrug, lighting up. He took a deep drag, then blew the smoke out in a long, satisfied breath. 'Don't mind if I smoke, do you? My manners, eh? Should have asked before. Oh, yeah, I've just remembered. You're an asthmatic, aren't you? I'm so sorry,' he concluded, with exaggerated, fake sincerity, looking around for an ashtray. Not finding one, he dropped the cigarette into Akaash's half-drunk cup of tea and fanned the air in front of his face.

'You want me to see how much you know about me, is that it?' asked Akaash, struggling to suppress a fit of coughing.

Curtis leaned forward. 'Bright boy,' he smiled, his face a few inches from Akaash's so that Akaash could smell the stale smoke and feel his breath on his face. 'We've just received a nice long file all about you. Came on the same boat you did. Funny that, eh? See, we're required to keep an eye on people like you 'cos you have a nasty habit of shooting retired Governors General. Ungrateful, I call it.' He chuckled. 'God bless the Railway! Get an enemy of the state to work for them! If there's a cack-handed way of doing something you can bet they'll find it.'

He leaned back, arms crossed, studying Akaash. 'Someone must have made the most almighty cock-up with your vetting! Mind you, to be fair, you don't look much like a threat to King and Country to me. But then your kind never really do, do they?'

'My kind?'

'Oh, you thought I meant…no, I mean you revolutionaries. Look at old whatsisname? Gandhi. A puff of wind would blow him away.'

'Are you here to arrest me?'

Curtis raised his eyebrows theatrically. 'You done something you think I should arrest you for? No? Well then, relax, Dr Ray. This is just a little "getting to know you" session.'

'Am I to be sent home?'

'Nah. No one seems in too much of a hurry to have you back.' He wandered around the room, paused at Joan's desk and leafed through a couple of the papers on it. 'What is it you're supposed to be doing here anyway?'

'I'm afraid I can't tell you. If I'm not being arrested, I'd like to join my colleagues.'

'"I'm afraid I can't tell you!"' mimicked Curtis in a music-hall Indian accent, wobbling his head. 'Good for you! Proper little soldier! And as for your "colleagues", I expect they'll be back with reinforcements any minute now. I'm surprised it's taken them this long. In the meantime, would you like to know a little secret?'

Akaash sighed. 'Do I have a choice?'

'You've got a smart mouth, son. You need to watch that. That could get you into trouble one day. Now I'll ask you again, and this time, I want you to be a little politer…'

'More polite.'

'What?'

'It's "more polite". "A little politer" is grammatically incorrect.'

'Fuck me! English lessons from a bloody Indian! You just can't help yourself, can you? Now let's try again, *more politely*, OK? Want to know that little secret?'

Akaash nodded, resigned.

'Good. See, between you and me, I don't give a tinker's cuss what you've done back home. In fact, to tell you God's honest truth I couldn't give a flying fuck about you, India or all her teeming millions. Stay. Go. Eat. Starve. It's all one to me. But what I do care about is this town, my people and this place. So don't you go trying any of your *communistic* bullshit here, OK? Not on my tic. Not on my tab. Got that?'

The door burst open and Phyl and Joan returned with a clearly unhappy Hartshorne.

'Ta-daa!' sang Curtis. 'Right on cue. Afternoon, Mr Hartshorne,' he said, rising. 'Just conveying the Chief Constable's welcome to your new employee. Don't work him too hard, sir. Asthmatic, you know,' he confided, tapping his chest as he headed for the door, where he paused and turned back to smile at Akaash. 'Look after that chest of yours, Dr Ray. You and I will be seeing each other again.' He raised his hat as he left the room. 'Mr Hartshorne. Ladies.'

Hartshorne was fuming, Phyl volubly outraged and Joan profoundly impressed by the police interest in Akaash. There was excited talk of formal complaints (Phyl), the precarious nature of personal freedom in a nation at war (Joan) and unacceptable state interference in the working of an independent commercial organisation (Hartshorne). Everyone, except Akaash, was talking over one another and paying no attention whatsoever to anyone else. Akaash finally spoke, urging them to forget all about it. Hartshorne and Phyl were far from satisfied with this and returned to the Chief Mechanical Engineer's office to place a call to the Chief Constable, with whom, Phyl was at pains to point out, her father had once played golf. Hartshorne trumped that by mentioning they were both members of the same Masonic lodge. Left together,

Joan looked at Akaash with something approaching awe. She picked up his cup and saucer, saw the cigarette end floating in the cold tea and grimaced. 'Eugh! What a disgusting swine! No better than the Gestapo!'

Akaash said nothing. He was still working through the implications of the visit. He was not terribly surprised that the police showed an interest in him. His political activities back in Calcutta were hardly secret. But he was surprised at how quickly they had tracked him down and how fully they seemed to have been informed about him. Most intriguing of all were the implications of the fact that he was neither being arrested nor returned home. That, he strongly suspected, did not bode well for the future.

'Special Branch,' Joan said, slightly breathlessly. 'Gosh! Political stuff! I say!'

Akaash looked at her thoughtfully. She seemed so young and gazed at him with such unalloyed admiration he found himself smiling in spite of himself.

'I've always wanted to meet somebody in the Congress party!' Joan enthused. 'Have you actually met Mr Gandhi or Mr Nehru?'

Akaash shook his head.

'But you must have been to meetings, rallies…marches? Heard them speak? I think non-violence is absolutely wonderful!'

'I'm not really a Congress man,' Akaash explained, noting the look of disappointment cross Joan's face. 'I'm a socialist, but more of a Marxist than the mainstream of the Congress party.'

Joan's eyes widened. 'Even better!' she enthused. 'So why are they interested in you? Have you, you know, blown up anything?'

'No. I'm not sure how much we'll achieve by non-violence but I am sure we can't yet win an armed struggle by ourselves. And current possible allies are likely to be as bad as the British. Any acts of violence right now will simply play into the oppressor's hands. Ultimately the revolution will triumph through the people taking up arms, but we're not there yet. All I've done so far is talk to student gatherings, attend the odd demonstration and organise a strike at college.'

'Well, that's a start, I suppose,' said Joan, secretly thinking that Akaash's struggle didn't sound much more radical than her own student life.

'Oh, and I threw a pot of red paint over a bust of Queen Victoria,' Akaash added. 'Or at least I tried to. You'd be surprised how difficult something like that actually is. Got most of it over myself. That's how they caught me. Red-handed. Literally. Still, it made headlines, which was the point.'

Joan laughed and held up her hand in front of her mouth. 'Sorry!' she said. After a moment's thought, she continued, 'You know, I have lots of friends in Oxford who are Marxists – or at least Marxians. You should meet them! They'd be thrilled to hear from someone who's actually on the front line of the struggle against imperialism.'

Strange, Akaash thought, how life works out. The previous evening he had been wondering how to make contact with the kind of people he wanted to talk to and, lo and behold, thanks to the British police no less, he was halfway to an introduction.

Billy was still thinking through what Keenan had said and reluctantly accepting the wisdom of it as he walked home at the end of the day. Approaching No. 23, he was surprised to see a taxi pulled up next to the cart outside the house next door. Motor vehicles were an uncommon sight on Ashton St and a parked car a rarity. The driver, leaning against the bonnet of the 1935 Austin and sipping a cup of tea, gave Billy a nod and a cheery greeting as he passed. Billy nodded back, even more surprised: whenever he'd encountered him before, sitting in his cab outside the station, he'd seemed a picture of misery. He walked up the pathway to the front door of No. 23, where he was met on the doorstep by a clearly troubled Sally.

'You've got a visitor, Mr Khan,' she whispered in a slightly accusatory tone, looking up and down the street as though afraid others might be lurking in doorways. Clearly, unexpected visitors were rarely a welcome surprise on Ashton St. 'I've put him in the front room.'

'Thanks, Mrs A,' he said. He couldn't help but notice she'd reverted to calling him 'Mr Khan'. That didn't bode well either. 'Do we know who this visitor is?'

'Said his name is Lockyer. Gave me his card,' she said, with a mix of pride and anxiety. 'From London!' she added, with the same tone she'd have used if she'd said he was from Sodom, Gomorrah or Berlin.

'Oh, Lockyer! Jolly good! Nothing to worry about, Mrs A. I've been expecting him to call.'

'That's his taxi. Mr Rimes from the station.'

'Ah. Right.'

'He's left the meter running!'

Whilst Billy found Akaash's frugality embarrassing and thought it symptomatic of a meanness of spirit, he found Mrs A's thrift oddly endearing. 'No wonder Mr Rimes is looking so pleased with himself. Oh well. It's not our money. Nor his, come to that,' he added on reflection.

'Should I lay another place?'

'What?'

'Will he be wanting his tea?'

'Shouldn't think so. Let's see what he does want and then let's, um, give him the bum's rush as soon as possible.' Billy was pleased at using a Cyn-ism he'd been looking forward to being able to deploy. 'Lockyer!' he shouted as he opened the door of the front room. 'Ah, there you are! Good to see you at last.'

Lockyer leapt up from the armchair, no easy feat for a man so tall who had been sitting folded like a collapsed deckchair into a seat so low and soft. 'My dear Mr Khan!' he said, advancing and offering his hand, 'I can't begin to tell you how sorry I am…'

Billy took a step back and held up his oil-stained and grimy hands. 'I've just looked in to say hello. We'll talk properly once I've cleaned up a bit. Do sit down. I'll only be, um, half a mo. Mrs A?' he called out as he left the room. 'Can we rustle up another cup of tea for Mr Lockyer? Thanks ever so,' he added, delighted he'd already managed to deploy two – no, *three* – newly learnt expressions in as many minutes.

Washed, changed out of his work clothes and carrying a cup of tea, Billy rejoined Lockyer in the front room. The Maharajah's man in London was stick-thin with a surprisingly young manner and a boyish face, and towered a good few inches over Billy. Only the wattle of red skin above his collar and the dark liver spots on the backs of his hands gave the lie to his youthful appearance. He was dressed formally – suited, with a stiff-winged collar and dark bow tie. There was a glisten of sweat on his forehead. On closer examination, Billy noticed the fine lines around his eyes and the broken veins on the sides of his nose.

'Mr Khan! I'm so sorry I wasn't at Southampton to meet you! I must have only just missed you. Delays on the railway…held up at Newbury. I understand Colonel Dawlish sorted you out there? He seems an interesting man…'

'Nothing to sort out,' Billy assured him, disinclined to engage in small talk or gossip.

'Well, maybe not there, but…' observed Lockyer, looking around the room with obvious distaste.

'Yeees?' said Billy carefully, one eyebrow raised.

'I've arranged rooms for you at the Goddard Arms. I understand it's the best accommodation available. This is hardly fitting…'

'Well, you can just go and un-arrange them. I'm settled here with my um, *muckers*, thanks.'

'But your…landlady told me they have you sharing a room! With some Bengali called Ray…'

'That's Dr Ray, if you don't mind. Now presumably you have some papers for me?' asked Billy stiffly.

'Oh, of course!' said Lockyer, mumbling further expressions of concern as he reached down to retrieve a briefcase by the side of his chair.

He took out a file and sorted through its contents. 'Let me see… we have a *laissez-passer* from the Durbar, letters of introduction to various friends of the Maharajah. Lines of credit with his tailor, bootmaker, wine merchant – don't imagine you'll have much need of that – and tobacconist. Nominations for membership of various clubs – the Duke of York, Royal Overseas League – they just need your signature. More letters to various institutes and professional associations to which I understand His Highness wishes you to be admitted, with details of various prizes, medals and contributions he is happy to fund to…shall we say, *ease* the process. I can deal with all of that for you. And this,' he concluded, handing over an envelope.

Billy tore open the envelope and skimmed its contents. It was an authorisation to draw on the Maharajah's private funds held at Coutts's in London together with a letter to the manager of the Commercial Road branch of Lloyds Bank in Swindon instructing him to facilitate the transactions. Billy's eyes widened as he saw the sums available to him. He carefully folded up the documents and slid them back inside the envelope.

'Excellent. Thank you, Mr Lockyer. Now unless there's anything else, can I suggest you go and cancel those rooms? We don't want to waste His Highness's money, do we?'

Lockyer closed his briefcase and looked up. 'Are you sure I can't persuade you to move to the hotel? It really would be so much more fitting.'

'Absolutely sure.'

'Well, I don't know how I will explain this to His Highness…'

'He doesn't need to be troubled with this. Anyway, there's something I am obligated to remain here to do.'

'Ah!' exclaimed Lockyer, touching a finger to the side of his nose. 'Say no more. How could I have been so slow! Wheels within wheels.' He nodded sagely, thinking of a recent conversation he'd had with the mysterious Colonel Dawlish.

'As you say,' said Billy, 'wheels within wheels,' wondering how Lockyer could possibly know about the faulty cistern. Perhaps he'd needed to spend a penny – another Cyn-ism – whilst waiting for Billy's return. 'Now, there are a few things you can have sent down from London for me…'

The next day was a Saturday and the working day Inside ended at midday. Vincent remained at No. 23, writing up his notes. It was late afternoon and he had stepped out into the backyard of No. 23 to smoke. Akaash had travelled to Oxford to address a gathering of Joan's Marxian friends. Billy was finally equipped to his satisfaction and was busy working on the cistern of the toilet, and Sally was ironing in the kitchen whilst listening to the wireless, humming along to a popular song Vincent was sure he knew but couldn't quite place.

He could hear children kicking a ball about in the alleyway that ran behind the houses. In someone's back garden, hens were clucking. He thought he could even hear what sounded like a piano lesson in progress further up the street. At such times it really was hard to remember there was a war in progress and that for those kids kicking a ball and that child at the piano, being at war was pretty much all they had known.

A weed-ridden cracked path and a sagging washing line led arrow-straight to the back gate. On either side of the path, stony soil was dug over and sparsely planted with a range of vegetables. Nearest to the back door outside which Vincent stood were a couple of rows of earthed-up potatoes. Then a patch of onions, a few carrots and, near the outhouse in which Billy was busily disconnecting old pipework, a wigwam of long birch sticks supporting runner beans, the pods of which hung thin and lank.

It struck Vincent that the garden could be much more densely planted, ideally with crops that would better match their palate. Spinach. Garlic. Coriander perhaps? He looked over the fence to the garden at No. 21. Now that was more like what he had in mind! Every scrap of ground closely planted in neat, straight rows. Even a few sweet peas entwined among the edible variety, and tall stands of chrysanthemums along the fence.

He'd occasionally glimpsed their neighbour at No. 21 but had not as yet spoken to him. Sally had told them people on Ashton St liked to keep to themselves, and his limited interactions with them had certainly confirmed that. Those at No. 25, the Adams, were deeply reserved. Methodists, Sally had said they were, although whether that had anything to do with their introversion Vincent had no idea. The father worked Inside and would nod to them if they left their front doors at the same time or returned home simultaneously. His wife, a small person who sniffed a lot and blinked rapidly, putting in Vincent's mind the image of some sort of nocturnal creature confused in the sunlight, did her best to pretend she hadn't even noticed they existed. The children were marginally more sociable at first but they too were wary of their new neighbours. Billy had reached into his pocket and presented them with a handful of boiled sweets when he'd first spotted them returning from school – sweets which their parents had made them return, tearfully posted back through the letterbox of No. 23. Thereafter, they fled in terror whenever they caught sight of a mystified Billy, and shrank away from his fellow residents as well.

The man living alone at No. 21 was called Ernie, Sally said. Ernie Norris. Had had a hard time of it in the trenches and never been quite the same, she explained. Been even worse since his wife passed on, she had added with a mix of genuine sympathy and unconscious satisfaction in the description of someone so much worse off than oneself. He made a living of sorts selling written-off stock, scrap metal and wood offcuts from the Works, which he collected and delivered on the handcart invariably parked in the street in front of his house.

As Vincent reflected on gardening possibilities, the neighbour came out of his kitchen door and, leaning on a walking stick, stared back over the fence at Vincent. 'Had a good enough look?' he asked. He shifted his balance, leaned the stick against the fence and began to open a tin of rolling tobacco.

'Yes, thank you,' said Vincent, not picking up the sarcasm. 'Care for one of these?' He stepped up to the fence, reached across the boundary between the two properties and proffered his packet of Woodbines.

Ernie continued to stare at him. Then he glanced down at the offered packet of cigarettes, thought a moment longer and wordlessly took one. Vincent lit a match and offered it to Ernie in cupped hands. Ernie drew hard on the cigarette and its burning red tip flared. He took the cigarette out of his mouth, studied it, looked back up at Vincent and nodded.

He was, Vincent guessed, in his late fifties or early sixties. His cheeks were sunken and covered in grey stubble, his eyes deep-set and small under bushy eyebrows and his complexion like old candle wax. He wore a flat cap, the top of which was greasy with dried sweat. The stiffening of the peak showed through the thin check cloth. His trousers looked as though they were too big for him and were gathered around his thin waist with a worn brown leather belt. He wore an old waistcoat over a collarless shirt with the sleeves rolled up to mid bicep, revealing tanned and surprisingly muscular arms. On his left bicep, Vincent could just make out part of a tattoo: a scroll under what looked like the bottom half of a Maltese Cross.

'The name is Rosario,' said Vincent, offering his hand. 'I'm...'

'One of the coloureds at the Works. I know who you are.'

There was an uncomfortable silence, interrupted by the clatter of dropped metal and a particularly colourful bit of muffled swearing from Billy. 'Your mate's sorting that bog for 'er then, is 'e?' Ernie asked, nodding over at the outhouse.

'Says it shouldn't take him long,' said Vincent with a smile. He continued to gaze contemplatively over the fence. 'Nice garden.'

Ernie looked round and shrugged. 'She could do a lot more with hers,' he said, casting a critical glance over Mrs A's efforts at planting and growing. 'Mind you, her Derek ain't much cop as a gardener either. Tried his hand at caulis once. Hopeless.'

Vincent mentally added cauliflower to his list. Cabbage too.

'I'm thinking of asking her if I can use part of the garden to grow some things from home,' ventured Vincent.

Ernie looked doubtful. 'Bit late in the year to be planting anything other'n winter greens.'

'I suppose so. Anyway, I'm not sure we'd be able to get the kind of things I'm thinking of.'

Without a word, Ernie turned and limped back into his house. Vincent was about to stub out his cigarette and go back in himself when Ernie re-emerged with a small booklet which he held out to Vincent. 'Seed catalogue,' he said. 'Want it back, mind.'

Billy emerged from the outhouse, unusually pensive, bearing a bag of tools. Vincent introduced him to Ernie.

'Shitter sorted?' Ernie asked.

'What? Oh, I see…sadly not. Proved a bit more tricky than anticipated. Odd fittings. Badly connected. Non-standard. Ball-cock misaligned. Nothing I can't handle, obviously,' he added hastily. 'It's just…'

'Wrong tools?' asked Ernie.

'Exactly,' agreed Billy, as Ernie and Vincent shared a quiet smile.

The schedule for fire-watching duties was posted at lunchtime the next day. Vincent was left off the roster as he was travelling so much but Billy was allocated a two-hour shift from midnight on the roof of Shop K with Elsie's best friend, Doreen, and Cyn, both of whom were old hands at fire-watching. Akaash was assigned to the same time slot with Phyl, for whom this was also to be a new experience, on the roof of the Pattern Store. The Pattern Store was a looming, rectangular five-storey building in the same brickwork as the rest of the Works but located just across Rodbourne Road from the Foundry, to which it was linked by a covered walkway. As the roof of the Store was entirely covered by a vast cast-iron water tank, the risk from fire bombs was minimal, and thus it was judged the ideal place to put new watchers if they couldn't be teamed up with anyone more experienced.

They received their induction training that afternoon after the final hooter sounded. They were issued with tin hats, three buckets of sand, a shovel, another bucket filled with water and a stirrup pump. Their main purpose, they were told in a bored voice by the chief of the Works' fire brigade clearly giving a speech he had repeated many times before, was to deal with incendiary bombs. They were advised that in the event of such bombs being dropped on their roof, they should use water to cool them down and cover them with sand before they could ignite. Any small fires could then be extinguished using the water and the stirrup pump. So far, both the town and the Works had escaped any serious bombing. The odd solitary daytime raider had dropped a stick of bombs and shot up the gasometer but compared to Coventry, London or even nearby Bath, Swindon had to date escaped very lightly indeed. The Chief Fire Officer sounded almost offended that the Luftwaffe had shown so little regard for the Swindon Works that they hadn't even attempted to give it a decent blitzing.

Not that there were any grounds for complacency, he warned sternly. As talk of the Second Front grew, the hub and heart of the rail network for southwest England must, he reasoned, inevitably become a higher priority target. They were asked if they had any questions, and then given a chance to practise using the stirrup pump. This caused much hilarity and some not terribly accidental squirting of one another. The Chief Fire Officer watched it all with bored tolerance. He looked forward with hope but no great expectation to just once training a group that didn't do exactly that. It wasn't the tomfoolery he found wearing, it was the fact that they always thought they were the first ones ever to do it. Then they were sent off home somewhat damp with instructions to be back and ready to take up their posts at least fifteen minutes before their designated shift.

Billy was delighted at the prospect of a midnight vigil with Cyn. Their being teamed up hadn't come as a complete surprise: it had cost him two packs of his rapidly depleting stock of Balkan cigarettes. Shame about Doreen being there too, but no amount of persuasion or inducements on his part could bend the rules that required a team of three watchers on the roof of Shop K. That, he was assured by the Roster Clerk as he gratefully lit up one of Billy's cigarettes, was that.

Almost inevitably, Billy had developed something of a crush on Cyn. He remained determined to respect the role and personal dignity of every one of his team in Shop B, but felt this responsible attitude and mature behaviour could reasonably be restricted to the time between the first and last hooters of the day. Before and after, he allowed himself to contemplate his colleagues not as a series of skilled – well, very semi-skilled – workers but as physical, sexual beings: women, with a glorious range of shapes and sizes of breasts, buttocks and thighs. Outside of Shop B, he could put aside his priest-like mantle of celibate professionalism and acknowledge that he was a man, with passions, desires and increasingly pressing needs that required satisfying.

It would have been impossible for him to avoid Cyn, even if he'd wanted to. She sat on all the Shop B Workers' Committees, which had been established to deal with employee grievances and the occasional disputes about trade demarcations, employment terms and wage rates, and which Billy nominally chaired. The innumerable regulations and arcane processes of the Works were as incomprehensible to him as they were uninteresting, but they seemed simplicity itself to Keenan, with a lifetime Inside and an encyclopaedic knowledge of the rulebook. He too was on the committees and their effective head. Billy confined his contributions to opening and closing the meetings and asking if anyone fancied another cup of tea. He then spent most of the time trying to follow the discussions, surreptitiously looking at Cyn, occasionally asking her what she thought and delighting in her wonderful Swindon accent every time she contributed. In everyone else he encountered, that pronounced west country burr, exaggerated pronunciation, odd additional syllables and seemingly arbitrary addition and subtraction of the letter 'r' sounded to him slow-witted and vaguely moronic. But in her it had a rhythm and charm all of its own. He particularly loved her nuanced use of 'Ahhh', which, depending on intonation, could mean anything from 'I quite agree with you' through 'Is that right?' to 'It was pretty obvious that was going to happen'.

This growing obsession with Cyn, constrained by his determination to keep their in-work interactions strictly professional, had three immediate results. First, the Shop B committees met far more frequently than those in any other shop. Second, the Shop B committees' Management side were the only representatives of the company to suggest possible grounds for disputes to the Union representatives sitting on the other side of the table. Third, Billy adopted ever more west country expressions, which had sounded so delightful when spoken by Cyn but when attempted by him caused considerable and poorly disguised mirth among his colleagues. 'Great' became 'gurt'. His accommodation at No. 23 was his 'digs', and his fellow lodgers his 'muckers' or 'oppos'. Anyone whose name he didn't know or couldn't promptly recall was referred to simply as 'Buggerlugs'. The growing heap of discarded scrap awaiting collection by Mollie and her cart horse became the 'glory hole' and anything deeply irritating or frustrating became enough to have him 'sent to Devizes', although he had no idea why. It did, however, lead him to regard anyone from that town with profound suspicion.

The prospect of a night with her on a workshop roof was already arousing him. The obvious problem was of course that they would not be alone. However, it would be very cold and bleak, which, he imagined, he should be able to exploit to his advantage. He wondered if there was a way of persuading Doreen not to join them, but dismissed the idea as unlikely, too obvious and even if successful would probably result in her immediate replacement, potentially by someone likely to be even more of a problem. He decided, at least for this first shift, to simply follow the rules. Doreen had said that they should each bring a flask of tea and some sandwiches to keep them going. Sally had already prepared this for both Akaash and Billy, as well as having taken out of mothballs a pair of her husband's woollen gloves and a scarf for Akaash.

Billy had also made some discreet preparations of his own. He didn't really think there was much chance of a romantic encounter with Cyn on the roof but thought it always wise to be prepared. He'd been advised by a tipsy shipboard acquaintance that a barber's shop was the place to go. And when the barber asked if you'd like anything for the weekend, well, that's how you acquired prophylactics in Britain. Even after a few drinks this had seemed unlikely to Billy, but having spent some time in the Works he now found he expected everything in this place to be done in the most obscure and illogical ways. In the hours before his watch therefore, he went for a haircut.

With hindsight, the framed image of the Virgin Mary on the wall of the waiting area should have given him pause for thought. The barber made no enquiries about his weekend at all and Billy's faltering attempts to raise the subject were met by a blank stare.

He'd also been told if all else failed, Boots, the chemist, was another source, but not to be recommended for the faint-hearted. In any case, by that time of day they were closed. Then Billy had a brainwave: if a chemist's shop stocked condoms, the pharmacy of the Medical Fund Hospital probably had some too. It was still open when he arrived, but the pharmacist was intimidating, female and in any case was, she assured him, only able to dispense what the doctor had prescribed.

Fortunately, or unfortunately, a white-coated Dr Falk emerged from her surgery as they were speaking.

'Mr Khan! What can I do for you?' she asked with a tired smile.

The pharmacist folded her arms and watched with ill-disguised amusement.

'Oh, er, nothing. It can wait…'

'He's after some…protection,' offered the pharmacist unhelpfully.

Dr Falk was clearly confused. 'Beyond what we've been discussing in the Safe Working Practices subcommittee?'

'I think it's his extracurricular activities he's thinking about,' said the pharmacist, who hadn't had this much fun in years.

Dr Falk frowned, before understanding dawned. 'Heavens! Give the poor man a pack of Johnnies, Mrs Richards, and stop being so mean! Honestly!'

Even though they had been warned just how long, cold and miserable two hours on a rooftop in Swindon in the middle of the night could be, the reality took Billy by surprise. Doreen, as the most experienced of the three, appointed herself team leader. This involved finding the most sheltered spot on the roof, wrapping a blanket around herself and promptly going to sleep. Cyn looked at Billy and rolled her eyes. As she often found, she was torn between the need to maintain and display solidarity with the people she represented and her personal dislike for several, in particular Elsie and Doreen. Faith in the proletariat and a determination to champion them against an exploitative management was much easier when the workers were an amorphous concept, a political construct, considered as a whole. When encountered as individuals, Cyn had to admit they could be every bit as petty, grasping and bloody horrid as the despised bourgeoisie. Elsie, determined to be a Foreman, could be dismissed as a class traitor. It was harder to justify her dislike of Doreen other than that Cyn thought her a gossipy, vindictive old cow.

As troubling as her dislike of an increasing number of her members was her fondness for their class enemies and a growing recognition that simple battle lines were easy to draw but difficult to maintain. Mr Hartshorne was a pompous old bugger but Cyn always felt his heart was in the right place. Yes, he'd started as an apprentice and risen through the years to leave his working-class origins behind him, but no one cared more about the Works than he did. Mr Keenan too wasn't such a bad old stick. Had it tough during the Great War, so her dad said, like a lot of the men. And as for Mr Khan…

She realised she'd been staring at him. She quickly looked away and made a great show of arranging the buckets and stirrup pump. 'Why should England tremble – eh? –' she quipped, 'when you, me and sleeping beauty over there are its first line of defence against Jerry? Sleep well, Swindon!'

He smiled and nodded. Cyn often said things like that, which left him uncertain where the boundary between sincerity and sarcasm lay. At such times he wasn't quite sure how he should respond. He found glancing skyward, nodding in agreement then rolling his head in wonder at the foolishness of mankind seemed to work well. Or at least he thought it did because it usually made her smile. In truth it left her totally confused about what he was trying to convey – assuming it was some exclusively Indian gesture, she smiled in response because she didn't know what else to do. She had a horror of appearing at all racially prejudiced and her every interaction with Billy was shaped by that fear.

The previous evening she'd asked her parents if they'd mind if she invited 'one of the Indians' around for tea one evening. Her mum was flustered and immediately worried about appearances. Her dad said he had no objection to any man on the basis of nationality or skin colour – just not that uppity bugger in Movements, he'd added. She'd reassured him that he wasn't the one she had in mind.

To Cyn, Billy represented a clear anomaly. Was he Management? It would be hard to deny that he was, even though he had his Union card, which with hindsight she probably shouldn't have offered him. But he didn't fit into her class-based perception of society – though in even thinking that, was she guilty of racialism? Just because he was an Indian, did that mean he couldn't be a boss and be entitled to all the negative connotations that title earned in her world view? And the fact that he came from some Maharajah's state she'd never even heard of rather than British India? What were the implications of that? Didn't that make him like some tsarist officer or royalist lickspittle? Maybe even an accursed aristo? Look at those trousers he wore. And that huge overcoat that he usually wore: astrakhan, someone said it was. Both were items she'd only ever seen before worn by the royal family and other knobs in the newsreels. She wondered idly why he wasn't wearing that coat right now. It would have been ideal up here. Probably didn't want to get it dirty.

Life could be so bloody confusing. Political theory and individual cases rarely sat comfortably together, she concluded. Especially, as she had to admit, since he was such a good-looking bugger. And no one could have failed to notice that he clearly fancied her. When others pointed it out, she dismissed it as so much tosh. But, much to her own annoyance, she found herself putting a bit more effort into her appearance when going to work. On one occasion, she even put a little bit of her last precious lipstick on – an act she did not repeat because it prompted so much smirking and teasing from her supposed comrades.

'Penny for them?' Billy offered. Another new expression he had learnt from her.

Cyn smiled and shook her head. 'Not worth even that. I was just wondering why you aren't wearing that fancy coat of yours.'

'Lent it to the good Dr Ray,' said Billy. 'He needs a...er, gurt big coat more than I do. You know he still hasn't bought himself any winter clothes?'

'I know. That Joan says he sends every penny he can get his hands on back home to his family.'

Billy looked surprised. 'Really? I thought he was just tight.'

'Deep pockets?'

He frowned, mystified. Cyn wondered about him sometimes. How could anyone who was so knowledgeable about engines and brilliant with machinery be otherwise so slow on the uptake?

'Deep pockets and short arms. So he can't reach the money in the bottom of them?'

'Oh, right, I get it! Deep pockets! Very good!' he cried, determined to use the expression as she had at the first possible opportunity. 'You know, it means exactly the opposite where I come from? Strange. Still, I didn't realise he was, well...I feel a bit bad about some of the things I've said to him now.'

'Well, you ought to be nicer to him. He's a good man.'

'Is he? I suppose he is. Seems a bit of a...' he groped for a suitable Swindonism but his colloquial vocabulary failed him. He wasn't sure if 'wassock' was a term a gentleman should use in front of a lady – '… twerp,' he concluded lamely.

'Well, I think you should all stick together. Support one another.'

'What, me, him and the Anglo? Why?'

'Well, you're all from the same place, aren't you? Unity? Solidarity?'

Billy did his head roll thing again. 'Funny, everybody says that about us, but I just don't see it. Maybe Akaash does because he's a revolutionary and a communist, as well as a deep-pocketed, short-armed twerp. But he believes in the triumph of the working class and he doesn't think Vincent and I qualify as members, so maybe he wouldn't, after all. As for me, I'm afraid I really don't feel I've got anything in common with either of them, except for the fact that we're all in Swindon. We come from completely different places, hundreds, thousands of miles apart. Different cultures, different languages, different food, music, gods. In fact, we could hardly be more different from one another if we came from separate continents.'

'You all seem the same to us. You're all Indians.'

'I suppose we do,' Billy conceded. 'But then you, the Italians, the French and the Germans all seem pretty much the same to us. You're all Europeans.'

Cyn acknowledged the fairness of the point with a grin and Billy's heart skipped a beat. He shivered and told himself firmly to pull himself together. 'Think it's too early for a sandwich and chai?'

'I love it when you try to talk like us! Go on then. But it's pronounced "char".'

On roofs all around town, yawning women and a few dozing men engaged in desultory, low-voiced conversations to pass the time and ward off sleep. There hadn't been sight or sound of an enemy aircraft for weeks. There was a heavy layer of cloud that presaged rain before dawn. No one thought there was much chance of a raid. The general consensus was that there was little point to all this except that it had to be done. The occasional flare of a match or the firefly glow of an illicit cigarette could occasionally be spotted, prompting a shouted reprimand about blackout requirements and a grumbled riposte as others cupped their cigarettes more carefully in their hands.

On the flat, cast-iron roof of the Pattern Store, standing slightly apart from the other buildings and with nowhere to shelter from the freshening wind, Akaash was profoundly grateful for Billy's gloriously warm overcoat. It was far too big for him – the sleeves extended beyond the tips of his fingers, the turned-up collar reached high above his ears and its hem nearly touched the ground. He'd been the subject of much hilarity when he'd reported for duty in it: who did he think he was, the Chief Fire Officer asked, shaking his head – Bud Flanagan? The reference had meant nothing to him. He looked to Billy who clearly had no idea either but it prompted a further wave of laughter from everyone else.

He probably did look pretty silly but at least he was warm. And it was indeed a very big coat. Room for two in it, as Phyl, his fellow watcher of the night sky, had sniffily, shiveringly observed.

'Are you, like, posh at home, Mr Khan?' Cyn asked, as they sipped their tea and ate a sandwich.

'Depends what you mean by posh. My senior cousin brother is a Sardar. I suppose that's a bit posh. But me? Not at all. We've got princes, maharajahs, lords, lots of rich farmers and wealthy bankers back home. I come from a very rich state and a noble family but sadly I'm the poor relation. And I've told you before, call me Billy.'

'I think we'll keep it at Mr Khan. You being Management and all. Posh and rich aren't always the same thing, are they? Anyway, I thought millions were starving in India?'

'So they say. But that's Bengal. Where Akaash comes from. Dying like flies, apparently. Not that I'd heard anything about it before I met him. But I'm from Gwalior and where I live we're doing fine. There was a late monsoon last year and a failed harvest a couple of years before that, but we have our own famine relief system and our Maharajah made sure no one died. I ran special food trains. Our Bulldog, *Jiyajirao*, pulled one.'

'Shouldn't you be helping Akaash's people?'

'Not our problem, nor our job. Even if we wanted to, there's nothing we could do. Like I said, it's a very long way away and not our land.'

'Well, that just seems wrong. People dying of starvation when others in the same country are doing fine. I suppose that's why I joined the Union. Things like that. Anyway, we were talking about you.'

'We were indeed! My father worked in the state administration: the public works department. My mother is from Indore. Father has passed but she's still with us. I was lucky enough to get a state scholarship to study engineering, and then a position with the state railway.'

'And no Mrs Khan?'

This was more like it, Billy thought. 'No. No Mrs Khan. What about you? No boyfriend away fighting for King and Country?'

Cyn shook her head. 'There was someone once, but you know, it didn't work out. Usual story.'

It was clear she didn't want to discuss the matter further. Billy asked her how she first got involved in Union business.

'It was our dad's idea. He's convenor over on Carriage side. Works in the Wagon Lifting Shop. He's always been dead keen on the Union, our dad. He said if any daughter of his was going to be working Inside, then by God she'd be a Union man! So I joined, and then I volunteered for this and that, and before I knew it, I was Shop Steward.'

'You enjoy it?' asked Billy doubtfully. Personally, he could think of few things less appealing than spending hours listening to people whining about real or imagined grievances and squabbling about piffling differences in pay scales.

'I love it! I love getting to understand how the place works and challenging why things have to be the way they are. Believe it or not, I have as many rows with the other Shop Stewards as I do with Management! Well, maybe not quite as many, but they're just as stuck in their ways as the bosses. There has to be a change coming after the war, or there'll be a revolution here too!'

'You sound like Akaash,' Billy smiled, shifting a little closer to her.

Cyn nodded. 'I was going to ask you. Your Akaash…' she began uncertainly.

'He's not *my* Akaash,' Billy insisted. He was not particularly keen to squander this glorious opportunity to be alone with her in talking about anyone else.

'Well, anyway, Akaash. Is he married, back home?'

Billy did not like the direction this conversation was taking and edged himself back to his former position. The move, small though it was, was not lost on Cyn.

'Yes,' said Billy stiffly. 'Two wives and lots of children. And another one on the way. Breed like rabbits, these Bengalis.'

Cyn laughed and Billy felt happy, sad, irritated and foolish all at the same time. 'That's not true, is it?'

'No.'

'Does he have a girlfriend?'

'Look, I really don't know! Why are we talking about him anyway?'

'Well it's just…'

'Oh no! You're not sweet on him, are you?'

'No, silly! It's just that he's so clever and serious and talks so wonderfully about politics, yet he seems so, well, little and delicate and in need of someone to look after him. Sometimes I just want to wrap my arms around him and tell him everything will be OK. He's not like you, big and strong and posh and confident. He's so… vulnerable. I'm thinking of inviting him round to our house for tea.'

'Really?' asked Billy, revolted by the image Cyn's words conjured in his mind. 'Doreen!' he shouted over his shoulder. 'About time you took a turn watching, isn't it?' he said as he crawled over to where a grumbling Doreen was reluctantly emerging from the little shelter she'd made for herself.

'She not interested then?' Doreen yawned as she passed Billy.

'Just look for the bloody Germans,' Billy snapped, turning up his jacket collar and folding his arms. One thing was sure, he told himself. Next time he was fire-watching, he'd be doing it in an astrakhan coat. With any luck, delicate, clever Akaash would catch pneumonia, curl up and die. Little bastard. From the next morning, Cyn would find herself reassigned from working directly with him on *Birkenhead* to joining Elsie's crew on *Tremayne.* And henceforth there'd be a great deal fewer Shop B committee meetings, that was for sure.

Akaash returned to No. 23 sometime after Billy. He hung up the coat, said a few words to Sally – who had got up to welcome them back and ask after their first experience of fire-watching – then went upstairs. Billy was already in bed, lying on his side facing the wall. Akaash quietly undressed and was soon asleep. After a few minutes, however, he was awoken by a rhythmic creaking of the bed across the room and the laboured breathing of its occupant.

'What are you doing?' he hissed.

'Never mind what I'm doing. Go to sleep'

'Well, there's not much chance of that with you making so much noise. What *are* you doing?'

'Can't you just shut up for once in your life?'

'You haven't asked me what my fire-watching was like.'

Billy gave a huge sigh. 'Ya'Allah! OK, what was your fire-watching like?'

'Interesting. Phyl and I got to know each other a lot better. Cold, though. Thanks for your coat, by the way.'

'You're welcome.'

'How was yours?'

'Frustrating.'

Akaash frowned. 'You're not...abusing yourself, are you?'

'I assume you went to a convent school? Yes, I am. And it's not something I want the sound of your voice associated with in my mind, thanks very much.'

'That's disgusting!'

'I know. It'll probably stunt my growth. I'll take the risk. This wasn't the way I'd hoped this evening would end but needs must. Now will you please shut up.'

'Can't you do that somewhere else? Eugh! You're going to make a terrible mess.'

'No, I won't. I'm using a Johnnie. And a sock.'

'One of yours, I hope.'

'Not sure. I picked it up off the floor.'

'Aaargh! That might be one of mine!'

'Probably is. Feels small. Don't worry. I'll wash it.'

'OK, that's it,' said Akaash, climbing out of bed. 'I'm going to sit downstairs. You've got five minutes. Keep the sock. And we are never ever going to talk about this again.'

'If only I thought that were true.'

Vincent's travels around the region left him little time in Swindon. On alternate days he repeated the journey up to Paddington. Through a mix of persistence, patience and politeness, backed up by his impressively drafted documentation, he gained access to the bombed-out shell of the old Movements office and looked through the water-damaged remnants of what material had been salvaged from there. On the days he did not head to Paddington, he took the train in the opposite direction, west through the bomb-damaged Georgian elegance of Bath Spa – where he had spent his night in the cells – to the dockyards of Bristol, Newport and Cardiff, or southwest to Exeter, or northwest up into the Cotswolds through plunging valleys to Gloucester and Cheltenham. He almost invariably caught the last train back to Swindon.

As he travelled the region, Vincent marvelled at the variety of station and place names. Some, particularly in the Cotswolds, were lyrical, if with idiosyncratic syntax: Bourton-on-the-Water, Stow-on-the-Wold, yet Moreton-in-, simply, Marsh. Others were quaint to the point of whimsy: Daisy Bank, Blowers Green, Kidwelly Flats. Yet others, he thought, would be better suited to movie posters than railway signs: Fenny Compton, Derry Ormond, Laira Halt. Some were clipped to the point of being brusque: Ash, Par, Box. Then there were the names with so few vowels they defied pronunciation: Blaenplwyf, Llanfairpwllgwyngyll – names that made it sound like the station announcer was clearing his throat rather than listing destinations. Oh, and one with a totally gratuitous exclamation mark – Westward Ho! All so linguistically diverse, yet – to an Indian railwayman at least – in such a geographically small area.

On every train he boarded he'd first introduce himself to the guard and show him (occasionally, her) his documentation, thereby ensuring that if later challenged by a wary traveller, he'd be vouched for. This became less of a performance as he became known and increasingly recognised as a familiar sight. When travelling in passenger trains, he'd wander up and down the blue-lit corridors, watching and listening. He'd realised early on that few people take kindly to having their observations – overheard or in response to a direct question – written down. It became his habit to carry as much as he could in his head, then slip into an empty first-class compartment or vacant toilet to scribble down his notes.

When riding in the guards van of goods trains, he'd get dropped off whenever possible at signal boxes, where he'd drink tea and chat with the lone signalman or signal woman only too glad for company. At stations, he'd check in with the Station Master before quietly inspecting each and every aspect of the workings of the place. As his confidence grew, he developed a fine sense of whether any observations on his part would be welcomed. If he thought they might, he'd willingly share his thoughts, discuss comparisons and suggest alternatives. Only once did he do this on the basis of contrasting how things were done in Bombay – it had not been a success. Thereafter he always offered his recommendations on the pretext of describing something he'd seen elsewhere in the region, at some invariably anonymous place.

Then he would sit – often with collar turned up and overcoat wrapped around him – in an unheated waiting room for the arrival of a connection or a return train. At stations large or small, mainline or branch, he rarely found himself alone. He was struck by how many folk were travelling, and how often they seemed to end up like him – hungry and cold, waiting for that last train, far from where they had started yet still distant from where they were going.

There'd be a few soldiers, the odd airman, sailors, merchant mariners, factory workers, dockers, nurses, worried wives and anxious mothers. He even met the odd travelling salesman or company rep still trying to pursue their pre-war occupation in these wildly transformed times. There was always someone needing to get to someplace else, and often someone stranded somewhere. Always someone happy, once satisfied that he wasn't an enemy agent, to pass the long hours chatting about their journeys – conversations that would invariably conclude with a resigned, 'Oh, well, mustn't grumble.'

Within two weeks he'd learnt all he could from visiting the stations, goods yards, depots and junctions reachable in a day trip. From the following Monday he intended to embark upon longer journeys that would require one or two nights staying away. His first such expedition would be to try to get to the bottom of why there seemed to be so many delays between Neath and Fishguard Harbour. Then he would carry out a detailed examination of the lines along the south coast from Dawlish through Devon and Cornwall to Penzance. This would need careful planning, extra permits and permission from the War Office, as large stretches were out of bounds to non-residents.

After dinner on Saturday evening, Akaash headed to the Mechanics Institute to discuss a possible talk with the Debating and Discussion Group. Initial reaction to the idea from the organising committee, comprising the librarian, Dr Falk and three supervisors from the Carriage and Wagon side, had been enthusiastic. They had explained that talks presented to date had had a distinctly local and practical focus: goods traffic on the GWR; the impact of the war on cider-making in Somerset; the secrets of successful beekeeping; first aid in the home. Something about India was bound to be a big draw, they assured him. After all, they'd been trying to get Billy to talk about the Gwalior State Railway since he'd arrived but he'd insisted he first needed to get a few slides sent over to do full justice to it.

Akaash's earlier meeting in Oxford with some of Joan's friends had been a disappointment to say the least. Only three had turned up, and they'd seemed much keener on telling him what they thought than listening to anything that he had to say. He was hopeful this evening's meeting might be an opportunity to make a greater contribution to the cause.

They met in the librarian's office – a cramped room cluttered with boxes of books awaiting accessioning – and sat around a small table on which was a stack of cards. 'Suggestions for future talks,' the librarian explained.

Akaash proposed that he talk about the Bengal Famine – its causes and its implications. The committee looked decidedly unimpressed. One of the supervisors picked up the cards and began sifting through them. 'Ah!' he exclaimed after turning over a few. 'This might suit better, Dr Ray: "Tropical Birds: Habits and Habitats". From Mr Cope,' he confided to his fellow committee members, who nodded and smiled.

'Loves his birds, does Mr Cope.'

'Can you talk about birds?' he asked Akaash, who shook his head.

'Shame,' sighed the supervisor, turning the card down and continuing his search. 'We'll have to disappoint Mr Cope again.' Although the look he gave Akaash made it clear where, in his mind at least, responsibility for this disappointment lay. 'Engine maintenance, no. Boiler design, no. Materials of the future, no. Ah! Exotic woods! Any good?'

'I really want to talk about the current situation in India,' explained Akaash. 'How about the Quit India Movement, or Mr Gandhi's arrest?'

'But that might sound like politics,' observed the librarian. The others looked vaguely uncomfortable.

'Well, it would be politics!'

'We don't do politics,' said the supervisor with the cards, offended. 'Can't you do anything about trains? Trains always go down well.'

'Yeah, your Mr Gandhi travels around on trains! Seen it in the newsreels! You could talk about the types of engines used to pull those trains…'

'Or the carriages he travels in. Carriages are good too.'

'In many ways, they're more interesting…'

'I have no interest whatsoever in trains,' said Akaash to a horrified committee. 'I'm an academic and a mathematician.'

'Hang on,' said the supervisor with the cards, doing another rapid sort. 'Yes! Here we are!' he cried, holding up a card in triumph. '"The History and Future of Mathematical Computation!"'

Akaash sighed with relief. At last!

'I don't think so, under the circumstances,' said the other supervisor who so far had not spoken.

'But that's something I could do!'

The one with the cards glanced at the name and his face fell. He showed the card to the librarian, who passed it on to the others.

'Best not,' she said.

'Why not?' demanded Akaash.

'Well, it was asked for by a young chap in the Wages and Salaries office, before he was called up.'

'Does that matter?'

'Well, not normally, no.'

'So?'

There was a long silence. 'He was reported as killed in action last week. Let's think again. You absolutely sure you don't know anything about birds?'

Whilst Akaash was at his meeting, Billy, having failed miserably to mend the cistern, was salving his bruised professional pride by attempting a range of other odd jobs: putting washers on taps; fixing a sticking drawer; repairing a long-unused mangle. As he busied himself around the house, Vincent and Sally sat in the front room listening to a programme on the wireless of British and American dance music introduced by Vic Oliver.

'Married to the prime minister's daughter,' Sally observed.

'Really?' said Victor. 'Sounds…foreign.'

'He does a bit, doesn't he?' she agreed, thinking how much he spoke like Vincent. 'I like his accent. Doesn't make a big deal about being Mr Churchill's son-in-law, they say. Do you like this sort of music?'

'Big band? Yes, I do. Why?'

'I noticed you tapping your foot.'

Vincent smiled. 'I used to be something of a dancer. In my younger days.'

Sally put aside her knitting. 'Oh, I used to love to dance! I'd be up at the Locarno on a Saturday night regular as clockwork before me and Derek…not that I was ever a great dancer, mark you. But I loved it, I really did. And watching folk who could really dance. I loved that too.'

'But not any more?'

'No. My Derek's not what you'd call a dancing man…' she concluded, resuming her knitting.

Vincent had previously asked her about the photographs on the wall and learnt that her husband Derek was now a sergeant, 2nd Battalion, Wiltshire Regiment. Fighting somewhere in Italy. Won himself a military medal for bravery, she explained, sounding somehow more mystified than proud. They'd been married twelve years and had one child – a girl, Sophia – who had died of scarlet fever in the winter of 1938.

She told Vincent all this in a matter-of-fact way, never looking up from her knitting. The needles clacked rhythmically and as she completed each line she tugged at the thread of bright blue wool, loosening more from the ball that lay in her lap before settling down to the next row. She sounded neither sad nor angry, just resigned. Accepting.

Sally had once asked Vincent about the photographs in his room, but he had seemed uneasy talking about his own family.

'You C of E?' she asked now, out of the blue.

'I'm sorry?'

'Church of England?'

'Oh, Anglican! Yes, I'm an Anglican.'

'I go to Christchurch. Up on the hill. You can come with me tomorrow if you'd like.'

'Thank you,' said Vincent after a pause. 'I would like that.'

He leaned over to the wooden chest radio set and turned one of the three Bakelite dials below the speaker a fraction, tuning it more carefully to the Home Service. 'Geraldo,' he said, as the opening bars of 'It's D'lovely' played by a full dance orchestra emerged through the last tweets and hisses of interference. He closed his eyes and with one finger conducted the music.

Sally smiled as she watched him transported by the simple tune.

A loud crash interrupted the tranquillity of the moment, followed by a burst of swearing in Hindi. Sally sighed, put her knitting aside and went to see what had happened. In the kitchen, Billy was sucking the forefinger of his right hand and glaring at the newly reconstructed mangle.

'Everything all right?' she asked, reaching to withdraw Billy's finger from his mouth and inspect the damage. 'Let me see.'

Billy showed her his damaged finger. There was blood under the nail and the tip was clearly swelling.

'The mangle is working,' he assured her.

'You put your finger in it?'

'Well…'

'You big silly!' she chided. 'Is that how you test things in the Works? Sit down and I'll make you a nice cup of tea. If you were little, I'd kiss it better for you.'

Vincent was leaning against the doorframe, arms folded, shaking his head slowly as Sally turned to the cooker and lit the gas under the kettle.

Billy gave him a huge leering grin, held up his injured finger and pursed his lips in a parody of a kiss.

On Sunday morning, Billy glanced at the alarm clock between his bed and Akaash's. It was 7.30. Akaash was still fast asleep. Billy was enjoying the luxury of not having to get up for work when he caught a distant hint of the first appealing cooking aroma he'd smelled since arrival. It was getting stronger – a gamey, salty scent. He got up, threw on a dressing gown and headed downstairs. In the kitchen he found Sally cooking with two pans. In one, two eggs were frying. In the other, long, thin strips of pink meat sizzled and spat. The kitchen table was laid for two. Vincent was already seated at the table, sipping tea and looking, Billy thought sourly, a little bit too much at home.

'Morning Mrs A! That smells wonderful,' Billy sighed. He treated Vincent to a curt nod.

'It's not for you,' said Vincent, buttering himself a slice of toast. 'You can't eat it. It's bacon.'

'I have no objection to bacon,' Billy assured him. He leaned over Sally's shoulder and sniffed appreciatively. 'I'm not even sure I know what it is, but it smells delicious.'

'It's pork. Pig meat.'

He looked back at Vincent, who was smiling in a deeply irritating way. Being prohibited by his religion from eating pork had never been of the slightest concern to Billy. The only pigs he had ever seen back in Gwalior were filthy, disgusting beasts rooting around in garbage and excrement and he could think of few things he would less want to devour. But this…

'I thought you said it was bacon,' he said, clearly sorely tempted.

'Bacon is cured pork,' Sally explained in the 'speaking to a simpleton' tone she often adopted when talking to Billy.

'Well, there you are, then!' cried Billy, happily. 'It may once have been pig, but now it's been cured. What can possibly be wrong with that. Shall I get myself a plate?'

'It's still pig.'

'Can we not be cured, Vincent? Isn't redemption possible? In a spirit of charity, I shall forgive it its past porkishness. And you need to watch that mean-spiritedness of yours. I've noticed it before. It's unkind and it's unattractive. Decidedly unchristian too, if you don't mind me saying.'

'I do mind.'

Several minutes later, Billy was satisfyingly full of bacon, egg and fried bread. He half-heartedly offered to help with the washing up, pretty sure Sally would never agree. She shooed them both out of the kitchen. Vincent stepped out into the backyard to smoke and Billy followed him.

'She really is a fine-looking woman, our Mrs A, don't you think?' Billy said, also lighting up.

Vincent raised an eyebrow but said nothing.

'I'm just making conversation,' added Billy. 'But you have to admit…'

'Can we talk about something else?' asked Vincent. 'Better still, can we not talk at all?'

'You notice the way she slices bread? Squeezing the loaf up close to her left breast and sawing away at it? I love it when she does that. I often ask for an extra slice just so I can watch her do it. Don't you ever find yourself thinking about all that woman under that housecoat?'

'Certainly not! She's a respectable married woman.'

'Come on! Not even once?'

'No! And if this is what eating pig meat does to you I think you'd better go back to avoiding it, cured or not. Didn't you have something you wanted to do today?'

Billy leered wickedly and gave a dirty laugh. 'I did indeed, but sadly you're taking it to church!'

Vincent looked skyward. 'God, you're disgusting.' He glanced at his watch. 'Right, I need to get ready. I'd offer to pray for you but I suspect that would be a waste of both God's time and mine.'

Billy was left alone with his thoughts, which, since the failure of his advances towards Cyn, had become ever more narrowly focused on sex. He was acutely aware that it had been a long time since he'd last been with a woman, and he was convinced extended abstinence was detrimental to a man's health, well-being and judgement. Proof was near at hand, he reflected, in the way the seemingly celibate Vincent and Akaash could be such depressing company and hold such odd views about things.

In fact, considered in that way, getting himself a 'shag' – he believed that was the appropriate local term – was almost a professional obligation he owed to both those he served and those he managed. It should also stop him having such troubling distractions: when he was supposedly supervising the work on the locomotives, he increasingly found himself staring for unhealthily long periods at his workers and completely losing his train of thought when, for example, one of them bent over to retrieve a spanner that had dropped into an awkward gap. This wasn't something he was proud of. He told himself that he should be thinking of the job he'd been sent to do. That he was letting himself, Gwalior State and the Maharajah down. When he found himself contemplating Elsie's massive bosom he realised things had got to such a worrying state that this was now a problem to be addressed with some urgency.

But where does one find a decent, uncomplicated shag in Swindon, he wondered?

Akaash got up well after Vincent and Sally had left for church, ate the slice of toast and jam left out for him and slipped out of the house without seeing Billy, although he could hear him whistling to himself as he sorted through his tools outside. He had been keen to avoid Billy as he didn't want to discuss his plans for the morning. Not that they were anyone else's business, just habitual caution. Plus, he found it difficult to talk to Billy without recalling his roommate's onanistic postscript to their night of fire-watching.

The proposal to meet had come from Cyn. She'd heard of his suggestion for a talk about India from Hartshorne's secretary and wanted him to discuss it with her father, who could make all the necessary arrangements for the lecture to be delivered at a Union-organised event if he was convinced that it would advance the cause of international socialism. The meeting was planned for immediately after church. Although Cyn and her father shared Akaash's view that religion was no friend of the working man, Cyn's mum remained a devout Catholic, so the entire family dutifully attended Holy Rood Church on Groundwell Road. Mrs Abbot also held that talking politics was incompatible with keeping the Sabbath holy, so Cyn and her dad planned to come upon Akaash to all appearances by happy accident. He would wait for them on one of the benches outside the town hall so that they could spot him, express their surprise and pleasure and tell him he'd be welcome to walk with them as they headed back to their home on Bristol St. The father and daughter were also pretty sure Mrs Abbot would not be able to walk back through town with a new acquaintance and turn him away at their door without inviting him in to share their meal – especially on a Sunday. If it looked like she might be thinking of doing so, Cyn intended to remind her of the bit in Hebrews about hospitality to strangers and welcoming angels unawares – thanks to rigorous Sunday schooling, she was remarkably well-equipped with biblical quotes for an atheist.

And if that failed, she'd play her trump card: asking innocently how it would look to the neighbours?

When she hinted to Akaash that he might be asked to stay for lunch, he had mentioned his vegetarianism, expecting the concern and confusion this had been met with by his landlady, but Cyn told him that one of her brothers was a vegetarian too. She'd asked if he'd got the special ration card issued to vegetarians – something of which he was completely unaware – and offered to help sort one out for him, but he had declined. He preferred to continue receiving and trading his eggs and meat for hard cash.

It was a beautiful morning as he crossed the deserted park, silent except for birdsong and the occasional passing train. A few late roses were in their final flush and there was the first real chill in the air. Leaves on one or two of the trees were starting to turn and there was dew glistening on what grass remained. He walked along Farringdon Road to the Medical Fund Hospital and then up Milton Road, passing the dispensary and the public baths that Mrs A's boarders visited rather than endure the tortured ritual of the tin tub in the kitchen of No. 23. At the top of Commercial Road he settled on a bench outside the imposing red-brick town hall and took out the notes he'd made in preparation for this meeting, to give them a final read through.

He was not alone for long.

'No rest for the wicked,' said Inspector Curtis cheerfully. 'Mind if I join you?' he added, sitting down without waiting for a reply.

They sat in silence for a minute or two. Akaash thrust his notes deep into a pocket, shifted as far as he could to the end of the bench and looked around.

'Don't worry, son,' Curtis murmured, not looking at Akaash but staring straight ahead. 'They won't be out for another fifteen minutes. I'll be long gone before they appear. Lovely morning, isn't it?' He screwed his face up, grunted and took a bottle of pills from his coat pocket. 'Indigestion,' he explained, popping a couple of pills into his mouth. 'You take anything for your asthma?'

Akaash didn't reply. Curtis chewed on the pills, swallowed with another grimace then took out a cigarette, lit up, took a long drag and exhaled with a long, satisfied sigh. 'Nothing like the first fag of the day.' He leaned back and looked up at the sky. 'I hear you're sending most of your wages back to the old folks at home?' said Curtis, singing the last few words, then thrusting out his bottom lip and nodding approvingly. 'That's nice. Yeah. I respect that. A man who looks after his family can't be all bad, that's what I say. Well done, you.'

He smoked in silence for a while. Then, as though the thought had just come to him, said, 'Mind you, it would be a bloody shame if all that hard-earned money wasn't getting to them, wouldn't it? Well, I say hard-earned but whatever you're up to doesn't look too much like hard earning to me. Do you and the lady la-di-das ever actually *do* anything? Anyway, let's let that one by. Now, where was I? Oh, yeah, your remittances. Imagine if it was all getting stuck in some bureaucratic balls up somewhere or other. That would be terrible, wouldn't it? There's mum and dad back at home, waiting, hoping every day for a little something to help them out, and all that money that you've tried so hard to get to them is just sitting in a post office in Port Said or some other shithole God knows where. How awful would that be?' He sniffed, took out a large handkerchief and blew his nose loudly. 'Heartbreaking! You heard from them at all? No? I bet your poor old mum is getting a bit peckish about now and thinking her little boy overseas has forgotten all about her. Life can be very unfair, can't it? But one or two words, a brief chat between mates could ensure that all these potential problems go away. I could do that for you, you know? I could guarantee you your money will be getting there.'

'But?'

'I knew you're a smart young chap! I said to my boss, I said, "'E's going places, that boy!" You've seen straight to heart of the thing. There's always a "but". Sometimes I think that's all there is in this life. The "ifs" and the "buts". See, I have the power to make all your problems go away. I'm your fairy godfather! If…if you do something for me in return. But…but you knew that, before I even started speaking to you.'

Curtis turned, resting his arm along the back of the bench and looked straight at Akaash for the first time. 'If you help me, then you can be pretty sure mummy and daddy will be tucking into a nice dinner tomorrow night. What do you lot eat back home? Curry? Rice? Some shit like that? Well, I can promise you they'll have enough money to pay for whatever they want. A nice bit of pud too, I shouldn't wonder. But…see, there's that word again! Life, eh? Ifs and buts. But if you don't help me out, well, you probably know better than I do what the next few days, weeks, months, will be like. I've been reading up on where you're from. Sounds bloody awful. Someone's cocked-up badly. No wonder it's not in the newspapers. Seems to me a good son like you would want to help me. Because that way he'd be helping out his old mum and dad. Pretty easy really when you look at it sensibly.'

'And what do I have to do?'

'Nothing much, really. I want you to talk. You like doing that. But I also want you to listen. And then, I want you to tell me what you've heard. I'm not asking you to betray any trusts, or to create any dramas. These will be public meetings. No secrets. No betrayal. All I want you to do is to give me the heads-up who said what, to who, where and when. Does that sound so hard? I don't think so.'

'It's whom.'

'What?'

'To whom. Who said what, to whom.'

'You really are a cheeky little fucker, aren't you? If I wasn't such a patient man…'

'You want me to betray my comrades? You want me to turn informer?'

'Such emotional words! Betrayal. Informer. But then that's you commies all over. So bloody overdramatic! Can't help yourselves. All think you have to talk like Lenin and Trotsky. Blood and guns and death to the Tsar! And you really think these people want to be your comrades? I'm already a better comrade to you than any of them will ever be. They wouldn't piss on you if you were on fire. I, on the other hand, would.'

Curtis paused, trying to read Akaash's mood and decide what would work best – carrot or stick.

'I'm not even asking you to tell me anything that won't be in the record of the meetings you attend,' he continued. 'I don't want you writing anything down. Just tell me what you see and hear. Seems to me you've got the best part of this deal. I could simply wait a day or two and read the minutes of who said what to *whom*, because your supposed comrades are breathtakingly obsessed with writing stuff down. You might want to watch that when you get home, by the way – and yes, that little bit of advice is for free: conspiracy for beginners! But right now, all I care about is knowing pretty damned quick what's discussed at the Union branch meetings you are going to speak to Abbot and his very fetching daughter about. Oh, yeah, there may be some slightly less public gatherings you'll be invited to attend in the Glue Pot which your fellow commies think nobody else knows about. That's all. If you help me out, mummy and daddy will eat well tomorrow night and every night thereafter. What's mum's favourite? I hope she enjoys it, I really do, and I'm sure she'll bless her little boy in her prayers for a good meal at last. But if you don't, well, I guess they'll be going to bed hungry. Again. Sad, eh? I have to say, if it were me, there would be no choice at all. I'd know where my duty would lie. What I owe, to *whom*, and for what. But then maybe you people think differently. They always say life is so much cheaper where you come from.'

Odd, thought Akaash, that there'd been no mention of the meeting Joan had arranged for him to address…

'Oh, and don't go getting the idea that I'm unaware of your little trip to Oxford yesterday,' Curtis added, as though reading his mind.

'You want me to inform on them too?' sighed Akaash.

'Nope. Someone will probably be asking you about it, but it won't be me. I care about what happens in Oxford only marginally more than I care about what happens in India. Not my tic. Not my tab. TTFN,' he added as he rose to leave.

'What?'

'Ta Ta. For Now.'

After church, Vincent called at Ernie's front door. When Ernie appeared, Vincent raised his hat politely and handed him back his seed catalogue.

'There's several things there that I'd like to get. Thanks for letting me see it.'

'I'll let you know when I send in my order. You can add yours, if you like.'

'That's very kind of you,' said Vincent, offering Ernie another Woodbine.

Ernie took one and put it behind his ear. 'No skin off my nose. The more I order the bigger the discount. Drink wine where you come from?'

Vincent was unsure if this was a general enquiry about life in India, his individual tastes or a specific invitation to have a drink. He nodded anyway.

As he had when getting the seed catalogue the previous evening, Ernie turned without a further word and limped back indoors, leaving Vincent on the doorstep. When he returned he was carrying a glass little bigger than a thimble with a cloudy brown liquid in it. He handed it to Vincent. 'Go on,' he urged. Cautiously, Vincent sipped. It wasn't precisely unpleasant. Just odd. Viscous. Very sweet. And clearly quite potent.

'Pea Pod, 1940,' said Ernie, taking the drained glass from Vincent and closing the door.

It was a new and thoroughly unwelcome experience for Akaash to be so unsure of how to react to a challenge or so uncertain about the right course of action to take. Following his latest meeting with Curtis, however, he had no idea what to do about the position he now found himself in. He had always thought it impossible to imagine any creature more despicable than a police informer. A vile traitor, profiting by wheedling himself into a position of trust and then selling out those who had placed their faith in him? Revealing their most intimate secrets to their most deadly enemies? Death was too good for such loathsome scum.

But now, having to either betray the local socialist and communist chapters or fail to help others avoid a slow, lingering death by starvation, things suddenly weren't quite so black and white. He had always told himself he was ready to die for the cause – if it would have offered a way out he'd willingly end his own life, ideally in a blaze of glory, taking some past viceroy with him. He'd thought that in coming to England he could achieve the two things most important to him: feeding folks back home and forwarding the prospect of full independence for India. How naive must he have been? Instead, he had made himself such an easy target for blackmail, coercion and manipulation and as a result put himself in this terrible, impossible situation.

He had been uneasy company at the Abbot home during lunch despite their best efforts to make him feel at home. Cyn had wondered if someone had said something to offend him as he seemed upset and distracted. Even when her father had agreed to arrange the 'Quit India' talk for him at the next NUR branch meeting, Akaash had seemed unenthusiastic, even though just the day before he had been enthralled at the prospect. He'd left them as soon as he could, barely bothering to thank them for their hospitality.

Akaash needed to think through what he should do now. He tried reading but even the German–English dictionary wasn't helping. He really could see no way forward. They had him precisely where they wanted him. He foolishly thought he had been using the system against itself but it turned out the system had all along been using him.

What could he do?

Could he somehow warn Cyn and Joan and all the others he would be coming into contact with that he was toxic without getting himself completely ostracised and thus of no further value to the cause or indeed the police? Could he, must he, compromise just enough to get his remittances back to Calcutta without doing any real harm? Curtis had said he was only interested in what went on in Swindon. Maybe he could still serve the cause of nationalism and remain true to India but it would have to be at the cost of betraying those around him here and now. Looking at it one way, he would be helping the British turn on one another. That didn't sound like a terrible thing. In fact it might actually help the cause. But the people who would suffer were the very people who were reaching out to help him. Wouldn't that make him as bad as those he opposed? Worse?

True, it would not be fellow Indians he would be betraying. That he knew he would never do, no matter what pressure they tried to bring to bear on him. He may not be betraying his country and his countrymen, but he was betraying those with whom he was united in the greater global struggle – fellow workers, brother and sister socialists.

Could he offer them something that would be more valuable? Something that would divert their attention and avoid the need for him to make this terrible choice. If only he could discover a fascist spy ring! Presumably they existed and presumably the police would be far more interested in them than the undoubtedly pretty mundane doings of local leftists. If he couldn't find one, could he make one up? They were working on ciphers, after all. Could he say he'd found some coded messages as part of his work…

In his desperation, he even thought about making up a story about Vincent, about how he was actually a German agent. After all, he wasn't a comrade and he wasn't a proper Indian either, so fair game, really. Looked like a spy too, with his noting things down and his flash clothes. As soon as the thought crossed his mind he realised how stupid this was. Who'd ever believe it? No – comrades, cause or country, something had to sacrificed.

Work was progressing well in Shop B. With every passing day the three best-preserved engines were looking more like they would shortly be ready for first testing. The various teams working under the joint supervision of Keenan and Elsie continued to develop their technical know-how at an impressive rate whilst reducing – although not yet sufficiently to Billy's satisfaction – the number of accidents and near accidents. Whilst it went against his principles and professional pride, Billy reluctantly accepted Keenan's advice about concentrating on the completion of just one of the three least dilapidated engines. So whilst his best workers focused on 3443 *Birkenhead*, the rest of the workforce was spread across all the engines and, to his pleased surprise, were proving very effective at moving work forward on a broad front.

Now that things were advancing so satisfactorily, Billy thought it might be timely to renew his brief acquaintance with Mollie, the girl who led the carthorse with which they'd nearly collided when they had first arrived. He'd come across her around the Works at odd times, invariably leading that huge brute of a thing that had clearly been so selectively bred for size that it almost seemed wrong to still call it a horse. He'd nodded to her when she came to empty the glory hole every other day. He couldn't help but notice that his scrutiny of her was invariably met by an equally bold and appraising stare in return. He found himself becoming quite aroused by the thought of her. No Cyn, perhaps, but a pretty little thing with an intriguing twist of wicked in her smile…

Reflecting on his lack of success with Cyn led him to question the best approach to adopt to this next attempted seduction: open and honest had hardly done him much good to date. Approaching Mollie as a mere railway engineer, albeit one from the other side of the world, might not be sufficiently romantic or mysterious to literally charm the pants off her in a place where you couldn't throw a stone without hitting an engineer much better qualified than himself. He realised that he was humming the tune of *The Sheik of Araby* as he mused, and smiled in gratitude. Inspiration!

He tapped the pack of Johnnies in his breast pocket. It was lunchtime – a time to feed an appetite and appease a hunger, as somebody probably once said. Shortly after the hooter sounded the start of the lunch break, Billy slipped out of Shop B and headed for the stable in which the huge horse – and Mollie – were based. He sauntered away with what he thought was exaggerated nonchalance, but which to Elsie, who nudged Doreen sitting beside her on a bench outside Shop B eating their sandwiches, looked more like a man with, as she put it, a load to get off his mind.

'Hello Mr Khan,' said Mollie brightly as he wandered briskly across the yard, pretending he intended to pass the stable.

'Oh, hello…er, Mollie isn't it? How nice to see you again.'

'Nice to see you too. You're a long way from Shop B. Anything I can do for you?'

Was one eyebrow arched? She was certainly smiling that smile at him. Important, though he told himself that he shouldn't misread the signals in a foreign country. However, he was pretty sure he'd seen that smile once or twice before among the bored wives of the Gwalior Residency.

'Er, yes, Mollie. As I'm passing I'd like to see that wonderful horse of yours.'

'Be my guest.'

He stepped into the stable and was immediately assailed by the fusty aromas of hay, dung and horse so out of place in this vast estate of machinery reeking of hot oil and burning coal. It made him feel oddly homesick. He told himself firmly to focus: that hadn't perhaps been the smartest opening. He'd never particularly liked horses – from childhood being far more interested in machines – and thus knew little about them other than that they shit, kick and bite. Ya'Allah, this one was a big brute of a thing, he thought. Absolutely terrifying this close up. Still, he supposed he'd better fake interest. Avoid face, feet and ass, he reminded himself. Warily, he approached the great hulking beast's flank.

'Never come up on the side of a Shire unless you've got room to get out of the way,' Mollie cautioned. ''E's a big softie but 'e's still three-quarters of a ton of bone and muscle with very little up top. And 'e's got a nasty habit of shunting sideways if 'e senses movement 'e can't see. If 'e catches you against the side of 'is stall you'll be squashed flat long before anyone will get 'im to shift 'imself. You'll be crushed stone dead,' she concluded with malicious glee.

Billy promptly stepped back, knocking over an empty bucket. Mollie stood watching him, arms crossed, amused. 'Bit different from the 'orses where you come from I 'spect?' she offered.

He smiled gratefully. 'He is indeed, my dear. I only have a small stable. Half a dozen racehorses.' He wasn't quite sure why he'd started talking like he was old enough to be her grandfather when there could only be a few years difference in their ages. And why had he suddenly started spouting off like some matinee idol in a Noel Coward production? This yarn-spinning wasn't proving as easy as he'd imagined it would be.

Still, it seemed to be working. She nodded, impressed. 'You 'ave a stable?'

'Oh, yes,' Billy assured her airily. 'Horses. A passion of mine.'

'Oooh! Passionate, are you? Do many railwaymen own racehorses where you come from then?'

'Ah! Well, you see, Mollie, there you've caught me out.' He stepped in closer to her, leaned forward and lowered his voice to little more than a whisper. 'Between you and me, I have a little secret.'

She looked up at him, slipped the scarf from her hair and shook her head, loosing long blonde tresses. 'I thought you might,' she said quietly.

He sighed. She was so beautiful! How could he ever have thought she didn't match up to Cyn? 'Would you like to know my secret, Mollie dear?' he asked, his voice low and slightly husky.

She nodded, running a hand through her hair.

'I'm not actually a railway engineer.'

'Coo! Aren't you just? And yet everyone says you're such a good one too. Strange that.'

'Well, that's very nice of them. Railways are a hobby of mine too.'

'Like 'orses.'

'Exactly. Like, um, 'orses. But more so.'

'So what are you then, if you ain't a railwayman?'

Billy took a deep breath, muttered a brief prayer for forgiveness for the act of *lese majeste* he was about to commit, and blurted out 'A prince.'

'A *prince*? Like royalty? You're one of them maharajahs?'

'Just a mere rajah,' said Billy, with a modest shrug, hoping this slightly assuaged his presumption.

'And you're repairing clapped-out old engines in Swindon?'

'Well, we must all do our bit to win this war, mustn't we?'

'Don't you have to be the rajah of somewhere? Like the whatsit of Hyderabad?'

'The Nizam. Yes, very good! Quite right. And I'm the Rajah of… Appam and Poha!'

'Of two places?'

'Well, yes. But they're very close to one another.'

'Imagine that!'

He could see she was looking doubtful. 'Why don't you show me around?' he suggested, recalling how the Maharajah of Gwalior acted on his occasional tours of inspection of the state railway. 'What an interesting stable.'

'You think so, Your Majesty?' she asked. Perhaps, Billy thought, she could have sounded a little more awestruck?

'Please! Not Your Majesty. A simple "Your Highness" will do. Shall we continue our tour?'

'Bucket. Oh, yeah. You're already familiar with the bucket. Net of hay. Pile of droppings. Rake. Shovel. Wheelbarrow. Brush. Big 'orse. Sack of feed. That's about it. Unless of course you want to see up in the loft,' she said, staring straight at him. 'We'd 'ave to climb that ladder and there's not much up there but loads and loads of 'ay. And it's very dark…'

'Why, that sounds most intriguing! Shall we?'

'After you, Your 'ighness.'

'So, explain to me again why you're 'ere,' Mollie said as she waited for Billy to make it up the ladder to the loft, 'Your 'ighness,' she added after a pause.

'Well, when the King Emperor asked…'

'What, our King? King George?'

He heaved himself up into the loft. 'Yes, that's right. He said to me, "Tiny," he said, "why don't you…"'

'Tiny?' she cried, with a snort of laughter. 'Sorry? The King calls you "Tiny"?'

He closed his eyes. Where the hell had *that* come from? 'Yes. Goes back to something that happened once when we were playing polo…'

'You and the King play polo?' she asked, halfway up the ladder.

'Often. "Tiny," he says to me one day, "you're good with these old railway engines. Why don't you come and help us out by repairing some for me in Swindon?"'

He reached down to help her. She looked up at him, shaking her head, and then took the offered hand. He gently hauled her up and into the loft where they sat side by side on the hay. Billy opened his mouth to speak just as the hooter sounded. She placed a finger on his lips.

'We both know that's an even bigger load of plop than that pile downstairs. But you've got such a lovely way about you I could listen to you talk bollocks all day. Now, we got ten minutes before the final lunchtime hooter...' She leaned in towards him, he could feel her breath on his face and he gasped as, seemingly accidentally, she let her hand run lightly over his swelling groin. 'Well, at least we know that's not why the King calls you Tiny. Just so we're clear, I don't go all the way, but I don't mind if you want to, you know, fool around a bit. So, what happens now, Your 'ighness?'

As Billy had headed towards the stable, Akaash had walked, head down, towards the main gate. Whilst Billy had been looking forward to his encounter with Mollie with growing excitement,

Akaash viewed his own lunchtime meeting with dread. He knew that no matter how well he managed to restrict his disclosures to the most inane and innocent, even if he could be absolutely sure no harm resulted to anyone, he would shortly take a step into a compromised, corrupted world from which it would be impossible to return. But as Curtis had said, what choice did he really have?

He'd decided to heed Curtis's advice about writing nothing down. He'd prepared in his head what he would say about the Union meeting he'd attended the previous evening and, just as Curtis had predicted, the subsequent discussion in the Glue Pot to which he'd been invited. In truth there wasn't that much to tell. No secret plotting. No treasonous conspiracies. Just a lot of enthusiastic comments about the glorious Soviets and positive words about post-war decolonisation for his benefit and, of all things, a surprisingly acrimonious exchange about a jumble sale to raise funds.

Curtis was waiting on a bench in the park, reading the *Daily Mirror* and eating a sandwich from a brown paper pack. Akaash sat at the other end of the bench and took out his own lunch. Neither acknowledged one another.

'Well?' murmured Curtis.

Akaash took a deep breath and began a simple summary of what was discussed at both the Union meeting and the Glue Pot gathering.

'Good. Who was there?'

Akaash listed who had been present. When he'd finished, he felt wrung out. Curtis sat for a while in silence, occasionally turning a page of his paper.

'Not bad, son,' he said eventually. 'At least for a first attempt. I'll give you…six out of ten for that. But don't worry, that's a pass mark. Mum and dad will get their tea tonight. I must be getting soft in my old age. Next time I won't be so generous.'

'What do you mean? I've done exactly as you asked.'

'And I thought we were getting on so well! Building up a relationship of trust and mutual respect. I know perfectly well who you were with last night.' He folded his newspaper and stood up, still not looking towards Akaash. 'You left Arthur Abbot and his daughter Cynthia out of your list. I may have been born at night, but it wasn't last night. And I'm not a fool. Don't make that mistake again.'

Billy returned to Shop B fifteen minutes after the end-of-lunch hooter still slightly shell-shocked and abstractedly humming *The Sheik of Araby*. Doreen put down her spanner and called across to Elsie who was supervising the removal of a panel on 3370 *Tremayne*. Elsie came over to join her and together they converged to block Billy's path.

'Everything all right, Mr Khan?' Elsie asked innocently.

'Hmm? What? Oh, yes, everything's better than all right, Elsie, thank you for asking. Everything's perfect.'

'We was wondering, see. You being a bit late back from lunch and all. I was saying to Doreen, I said, "That's not like him," I said. "Not like him at all."'

'Yeah, she did. That's what she said. Nice lunch, was it?' chimed in Doreen. 'Porridge, by any chance?' she added, glancing across at Elsie, her tongue making a large bulge in her cheek.

Billy frowned. He was pretty sure porridge was only ever eaten for breakfast. And even in his present state of bemused euphoria he could sense they were setting him up.

'No, Doreen,' he said, trying to sound stern. 'It was not porridge. Why do you ask?'

''Cos you look like a man who's just had his oats!' cried Doreen. Keenan came over to see what the fuss was about as Doreen and Elsie headed back to work amid shrieks of laughter.

'Take no notice of them, Mr Khan. No respect, those two. Never have had. I could tell you a tale or two about that Elsie when she was younger.'

'What does "have his oats" mean?'

'Is that what they said?' Keenan asked, tutting and shaking his head in disgust. 'Smutty cows. It means, well, how can I say it? A bit of "How's your father?"'

Billy was clearly none the wiser.

'You know! A touch of the old slap and tickle.'

'Slap and tickle? Is that like Bubble and Squeak?'

Keenan laughed. 'Only after you've been married a long time! Otherwise it's more like Toad in the Hole.' He could see Billy was still struggling. 'You *know*...' He leaned in close, nudged him with his elbow and spoke behind the back of his hand, extenuating every syllable. '*Sex-u-al in-ter-course*!'

Billy's eyes widened in horror and his hand instinctively leapt to his crotch where he was hugely relieved to discover his flies were securely buttoned up. 'How could they...think such a thing?'

Keenan spread his arms wide, stuck out his bottom lip and grimaced in a gesture of resigned incomprehension. 'Who knows what nonsense goes on in a woman's mind. I tell you, I'll be bloody glad when the lads come back, Bolshie sods though they usually are. At least you understood what was what with them. Women, eh? By the way, you've got some straw in your hair.'

That morning, Joan and Phyl had noticed Akaash had reverted to sullen introspection and had done their best to chivvy him back to better spirits. Joan had lent him a book of Bengali folk tales. Phyl had told him to buck himself up. All three at least had agreed that further study was unlikely to be worth the effort. Unfortunately they were proving far more adept at breaking one another's attempts at encryption than at developing anything the company was likely to think worthwhile. Time was passing and they were scheduled to present an outline at a Board of Directors meeting that was approaching with depressing rapidity.

Akaash returned to their office after lunch. For him, everything had changed over that lunchtime. He was compromised, conflicted, sullied. For Joan, it had just been another lunchtime. She spoke excitedly about her latest idea for a new code, betting gleefully neither he nor Phyl would break it in a hurry. Akaash tried hard to concentrate but the words just wouldn't register.

Phyl, who had left early for an appointment with Dr Falk, returned late and on arrival seemed reserved, even for her.

25

The next Sunday, Akaash made a further visit to Oxford to talk with another set of Joan's friends. Whereas the first group to which she had introduced him had been earnest political types, declaiming the triumph of the proletariat and denouncing imperialism, these were urbane, loose-limbed aesthetes. The men wore their hair long, the women close cropped. Aspiring artists, he assumed. Calcutta was awash with them. The clothes and coiffure might differ but the carefully constructed indifference didn't. They seemed to Akaash so young, albeit desperately aping the trappings of maturity. Corduroys. Cardigans. Scarves. Pipe-smoking, sherry-sipping. Responding to whatever he said with wry, cynical observations and regarding him through horn-rimmed spectacles as an exotic reflection of their pretensions. They could hardly be bothered to fake interest in the Quit India Movement or the famine in Bengal, only really engaging with him at all when Joan asked him to join her in reading Tagore to them in the original Bengali.

Vincent once more accompanied Sally to church. She took with her a small bunch of chrysanthemums for her daughter's grave that she had surreptitiously picked early that morning from those in the garden next door growing close to the fence. She thought Ernie wouldn't notice, unaware of him watching her from behind a grubby net curtain through his kitchen window.

As soon as she and Vincent had crossed the road into the park, Billy dashed out of the front door, searching up and down the street until he spotted the van with two men sitting in the cab. He waved them to approach and they drove slowly up to No. 23.

When Vincent and Sally returned – both reflecting on the sad little grave where he had watched in respectful silence as she had tugged away grass from around the gravestone, unsure if he should help or not – Billy was at the front door to greet them.

'Cistern fixed?' Vincent asked unenthusiastically. It was a fair deduction from the smug expression on Billy's face that it was.

'I've gone one better. Come, Mrs A, to the inaugural flush of the "Deluge".'

Billy led them through to reveal a newly installed tank, in gleaming white ceramic decorated with an elegant blue coat of arms, mounted on ornate brass brackets. There was a stunned silence as he proudly pulled the chain.

'It's beautiful. But I could never afford anything like that,' Mrs A said very quietly.

'It's a gift!' Billy assured her, hoping desperately that the tears welling up in her eyes were of joy and gratitude.

She took out a handkerchief, sniffed, and shook her head. 'I can't accept it. I'm sorry but I just can't. My Derek…' She turned and half ran back into the house, the kitchen door slamming behind her.

'I don't understand,' said Billy, stunned.

'You really don't, do you?' said Vincent. 'You think you can just buy your way into and out of everything without a care for other people's feelings.'

'But I was being kind,' insisted Billy.

'No, you weren't. You were showing off. As per usual. And in the process sneering at all her efforts to get by and sort things out and make the best of things. Jesus! It would be bad enough if it was your money you're acting the big shot with. You're no better than these Americans everyone grumbles about, flaunting your fat pay packet and expecting everyone to think you're great and bow down and suck up to you. You're just another overpaid, arrogant foreigner throwing someone else's money around. And why? To hide the fact that you, the great engineer, couldn't even fix a toilet. How appropriate. You make me sick. You and all your kind.'

'Ya'Allah, you're always a sanctimonious bastard but you're particularly awful when you go to church! If you're so bloody all-knowing then tell me how I put this right with her.'

'Where's the old cistern?'

'Round the side.'

'Can it be put back up?'

'I suppose so.'

'Then go and say sorry to her and this afternoon we put the old one back. Then on Monday you pay a fraction of what this monstrosity cost to get a plumber to come and get the damned thing working properly.'

'What do I do with this one?'

'Who cares? Send it back.'

'To London?'

'Good God! How much did you spend on this? No, don't tell me. Just give it to Mr Norris next door and ask him to get rid of it for you. And then whatever it raises I suggest you put towards the Works' Christmas party for the kids.'

That evening, the old cistern securely back in place – and by some marvellous accident or cruel humour of the gods, actually restored to better working order – and the majestic, rejected 'Deluge' loaded onto Ernie's cart, tranquillity returned to a near-deserted No. 23. Akaash and Billy were fire-watching – both now practiced hands, they were teamed with men from the Carriage and Wagon side they'd not met before, and were settled on various roofs. Akaash was trying to read by torchlight under a blanket, and Billy was smoking, sharing round his hip flask, yarning and joking. Sally had also absented herself, off to visit her mother-in-law on Walcot Road as she did most Sunday evenings. Vincent had the house to himself for the first time.

He settled in the front room and tuned in to *Gala Night* on the Home Service. Ann Zeigler and Webster Booth were halfway through *We'll Gather Lilacs* when he could sit still no longer. Adopting the appropriate stance, arms lightly holding an invisible partner, eyes closed, he began to dance – slow sweeps, heels raised, back arched. Soon he was transported far from a small front room on Ashton St, no longer dancing on a threadbare carpet but on the highly polished sprung floors in ballrooms and dancehalls in Mazagaon and Byculla. Not a forty-something far from home in a strange and not particularly welcoming place but back in his late teens, winning first prize in the Railway Colony dance competition.

He had no idea how long Sally had been watching him. She had removed the headscarf she invariably wore outside, and it hung in her right hand. Her coat was undone and she had a sad smile on her face.

'Can anyone cut in?' she asked.

He paused, as though momentarily uncertain quite where he was. Then, unspeaking and unsmiling, reached out a hand. She let the coat slip off her shoulders and let him lead her into a waltz. She was a good dancer, confident and well-attuned to his lead, picking up immediately when a step or turn needed to be foreshortened to avoid the furniture that surrounded them. They danced as partners, but not as a couple, moving in unison yet entirely separate in their enjoyment of the movements and with a respectful distance between them. The radio orchestra moved from one tune to another and they, attuned, changed their steps with the altered tempo.

They danced on until the programme ended. Then they stopped, still holding each other lightly, bodies apart, strangely formal yet neither seeming to want to be the first to break away as the concert music gave way to hymns for evensong. Sally leaned forward, rested her head briefly on his shoulder, and then stepped back. 'Thank you,' she said. 'That was lovely.'

She turned, picked up her coat and hung it up in the hall. Vincent stood for a while, then turned the wireless off and went up to his bed.

The lunchtime encounters between Mollie and Billy continued. At the sound of the first lunchtime hooter, he would abruptly conclude whatever he was doing, wash his hands, grab his sandwiches and head over to the stable where they would kiss and impatiently explore each other's bodies. Mollie maintained strict rules of engagement. He could touch any and every part of her, he could kiss her neck and breasts but no lower. Stern murmurs warned of boundaries being approached; encouraging sighs conferred approval. After, they became oddly formal. He would thank her as she wiped her hand on the handkerchief he'd give to her and she would smile and tell him he was welcome. They wouldn't look at each other as they dressed. Then, fully clothed, they would share their sandwiches and chat about small things that had happened that morning and about the co-workers they had in common. Mollie knew most of the women in Shop B and proved to be a rich source of gossip about several. They'd part with a careful clothing-and-straw check and a chaste peck on the cheek. Then Billy would stride away, his heart feeling like it would burst with an overwhelming affection for this sweet girl.

He had no comprehension of the nature or extent of her enjoyment of their encounters. He'd been brought up to believe sex was something men sought and women endured. The fact that Mollie seemed to want nothing from him beyond these snatched moments of shared passion confused him. Whilst they were rarely lost for something to talk about, they hardly spoke about each other's life outside the Works, as though that would be an intrusion. As though they didn't really have that right. Once, Billy had suggested that they meet up for a drink in a pub or a walk in the park but Mollie, not very convincingly, pretended that she hadn't heard him. Reluctantly he accepted that she either didn't want to or wasn't able to and didn't ask again, although he did try to explore if she was, like some fairy-tale princess in need of saving, trapped by cruel parents and unable to follow her heart. It soon became clear even to him that whilst this was an appealing romantic fantasy, it was also arrant nonsense. She was, he resentfully suspected, an independent spirit from a happy home, free to go out to work and socialise and in need of neither champion nor saviour.

She was fond of him, he was sure. They liked each other and were powerfully drawn to one another. Affection and desire combined. Wasn't that all love was? So why didn't she ache and pine for more like he did? Once Billy had come to terms with the fact that she enjoyed their passionate lunchtimes and subsequent amiable, trivial conversation, he struggled to understand why she didn't seem to want to spend every waking and sleeping hour with him, because that was how he was starting to feel. When he wasn't with her, he yearned desperately for her company, going over in his mind all that had passed between them. He spent day and night in a state of semi-arousal, replaying carnal images of the hypnotic movement of her breasts and the breathtaking whiteness of her thighs whilst simultaneously trying to compose poems to celebrate her purity like some medieval swain lost in virtuous worship of a chaste maid. Billy cherished the fact that she was still a virgin – well, she must be, he told himself, why else would she so determinedly police her panty-line against all attempted incursions on his part? He dreamed at night of the lustful act of consummation of their love and daydreamed about where and how and when that glorious moment would be.

Unfortunately, or perhaps fortunately, Mollie did not share his obsessive passion. For her this was nothing other than a pleasantly wayward adventure. A secret little fling. An agreeable, delightfully sensual but essentially transient fling. In many ways she thought about 'His Highness' as she did her horse: lovely to look at, a delight to touch, wonderfully strong, beautifully constructed – but strictly confined to the Works. She did, however, share another of Billy's delusions: that no one else had noticed their mutual lunchtime absences and deduced their cause.

Billy, following his uncomfortable encounter with Elsie and Doreen, took great care to return to Shop B before the final lunchtime hooter and the start of the afternoon shift properly dressed and well groomed. Molly returned to her rounds, collecting scrap. Whenever she called at Shop B, she kept her head down and avoided eye contact with Billy, who invariably found something that needed all his attention at the most distant point in the shop from the glory hole.

They could hardly have been more obvious if they'd tried.

Their naive confidence in their discretion and the lack of inquisitiveness of others were totally unfounded. Everyone in Shop B was perfectly well aware of what was going on between them and all discussed it with varying points of view ranging from 'none of my business what other people choose to get up to' through amusement and tolerance via occasional envy to downright disgust.

Elsie, to no one's surprise, was at the revulsion end of the spectrum. 'That Mollie Bowen is no better than she should be.

Little trollop,' she said to Doreen as they watched Billy return one afternoon. 'She'll be smiling on the other side of her face when she pops out a brown baby.'

'Listen to you!' scoffed Doreen. 'You'd have been all over him thirty years ago. Live and let live, that's what I say.'

Elsie frowned. 'Here, what do you mean "thirty years ago"? Cheeky cow!' She placed both hands under her ample bosom and thrust up. 'There's many a good tune played on an old fiddle.'

'If he prefers mutton to lamb!'

Elsie removed her hands and her breasts sagged. Both laughed. 'Still,' said Elsie as they returned to their work, 'it's not right. Not right at all. Someone ought to do something about it.'

Someone did.

It was a Wednesday. It had poured all morning and the rain showed no signs of letting up. Billy ran across the yard to the stable, splashing through oily puddles and holding a sheet of tarpaulin over his head. Reaching shelter, he stepped in, and turned to shake the tarpaulin vigorously. He then turned back to be confronted by a stocky elderly man holding Mollie's long-handled broom across his chest like a rifle held at port. He stared, cold-eyed and stony-faced, up at Billy.

'Where's Mollie?' Billy asked.

'Mollie ain't coming no more,' the old man snarled through gritted, yellowed teeth. 'I'll be looking after Boxer from now on.'

Billy wasn't sure what to say or do. He stood silently, listening to the rain, breathing in the smell of the horse and the hay and feeling a vast – and, as even he admitted to himself, totally selfish – sadness. He looked at the angry face of the man still holding the broom as though it were a weapon. 'Is she all right?' he asked.

'She's fine. She just ain't working here any more. And don't you go bothering her neither. She don't want anything to do with your sort. *Theek hai?*'

'Indian Army?' asked Billy, thinking that would explain a lot.

'No. Royal Artillery. But eight years out there. You leave her alone, you hear? From now on you eat your sandwiches elsewhere. Now, *jaldi chalo*.'

Billy turned, dragged the tarpaulin back over his head and shoulders and listlessly retraced his steps. He felt sick. He wondered how he'd ever survive without Mollie in his life. He couldn't, he was sure. He must either persuade her to run away with him or he would pine away and die of a broken heart. But then he couldn't run away just yet as he had his duty to perform. He had no choice but to stay. But how could he stay in this shitty little town, in this miserable grey country, without seeing her, being with her, holding her? To think that glorious body would never be touched and kissed by him again. Worse, imagine it pawed at instead by the grimy hands of some beer-swilling, semi-skilled labourer. She, who had been loved and caressed and worshipped by a true Gwaliorite? He'd kidded her about him being a prince but compared to these…peasants he was as good as. And who the hell did that superannuated squaddie think he was talking to? *Jaldi chalo* indeed! If nothing else, Billy was Management and should be spoken to with respect.

He paused, considering going straight to the Chief Mechanical Engineer's office to complain about such insolence, but a millisecond's reflection changed his mind. Could she really have agreed to this brutal separation? Impossible! But then, maybe she'd wanted this to end: maybe this cruel termination was actually all her idea. After all, he had to admit Mollie hadn't always listened to him as attentively as he'd have liked. Sometimes it seemed she'd have preferred it if only his body had turned up. She could be impatient of his conversation and actually a bit dismissive of his post-fumble reflections. Almost as though she was getting bored with his company.

And he had to admit that she was really a bit…common. Plus, she'd obviously told others about his initial attempts to impress her because he was bloody sure he'd heard Elsie and her bunch call him 'His Highness' when they thought he was out of earshot.

He frowned, paused, turned to walk back to the stables and then turned again and continued to Shop B. If he were to be honest, he felt a little bit used. In fact, the more he thought about it, he felt quite a lot used. Taken advantage of. He shook his head. Had this all been a massive mistake? But those breasts… her neck, like a swan's… actually a swan's neck wasn't exactly the most erotic thing he could imagine, but it sounded nice. He was getting excited at the thought of Mollie's neck. The tilt of her chin. That tiny mole on the side of her nose.

He had to find a way to see her, at least once more. To make sure she was OK. To find out if this really was what she wanted.

But then again…

Billy was still so preoccupied with these thoughts that when he entered Shop B he initially failed to register the celebratory buzz. Keenan came rushing over, face flushed, and grabbed his arm. 'So glad you're back early, Mr Khan! You must see this…'

Billy shook his arm free. '*Birkenhead*'s ready for testing?' he asked unenthusiastically. This would be welcome news but hardly that much of a surprise: they'd been well on schedule for the end of the week as planned.

'No! I wouldn't have believed it if I hadn't seen it with my own eyes!'

'What?'

'It's *Tremayne*! Elsie's girls have got *Tremayne* sorted first!'

Billy stared at him in disbelief. Whilst he'd concentrated most of his attention on *Birkenhead* in the past few days, he'd kept his eye on the progress on all the other engines as well, and he'd have sworn *Tremayne* wasn't anywhere near ready. Admittedly, he hadn't followed her progress as closely as the others' in recent days; since transferring Cyn to work on *Tremayne* with Elsie he'd felt embarrassed and a little bit ashamed of himself and had thus left inspections to Keenan in order to avoid having to encounter either of them.

'You had no idea?' Billy asked doubtfully, feeling somewhat piqued that his scheduling had been so spectacularly derailed.

'Well, I knew they were cracking on better than we'd expected, yes. I see now why you put young Cynthia in with them. She's the one who made the difference! I said to my Edie, I said, "That Mr Khan is a clever bug…one."'

'And you didn't think to mention it to me?'

'I was going to, 'course I was. But young Cynthia begged me not to! Wanted to surprise you, she said! Women, eh? Soft-hearted, see? Between you and me, I think a couple of her brothers have been lending a hand after hours. No names, no pack drill, but I can't see how they could have sorted that reversing rod by themselves. You got to hand it to them though…and to you! Well done, Mr Khan!'

Billy looked across with deep loathing at the women gathered below *Tremayne*'s smokebox door. Elsie stood in the centre of the group, feet apart, armed folded, triumphant. Cyn was chatting to an older woman leaning on the coupling hook. She paused, looked across at Billy, raised her chin and smiled.

'You've carried out a full inspection?'

'Just done it. She looks ready to move on to me. First engine out!'

'Well, let's just make absolutely sure,' said Billy, shedding his jacket and grabbing a clipboard and pencil. He was pretty confident he'd be able to find something that would require further attention and get things back as they should be.

He dropped down into the inspection pit, tapped wheels and rods with his sounding hammer, walked slowly along both sides, tugging at pipe fittings, running his hands over surfaces, then climbed up into the cab where he shifted levers, checked dials and twisted wheels. All looked infuriatingly in order. Until they got steam up, which they couldn't do in the Erecting Shop, there really wasn't anything he could find fault with. How the hell had they done it?

Elsie, horribly triumphant, drew his attention to the firebox. Doreen's head popped out through the narrow firebox door – designed for having shovelfuls of coal flung through it rather than allowing human entry – and called cheerily to him, 'Give us a hand out and you climb in here and have a look, Mr Khan. You wait till you see what we've done in here.' Slowly, painfully, she eased herself through the firebox door with Billy's help and rolled out onto the floor of the cab.

Billy squatted down beside her on the cab floor, leaned forward and peered in. 'That's OK, Doreen. I can see from here.'

'No, you can't. Get in there and just look at them lovely boiler rods…'

'No, Doreen. I said it's OK. I'm sure Mr Keenan took a good look when he did his inspection.'

'But…'

'I said no! What is there not to understand about that? Are you stupid?'

Cyn was taken aback at this uncharacteristic outburst. She knew Billy's pride would be wounded by their success but she was surprised at how he'd snapped at Doreen. He'd never spoken to anyone like that before.

Billy climbed down to an uncomfortable silence. Doreen, unperturbed, clambered down from the cab after him. Elsie handed her an old towel and she wiped her hands.

'He's not a happy chappie,' said Doreen as Elsie and she walked away from the engine.

'You know what I think?' mused Elsie. 'I think His Highness is averse to tight, dark holes.'

'Wish my Jack'd suffered from that problem when he was younger. I wouldn't have had to marry the bugger.'

'You know what I mean. Don't like confined places.'

Doreen shrugged. 'Who does?'

'I mean, like a real fear. What do they call it? There's a name for it...'

'A touch of the collywobbles?'

'No! You know, a phobia.'

'So?'

'So nothing, just saying. Mind you, might just be that he's like that bloody big horse: pining 'cos Mollie Bowen ain't giving him his oats no more.'

Could this day get any worse? Billy wondered miserably, overhearing the last of the exchange.

It could. It did. Almost immediately. Hartshorne, in shirtsleeves – a sight unseen outside his office – burst in with his flustered secretary in his wake carrying his jacket. 'Is it true? *Tremayne*! I thought we were looking at *Birkenhead* by Friday?'

Keenan stepped forward. 'That's right, er...Chief. So we were. *Are.* We weren't sure we could deliver on *Tremayne* so we didn't want to raise false hopes.' He looked towards a stony-faced Billy. 'As Mr Khan always says, don't promise what you can't deliver. We wanted to surprise you.'

Hartshorne looked from Keenan to Billy, sensing the tension between them but unsure what it was all about. 'I don't like surprises, Mr Khan, as Mr Keenan should know very well. Surprises are bad engineering. Well, well, well. *Tremayne*, eh? Who'd have thought it? Ready for roll-out this afternoon for full testing and painting?'

Billy, unsure if he was being congratulated or reprimanded, nodded glumly. Hartshorne placed a hand on his shoulder, 'And by a crew led by that dreadful woman, Coggins! You are a remarkable man, Mr Khan. One day you must tell me how you did it! And we're still on schedule for *Birkenhead* by Friday? Two engines when I'd only asked for one, eh?' he added, with a meaningful look at Keenan. 'We'll have to revisit those targets of yours, won't we? Miss Jennings?' he shouted, and then turned, surprised to find her at his elbow. 'Oh, there you are!' She held his jacket up for him to slip his arms into the sleeves. 'Now don't tell me *this* doesn't warrant one of our special cups of tea!'

Swindon, everyone said, had been lucky. Not only had it been spared the serious attention of the Luftwaffe but it had also avoided the large-scale invasion of American troops that the rest of southwest England had endured. The old joke was that there were only three things wrong with the American GIs: overpaid, oversexed and over here. And it was funny because there was so much truth in it. In a country starved of comforts and worn down by war, with huge numbers of its own manhood conscripted and sent off for years on end, the impact of the arrival of tens of thousands of fresh-faced, fit young men with pockets bulging with money and with access to seemingly limitless mountains of goods was instant and seismic. How could such men not be profoundly attractive to hungry, sexually frustrated younger women who saw their prime being ground down into a premature, celibate, grey middle age through years of privation, rationing, making do, mending, mustn't grumbling and getting by?

With the American troops came American policies, including the allocation of different parts of the county to different ethnicity of soldiers. For the first time in mainland Britain, segregation of the races was imposed. It only applied to American troops, but it was clearly signed, uncomplainingly adopted and rigorously policed. Some villages and towns – where the entire population was almost invariably entirely white-skinned – were designated Black, and only African American GIs would be posted in the surrounding area. In places where troop allocations made such stark distinctions impracticable, pubs, cafes, clubs and cinemas would be segregated by day of the week. Typically, Mondays, Wednesdays and Sundays being designated 'Coloured' days and all others reserved exclusively for whites. This was both possible and legal because the US, while being one of many nations gathering troops for the approaching invasion, was allowed to impose their own military legal code on British territory and police their own forces, something that had never happened before.

As a result, for the first time in well over a century in mainland Britain, convicted men faced the gallows for rape. A British hangman was contracted by the American army to carry out the task in the two-storey execution shed hastily erected in red brick at the side of the 400-year-old grey stone Shepton Mallet prison. It did not pass unnoticed that although African Americans made up only 10 per cent of the US Army, they comprised 100 per cent of those executed for rape. Whilst the statistic was incontestable, what it evidenced was subject to considerable heated debate: to some it demonstrated the danger the arrival of large numbers of Negro troops represented, which justified the policies of segregation. To far more – among them Akaash, Cyn and indeed the whole Trade Union movement – it demonstrated the racism and prejudice of Britain's ally to the west and its enthusiasm for state-authorised lynching.

Seaports and cities in the Great Western region, in particular Swansea, Cardiff and Bristol had, as long as anyone could remember, comprised a typical entrepôt population. Significant minorities of many races and numerous colours lived there, speaking the language of the land in the accents of the region, with more than a few examples of marriages that crossed racial divides. With the arrival of large numbers of Americans to whom such a thing was an obscenity, problems were inevitable. Black Englishmen and brown Welshmen were threatened, abused and beaten up by gangs of white GIs simply for walking along the street with their white wives, who would as often be spat at and called nigger-loving whores.

Vincent had witnessed one such incident himself, just near Cardiff Docks. A neatly dressed couple in their fifties were waiting for a bus – the wife was white, the husband of African or West Indian origin. They were chatting to one another in a strong Welsh lilt when a small group of white GIs began jostling them and calling them names. It was trivial stuff by comparison with some incidents Vincent had heard talk of. It seemed to him from the wary reaction of the couple that this wasn't the first time this had happened. They kept their heads down, eyes averted, waiting for the troops to grow tired of picking on them and move on. Vincent, similarly born and bred in a huge port, was all too familiar with the sense of entitlement and off-duty excesses of drunken men in uniform. What he found most shocking was the bitterness and the rage this innocuous couple engendered in these American GIs, and the fact that it was mid-morning and these angry men were stone-cold sober. Passing locals, though clearly offended, seemed not to want to get involved.

Such incidents, sparking local outrage and fuelling growing resentment though they might, went largely unreported and were dealt with not by the law of the land but by courteous and sympathetic middle-ranking American officers offering sincere regrets and presenting large hampers of luxury goods.

Swindon had indeed been lucky not to have an American garrison nearby. But it was not so lucky as to be spared occasional boisterous gangs of GIs out on a spree, a sufficiently regular occurrence for the town to have its own small US Military Police presence, just in case. And it was particularly unlucky that such a bunch of drunken GIs found themselves thrown off their train at Swindon station as a result of their raucous behaviour on the very evening of the celebration of *Tremayne*'s resurrection.

Celebrations started in Shop B at 3 p.m., by which time Billy's mood had improved. He was secretly hugely impressed by what the *Tremayne* crew had pulled off and chastened that they had managed to do it right under his nose without him having the slightest clue. Humbled, he was magnanimous in his determination to celebrate what they'd managed and generous in his praise for their achievements. To show his pride in them, he raced back to No. 23 and quickly donned his full dress uniform, this time waving delightedly at the wolf whistles and cheers that welcomed him on his return, sensing as much affection in it as mockery.

Shop B was unusually flooded with light as the huge double doors were flung open. Just outside the doorway an 850 Class saddle tank engine, of a vintage even older than the Bulldogs, stood in steam and ready to tow *Tremayne* off to the next stages of her return to service. An urn had been set up on the table normally reserved for paying out the wages on Friday. Invited guests were being served mugs of steaming tea. As well as any family members of the *Tremayne* women who were also employed Inside – which included an alarming number of Abbots – Hartshorne and Miss Jennings were there, as was Mrs Deakes and Dr Falk, who had developed a special affection for Shop B.

Billy wasn't quite sure why he'd invited Akaash and his two colleagues to be present, but he did. Akaash had been so distant and self-absorbed of late that even Billy had noticed and felt concerned about him. He raised a hand to him as Akaash eased himself unobtrusively into the Shop, his head down, avoiding eye contact. Cyn gave him a welcoming wave and pointed him out to her family, who went over to stand with him. A moment later, Joan and Phyl arrived.

'Here come the Debs! Afternoon girls!' Elsie called out cheerily as she watched them pick their way around the workbenches and bins. They looked over, smiled and waved in acknowledgement. 'Mind you don't get those lovely clean clothes all mucky,' she added, one eyebrow raised.

Elsie struck a match on *Tremayne*'s coupling hook – an action that she regarded as her exclusive right – and lit her cigarette. She took it from her mouth, blew on the burning tip until it glowed and lit one for Doreen off it. 'Look at those daft cows,' she muttered, handing the cigarette over.

'What about them? They seem like nice girls. Bit posh, but they can't help that,' said Doreen, taking a deep drag.

'Well, I mean! You ever seen anyone wear work clothes that clean? They come in every morning with us like butter wouldn't melt, dressed like they're here to do a real job, then off they trot to the offices. Look at those boots. Polished! And neat creases ironed into their overalls! Proper little madams.'

'So what?'

'Well, they're obviously up to something. Like them mini-submarines in Shop X that no one's supposed to know about. All hush-hush, top-secret stuff. But they're working in the offices.'

'Well, it's none of our business. Not if it's hush-hush. Let them get on with it, I say.'

'This is why it's taking us so bloody long to win this war! They dress them up like factory girls, then put them in the offices where they'll stick out like sore thumbs! They may as well put a big sign out saying, "Oy, Adolf! Secret work being done here." Why don't they just dress them like everyone else in the office? It's a disgrace! And an insult to those of us doing the actual work. I tell you, if I was in charge things would be different.'

'Listen to you!' laughed Doreen. 'I hope all this isn't going to your head, Elsie Coggins! You'll be too grand to talk to the likes of the rest of us before you know it. Oh, look out!' she warned, taking another drag on the cigarette and then carefully pinching out the tip to save the butt for later. 'Looks like His Highness is about to grace us with a few words.'

'Ladies!' cried Billy, from the footplate of *Tremayne,* beckoning to the groups of workers who stood beside their respective engines to come and join the visitors. 'It's three o'clock. Gather round, please!'

The women came together and stood around the cab of *Tremayne*. He couldn't help but notice and sympathise with the fact that a very dispirited-looking *Birkenhead* crew were last to join thc crowd.

Billy looked to Hartshorne, who shook his head. 'This is your Shop, Mr Khan. You carry on.'

Billy glanced down at the upturned faces and felt suddenly deeply moved. He remembered standing exactly like this and first addressing these women just a few weeks earlier. What had then been a bunch of anonymous and slightly intimidating strangers were now colleagues, fellow workers, his girls. And just consider what they'd managed to do together so far!

'We are about to see one of the most glorious sights known to man! Or woman. Something no one has seen since before most of us were born. A 3300 Bulldog Class GWR locomotive being rolled out from its Erecting Shop! Mr Keenan, if you please!'

'Right you are, Mr Khan!' With a huge grin on his reddened face, Keenan heaved the loop of the steel hawser over *Tremayne*'s coupling hook and signalled to the driver of the ancient shunter standing just beyond the doors.

'Well, I'm sorry,' said Elsie, arms crossed and trying hard to look bored, 'but I'd sooner have a few bob extra in my pay packet on Friday than all this hullabaloo.'

Cyn shook her head. Her eyes were bright and her lips trembled as she spoke. 'Can't you see it?' she shouted over the noise. 'Look, she's moving! This is us! What we've done! It's beautiful!'

One or two women began to clap. Others joined in and the applause grew. The ancient crane operator took off his cap and called for three cheers. Cyn's father, brothers, uncles and cousins bellowed out hurrahs and threw their caps into the air. *Tremayne* moved forward a foot or two then stopped, to a disappointed groan, as Billy waved his arms to halt the shunter. 'Isn't it traditional here to sound the shunter's whistle to salute a newly built engine when it first rolls? Well, I think that must apply to a newly rebuilt one too!'

Keenan beckoned Hartshorne forward. 'Go on, Fred,' he whispered as Hartshorne passed him. 'For old times' sake.'

Hartshorne, clearly delighted, waved in acknowledgement of renewed cheering and climbed up into the tank engine's cab, shook hands with its surprised driver, who quickly doffed his cap, and reached towards the dangling whistle chain. He touched it contemplatively, the years disappearing... then he shook his head and withdrew his hand. 'No,' he said, regretfully to himself. 'Not this time.' He leaned out of the cab and called out, 'You're right, Mr Khan, but that honour always goes to the most junior lad in the shop. Who's the youngest person here?'

The crane operator raised an arthritic hand to a good-humoured cheer. There was a series of muttered conversations – claims, counterclaims and vehement denials, and then Cyn found herself pushed forward. Billy tried to look indifferent but even he was grinning as he climbed down to stand next to Keenan.

'No one more appropriate,' cried Hartshorne, reaching a hand out to her. 'Up you come, Miss Abbot!'

There was a huge roar as Cyn clambered up and gave three long blasts on the whistle. Keenan and Billy turned to each other, broad smiles on their faces and, both feeling far more emotional than either would ever later admit, shook hands.

Celebrations continued until the afternoon hooter sounded. Then for Billy and several others came a brief dash home, a tea bolted down and a change of clothes before they were off to an evening of tales about fine engines, old characters, narrow scrapes and exaggerated achievements in the Queen's Tap.

It was the first time Billy had actually been in that pub. He was well-acquainted with hotel and lounge bars elsewhere in the town but a proper spit-and-sawdust working man's pub: this was new and foreign ground. He headed for the lounge but was met at the door by an already tipsy Keenan, who steered him away towards the more starkly furnished and smoke-filled saloon bar where he was greeted on entry by a cheer, handshakes and offers to stand him a beer.

Akaash, following in his wake, was greeted solemnly as a comrade in the struggle by several serious men present. He had now attended and reported back to Curtis on two of their clandestine gatherings in the upstairs room at the Glue Pot but had never actually sat and drank in a bar with them as they would that evening. He hadn't wanted to go along at all but Sally – who promised to drop in at the lounge bar and let Billy buy her a congratulatory port-and-lemon after she'd finished the washing up – had virtually pushed him out of the front door, insisting it would do him a world of good to get him out of himself for a while.

Akaash advanced into the bar, wheezing in the wet-dog reek of stale smoke, spilled beer, damp clothes and honest sweat, and was immediately absorbed by the Abbot clan – several generations of which seemed to be there. He ended up in a corner with Cyn and her vegetarian brother, sipping unenthusiastically at a half-pint of Arkells 3Bs and debating the difference between cooperativism and collectivism.

Ernie Norris sat alone at the bar, his stick leaning against his stool, meditatively sipping a Guinness. They said hello to him but he just ignored them as he did everyone else around him.

It was around ten, not far off last orders, when the Americans arrived. Sally had, as promised, popped in for one drink and then made her apologies, reminding Billy – who was trying to persuade her to stay for at least one more – that Vincent was due back that night and explaining that she wanted to be back to get him his tea when he arrived. Keenan had long before excused himself and, slightly unsteadily, made his way home, as had Cyn's father and most of her relatives. Akaash had promised he'd walk Cyn – who was still deeply engaged in a debate about the difference between a party and a movement – home in half an hour. In the Abbot household, politics trumped curfews – at least when Mrs Abbot wasn't present. The last hangers-on were getting to the reflective stage of the evening. There'd been a sing-song earlier but now things were more muted.

There were seven of them. So long drunk they'd sobered up once and were now drunk again – bad-tempered, blurry-eyed, sour-faced, vomit-breathed drunk. And they were looking for trouble. The sight of a dark-skinned man leaning deep into a conversation with a white woman was just the kind of opportunity they'd been hoping to be given all day.

They ordered beers and looked around them, pretending to register Akaash and Cyn for the first time.

'Woah! What the… Hey guys, see what the little coon sniffin' up the leg of! Lady, you should be with yuh own sort. I can give you better than anything he's offering.'

'Yeah.'

'Shit!'

'S'right.'

Akaash stood and removed his glasses, tensing for a beating. He was determined that there would be as much distance as possible between himself and Cyn before it started. Billy stepped away from the bar and stood between the drunken soldiers and Akaash.

'Gentlemen, I think…'

He got no further.

'Who the fuck you talkin' to, boy?' slurred the largest of the GIs, squaring up to him. 'Watch me, boys! This fukkah gonna get a whuppin'.'

Billy, having boxed for the engineering school of his college in his youth, automatically adopted orthodox stance, head drawn down, shoulders forward, fists up and legs apart. The other GIs started chanting '*Coon! Coon! Coon!*' His evident readiness for a brawl left the American facing him momentarily nonplussed. The aggressive chanting by the soldiers was met by embarrassed, confused silence from the regulars, but no one made a move.

Then Ernie Norris, without glancing up from his drink, picked up the heavy glass 'Senior Service' ashtray he'd been flicking his cigarette ash into and brought it crashing down hard onto the bar. Everyone turned towards him.

'I don't want any trouble, Ernie,' warned the landlord anxiously.

'There's not going to be any trouble, Harry,' Ernie assured him. 'I know these Yanks from the last lot. They never fight anyone they don't outnumber ten to one.'

'What the fuck this got to do with you, grandad?'

Ernie turned to study the speaker. 'I suffer from my nerves, son. And you're getting on them. So I'm telling you nicely, either pipe down and drink quietly or clear off out of it. These lads are my neighbours.'

There was a chorus of contemptuous laughter from the Americans. 'You fuckin' crazy, pops?'

'And they're Union men,' called out Cyn, leaping up and stepping forward to stand beside Akaash.

A slow smile spread across Ernie's face. 'Really? Got their cards on them?' he asked.

At Cyn's urging, Akaash took out and held up his Union card. Billy, eyes never leaving the face of the largest American, right fist still raised, ever so slowly reached his left hand into his jacket pocket and did the same. Ernie chuckled. 'This just gets better and better. Gentlemen?'

All around the bar, men took out their Union cards. Two old boys playing shove ha'penny on a table over by the toilet door, deafened by years in the Foundry, were oblivious of what was going on until someone tapped them on the shoulder. Stony-faced, they felt in their pockets and held up tattered and creased cards.

'Harry?'

'I'm asking you nicely, Ernie…'

'Card, Harry.'

The landlord sighed, reached into the breast pocket of his waistcoat and took his Union card out.

'Retired Section,' explained Ernie with a dangerous smile. 'You see, you lads have typically misread a situation. You come in here all full of spit and vinegar, see a couple of dark-skinned men in a bar full of white blokes and you think we're going to stand by and watch while you act like the cunts you are – apologies for the language, Miss Abbot – and kick seven bells out of them. 'Cos that's all you see. But we see this picture a bit different. This is a railwaymen's pub. In a railway town. And, surprise, surprise, it's full of fucking railwaymen! All except for you lads. And you take on one railwayman in this town, Sonny Jim, you take on all of us. That's why you're going to finish your drinks nice and quiet and then you're going to toddle on out that door and walk away.'

The GIs looked around at a roomful of hard and resolute faces.

'Actually,' added Ernie. 'I've changed my mind. Fuck your drinks. Just piss off out of it now. Apologies again, Miss Abbot, but ladies really should be in the lounge.'

'We'll see you later,' snarled the last of the GIs to leave. 'This isn't over.'

'No? Bring a few more of your mates along with you if you're looking for a scrap,' sneered Ernie, returning to his beer. He took a sip, regarded his quarter-filled glass with distaste and placed it back on the bar. 'I always say you can't leave a Guinness standing,' he sighed. 'Give me another, Harry.'

'I think you'd better be on your way, Ernie,' said the landlord. 'And someone'd better see these lads home safe too,' he added, looking anxiously across at Akaash and Billy. 'Young Cynthia as well.' He glanced up at the clock above the door. 'I'm calling Time, gentlemen. Drink up now, please!'

Akaash protested that he'd promised to escort Cyn home but three burly Foundry men who lived in Prospect Place insisted they'd see her safely to her door. Just then two of Cyn's cousins – who had been drinking in the Great Western across the road and had heard there was trouble at the Tap – ran in, sighed with relief at seeing her safe and joined her escort. Cyn gave Akaash a quick peck on the cheek as she was ushered out. She smiled at Billy as she passed him. 'Quite a day,' she said, offering him her hand. 'Thanks, Mr Khan.'

A group of engineers said they'd be proud to walk along with the man who had repaired the Bulldogs. Billy called across to Akaash, assuming he'd join them, but Ernie shook his head. 'I'll see him safely back to his billet.'

'By yourself?' the youngest of the engineers surrounding Billy asked doubtfully.

Ernie looked at him. 'You Arthur Wickes's lad?'

'S'right, Mr Norris.'

'You tell your dad that Ernie Norris sends his regards. And you ask him to tell you what would have happened if you'd disrespected me like that twenty years ago. Now, we've still got ten minutes drinking-up time. Skinny Jim over there's going to sit with me while I finish my Guinness and then he and I'll walk home together. Neighbourly, like.' He glanced over at Akaash. 'All right with you, son?'

Akaash dearly wanted to go with Billy and his tough-looking companions but, intrigued and intimidated in equal measure by the man at the bar, he nodded.

'Good. Off you lot go. And tell Sally Atkinson to put the kettle on. I'll bring her lodger back shortly. What's your name, son?'

'Akaash Ray.'

'Ernie Norris. Pleased to meet you.'

'Likewise.'

'You've been in the wars.'

'Not me.'

'But you've taken a kicking or two. Come over here and stand at the bar. Real men don't drink at tables.'

Akaash crossed the room and stood beside Ernie. Harry put a Dewar's whisky in front of him. 'Time's been called. This is on the house,' he muttered. Akaash had no idea what that meant but grasped that the drink was free. Not surprising, he thought after he took a sip: it burned his throat and seemed to him every bit as revolting as the beer but with the single advantage of being much smaller in volume. Why did people do this, he wondered?

'Kickings?' Ernie reminded him.

'Oh, yes. One or two,' he admitted, his voice hoarse. 'Demonstrations. Marches for freedom. Why?'

''Cos you didn't flinch when it looked like those Yanks were gonna beat the living daylights out of you.'

'Nor did Billy Khan.'

'Captain Toilet Cistern? No, he didn't. But he did put his fists up. He was ready to fight. You weren't gonna defend yourself. You were just gonna take it, which is pathetic, but you weren't scared, which is interesting.'

'Why?'

'Because that's not natural. That's fucking strange. I don't get it.'

'It's called non-violence. The only true strength the weak and the vulnerable have.'

'What? Having the shit kicked out of you and not sticking up for yourself? That's bollocks. Makes no sense.'

Akaash smiled for the first time in days. Maybe this alcohol-drinking did have a point after all, he thought. 'No, it probably doesn't,' he agreed. 'But it's a fundamental principle of mine. Now I'm going to break a different fundamental principle. I'm going to buy you a drink, Mr Norris. As a brother in the Union.'

'No, you're not. Time's been called. Adolf might march up The Mall and have tea with the King but even he'd never get Harry to sell a drink after he's called Time. That's a fundamental principle too; another bloody stupid one.' Ernie belched, stood and leaned on his walking stick, bending his left leg stiffly. 'Come on. Let's get you home.'

And they were so nearly there – just across the park on Farringdon Road, at most five minutes from their front doors – when they encountered four of the GIs who'd invaded the Queen's Tap.

One was vomiting into the privet hedge that surrounded the park. The other three were standing around, waiting for him to empty out and straighten up. Akaash and Ernie had just started to cross the road towards them when they spotted the Americans. Akaash paused but Ernie kept walking, his limp noticeably worsening.

The four GIs, one wiping his mouth with the back of his hand, formed a line, barring their way.

'Well, well, well. We meet again,' slurred the one who had squared up against Billy.

'Let it go, Al,' pleaded the youngest of the four.

'Shut the fuck up, Woody. Not so brave now, are we, pops?'

Ernie shrugged, as though considering the matter. 'Don't know about you but I'm pretty much the same, now you mention it.'

Akaash stood very still. He was relieved his glasses were still in his pocket. He looked at their adversaries, who were engaged in a rambling debate about what should happen next. By a majority of three to one, an act of concerted brutality seemed to be the consensus, with him the primary recipient. The three for violence seemed clearly fighting drunk beyond reason. The fourth, the one called Woody, argued for just walking away. He looked wretched, uncertain, tired. Just an unhappy boy far from home and in need of his bed.

Ernie seemed suddenly a lot older than he had a moment before. He leaned heavily on his stick, hunched over. He coughed, spat and took out a grubby handkerchief with which he covered his mouth. 'Right, son,' he whispered. 'Now might be as good a time as any to reconsider that non-violence principle…'

'Are you crazy? There's four of them! And they're soldiers. Trained fighters.'

Ernie shook his head, still coughing. 'They may be dressed like soldiers. They may think they're soldiers, but believe me, son, until you've fought and you've found out you can kill, you're no more than a farmhand in uniform. Now, I need you to keep the puker occupied until I get to him. OK? I'll put down these two on the right.'

'What about the fourth one?'

'Don't worry about him. He'll run, or he'll stand, but he ain't gonna fight.'

'How do you know?'

'Just take my word. No time at present…'

With that, Ernie brought up his stick fast, the ferrule catching the soldier to the extreme right under the chin, snapping his head back and causing him to stagger backward a couple of paces. 'Move!' Ernie shouted to Akaash as he swung the stick into the side of the head of the second GI and then struck again at the first.

Akaash let out a high-pitched scream and leapt up on the third GI. Totally unsure what he was doing, he threw his arms around the startled soldier's neck, still screaming. He brought his knees up into his chest, and bit hard on his left ear. The soldier roared in pain and shock, falling backward, torn between trying to keep his balance and clawing his seemingly demented attacker off him. Akaash held on for all he was worth, eyes closed, teeth clenched on the ear, heart beating furiously. The two of them tumbled over the low wall that surrounded the park and ended up tangled in the hedge, when Akaash realised Ernie was dragging at his shoulder.

'For Christ's sake, enough. Jesus! Get off him so I can lay him out.'

Akaash released his grip as Ernie dragged him roughly back, almost throwing him out of the way. He spat what he suspected was blood out of his mouth and immediately retched up acid whisky and rancid beer. He slumped down onto the wall, shivering desperately as Ernie stepped back. Holding his stick like a golf club, he lined up the swing and delivered a sharp blow to the side of the moaning GI's neck.

'Old trench warfare tactic,' he explained calmly. 'Learnt that when we were sent over to bring a Hun or two back for interrogation. A smart smack on the side of the neck: keeps them quiet but doesn't significantly disable them. Well, not usually. Long as you get the angle right…'

Akaash looked at the profound consequences of what had been a mere few seconds of intense aggression. The two GIs Ernie had first tackled were laid out, side by side, still as corpses. The third was curled, slumped in the privet hedge. All three were breathing heavily. Ernie turned each to lay them on their sides.

'You have to make sure they don't swallow their own tongues or choke on vomit. They're not worth a murder charge. Now, what do we do with you?' he asked, turning to consider the last GI, who stood trembling and deathly pale.

'I didn't want any part of this,' he pleaded, holding up his hands. 'I…'

'I know, son,' said Ernie, nodding sympathetically as he brought the handle of his walking stick down hard on the bridge of the boy's nose. Blood burst forth and the young soldier fell to his knees, holding his face and wailing in shock, pain and horror.

'Why did you do that?' Akaash cried. 'He tried to stop them!'

'Indeed he did. And what's his life gonna be like if his mates wake up severely fucked and he's right as rain?'

He swung the stick again, striking the boy on the neck just as he had the others. The kneeling soldier fell sideways with a sad whimper. As he had with his comrades, Ernie knelt and turned him onto the side, giving him an avuncular pat. 'One day, when he's old and grey, he'll thank me for that. Give me a hand up… are you all right?'

Akaash nodded dumbly. He wasn't quite sure what he was or what he thought or felt. He had never witnessed such an exhibition of unbridled, concentrated viciousness before. Lathi charges and riot squads back in Cal seemed amateur and ill-trained compared to what he had just seen. He stared down at the silent bodies, secretly convinced that they were dead.

Ernie seemed to read his mind. 'They'll be right as rain in an hour or two. Might be a bit uncomfortable if they're ordered "Eyes Right" in the next few days. Other than that, they'll be fine.'

They heard the approaching vehicle well before they saw it. The streets were silent, and a truck moving at speed at that time of night couldn't help but be heard from quite a distance. An American Military Police lorry – a one-and-a-half-ton Ford 'Burma' Jeep – careered around the corner from Cambria Bridge Road onto Farringdon Road and screeched to a halt beside them. Three Military Policemen, with 'MP' on their white helmets and armbands, leapt out and shone torches on the prone soldiers.

'What's happened here?' demanded the master sergeant in command as the other two checked the unconscious soldiers for vital signs.

'Don't know, son,' said Ernie, again suddenly aged. 'Looks to me like these lads bit off a bit more than they could chew.'

'They were fighting among themselves, sir,' said Akaash, standing next to Ernie, his hands behind his back. 'We saw them from across the road.'

'Laid out mighty neat for guys who've knocked each other out in a brawl,' observed the master sergeant.

'We tried to help them. Administered first aid.'

'They seem to be OK, Sarge,' said one of the other MPs, rising from his inspection of them and brushing dust off his knees. 'Breathing normally and all. Stink of booze.'

'Load them in the truck and they can sleep it off in the cells. You two know what they were fighting over?'

'Which of them got to beat my pal here to death,' said Ernie. Akaash sighed and shook his head sadly.

'Strange they all got those same kinda marks on their necks.'

'Yeah. Funny, that.'

The master sergeant yawned hugely and glanced up and down the deserted street as the MPs heaved the unconscious GIs, none too gently, up into the back of the lorry. 'You know, this whole thing sounds like a crock of shit to me.'

'Which part?' asked Ernie. 'I thought lynching darkies was a national pastime where you come from.'

'Watch your mouth, pops.'

Ernie lifted his stick slightly. 'Or what? And you watch who you're calling pops.'

'Steady, old man,' warned the sergeant, taking a step back and resting one hand on his holstered pistol and the other on the handle of his nightstick. 'We're not a bunch of drunks you can roll. We're sober, eyes-on and carrying.'

'Yeah, guns and sticks which you can't use on British citizens whatever colour their skin is. They're no more than dead weight on your belt, pal, or a ticket to the glasshouse if you've got the balls to use them. And when you get out, you won't be pansying about in your fancy white helmet. You'll be sent off to where the real fighting happens. So why don't you go for your gun, Roy fucking Rogers, and let's see what happens next?'

Akaash stepped between them, adopting a conciliatory, almost obsequious tone, an exaggerated accent and an ingratiating smile. 'Sir, please forgive this elderly gentleman. We've both had a very frightening experience. But can I very respectfully suggest we just pause to think for a moment what's best for everyone here? A drunken brawl between GIs is a matter that stays purely within your jurisdiction. For you to deal with however you will. But if this is a case of a fight with civilians, it becomes a criminal matter, which the British will need to be involved in. And with respect, sir, an attempted lynching, by four strong young soldiers, the pride of the United States, of my humble self who has come here just as you have to help Britain in its hour of need? Not good, sir. Not good at all. The same four soldiers knocked for six by an old cripple and a simple little Indian like me? Even worse.

Does that even sound likely?' He paused, weighing the effect of his words. Then he added, toning down his put-on accent, 'More importantly, does that sound like a story you want to be telling anyone tomorrow morning?'

The master sergeant glared steadily at them both. 'All right,' he said finally. 'We'll play it your way. But if these boys have a different story to tell when they wake up, you'll be seeing us again.'

'Can't wait,' said Ernie.

'Thank you, sir,' said Akaash, with an exaggerated head wobble of gratitude and acquiescence.

'And whatever happens, I'll be remembering you two.'

'In your prayers, I hope,' said Ernie. 'Kindly.'

'Fuck you, grandad.'

'And a fuckety doodle doo to you too, mate,' muttered Ernie under his breath.

Akaash and Ernie stood in silence as they watched the MPs drive away with their load of slumped bodies rocking from side to side in the back of the lorry. As the vehicle disappeared, Akaash let out a long sigh and Ernie bent forward, hands on his knees, and roared in delight.

'I'm sorry I wasn't more help,' said Akaash. 'You should have had Billy with you. He would've been more use than me.'

'Rubbish,' said Ernie, straightening up and slapping him on the shoulder. 'With a big tough-looking bugger like him along we would never have got away with that tale. And he'd never have managed that act! Genius! Think about it, son. You and me! We've laid out twice our number, twice your size, half my age and not a scratch on either of us!'

Akaash brought his hands out from behind his back and held them up. The knuckles were severely grazed, skinned raw and bleeding from crashing through the hedge with the American he had leapt upon. 'Well, OK,' conceded Ernie. 'Maybe one or two scratches. But imagine! We won't be buying our own beer till Easter when this story gets out! Now let's get you home and cleaned up. Ha! What a night!'

Unusually, the on-duty Station Master came out to greet Vincent off the last Down train and asked how he was. Vincent assured him that he was fine. There was a buzz of excited chat among the working girls who were now boarding the same train. Something was going on.

'Good, good,' said the Station Master, clearly agitated. 'I'm going to have someone walk you home. OK?'

Vincent was confused. This was something new that didn't really make much sense. 'It's just a five-minute walk,' he protested.

'Then he'll be back in ten,' insisted the Station Master. 'Patrick!' he shouted. A porter came over, touched a finger to his forehead and nodded to Vincent. 'See the Bof to his door. Make sure he gets home safe, and then come straight back. Oh, and wait a minute…' He strode back to his office and returned with a poker from the fireplace. 'Take this with you.' Not for the first time, Vincent was conscious of how many of the men in the Railway had seen service in the Great War. Formed, deformed, enabled and disabled in battle, all seemed comfortable handling weapons, improvised or otherwise, and appeared oddly indifferent to the prospect of sudden violence.

When Vincent reached No. 23 it sounded as though a party was in progress. He thanked Patrick – who grunted a goodnight – let himself in and found Ernie sitting at the kitchen table with Billy and Akaash. Akaash was shivering as though chilled with his hands resting palms up in a bowl of bloody water. Sally was standing by the sink in her dressing gown cutting up strips of pink sticking plaster. She gave Vincent a huge, relieved smile and lit the gas under the saucepan of water over which his plated meal rested. There was a bottle on the table, of what Vincent hoped was disinfectant but secretly feared was another sample of Ernie's homemade wine.

He was greeted with an unexpected display of relief. 'Ya'Allah, the wanderer returns!' Billy cried, leaping up and coming over to help him out of his coat. 'You're OK?'

'Of course I'm OK,' said Vincent, shrugging off the proffered help. 'What's going on?'

Billy gave him an unwelcome hug, hugely relieved. 'We've had quite a day. First, *Tremayne* was rolled out.'

'*Tremayne*? I thought your first roll-out was going to be *Birkenhead* on Friday?'

'Things change. Keep up. We've also had quite an eventful evening.'

'What's happened to Akaash?'

'Well, among other things,' said Ernie, reaching over to give Akaash's shoulder an approving pat, 'your little vegetarian has developed a taste for American meat.'

Sally, Billy and Vincent shared a bemused look whilst Ernie and Akaash laughed, the latter's laugh too high-pitched and fast for it to be anything but a stress reaction.

'What, like Spam?'

'Nah, he likes his Yankee ham fresh and on the bone!' said Ernie, leaning on the table and getting stiffly and slightly unsteadily to his feet. 'Right, time for me to head up the wooden hill to Bedfordshire. Keep the rest of the bottle.'

'Are you sure you don't want to take it on home with you?' asked Sally hopefully.

'No, no. Let these young blokes enjoy it. I have to say, lads, it's a pleasure to have you around. Haven't had this much fun in years.' He leaned over to Akaash. 'You're all right, son,' he added with a belch. 'Oops. Sorry. We did good tonight, you and me. God bless the King and confusion to his enemies!'

After they'd watched Ernie weave his way down the path of No. 23 and back up the path into No. 21, Sally led them back into the kitchen and picked up the bottle of wine he'd left.

'Down the drain?' she asked. There were no dissenting voices.

28

Akaash arrived at the Works the next morning to an unexpectedly warm greeting, at least by Swindon standards. Nods of acknowledgement, a grunted greeting here or there and the occasional gruff 'aright?' but a very great deal more engagement than he'd ever received before. His hands, professionally bandaged and reeking of iodine, had been checked and dressed by a yawning Dr Falk, who had turned up shortly after Ernie had left. As the on-duty police surgeon the previous night she'd been called out to check on the condition of the Americans, slowly returning to consciousness. Having been told that 'one of the coloured lads' might have crossed paths with them, she knew where her next call needed to be.

She had assumed their potential adversary had been Billy and was concerned to check that he wasn't too badly hurt. Shop B solidarity and professional responsibility primarily directed her steps to No. 23, but she was also keen to investigate the cause of the inexplicable, near-identical livid bruises she had noted on the necks of the four GIs. When asked, however, no one in No. 23 seemed to know what she was talking about. Even Akaash, grateful to be spared Sally's compassionate but inefficiently painful bandaging of his hands, feigned no recollection of the details of his narrowly avoided lynching.

His new status as a local hero was evident in the office, where Joan in particular wanted to hear all the details and talked over his edited account with references to the Scottsboro boys, Jim Crow and Joe Hill – all completely lost on him. Akaash basked in the adulation and attention. He suspected, rightly, that the less he said the more his reputation would be enhanced, and so shrugged off the whole affair, silently implying that knocking four big soldiers flat more or less single-handedly was all in a day's work for a revolutionary socialist of his calibre.

Hartshorne called by, enquired after his injuries, apologised that he'd been the victim of racialist abuse and violence in 'his' town and – despite Akaash urging him to forget all about it – assured him that he would be contacting both the US Army liaison office to complain and the local Member of Parliament to get the matter raised in the House. He asked Akaash if he'd like to take the rest of the day off, an offer that clearly didn't come easily to him, and was relieved when Akaash assured him that he'd be fine.

'Call for you, Mr C,' the desk sergeant said. Curtis picked up the phone.

'I am speaking to Inspector Curtis.' All the distortion on the cracking line could not disguise the clipped accent and the fact that it was a statement rather than a question. Curtis, convinced his dyspepsia was going to be much worse by the end of this conversation, reached for his chalk tablets and confirmed that the caller was, indeed, speaking to Inspector Curtis.

'My name is Dawlish. You're the local Special Branch chappie?'

'I'm the officer in charge of the Special Branch here, sir, yes. How can I help you, Mr Dawlish?'

'You are the entire Special Branch there. And it's Colonel Dawlish. Keeping an eye on our Indian visitors?'

'I'm not at liberty to discuss…'

'Yes, you are. With me at least. I outrank you in every possible way. Answer my question, please.'

'I am not authorised to discuss any operational matters with you, sir,' replied Curtis doggedly.

'Give me strength,' Dawlish sighed. 'Very well. Stay where you are and await a call from your Chief Constable. We will speak again in thirty minutes.'

Precisely half an hour later, Dawlish called back. 'All clear now? The three Indians?'

'As far as I'm concerned, colonel, there is only one of any interest to us – Dr Akaash Ray – and my only interest in him concerns his political activities here.'

'Well, sadly some of us have a rather broader remit. I trust your Chief Constable has instructed you that you are to give me every assistance?'

The silence at the other end of the line was sufficient confirmation. Curtis could almost hear Dawlish purring with satisfaction.

'There are three of them, Inspector, as you well know. Ray, you are already well acquainted with. Khan, you can forget about. He's one of us. The third, Rosario, is a person of interest. I want you to keep an eye on him as well.'

'Can I ask why?'

'By all means. He's been making a bit of a nuisance of himself in some very sensitive areas. Asking questions we would rather people weren't asking just now. I need to know what he's up to and who he's talking to. Can you do that for me?'

'I can.'

'Good man. Everything we have about him will be with you first thing tomorrow morning. I'd sooner this was handled with discretion.'

'That's the way we usually do things in Special Branch,' Curtis replied.

'Not in my experience. Weekly reports? And I'll give you a number to call if, God forbid, anything untoward should happen.'

'Untoward?'

'These are dangerous times, Inspector. Goodbye.'

29

Vincent, having visited every part of the railway network and checked every junction of any significance – blissfully unaware of just how many feathers he'd ruffled – felt ready to write up all he'd heard and seen. A single comprehensive report would do the trick, he thought, with simple, clear and hopefully implementable proposals for action.

He returned to the Movements office, where he was still viewed with deep suspicion but now with a far more wary regard that was edging towards grudging respect. He certainly wasn't welcome, but nor was he simply despised and dismissed. He had been offered a proper desk. When the tea trolley came around a cup would now wordlessly be placed at his elbow, and one or two of his colleagues had even asked, with exaggerated casualness, what he thought of things now that he'd had a good look around. To all such enquiries he had replied politely that he was impressed by lots of things but still had much to check.

Vincent placed his observations and records – now filling two dog-eared notebooks – on the blotter beside a pile of paper and began to write. He was desperate for someone to help collate the vast amount of information he'd gathered and to check assumptions and challenge deductions. He thought of Lapworth, the Deputy Head of the Movements team. Lapworth had seemed the least reserved in their office, often sauntering over to chat. He too had asked about Vincent's conclusions but his enquiries had seemed less motivated by defending the status quo than by genuine interest.

Reluctantly, for Vincent was not someone who found it easy to seek aid or confide in others, he asked Lapworth if he might perhaps be able to assist him. Lapworth was more than pleased to do so and promptly went off to seek the permission of the head of the team. In the hope of infiltrating a spy into the operations of someone he still thought of as an invading enemy, the head readily agreed to allocate him full-time to work with Vincent.

'Can you see how you can help them improve their performance?' asked Lapworth. Vincent noted but didn't comment on the fact that he referred to the Movements team as 'them', not 'us.'

'From the moment I arrived in Southampton,' Vincent assured him. 'That's the easy part. The real problem is how to tell them in a way in which they will be willing to accept my conclusions, a way in which they will still be listening to me when I get to the end. They resent me being here, and I suppose in a way I understand why. No one likes a foreigner coming in and telling them what to do. But whilst they may dislike all us Indians,' Vincent continued, 'at least Dr Ray and Billy Khan are doing something the British need doing but don't want to or can't do themselves. But in my case, they hate the thought of being told by someone like me that I know how to do their jobs better than they do.'

'So what are you going to do?'

'I honestly don't know. The key to the problem is that they see the railway network and everything that runs on it as separate and distinct entities. Elements of a bigger system to be sure, but still perceived in bits, each of which can be enhanced and then all fitted back together so that the whole runs better. That's mistake number one.'

'And you see it as what? One great big machine?'

'No! That's mistake number two. A machine is something you can disassemble, enhance an individual component, then put it back together and expect it to run more efficiently. It's not a machine, not even a system. A railway is a living thing! I don't see locomotives moving along tracks pulling trains. I see pulses of blood circulating through veins and arteries. I don't see junctions, stations and terminals. I see organs being fed, fuelled and sustained by that lifeblood!'

Lapworth smiled at Vincent's animation. Normally so wary and constrained, he was speaking fast, eyes wide and hands gesticulating.

'And life involves risk, growth and change,' he continued. 'And that's where they make mistake number three. Every time there's a decision to take, they go for the tried-and-tested way. They are loading and timetabling as though they were still running a peacetime railway. They're too big and too old and they've been doing this for too long. They're obsessed with craftsmanship at the expense of efficiency. Experience and seniority matter far more to them than energy and intelligence.'

'So what kind of living thing is it that you see?' wondered Lapworth. 'An ageing lion? A slow, old carthorse?'

'No. A rat king.'

'A what?'

'A rat king. When a large number of rats are trapped in a confined space, their tails become hopelessly entwined. They are forced to live together as one or all perish, yet they can't function as a single being or even a successful community. They all pull in different directions and starve, or turn in on one another. Either way, they're doomed. Look at all the things the company does. In addition to maintaining thousands of miles of track, tens of thousands of units of rolling stock, thousands of motive units and hundreds of bridges and tunnels, they've got their own docks, steamships, warehouses, factories, houses, hospitals, hotels and fleets of vehicles. They've even got their own airline, for God's sake! People look at the GWR from outside and see a vast but single entity. A coherently functioning whole. But it isn't! It never has been! It's a company that never set out to be so huge and diverse, but which took over hundreds of other operations – many of them specialised – and is still trying, decades later, to absorb them. That's why there's such a huge range of different engine types, a totally illogical spread of stations and such a patchwork of workshops and depots. It's a mess and no one seems willing to drag it into shape. It isn't something that has grown naturally and expanded to meet new demands and opportunities. I looked for a single, vast living thing, but I found a lot of separate, often antagonistic, creatures. I found a rat king.'

'That might not be the best way of explaining your findings.'

Vincent smiled, slightly embarrassed by sharing so much of his private thoughts. 'Probably not. But something has to change, and fast. I've been over what statistics exist about the past few months. Outside of peak travelling times, almost all passenger trains run less than half full. Numbers of carriages could be cut. Many of the trains could be combined. And there's no logic whatsoever to the pattern of first and last trains of the day, as I have learnt to my cost. I could increase capacity massively if they let me. Like I said – I know what needs to be done. I even know how to do it. I just don't know how to get anyone to agree.'

'May I look at it?' asked Lapworth.

Vincent hesitated. 'On the basis of strict confidentiality?'

Lapworth reached out his hand. 'You have my word.'

30

Birkenhead's roll-out, whilst in practical detail a repetition of that of *Tremayne* two days earlier, couldn't help but seem anticlimactic by comparison. Polite words were said, tea was served, whistles sounded and cheers called for, but it wasn't, couldn't be, the same. Attention in Shop B had already turned to the next to be completed, *Sir Stafford*, which Billy was content to leave under the supervision of Keenan whilst he gathered the most able of the women, including Cyn, and with them focused his efforts on the most decrepit of the engines. Three would need to be taken completely apart and rebuilt, which was an enterprise he was looking forward to with renewed enthusiasm. If only he could slake his nagging passion for Mollie…

His opportunity to confront Mollie about her precipitate departure arose sooner than he could ever have hoped. Walking back from a visit to Lloyds Bank three days later – he now had lots of time for errands during his lunch break – he saw Mollie leaning her bicycle against the window of Woods the butcher's, just below a chalked sign announcing 'We Have Chops!', and joining the back of the queue of hopeful customers.

He strode across to her, unsure quite what he was going to say but knowing that he was unlikely to get a better opportunity and that he must speak with her. She saw him coming, and quickly looked away.

'Hello, Mollie.'

'Leave me alone! I got nothing to say to you. We ain't got anything to say to each other.'

'But Mollie, I just…'

'I told you,' she hissed, looking around. Heads were turning to watch. Others were exaggeratedly looking the other way. 'Leave me alone!'

'Yeah, clear off!' added a woman three places ahead of Mollie. 'Can't you see you're upsetting the poor thing?'

There was a murmur of support and more resentful faces turned towards them. Conversations about what swine men were started up. Foreigners, by general agreement, were the worst. All just interested in one thing. Look at the bloody Yanks…

'Just answer me this,' Billy said desperately. 'Then I'll go. I promise. Was it your idea to stop coming to work?'

She shook her head vigorously. ''Course not!' She looked up at him and he could see the tears in her eyes and the anger twisting her mouth. He reached out to her.

'Don't you dare touch me!' She sobbed, jerking her arm out of his reach. 'I never, ever wanted to leave! I loved that job. But mum said I 'ad to. 'Cos of the talk.'

'Oh Mollie...'

'I miss 'im so much,' she wailed, burying her face and blowing her nose wetly in what Billy couldn't help noticing was the handkerchief that he had given her. 'And I know 'e misses me. Uncle Jim says 'e's off 'is feed. And 'is movements ain't regular. I loved that 'orse!'

Billy retreated, pursued by glares and mutterings. He was taken aback by her pain and anger but somewhat to his surprise, not as upset as he would have expected. This was a sad and tawdry end to what for him at least had been a delightful little romance, but it was already starting to dawn on him that there might just be a positive aspect to all this. Maybe on reflection the whole thing had all been a bit of an error of judgement on his part? She was, after all, little more than a simple girl, understandably bowled over by his exoticism and maturity.

What he needed, he concluded, was a relationship – a full, consummated relationship, with a real woman of intelligence and experience with whom he could also have a sensible conversation. In short, with someone more of his own class. He resolved to look over that very evening the list of the Maharajah's acquaintances that Lockyer had left with him.

Lapworth proved far more valuable than Vincent had ever hoped or imagined. He quickly picked up the main thrust of Vincent's thinking and quietly pointed out what, once identified, were obvious and glaring errors – mistakes which, had they gone unnoticed, would have proven to be cheap ammunition for anyone determined to discredit and dismiss Vincent's ideas. Lapworth was also immensely helpful on the format and structure of the report itself. Brought up on the way such documents were presented in the GWR, he took responsibility for style and tone, and together they produced a weighty draft that contained no less than eighty-two recommendations. There were a further twenty-one suggestions not directly related to the task at hand, concerning catering arrangements at mainline stations and toilet facilities on branch lines, annexed at Vincent's insistence. Finally, and much to the irritation of his colleagues, Lapworth was also highly circumspect in discussing what the report actually contained, saying it was still a work in progress and it was for Vincent rather than him to decide when and to whom the contents would be revealed.

Lapworth was checking through the final draft for typing errors when he glanced up to see Vincent's gaze following the most junior member of the office as he walked across the room. Vincent had been reflecting on how the youth moved, light-footed, loose-limbed and almost liquid, contemplating sadly how he too had once moved like that.

Lapworth followed his gaze. 'A thing of beauty, our young Mr Brooks. "If youth knew, if age could…"'

'I was just thinking what a good dancer he must be.'

Lapworth looked steadily at him. 'Of course.' Gently, he rested his hand on Vincent's sleeve. 'There are places, you know,' he said quietly. 'Where people of like tastes can…'

Vincent jerked his arm away, angry with himself for giving Lapworth, whom he had assumed for some time to be a homosexual, the opportunity to make any assumptions about him. It was not the first time his fastidious attention to dress, precise manner of speech and perhaps most of all his love of dance had led others to draw such conclusions about him. He knew several attendees at Thursday evening dances back in

Bombay who were openly attracted to other men. He felt neither kinship with them nor disapproval of their preferences. Nor was he particularly offended that he should be thought to share them. He would have been equally angered if Lapworth had been discussing his contemplation of a woman. What mattered was that a line that separated the personal from the professional had been crossed and he was annoyed with himself that his own reverie had been the cause. For he valued and liked Lapworth and he didn't want to lose him as a colleague.

He looked at Lapworth, who glanced away. 'The report?' he asked.

'Of course. The report. On page 32…'

Shrinking days faded into long twilights and magnificent sunsets. Clear, starlit nights held the hint of future frosts. Dawns were misty and chill. Cobwebs in hedges and bushes were silvered with dew. Bright days and frosty nights were in balance as they approached the start of a lengthening dark. Starlings gathered in ever greater numbers on telephone wires, as though plucking up the nerve and finding comfort in companions as they readied themselves for the long migration ahead. They would all rise together, swarm, swoop and spread, forming brief yet magnificent patterns in the evening sky before the swirling murmuration flushed back down to huddle onto perches, not quite ready to set off…not just quite yet.

The thought of those tiny creatures preparing to head south en masse across Europe – indifferent to the conflict enveloping all below – to the heat and the peace and the sun made Akaash uncharacteristically homesick. He had grudgingly succumbed to Sally's nagging and purchased, second-hand, a heavy woollen three-piece suit. It was a bit worn, as the widow of its previous owner acknowledged as she accepted his shilling, but still warm. He also bought some good solid brogues. Vincent used a few of the clothing coupons he'd been collecting to invest in long johns. Billy, to no one's surprise, produced from the luggage he kept in storage a cold-weather suit as well as a shooting jacket, a cape and plus fours.

That Sunday was Harvest Festival. Christchurch was for a day transformed, at least in Vincent's novice eyes, from dour Anglicanism to a more pagan celebration of the cropped bounty of the fields and the fecundity of the land, of the harvest moon and the autumn equinox. Sheaves of barley, ears heavy with corn and sacks of potatoes smelling of earth and damp hessian replaced the usual arrangements of dried heads of hydrangea and branches of laurel. Spread across the altar on a bed of sweet hay lay wicker baskets of fruit: pink plums, greengages, yellow pears and near-black, dusty damsons. Three great phallic marrows lay beside neat bunches of orange carrots tied with raffia, and in pride of place, a loaf of freshly baked crusty bread shaped like a wheat sheaf.

This riot of ripened colour and fleeting abundance was tensely echoed in kitchens across Swindon. At No. 23, Sally, humming the tune of 'We plough the fields and scatter, the good seed on the land' and repeatedly singing the refrain 'All is safely gathered in, ere the winter storms begin' as though to stress the urgency of her task, seemed suddenly obsessed with pickling, salting, drying and preserving. Every flat surface throughout the house – shelves, table, the uncarpeted edges of the treads of the stairs, even the dressing tables and washstands in their bedrooms – were all spread with newspaper on which apples, pears, shallots, parsnips and onions were carefully laid to ensure they didn't touch one another. A shallow clamp was dug in the back garden to overwinter potatoes. Tall saucepans of vinegar were boiled up and wide pans of fruit bubbled away as pickles and jams were made. Rows of freshly sterilised glass jars stood ready to receive the new season's preserves, to be topped with greaseproof paper once cooled, and then secured with string and neatly labelled. Runner beans, beetroot, carrots and tomatoes were traded for rhubarb, plums, gooseberries and greengages. Brambles heavy with blackberries entwined in hedges in the surrounding countryside were stripped by enthusiastic gangs of children who, with fingers and mouths stained red with juice, bore them home to waiting mothers along with rose hips, elderberries and cobnuts to be added to pies and crumbles. And amid all this furious baking and boiling, everyone faced the same dilemma: insufficient sugar.

The weekly ration was hardly sufficient to meet the normal demands of even austerity recipes in a country with a fondness for cake and where a cup of hot, sweet tea was a panacea for all ills. Sally, like every other prudent housekeeper, had ferreted away a little each week to build up a reserve for the preserving season, but her stockpile, even with the additional one-off ration issued for jam-making, simply wasn't enough. Like a soul possessed she pursued every rumoured source of illicit sugar without reflection on or consideration for the needs of others. Normally a law-abiding and considerate soul, well thought of by all and generous to a fault, she engaged without compunction with spivs and black marketeers, lied to her neighbours, dissembled to relatives, deceived her guests (she assured Akaash, eyes averted but without a blush, that his weekly egg had broken and been discarded when in fact she'd traded it for three ounces of Tate and Lyle's demerara) and misled dearest friends in her single-minded search for the vital but scarce ingredient. There was a new war on: against the inexorable process of rot and decay. Sally was agonisingly aware that minute by relentless minute, soft berries were reducing to pulp, slight bruises were spreading and deepening on pears and mould was furring overripe damsons.

Vincent was begged, but refused, to return to his travels in order to raid stations throughout the region on her behalf. He assured her that sugar bowls were a thing of legend in buffets, where teaspoons were routinely chained to the counter. Her paying guests had also resisted her suggestion that a Sunday afternoon spent blackberry-picking would be a novel and enjoyable experience for them. Billy was happy to imagine himself wandering the lanes and tracks up towards the Ridgeway with his landlady in pursuit of forbidden fruit in some bucolic erotic adventure involving ripened fruit, dribbled juice and naked flesh. However, the thought of spending more time than necessary with his fellow lodgers scavenging, as he put it, through hedges and ditches like some bloody tribal, really didn't appeal. He considered ringing Lockyer and ordering a 56-pound sack of sugar from Fortnum and Mason and bugger the coupons, but had been wounded by the debacle of the 'Deluge' and thought better of it. Akaash couldn't see what all the fuss was about but Vincent, moved by her evident anguish, relented so far as to promise to at least make a trip up to Paddington early the following week to see what he could scrounge. Determined not to be outdone, Billy tried to persuade Akaash, who invariably had two heaped teaspoonfuls in his tea, that he'd heard on good authority Gandhiji had demanded all his supporters forswear sugar. Neither strategy met with success.

And of course, there was an overabundance of ripe, fresh produce to consume. For a couple of weeks, their meals skimped on the meat and potatoes in favour of piles of fruit, many of which were entirely new to them or had only been read about before. The three men wondered at the fine distinctions made between, for example, different types of English apple. To them, whilst skin colouration may vary from russet through green to red, they all tasted pretty bland, and pretty much the same

Presented each evening with bowlfuls of them, they discussed the matter at length.

'A Cox's Orange Pippin is sweeter than a Worcester Pearman,' thought Billy.

Akaash nodded. 'A Cox's Orange Pippin,' he concluded, 'is an apple which in its next life wants to be a mango.'

'You believe in reincarnation of fruit?' Billy asked.

'I don't believe in reincarnation of anything. I'm an atheist, remember. But if I so illogically did, I wouldn't be so narrow-minded as to exclude fruit.'

'Well, I don't think…' began Billy, before Vincent cut him off.

'Apples and pears,' he said. 'Stairs.'

The other two stared at him.

'It's a London way of speaking. Cockney rhyming slang. Frog and Toad: Road. Trouble and Strife: Wife.'

'You mean there's yet another English we have to learn?' cried Billy aghast. 'I've only just got the hang of all this "gurt" and stuff.'

'I wouldn't worry. I don't think it matters here.'

'But London's just seventy-five miles up the line,' said Akaash.

'So bloody tribal, these people,' Billy concluded. 'Could benefit from one language they all spoke and understood.'

He looked at the solitary piece of fruit left in the bowl on the table. 'Anyone want that last "Stop and Stare"?' He looked around proudly. 'Come on! I thought you chaps were meant to be smart! "Stop and Stare"? Pear?'

'I don't think it works like that,' smiled Vincent. 'There's a pattern.'

'Of course there is,' sighed Billy. 'There always is. Bloody British. Bastards.'

'We'll make a comrade of you yet,' said Akaash, reaching for the last pear.

'Not on your bleedin' Nelly,' Billy assured him, snatching it up.

'Cynthia Abbot?' wondered Vincent.

'Elsie Coggins,' Billy mumbled, mouth full. 'Hers have so much more – ' he spat a pip into his hand, '– pith,' he concluded.

'You mean they're more pithy.'

'Isn't that what I just said?'

One evening, their meal consisted entirely of fruit. Fresh, boiled and baked.

'It'll keep you regular,' Sally assured them, noting their marked lack of enthusiasm.

'Any idea what that means?' asked Akaash – who was developing a serious dislike for apples – after she'd gone.

'No idea,' said Vincent, reaching for a pear.

'Nor me,' said Billy. 'Sounds like a nice thing though.'

They found out several hours later when, on a thankfully dry if bitterly cold night, all three headed for the outside lavatory within minutes of each other. Akaash made it first.

'Ya'Allah!' cried Billy on finding the toilet bolted. 'Bengali bastard!' He banged on the door. 'Come on! How much longer are you going to be?'

Billy turned and shone his torch beam on Vincent who had appeared behind him, slightly bent over and walking very carefully. 'I really need to get in there,' Vincent moaned.

'There's a queue,' snapped Billy, hopping from foot to foot. 'You're half bloody British: grasp the principle. I'm ahead of you. You're after me. Wait your turn.'

'I don't think I can.'

Billy cursed and hammered on the door again. 'Come on, arsehole! You want us to shit ourselves out here?'

'Bloodsucker, I'm shitting myself in here,' Akaash called out. 'Sorry, but I'm not coming out.'

Salvation came in the unlikely shape of a pyjama-clad Ernie, peering out of his bedroom window at the beams of light in the garden next door.

'What the fuck is going on out there?' he grumbled. Then, spotting the shivering, hunched figures outside the outhouse next door, grasped the problem. 'Jesus Christ!' he groaned. 'All right, come round the back and use mine. But there are two sayings you'd both better know by now: "Shipshape" and "Bristol-fashion", 'cos if my bog isn't both those things when I go for my morning wazz, we'll be having words.'

Vincent had begun edging towards the gate whilst Ernie was still speaking. Seeing Billy turn to head in the same direction, he ran as fast as the need to keep his buttocks tightly clenched would allow.

Billy roared in anguish and frustration. He shone his torch along the fence between Nos. 21 and 23. Whilst it would be easily leapt in normal circumstances, he decided any attempt to do so in his present state would be catastrophic. With a snarl he dashed after Vincent, catching up with him in the alley and getting through the back gate to Ernie's with an unassailable lead.

Fortunately, Akaash staggered out of the outhouse at that moment and Vincent returned to take his place.

'Regular, the bloody woman calls this!' Akaash muttered as Vincent elbowed his way past him. 'I hate this place.'

Next door Billy, relieved, sighed in ecstasy. When he pulled the chain to flush Ernie's toilet, he was not at all surprised to hear above him the magisterial gurgle, roar and gush of the 'Deluge'.

EXHIBIT

WORKERS' PLAYTIME

BBC Light Service

TRANSCRIPT OF RADIO BROADCAST. DATE UNCERTAIN. NOVEMBER OR DECEMBER 1943 (EXTRACT)

Theme tune fades.

(Announcer) 'Well, today, workers, we're continuing our series of Home Front visits to the factories of Britain and this time, it's the turn of the Railway!

Whistle sounds.

'I can't tell you where I am but believe me, it's a wonderful sight! I wish you could see it. As far as the eye can see, dozens – hundreds – of ladies working hard to keep the trains running. And I'm here to see some fine old ladies of the track and meet the remarkable girls who have picked up the tools left by the lads at the front. And a fine job they seem to be making of it too!

'I'm standing next to a newly restored engine, a grand old workhorse from a bygone era brought back to tip-top condition by a charming bevy of lovelies. Let's speak to one... Ah, here we are! Hello there! And what's your name?'

'Elsie. Elsie Cog...'

'Lovely! And your young friend here?'

'I'm Cynthia.'

'Lovely! And what have you and your pals been up to, Cynthia?'

'Well, at the moment we're working on these boiler rods...'

'Hard work for you girls, I shouldn't wonder! And do you enjoy it?'

'Oh, yes! Very much. We...'

'Lovely! And what about our broadcasts of music while you work? They keep the spirits up, I'm sure?'

'Well, we can't really hear anything above the noise...'

'Lovely! Well, listeners, it's almost time for our next number. Here's Bing Crosby singing 'I'll Be Home for Christmas', but before we let these lovely lassies get back to doing their bit, let's all give three hearty cheers for the ladies who keep the trains running. And if this is what Total War looks like, I have to say it's pretty jolly... fetching! Take it away, Bing!'

Work in Shop B progressed well. *Sir Stafford* joined *Tremayne* and *Birkenhead* in the queue of engines in the marshalling yards slowly advancing towards testing. Delays – though frustrating, as everyone who had worked on them was keen to see a Bulldog in full steam – were inevitable. The reconditioned engines had to be squeezed into the pre-existing maintenance schedule for the thousands of engines currently in service – a schedule under pressure to repair units damaged in bombing raids as well as commissioning new units regularly coming off the Shop A line.

With the best-preserved engines having now been dealt with and dispatched, work inevitably slowed. Billy and Keenan concluded that two of the oldest, *Vulcan* and *Eclipse*, were beyond any realistic prospect of repair, and so persuaded a reluctant Hartshorne to write them off and authorise their cannibalisation for parts that could be used in others or for the creation of patterns for the manufacture of new components as required. The teams working on the two condemned engines resisted their dismantling as long as possible, making one excuse after another, as though feeling the decision was a reflection on their competence and belief in their machines. Billy did his best to reassure them, pointing out the incredible amount they and others would learn from some real stripping down. This time, no one smirked at his use of the expression, interpreting it solely in its engineering sense. They were far past double entendres when discussing Bulldogs.

Not that all was happiness and light with the women working on the other locos. There was an ongoing problem with pay and conditions. Week after week, pay packets were hopefully torn open to reveal exactly the same wages as they had received before their move to Shop B when employed in far less demanding roles. No promises had been made about increases in remuneration but there were local and national agreements that set the ground rules for a fair rate for each job – rates which, week after week, were not getting paid.

Cyn raised the matter every Friday afternoon with Billy, supported by a posse of increasingly frustrated women. Billy just looked pained and told them to talk to Keenan about it. He in turn referred them would the Wages Clerk responsible for Shop B – a well-meaning, bespectacled Cricklade man, who listened politely and then assured them that there was nothing he could do about it. He simply paid out what he was told to.

Cyn gave Billy formal notice of her intention to escalate the matter to the main Remuneration Committee. It was a threat she clearly expected would trouble him but which, infuriatingly for her, struck him as an excellent way to offload the problem – so much so that he offered to do it for her. She thought he was mocking her until, that very afternoon, he did.

Perhaps because the committee was constituted entirely of men, both Management and Union sides showed scant concern for the demands of these temporary and troublesome women. Their claims were deferred to the next meeting to be raised under 'Matters Arising', and in all probability would be kicked on further.

'Things,' Cyn muttered glumly to Akaash one evening in the Queen's Tap, 'can't carry on like this.'

'What delights have you for us tonight, Mrs A?' asked Billy as he and Akaash sat waiting for their evening meal.

'Welsh rarebit,' Sally said proudly, placing a rubbery yellow mix on a slice of toast in front of him. Vincent, Billy noticed, seemed to have rather more of whatever it was on the plate put aside for his late return. 'Yours is just cheese on toast,' she assured Akaash with a motherly smile.

Billy studied the plate in front of him. 'Doesn't look much like rabbit,' he said.

'*Rare*-bit. Not rabbit. It's cheese and powdered egg. I'll put the kettle on.'

Billy began to laugh. 'I heard a joke about this.'

'Hard to believe anyone could find anything funny in that,' Akaash said, ladling a generous spoonful of piccalilli onto his plate.

'What do you call a virgin in Cardiff?' Billy asked.

Akaash shrugged.

'A Welsh rare-bit!' cried Billy.

'I don't get it.'

'Well, I'm not sure I do either,' admitted Billy, 'but apparently it's very funny. They like jokes about the Welsh here.'

'They like jokes about anyone but themselves.'

'Doesn't everyone? Want to hear another?'

'Do I have a choice?'

'Two men are talking in a bar. The first man says, "Wales: a nation of prostitutes and rugby players." The second one says, "My mother is Welsh." "Really?" the first man replies. "What position does she play?" Good eh!'

'I see a pattern emerging. Where are you getting these so-called jokes from?'

'Shop B. At breaktime. I've tried to come up with some jokes myself, but any I know are either too rude for mixed company or don't make sense in translation. You know any?'

'What do you call a thick Muslim with too much money?'

'I don't…oh ha, ha. Very funny. Pass the piccalilli. Arsehole.'

'We're getting nowhere,' sighed Phyl.

Joan nodded sadly. 'I feel like such a fraud. Our one chance to really help defeat fascism and we're no further forward than we were when we started. I still have no idea what we need to do or even what they expect of us. None of us seem capable of creating a code the other two can't break within hours. We're so useless. And it's so unfair! A system of secure communications isn't something that three amateurs can just make up, no matter how clever they are. All these weeks and what have we achieved?'

'Well, we've examined the pattern of messages that are currently dispatched in breathtaking detail,' said Phyl. 'Not that we've learnt anything much from that.'

'I'm not so sure,' said Akaash, trying to lift the mood of despondency. 'We've learnt that virtually all GWR signal traffic comprises numbers, times, loads, routes and destinations. We've learnt that the vast majority of the signals at present describes routes that are timetabled and public knowledge. We've learnt that very little currently needs any classification.'

'It makes you wonder why they bother about coding anything at all,' said Phyl.

Akaash was about to make a supercilious comment but paused: the question was so simple it had never occurred to him. He had been told and had accepted that this assignment was important. Worth travelling halfway across a war-torn world to carry out. He had not given any thought as to whether it was even necessary. So much for academic rigour and scientific methodology! 'Say that again,' he said.

'Why bother about coding anything at all?'

'To disguise movements of troops and equipment from the enemy,' answered Joan. 'Obviously.'

'And why do we want to do that?' asked Akaash. 'I know it seems like a silly question, but just bear with me.'

'All right. To enable those movements to be safer from bombing. To ensure that the direction and scale of movementsdoesn't tip the Germans off to where any invasion might take place.'

'But surely if we suddenly start sending coded messages, it will alert the enemy to the fact that something is going on and attract the very attention you want to avoid...even if they couldn't break the code, the weight of traffic alone would be enough.'

'It could. In fact, it might. But there's no alternative.'

'Isn't there?' wondered Akaash. 'Why not progressively increase signals about the amount of traffic in all directions, prior to the build-up? Don't bother coding it at all! I guess we can assume the big push won't happen in the middle of winter so we've got a few months yet. If we started now and worked incrementally, no one would probably even notice!'

'Could that work?' asked Phyl.

'As long as we set up a system which ensures the recipients of the messages can tell which relate to genuine movements and which they can safely ignore, I can't see why not.'

'That you can do with a simple phrase, word, letter or number,' pointed out Joan, sitting forward on her chair bright-eyed.

'Absolutely! Then as the movements begin to build up in earnest, replace the fake messages in that area or in that direction with real messages about those movements whilst maintaining the fake messages, the noise, in other directions!'

'There'd have to be a lot of people in on it,' warned Phyl.

'No more than those who would have to have been given access to the codes if we used a cipher system,' Akaash insisted.

'You're right. As long as the way in which anyone can tell which messages are genuine and which are fake is kept secure, we will have achieved everything we could have done with coding, just far more simply, cheaply and reliably.'

Phyl, for the first time in weeks, smiled at Akaash. She nodded and began to laugh, then glanced across to a grinning Joan. 'I think he might just be the genius everyone said he was!'

Joan leapt to her feet. 'I think he might have just thought us all out of a job! Three cheers for Presidency College! Let's get this down on paper and see if it reads as good as it sounds.'

Just then, the telephone on Phyl's desk rang. It was for Akaash. A request from the police. There was a sudden need to check his papers at the police station, soonest.

On arrival at the police station, Akaash was shown through to Curtis's office. 'Thought it better if we meet here from now on, young Bish-Bash,' said Curtis, waving him to a seat. 'Away from prying eyes. Anyone asks, there's a problem with your identity card.'

'But there isn't.'

'I think there is. Show it to me,' said Curtis, holding out his hand. He took the card that Akaash had clumsily removed from his breast pocket with a bandaged hand, and tore it in two. 'There, told you there was a problem! Government property, damaged and defaced. Very careless, probably illegal. We'll issue you with a provisional document but whilst a replacement is being prepared, you'll need to call in to the station every day under the Alien Registration provisions. All quite legit. No reason anyone should be surprised. Who knows? Might even improve your standing with the comrades. Under police surveillance. Ooh! Very glamorous!'

Akaash sighed. 'What do you want? There haven't been any more meetings since we last spoke.'

'Maybe I just enjoy your company. Maybe I want another lesson in how to speak English proper – and I did that deliberately so don't bother correcting me. Or maybe I want to know a bit more about your half-caste oppo.'

'Who?'

'Rosario.'

'Oh, him! Why?'

'None of your business. Just tell me about him.'

'Not much to tell. Comes from Bombay. Railway family. Anglo-Indian. They don't like being called half-caste. I don't like being called Bish-Bash, come to that.'

'As if I give a shit. What's he doing here? And don't give me the secret stuff again.'

'He's supposed to be quite brilliant at shifting trains around back home so he's advising on how the GWR can improve their traffic movement.'

'That must make him popular!' chuckled Curtis. 'I'm starting to warm to him. Know anything about his politics?'

'Not sure he's got any. Proper little Empire Loyalist. Proud to serve the mother country. All that nonsense.'

'Conservative?'

'Compared to me, yes.'

'Trotsky's conservative compared to you. Could he be a fascist supporter?'

'Could be. He's very dismissive of the struggle for freedom.'

'I'm getting the impression you don't like him.'

'No, I don't. Not very much.'

'Is that him, or his type?'

'Both. Neither. I don't like him individually and I think people like him have no future in a free India.'

'Getting the knives out early, are we?'

'No. Just preparing for the future. Anything else you want to know?'

'Where he's been. Who he's been speaking to. What he's been saying.'

Akaash laughed. 'That's easy! He's made copious notes on everything he's done from the moment he arrived. It's all in a couple of notebooks.'

'Can you make copies?'

'You do understand what "copious" means?'

'Is it like "irritating little shit"? 'Cos I know what that means.'

'There's hundreds of pages of tiny scrawl. It would take forever.'

'Any way I can have a dekko at them?'

'Why don't you just ask him?'

'Not the way it works. Where does he keep these books?'

'Right now, in the Movements office. Under lock and key, I think.'

'And I suppose he's the only one with that key?'

'I don't know. I wouldn't be able to get it for you. But there's a man he works with. A Mr Lapworth…'

Curtis smiled broadly. 'Not "L-L-Lucy" Lapworth?'

'You know him?'

'Went to school with him. Bit of a Cottager, even then. Shoved his head down the toilet in Clarence St Boys more times than I can remember. Ah, happy days! Right, that will do for now, young Bish-Bash. Show your damaged ID to the desk sergeant and tell him I said you're to have a temporary card.'

'Do I get paid for this?'

Curtis looked confused. 'You don't take money for grassing up the comrades but you will for selling out one of your own? You're a strange lad. No, I'm afraid you're doing this for King and Country, and to make sure those remittances keep getting through to mum and dad. TTFN.'

Three days later at 7 a.m., a yawning and unshaven Curtis returned Vincent's notebooks to Lapworth, who had acquired them for him the previous evening and whose self-loathing made Akaash's crisis of conscience seem trivial. It had taken him a while to make sense of the scribbles. At one point he'd thought the spidery scrawl must be in code or some foreign tongue until he realised that it was simply fast, bad handwriting. He was too troubled by what he'd read to bother reminding the ashen-faced

Lapworth of the fate in store for him if he told anyone that he'd allowed a policeman to glance through them.

Curtis thought Vincent would have made a fine spy: an eye for detail and an ear for intelligent insights from the most unexpected sources. He wondered what to do about so much vital information now being in the hands and head of a foreigner. He picked up the phone, then put it down again. He knew he had to call Dawlish but hated the very idea of doing so. How could the GWR be so bloody stupid?

All three of them received the invitation – to a 'Hands Across the Seas' event at a grand house in Liddington, one of the neighbouring villages up towards the Ridgeway on Ramsbury Road – but only Billy accepted. 'To say a small thank you to those who have come to our aid in our hour of need', the invitation stated. What could be more pleasant?

Akaash took one look at the embossed coat of arms on the card and promptly declared he would sooner die than be fed scraps from the table of the aristocracy. Vincent was equally unenthusiastic, simply saying he had far too much to do. Billy thought it sounded like super fun.

It was to be an evening event on a Saturday – cocktails and a light supper. Billy couldn't decide between his uniform and evening dress but finally opted for the latter, despite it being seriously creased from long storage in his trunk, because the former was on inspection soot-soiled and oil-stained probably beyond saving. Sally cooed over the elegance of his clothes and was particularly taken with his silk shirt. She had offered to wash and iron it for him but Billy, wary of her overenthusiastic use of the repaired mangle, took his clothes to a tailor on Victoria Hill to have them laundered and pressed professionally.

Billy arrived at the party by station taxi, fashionably late, only to find that almost all the other guests were military types who had turned up on the dot. There were Poles, Czechs and Lithuanians in RAF blue, Free French, Australians and Canadians in khaki. There were also numerous Americans in olive drab. All were officers. All had glasses in their hands. Billy was profoundly grateful he'd opted for civvies.

Their hostess was a striking woman in her mid-forties dressed in well-cut utility-style jacket and skirt. She welcomed him and, with a hand lightly on his elbow, guided him towards a tray of glasses, making introductions as she went. She reminded Billy of a majestic ship parting the waves as she moved through the uniformed men. Not particularly good-looking, he thought, but certainly attractive. As tall as him, with a full figure, a wonderful laugh and a complexion, stride and tone of voice that spoke of the outdoors, long walks and instructions rarely challenged and seldom repeated.

'Been looking forward to your arrival,' she assured him cheerily. 'There's someone here who's particularly keen to meet you.'

An American colonel came over, hand extended. 'Helmick. Ely Helmick. 116th US Army. Mr Ray?'

'Afraid not,' said Billy, shaking the offered hand. 'Sends his apologies. I'm Khan. Billy Khan.'

'Ah. The other one. I just wanted to apologise about my boys' behaviour. Inexcusable. If there's anything I can do…'

'Water under the bridge, old chap. Think nothing more of it.'

'That's mighty good of you. But they were way out of line.'

'From what I hear, they came off worst.'

'You weren't involved?'

'No. Sadly, I missed all the excitement. Safely back in my, er, billet long before it happened.'

'That's a pity…not that you were home safe, of course! It's just I was kinda hoping you could enlighten me a little about their injuries.'

'Oh, dear. Hope they weren't too badly hurt?'

'No, no. They're fine now. Fighting fit. Or they will be when they're off punishment parades. Hope you liked your hamper of humility.'

'My what?'

'The Adjutant General's office usually sends someone round with a basket full of goodies to say sorry on behalf of Uncle Sam. Not had it yet? Guess they got a backlog of bad behaviour. I'll chase them up.'

'What, um, might be in one of those hampers?'

'Tinned fruit and meat. Cookies. Cigarettes. Candy bars. Booze, if you'd like it. Coca-Cola if you wouldn't.'

'Any chance we could throw in a bag or two of sugar?'

'No problem. Granulated, castor, demerara or muscovado? Not sure? Shoot, I'll just get them to send some of each. We're pretty keen this whole thing stays out of the papers.'

'Absolutely! And I think you mentioned booze? Not a half-decent single malt by any chance?'

'Could very well be. Kentucky bourbon at the very least. Now, the licking my boys got…'

'Which they richly deserved.'

'You won't hear disagreement on that from me,' Helmick assured him, then paused, looked around and continued in a lowered voice. 'But I gotta say, that was a pretty tidy handling your Mr Ray dished out.'

'It's Dr Ray, actually,' said a well-modulated voice.

Billy looked around, surprised. 'Hello, Dawlish! Didn't know you were in this neck of the woods.'

'Just passing through. Jessie kindly invited me along. Should have taken out the old Mess Jacket. Feel naked in mufti among all this brass and braid.'

'Jessie?'

'Lady Jessica. The chatelaine.'

'Oh, right. Have you met Colonel Helmick?'

'How are you, Mr…'

'Delighted,' said Dawlish, not looking at the American. 'Frightfully poor show about your soldiers in Swindon. How are they coming along?'

'As I was just telling Mr Khan here, they'll be fine. But…'

'Well, that's all that matters, isn't it? Lovely to meet you, Colonel Helmick. Now if you'll excuse us, I just need a brief word with my old friend Mr Khan.'

Dawlish, who clearly knew his way around the house, picked up a couple of glasses and a decanter of whisky and led Billy through to the library, kicking the double doors closed behind them with his heel.

'How have you been, Billy?' he asked amiably, putting the glasses down on the desk and pouring them both a large measure.

'Well, thanks. Three engines brought back into service and ready for testing. Pressing ahead with the rest.'

'Marvellous. And the other two musketeers?'

'Also doing well, I think. Rosario is near to presenting his recommendations and Ray thinks he's got the answer to the coding thing he's working on. All looking tickety-boo.'

'What do you think of Rosario?'

'Can't say I've taken to the man but he seems sound. Certainly knows his way around a railway.'

'Perhaps a little bit too well.'

'How's that?'

'He's been seen in some sensitive places.'

'Well, he would be, wouldn't he? Can't do the job they've asked him to without looking at the docks and harbours and junctions and stuff.'

'The problem is, he might just be a bit too good at that job. For all our sakes.'

'Don't follow you, old man.'

'What do you think Jerry would give for such a detailed, up-to-date report on the railway network in the region from which the invasion may well be launched? Weak points? Location of troops? Holding areas? Supply depots?'

'Quite a lot, I suppose. So what?'

'So what if Rosario turns out to be a fifth columnist? A Nazi sympathiser?'

'Don't be ridiculous! I can't think of anyone less likely to be an enemy agent. It's unimaginable.'

'It's my job to imagine the unimaginable. Would you vouch for him personally?'

'Well, I don't know him that well, but I'm bloody sure he's no traitor.'

'Willing to stake your life, and the lives of thousands of others, on that? What if I told you he's got a German–English dictionary in your house?'

'What? Oh, that! That's bloody Akaash's. Daft bugger borrowed it from the Mechanics Institute ages ago. God knows why. Something to do with his work. Don't ask me what.'

'Not Rosario's?'

'No.'

'It's in Rosario's room.'

'How would you know that?'

'Never mind how I know. It just is.'

'Well, everything's all over the place at the moment because of all the bloody fruit laid out everywhere. Our landlady is a goddess among women, and I won't hear a word said against her, but an ability to remember what belongs to whom is not among her many gifts. Didn't come across a pair of my gold cuff links when you were grubbing around in Rosario's room by any chance? I know he's had his eye on them.'

The sneer and the sarcasm weren't lost on Dawlish, who treated Billy to a long, silent stare.

'Look, the man's an irritating, sanctimonious blighter, like every other Anglo I've ever met,' continued Billy in a conciliatory tone, 'but I honestly think you're barking up the wrong tree here. He's a railwayman, through and through. I really don't think he'd betray this country and I'm damned sure he'd never do anything to harm the Railway.'

'What if someone got to him?'

'What, you mean like blackmail?'

'Or threats. Or a bribe. Every man has his price.'

'Well, I suppose if someone threatened his family back home...'

'I don't think you need to worry about that.'

'No? They're pretty close, these people. He's got pictures of his parents and brothers and nephews and nieces in his room. But you'd know that too, no doubt?'

Dawlish appeared about to say something but thought better of it.

'Can't see it,' concluded Billy. 'Not him.'

'Well, perhaps you could keep an eye on him for me?'

'I could, but I won't.'

'Why not?'

'Because I'm not a bloody sneak, that's why not.'

'You seemed happy enough to help out when we met in Southampton.'

'Totally different. I didn't know either of them from Adam then. Now, well, we're, um, oppos.'

'Really? You surprise me. You still have my card? Call me if you have any suspicions, no matter how vague, no matter how small.'

'I thought you chaps were more interested in our Bengali revolutionary. You hear how he laid out those Yanks? I think you'll also find that dictionary is overdue for return. The little bugger's subverting the war effort at every turn.'

'I fear Dr Ray is about to have bigger problems than an overdue library book. You can safely leave him to me.'

Before Billy could pursue that comment, their hostess opened the double doors. 'Roddie, you've hijacked my guest long enough. Come with me, Mr Khan, we're about to eat. I want you to sit next to me and I particularly want your opinion on the venison. Shot it myself. Shockingly illegal, I expect! Staying for a bite, Roddie?' she called back over her shoulder, an obligatory invitation offered with little enthusiasm.

'Sadly not. Need to head back. Remember what I said, Billy.'

'We'll have sandwiches made up. Give my love to Celia.' She put her arm through Billy's as they walked back towards the reception room, where voices were noticeably louder and conversation considerably more animated. 'Isn't Roddie Dawlish just the ghastliest man?' she whispered. 'All this cloak-and-dagger stuff! Wouldn't have the blighter in the house if he hadn't been such a great chum of the Late Lamented. So, Gwalior! Beautiful in the winter, I hear. Marvellous fort…'

Billy enjoyed the meal. The food was well-cooked, portions generous and the venison excellent. There was good wine from a pre-war cellar and the company was enjoyable. Colonel Helmick – slightly the worse for wear, tie loose and jacket undone – invited Billy to visit his headquarters in Calne and dine at their mess. He offered to send a jeep to pick him up and assured him that he wouldn't forget about the sugar. After the meal was cleared away there was a dewy-eyed sing-song of mawkish ballads about homes far away and sweethearts left behind. Then, as Billy had noticed was often the case here when people became too sentimental, came an abrupt change of mood and a round of cheery songs full of double entendres or, for those in foreign tongues, accompanied by vulgar gestures that made the meaning abundantly clear. There was laughter, cheering, backslapping and bonhomie. Throughout, their hostess drank as steadily as her guests, clapped as enthusiastically and cheered as loud. Once or twice Billy caught her looking at him contemplatively. It made him surprisingly uncomfortable, feeling like a prize specimen being appraised at an auction.

Gradually the party dispersed. First to go were the airmen, who were on a curfew. They had been markedly quieter than the soldiers and watchful of their alcohol consumption. Near to last were the Canadians, who were keen to perform *The Shooting of Dan McGrew* but couldn't agree on the words and needed gentle urging to depart, still arguing as they staggered to their truck. Finally only Billy remained. He'd planned to leave much earlier. He'd told Mr Rimes to return to collect him and he was well aware that the station taxi sat outside with the meter running. However, every time he started to make his farewells, Lady Jessica insisted he remain. He was half excited and half troubled by her evident interest in him.

'One for the road?' she asked, picking up a bottle. She looked at it disapprovingly, then turned it upside down. 'Another dead soldier. Oops. Poor choice of words. There must be something to drink left somewhere.' She squinted around the room and weaved unsteadily over to the sideboard where several more bottles stood.

'I'm fine. Honestly,' said Billy. 'I've had more than enough.' As have you, he thought.

'Really?' she asked, pouting disappointedly. 'Can't persuade you? Ah!' she cried in triumph as she found a sherry bottle still half full. 'Bloody awful drink, sherry. Old maids and mincing vicars. Still, needs must…' she concluded, sloshing a measure into a tumbler and slumping into an armchair. 'You're a cruel man, to let a woman drink alone.'

'I really think I ought to be going…'

'You could stay and take advantage of me if you wanted to. The staff are long abed. I'm all alone, a poor, defenceless woman in this big, empty house…'

Billy recalled the well-stocked gun case in the hallway. Three – no, four – shotguns and as many hunting rifles. And the baying he'd heard at various points throughout the evening didn't sound like it emanated from a lapdog. 'It really is time for me to go. I'm very sorry. Thank you for a lovely evening.'

'I'll only let you go if you promise you'll come and visit me again.'

'I'd be delighted. Any time.'

'Next Sunday. After lunch.'

'Er, fine. Thank you. That would be very nice.'

'Yes, it will be. Don't forget. Come for tea. And come alone,' she added, leaning her head back and closing her eyes.

'You can butter my scones,' she called after him with a drunken guffaw as he picked up his coat and headed for the door.

Habits form – unintentionally, inexorably. At No. 23, with Billy out at the reception and Akaash at yet another discreet gathering at the Glue Pot, Vincent Rosario and Sally Atkinson began a pattern of behaviour that would have unforeseen and far-reaching consequences for them all.

They had tea in the kitchen, as usual. She did the washing up and he stood beside her and dried the plates and cutlery, as usual. He stepped out into the back garden and smoked a cigarette, again, pretty much as usual but with a highly unusual fluttering of nerves and a quickening of his pulse. As he stepped back indoors, she suggested they 'have a little listen to the wireless', which was again something they had often done together before, but this time both knew it would not be quite as usual.

Though never discussed, both changed their clothes and dressed formally for their shared evening in the front room tuned to *Accent on Rhythm* on the Home Service. At 7.45 p.m., the programme of light music began. Without a word, they took up position and began to dance. Prim and formal as a church social, holding one another respectfully, they'd spin, turn and dip. At the end of each number, they took a step back from one another, him still lightly holding her right hand in his left. He'd bow slightly, she'd curtsy and they would avoid each other's eyes and stand in silence until the next tune began. When the programme ended forty-five minutes later, he thanked her, she thanked him and they retreated to the kitchen for a mug of Ovaltine. The front room was shortly to become a singleton bedroom once more.

Where was the harm? What could be more innocent? Who could possibly know or even care?

The curtains were firmly drawn.

But shadows were cast.

Vincent was mystified by Lapworth's sudden change of behaviour when they met on Monday morning. Monosyllabic, unwilling to meet his eye. Nervous movements. His speech hesitancy much more pronounced. Clearly something was wrong but Vincent had no idea how to broach what it might be. Their report was virtually completed. It was to be presented to the Head of Movements, copied to Hartshorne.

Perhaps Lapworth was nervous about the reaction it would receive? That would be hardly surprising. Lapworth had done his best to tone down Vincent's most trenchant observations and present the recommendations in the best light, but all the tactful editing in the world could not hide the fact that it was a report deeply critical of present ways of working – one that was going to make for uncomfortable reading. Vincent was entirely satisfied as to the validity of his conclusions and workability of his suggestions. He was also realistic enough to know that being right mattered not at all in this case. His proposals being adopted was all that really counted.

'Perhaps we should condense it down to just a few pages. Make just one or two key recommendations?' Vincent mused. 'Then if we can get them accepted, we can go to the next level, and the next.'

Lapworth seemed to need to drag his attention to Vincent's words. He thought for a while. 'Could you reduce it to just one thing they need to do? Say it all in just three words?'

Could he? Yes, he thought he could. 'Right,' he said, stubbing out his cigarette and getting to his feet. 'Let's go.'

'Run empty trains?'

'Yes.'

'After three months and thousands of miles of free travel around the region, that's the best you can come up with?'

'Yes.'

'Well, thank you for proving me right all along,' said the Head of Movements, rising from his chair.

'I think you should hear the rest of what Mr Rosario has to say,' offered Lapworth quietly.

The Head of Movements glared at him. 'Oh, very well,' he sighed slumping back into his seat. 'Get on with it.'

Vincent looked towards Lapworth, who gave him an encouraging nod.

'I have pages and pages of recommendations on how you can improve goods and passenger movements over the whole region, but I was asked here specifically to address this problem of pre-invasion traffic management, so let us concentrate solely on that. It will involve a lot of traffic, all moving broadly in the same direction in a relatively short time, but I don't think it will involve the bulk of the network. Basically, it will all be heading east or south.'

'How can you possibly say that? No one knows when or where the invasion will be.'

'No, but it's not that hard to hazard an intelligent guess, is it?' Vincent unfolded a map of the railway network and spread it out on the table. 'Look at where the troop build-up is – namely, right here – and look at where the Germans are. The invasion force has to embark from the south of England somewhere and aim for France or Belgium. If the invasion is launched from anywhere east of Portsmouth, our responsibility will be to get everyone and everything currently in our region east to the Southern Railway. One of my recommendations is about liaison and greater cooperation with them, by the way. If it's launched from anywhere west of Portsmouth all the way along the coast to Land's End, we will be running trains south to the coast. We have no choice but to utilise existing permanent way. There's no time to build more. The issue comes down to identifying the likely key junctions and ensuring that we reduce delays there to an absolute minimum.

'You will see I've circled in red those I think we need to focus on. Reading is working adequately. So is Bristol Temple Meads, although I have suggestions on platform allocation for both that, when adopted, will significantly improve things. We need to concentrate on Westbury, Newport and Gloucester. And of course, right here in Swindon. All are potential bottlenecks. And although it's not part of my remit, I'd also recommend beefing up the air-raid defences around Westbury. If the Germans manage to destroy any of these junctions, we'd be crippled. Those in cities or near docks seem well-protected, but Westbury…'

The Head of Movements, against his instincts, leaned forward and studied the map, intrigued. 'The empty trains?'

'We need to create space and increase capacity. We need to start running ghost trains to some of the likely departure points to check timings and to identify now where possible holdups occur so that we can put them right before we start moving troops and materiel in earnest.'

'We?'

'Very well. You.'

The Head of Movements sat in silence, pensively biting at the skin at the corner of the thumbnail of his right hand. 'Has a copy of this gone to the CME?'

'Not yet,' said Lapworth. 'We wanted to consult you first.'

'Well, I'm sorry, but it's simply impossible. I understand the arguments and don't think I'm not impressed by all the hard work. Let me have chapter and verse on these bottlenecks of yours and I'll see they're passed on to the right people. But as for increasing traffic, it's no can do. We are running beyond full capacity already.'

'Only because you're allowing unnecessary safety margins at junctions! Since the accident at Norton Fitzwarren your signalling regulations are far too cautious.'

'Twenty-seven people died in that accident. We're determined it won't happen again.'

'Well, I think I can assure you…' Vincent began, but Lapworth cut him off. 'Thanks, Mr Gardiner,' he said, folding up the map and picking up the brief report. 'We'll send you the recommendations on the junctions as soon as possible. Mr Rosario?'

'What do I do now?' wondered Vincent, once they were out of earshot of the Head of Movements.

'I'm not sure,' admitted Lapworth. 'I know you're right about this. We just have to come up with a new approach.'

'We?' asked Vincent, bitterly.

'Yes, we,' insisted Lapworth. 'If you're willing to have me stay on board.'

'I'd be happy to,' said Vincent, touched by this unexpected show of solidarity.

'In that case, I have something I have to tell you.'

Billy strode angrily up to Office No. 6. Ignoring the sign prohibiting entry to any but authorised personnel, he threw the door open and stormed towards Akaash, fists clenched. Behind him, clearly still trying unsuccessfully to get him to stop for a moment and talk to her, came Cyn.

'You got my girls to go on strike, you *behenchod*?'

Phyl and Joan looked up, shocked by the sudden intrusion. Akaash, less surprised, put aside the document he had been studying and carefully removed his glasses.

'You're not meant to be in here,' he said, pleased that he sounded a great deal more confident than he felt. 'And you should know Miss Fraser understands Hindi.'

'Oh,' said Billy, momentarily taken back. 'Sorry.'

Cyn came around Billy to stand behind Akaash and placed a supportive hand on his shoulder. 'They're not girls. They are women.' She shook her head in frustration. 'Actually they're workers. Who have rights. Anyway, whatever they are, they're certainly not yours.'

She leaned over to Joan and asked quietly, 'What did that mean? What he just called Akaash?'

Joan cupped her hand and whispered a translation in Cyn's ear. Cyn winced. Then Joan added, 'By the way, you shouldn't be in here either.'

'Well, the female version of that to you too, you stuck-up cow!'

'This is not about you or me, Billy,' said Akaash quietly. 'It's about what's right. All I've done is point out the only way their claim will ever be taken seriously.'

'Absolutely,' agreed Cyn. 'My ladies…the workers in Shop B are entitled to the same pay men would get for the same work after nine weeks. That's not just a local agreement. That's the law! They've all been working here for months before you arrived but they're still on lower wages. "To accept injustice is cowardice." That's your Mr Gandhi,' she concluded, earning her a proud nod from Joan.

'And all I've done is to support my comrades in their struggle for what is right,' said Akaash. '"No man can be actively non-violent and not rise against social injustice, no matter where it occurs",' he quoted, amid supportive noises from Joan and a comradely pat from Cyn. He liked having her hand on his shoulder. 'That's our Mr Gandhi too.'

Billy was about to tell them both that what he'd just implied Akaash did with his sisters they were more than welcome to do to their Mr Gandhi when Hartshorne appeared demanding to know what was going on. He ordered Billy and Cyn into his office. With an unpleasant glare at Akaash, he instructed that from now on the door to Office No. 6 was to be kept securely locked at all times.

'You stole my notebooks and showed them to the police?'

Lapworth nodded miserably.

Vincent frowned, more confused than upset. 'Why?'

Lapworth sniffed. He couldn't meet Vincent's questioning stare. 'They made me. He, they, said they'd charge me with gross indecency…'

Vincent shook his head. 'I'm not asking you why you stole them,' he said impatiently. 'I'm asking you why anyone other than the Railway would care what was in them.'

'I don't know.'

'Why didn't they just ask me? As long as Mr Hartshorne agreed, I'd have shown them. There are no secrets in them.'

Lapworth shrugged. He looked so crushed that Vincent felt sorry for him. His hands shook and he seemed near to tears.

'You gave me your word.'

'About the report,' pleaded Lapworth. 'And I didn't tell them anything about the report. I swear!'

'Did they ask?'

Lapworth's silence was confirmation enough.

'Who else knows about this?'

'No one. Honestly. I've told no one.'

'Let's keep this between us.'

'I understand. I also understand that you'll want me to return to my usual duties.'

'Let's concentrate on what we have to get done.'

'But I've betrayed you...'

'As you said, your promise was about the report. There's nothing secret in those notebooks. Nothing anyone couldn't see with their own eyes.'

In Hartshorne's office, Billy tried to calm himself as he recounted how thirty minutes earlier the staff of Shop B had downed tools and walked out. Cyn explained that this was legitimate industrial action and reminded Hartshorne of the legal right to equal pay that was being ignored and the numerous representations to Management that had ultimately led nowhere. Hartshorne nodded, closed his eyes and pinched the bridge of his nose.

'I'm well aware of the rights your members have and that we have not yet properly implemented the pay arrangement. I will be honest with you, Miss Abbot, the problem is that this work on the Bulldogs is not, as yet, formally approved by the Directors of the company and until I can show them at least three locomotives fully tested and ready to pull trains, I don't particularly want to bring it to their attention. I've asked the Pay Clerks to calculate the money owed and it's more than I can approve. If I go to the Directors, chances are the work will be stopped, in which case most of your members will be reassigned to lower-grade work or laid off completely. Either way they won't see the money they're owed. And the war effort will be adversely affected. They lose. We lose. The country loses. Surely that's in none of our interests?'

Billy frowned. 'Is this only about money?'

'This is a commercial enterprise,' observed Hartshorne dryly. 'Everything's ultimately about money.'

'And that's capitalism for you in a nutshell!' cried Cyn, triumphantly if unhelpfully.

'Well,' said Billy, brightening. 'In that case we can sort this out immediately. I'll make up the difference!'

'You?' asked Cyn incredulously. Hartshorne laughed and shook his head.

'Well, not me personally, obviously! Let me dash off a telegram to Gwalior and the palace will arrange for the Maharajah's London bankers to make the necessary payments. I am sure His Highness will be happy to authorise the funds.'

Cyn shook her head in disbelief. He really was from another world! 'And if he did do that, what do you think will happen next?'

Billy shrugged. 'Everyone is happy and we all go back to work?'

'No! Everyone comes out on strike. The whole site. This isn't just about money. It's about what's fair, and what's right. It's about people being paid what the law requires and justice demands. Whether they are male or female. You can't make this problem go away with anyone else's money. The company has to do the right thing.'

'I agree with Cyn,' called out Akaash, who had followed them and now stood at Hartshorne's door.

'Can I just point out that no one actually gives a tinker's cuss what you think?' asked an exasperated Billy. 'Sorry,' he added to Cyn, just in case the expression constituted swearing.

'Can you speak to Dr Ray with respect please?' insisted Cyn.

Billy thought about that for a moment. 'No, I honestly don't think I can,' he confessed.

'Go back to your office, Dr Ray,' said Hartshorne impatiently. 'You do have work to do.'

'How can we sort this out then? What can we do?' asked Billy.

'I don't know,' admitted Cyn sadly. 'But until my members get paid a proper rate for the job, Shop B remains closed. We'll fight for what's right.'

'"Wrong cannot afford defeat, but right can",' Akaash called from the outer office, where he was ever so slowly making his way back to his office.

'Not Mr Gandhi again right now. Please,' begged Billy.

'That one was Tagore.'

The strike held, the women's solidarity in the face of serious hardship won the grudging support of the local branch of the NUR, which had until then been convinced that a bunch of gossipy females lacked the spine for sustained industrial action. Swayed in no small part by a passionate speech from the normally taciturn Arthur Abbot, they declared the dispute official. As a result, the women received strike pay, a small proportion of what they had been earning even on their old wages, but a welcome help nonetheless. Several had already been forced to turn to the tallyman to tide them over.

A number of other consequences flowed from that declaration. No NUR member would enter Shop B. No member of any other trade union would cross their picket line and all work that they would otherwise have done was effectively blacklisted. The local Cooperative Society made arrangements at its shops for credit facilities to be extended to the strikers. The lady who ran the corner shop near Ashton St didn't ask for end-of-week settlements of accounts.

Billy swung from impotent rage to desperate pleading to unsubtle attempts to bribe Elsie and her cohort, but nothing he tried would persuade a single one of the resolute band of workers to break ranks and turn scab, another new if unwelcome addition to his vocabulary. He stood with Keenan, thumbs in his waistcoat pockets, morosely watching the women huddled around a brazier, waving in acknowledgement of the cheers, thumbs ups and encouraging calls of passing fellow Union members. They greeted Billy cheerily too. There was no ill will towards him. He wasn't the enemy. He wasn't the problem. Indeed, as a Union man himself, he was actually officially on their side.

'You gotta feel for the poor bugger!' Doreen observed to Elsie. 'Comes over here to help us out and he ends up mucked about like this. Not right. Not fair at all, if you ask me.'

There was a can of water on the brazier nearing boiling point. Packets of tea and sugar were produced and a can of condensed milk opened.

'Cuppa, Mr Khan?' Doreen called out. 'Come on! You too, Mr K. No sense all of us standing here freezing our tits off.'

Billy and Keenan joined them around the brazier. It really was getting cold. They gratefully accepted the steaming mugs of sweet tea. 'Soon be Christmas,' said Keenan conversationally.

'What's Santa bringing you, Mr Khan?' asked Elsie with a smirk. 'I hear you're getting very pally with her up in the big house on the hill. She gonna be filling your stocking this year?'

Was nothing ever secret in this bloody awful town, Billy wondered miserably.

Billy had spent the first week of the strike in a growing fever of erotic anticipation as his Sunday afternoon assignation with Lady Jessica approached. The instruction to come alone, the looks she had given him during the reception, the urging that he stay after everyone else had left all seemed obvious indications that he was at last on the threshold of the sexual encounter that he'd waited for for so long. He pictured her awaiting his arrival draped across the sofa in a flimsy negligee, breathless in anticipation of his manly attentions. He was excited, nervous and just a little intimidated.

He'd asked with exaggerated casualness about her and learned that her husband's family were local grandees – major landowners who had been the effective lords of the manor before the depredations of war and death duty taxation eroded their property and the GWR drew labourers from the fields to the Works. Their wealth and power faded but they clung doggedly on to their status and social influence. Lady Jessica in particular was on all sorts of boards and patron of all manner of bodies such as the local Women's Institute and the Land Army, besides being a school governor, a parish councillor and on the bench with Hartshorne as a fellow justice of the peace. Widowed in her thirties, the word was that she had a weakness for strapping young men.

Billy turned up the following Sunday as invited, glowing from having spent the morning in the Turkish bath on Milton Road , in an immaculately tailored suit. However, he found to his disappointment and confusion that Lady Jessica was not waiting as he had imagined her in his erotic fantasy, and was instead in her garden pulling up pea stalks and birch canes. A huge long-haired dog lay sprawled on the gravel path beside the muddy bed in which she worked. The creature sat up on seeing him approach, offered a low growl almost as a matter of form, studied him for a further moment and then, with a massive yawn, flopped sideways and closed its eyes.

She looked up, alerted by the growl, and was politely bemused by Billy's sudden appearance. 'How lovely to see you again, Mr…?'

'Khan. Billy Khan.'

'Of course!' She studied him with a polite, enquiring smile. Billy noted that she was dressed in a tweed jacket, skirt, headscarf and green Wellington boots.

'You invited me. After the reception last week. Told me to… well, to come and see you this afternoon.'

She threw down a handful of canes, straightened, arched her back with a pained expression and looked at him doubtfully. 'Did I?'

'You did. You mentioned scones.'

She put one hand to her mouth. 'Was I blotto?'

'Well…'

She chuckled and shook her head, the indulgent adult amused by the mischievous stupidity of another, younger self. 'No recollection whatsoever! Give me a hand to clamber out of here and I'll get some tea organised.'

Lady Jessica took him for a tour of the requisitioned flower beds and the walled vegetable garden at the rear of the house. She assured him that he was not seeing them at their best, describing her plans for tasks over the coming days as long as the weather held and boasting of how well her French beans had done that year. After his initial disappointment, Billy realised that he was actually rather relieved that the anticipated frenzy of sexual gratification he had imagined all week didn't look like it was going to materialise. He had spent so long thinking about it that his lust – and supply of prophylactics – had over the week been almost exhausted and progressively given way to nervousness, introspection and a growing trepidation over quite what was going to happen when they finally met.

The light was starting to fade when they returned to the peas and she gathered up her bean sticks and tools. He offered to carry them for her but she told him not to be silly. Her wolfhound, which had loyally if unenthusiastically padded along at her heels throughout the tour, was joined as they approached the house by a small terrier that took an instant and noisy dislike to Billy, yapping and growling at him and ignoring his mistress's sharp demands for silence. She thrust first one foot then the other into a cast-iron bootjack by the door and led Billy into the house in her thick socks, leaving her discarded boots lying at right angles to one another in the hallway. She waved him towards the reception room, telling him to make himself at home whilst she headed towards the stairs, calling to invisible staff for tea to be made.

Not seeing things at their best applied as much to the house as the grounds. On his previous visit, illuminated by gas lamps and candles and warmed by roaring fires, the place had seemed grand. In fading daylight the threadbare carpets, worn furniture, cold ash-filled grate and dusty cobwebs in the corners of high cracked ceilings seemed to mourn better days, greater care and happier times. Lady Jessica too, he couldn't help noticing as she'd plodded along beside him, was older than he'd thought, considerably less glamorous than she'd previously seemed to him and somewhat more solidly built than he recalled. But even without make-up and done-up hair, to Billy she remained an appealing proposition. Shame it looked like any sort of romantic encounter seemed so clearly off the agenda. At least, he reminded himself, she was a woman with whom a chap could hold a sensible conversation. But he'd have preferred such conversations conducted in a decent bed, postcoital.

When his hostess returned Billy found the dowdy woman in Wellingtons with whom he had entered the house had been transformed into his hostess of a week earlier. With artfully applied make-up, hair tied up and a three-quarter-length V-necked dress that flattered her figure, she was once again the Grande Dame. She smiled at his gaping at her. 'Tea not arrived yet?' she asked. 'Honestly, if you want something done… ALICE!' she bellowed. 'Deaf as a post, daft old bat. Ah, there you are.'

An ancient, bent woman entered, treated her employer to a scowl and Billy to a disdainful glare and took the order for tea '…and whatever cakes, biscuits or buns you can rustle up,' Lady Jessica added, indifferent to the mumbled grumbles.

She flopped onto the sofa, tucking her legs beneath her and indicated an armchair into which Billy settled himself. In this avatar she was once again an object of massive desire for him and he seemed suddenly lost for anything to say. She reached for a silver cigarette box, took one and offered the open box to him. He leapt up, took a cigarette for himself and lit hers for her, hands shaking slightly. She smiled at his nervous gallantry.

She asked a series of questions about his home. She had never visited India, she explained, although 'the Late Lamented' had been on the Prince of Wales tour. Billy had assumed her husband had died in the Great War or the subsequent Spanish flu epidemic, but the tour had been in the early 1920s so evidently not. Billy described Gwalior, the palaces, the fort and the surrounding countryside. He talked of rivers and plains, nullahs, maidans and tanks, of tribes and dacoits, conjuring up for her a place of exotic mystery that she clearly enjoyed listening to him talk about.

Tea arrived, with a plate of somewhat damp digestive biscuits. Long, dusty drapes were drawn and gas lamps lit. They chatted about the reception, the various nationalities present, joked about the Americans and wondered about the war. Billy realised that he was enjoying himself and feeling very much at home.

'Would you like me to get the fire going?' he asked.

She nodded, reaching for another cigarette. There was something intimate, comfortable and companionable in the way she tossed the matchbox over to him. He knelt by the fireplace, took a small brush and cleared as much ash as possible from the grate, screwed up balls of newspaper, made a neat stack of kindling and set it alight.

'Draws well, that chimney,' Lady Jessica observed. 'There's a log basket in the hallway.'

Billy brought the half-full basket through and again sat by the fire. The flames had taken hold and he fed a couple of the smallest logs into the blaze. The flickering firelight made the room seem more alive. He looked around at Lady Jessica, who was studying him thoughtfully. She suddenly got up. 'Sherry? Or something stronger?' she asked, walking towards an occasional table by the window on which a series of decanters and a soda syphon stood on a tray with a set of glasses.

'I think something stronger, please. I recall someone once telling me sherry is for old maids…'

'…and mincing vicars? Whoever said that must be very wise indeed. Scotch or brandy?'

'Scotch.'

She poured two measures, they toasted one another and sipped their drinks. She looked steadily at him and he returned her scrutiny. Was she waiting for him to make the first move, he wondered? He lowered his head, inhaled her perfume and closed his eyes. She raised her face. He could feel her breath on his. She let out a little sigh, almost melancholic, as though reconciled to the inevitability of embarking upon a not terribly wise course of action she had been considering for some time. She took his glass from his hand, spread her arms and kissed him, at first diffidently, then with greater passion, mouth opening and hips pressing forward. He pulled her close to him. He could feel her bra strap through her dress as he stroked her back. One hand slid down to caress her buttocks, gathering up the cloth of her dress.

'Steady, tiger,' she murmured, her mouth still on his. 'Let me get rid of these glasses.'

Reluctantly, he let her go and stepped back, panting slightly.

'There are ground rules,' she said matter-of-factly as she walked over to place the glasses on the drinks table.

'What?'

'Do you like me?'

Why do women do this sort of thing, Billy wondered, desperate to be touching her again, screaming and aching inside. 'I think you're the most beautiful woman I've ever seen,' he assured her, crossing the room towards her.

She held up a hand, warning him off. He briefly recalled the dogs and the guns and reluctantly paused.

'That's unlikely to be true and anyway isn't an answer to the question I asked.'

Billy frowned. 'Well, I suppose so, yes.'

'Why? You hardly know me.'

'I don't bloody know! Because you're clever and…'

'Available?'

'If you like,' he said, exasperated. 'Look, I really, really want to…'

'Yes, I can see that,' she observed wryly, looking at the bulge in his trousers and the tiny damp patch evident. 'I'd quite like to, too. But there are…'

'Ground rules. Yes, you said. Like what?'

'Like that whatever happens here remains between us. No boasting to your friends. No indiscreet comments. I have a position to maintain and a reputation to protect.'

'Fine, fine, fine. Agreed. Mum's the word. Now can we…'

'And this is only about…you know. It. And respect. Not affection, romance or, God forbid, love.'

'Agreed. Absolutely. A hundred per cent. No love whatsoever. Perish the thought! Any more rules?'

'Only one more,' she assured him, reaching up to the mantelpiece above the fireplace and taking down something he couldn't make out which she slipped behind her back. 'I'm always in charge.'

He dropped his trousers to his knees and she quickly, inelegantly discarded her knickers. They threw themselves at one other, fumbling, clutching and clawing. She fell back onto the sofa and he fell on top of her, throwing up the skirt of her dress and parting her thighs. She was kissing him, cursing him and urging him on. He entered her with a moan of triumph and she welcomed him with a groan of possession. He knew he had to calm himself or it would all be over too soon. He tried to focus his thoughts far away to delay his orgasm but found physical stimuli fighting against his best endeavours. Her moaning chorus of delight and desire, the sensation of her enclosing him, the scent of their lovemaking, the warm embrace of her strong, silky smooth thighs gripping him, the sudden sharp pain in his left buttock…

'Ow!' he cried as the sting was repeated. He instinctively thrust forward to avoid the source of pain and she spat out her satisfaction as he drove deeper into her.

'Yes! That's more like it! Come on, you bastard! Yes, you useless piece of shit. Yes! Yes! Do it, damn you, sir! Come on! Do it!'

Her furious demands, snarled through gritted teeth, were accompanied by ever more rapid lashes at his backside. If nothing else, he reflected grimly, it was certainly distracting. He rammed himself into her, thrust his hands under her buttocks and rolled them both off the sofa and on to the carpet, her now on top of him. She straddled him, her knees compressing the sides of his ribcage so he could hardly breathe as she continued to bring the riding crop down, now striking at her own calves and ankles as frequently as at him.

She rose and fell on him, increasing the pace and the fury of her curses. The thought flitted across his mind that sex with this woman involved a great deal more slap than tickle. Finally, she shuddered, snarled, swore and blasphemed and collapsed onto him with a grateful moan that sounded to him like, 'That's my Sampson.' His own orgasm moments later, a muted and almost resentful echo of her spectacular, violent climax, generated nothing more than a contented acknowledgement from her.

After a stunned moment, he rolled her over onto her back, withdrew and climbed to his feet. 'What in the name of all that's holy was that?' he cried, craning round to check if he could see the welts he was sure she'd inflicted.

She chuckled as she lay aside the riding crop and pulled down the hem of her dress. 'Don't be such a baby.'

'And who the hell is Sampson?'

'Ah, Sampson,' she sighed, a nostalgic smile on her flushed face. 'I had my first orgasm astride Sampson.'

'Really? I think I'm bleeding.'

'Not on my carpet, you're not.'

'So who was Sampson? The gardener?'

'No, silly. My first real horse. It was the New Year's Day hunt. I was driving him hard to take a high hedge with a ditch on the blind side when it just happened. I nearly fainted but we cleared that jump! Ever since, I associate a good come with dear old Sampson.'

It suddenly struck Billy how both his sexual experiences in the UK had indirectly involved dominant horses. He hoped this wasn't going to leave him with similarly troubling equine associations with orgasm. 'And the whip?'

'It's called a crop. And I told you, I was driving him on. He was a sweetheart but he could be a little… lacklustre at times. Not unlike some others. I believe I detected a momentary lack of application?'

'I was trying to be a gentleman. And I don't care what it's called, it really hurt.'

'Don't be such a big softy. I just tickled you up a bit.'

'Where's dear old Sampson now?'

'Dispatched to the glue factory years ago.' She gave him a mischievous grin. 'Don't worry, I think there's a few more miles in you before the knackers come calling.' She raised her knees, slowly spread her legs and let her dress fall away. 'Up for another canter before we put you away wet?'

God, those thighs! So white! He felt himself hardening. 'No more whip?'

'No promises,' she sighed as he placed his hands on her knees and gingerly knelt between them. 'Remember the ground rules. I'm always in charge.'

The Shop B dispute having been declared official, there was no longer any possibility of Hartshorne keeping the unapproved repair of the Bulldogs from the Board of Directors, who descended en masse on the Works to hold an ill-tempered extraordinary meeting, replete with rancour, blame and criticism. One of the many repercussions of this was that the three locomotives awaiting testing were jumped up the queue so that Hartshorne might have some successes to defend his decision to embark on their recommissioning. Minor problems were identified with one of *Sir Stafford*'s driving wheels that would require further, more detailed inspection but the other two passed with flying colours.

Despite the ongoing industrial action, and against the instructions of the local NUR convenor, all involved in their renovation turned out on a wet Tuesday afternoon to watch *Birkenhead* and *Tremayne* – with gleaming, newly repainted tenders now attached and looking incongruously pristine behind the still unpainted engines – get up steam and move under their own power for the first time in this resurrected incarnation.

'Proud?' Billy asked of a pensive Cyn, who had silently taken shelter under his umbrella as they watched *Tremayne* being reversed onto the turntable prior to being shunted to the Painting Shop.

'I am. You?'

'This should be your moment of glory but yes, I am too. Nothing sounds like a Bulldog in steam. How about we…'

'Sorry, Mr Khan. All offers have to be addressed to Branch level or above. I'm not even supposed to talk to you.'

He couldn't miss the wistfulness in her voice. The matter had been abruptly and comprehensively taken out of her hands. She wasn't involved in discussions of what should happen next, no one asked her opinion and she wasn't part of the Union's negotiating team. She was simply told what to do and expected to do it without question. Industrial action, she reflected, was depressingly like being at work: being ignored most of the time and for the rest, being ordered about by middle-aged men who really didn't care to hear what she felt or gave a damn what she thought.

She knew, or at least assumed, that this was how things had to be. But just at that moment, standing beside Billy watching their engines in steam and knowing there were several more gathering dust and rust in the locked-up Shop B, she wondered if perhaps she shouldn't have been quite so abrupt in her dismissal of his attempts to find a way around the problem. Still, too late now. As her dad liked to point out, compromise was not an option. Short of divine intervention, one side or the other had to capitulate and right at that moment, neither seemed at all willing to do so.

She smiled sadly, nodded to him and stepped back to join the women smoking under the shelter of an overhanging roof.

Both Vincent's and Akaash's assignments having been fully approved and authorised by the Board, Hartshorne was keen to assuage some of the Directors' ire by making a show of their success. Dismissing the Head of Movements' deep reservations, he instructed Vincent to explain his findings and conclusions at the meeting whilst Lapworth handed round copies of the various maps, charts and tables required to support his recommendations. If not the emollient Hartshorne had hoped, Vincent's proposals certainly diverted the Board's attention, prompting lengthy and occasionally heated debate about the feasibility of his ideas. The Deputy Permanent Secretary of the Ministry of War Transport, an ex officio member of the Board, whom all referred to simply as 'Sir John', asked numerous questions about exactly where Vincent had been and what he had observed. He then requested any decisions be held over to their next meeting to allow him time to explore the implications of the idea with his officials back in the ministry. After a polite glance around the table to check for dissent, he suggested they move on to hear about how the development of secure communications was progressing.

Phyl, Joan and Akaash had been on standby to appear all day but it was only after the Board members returned from a private lunch at the Great Western Hotel that they were called in. Phyl gave a low-key but complex account of their work to date, the three of them having agreed that they would try to throw dust in the eyes of the Board by talking at length about cyphers, codes and encryption algorithms considered and reasons for their rejection before hinting in conclusion that a more simple alternative might be possible, just to test the water.

To Joan and Akaash's surprise, the man from the ministry was generous in his praise of their work and enthusiastic about their emerging ideas. The reason for his positivity, and the contrast with his forensic analysis of Vincent's report, might have had something to do with the fact that as they withdrew, Phyl let slip a parting, 'Thank you, daddy.'

The strike had not only caught the attention of the Board of Directors but also of the media – at first locally, then nationally. The *Daily Mirror* heralded the women of Shop B as heroines, worthy workers typifying the Bulldog spirit (pun very much intended) and lauded their refusal to be taken advantage of. Isn't that, the paper asked, precisely what we are fighting for? The *Daily Mail* denounced them as traitors and Trotskyists, undermining the war effort and trying to advance a communist takeover of the world. The *Telegraph* wondered if this wasn't an inevitable consequence of women in the workplace and reminded its readers that patriotism and paternalism sprang from the same source. The *Daily Sketch* highlighted the presence of Indians on both sides of the dispute and seemed unable to decide if this was to be applauded as yet another example of the empire coming to the aid of the mother country in her hour of need or decried as evidence of a Gandhian conspiracy to undermine Britain by exploiting tensions in her industrial heartland.

The *Times* ignored the matter entirely, as did the BBC.

All this focus raised the stakes and resulted in the women's campaign, which until then had been regarded with a mix of bemusement, affectionate tolerance and grudging respect, being denounced as self-centred and conducted by lightweights. The strikers were mocked as strident, unstable females – their demands contrasted with the real Management–Union struggles of the '30s – and denounced as housewives playing at industrial strife. Attitudes hardened and common courtesy gave way to waspishness and impatience. Cyn found herself shunned, muttered about, sneered at and on one occasion, actually spat upon.

A breakthrough came not because either side weakened but because each had bigger fish to fry. The Union wanted to focus all its attention and negotiating power on a proposal to restructure differentials. Management had a shareholders' meeting due in a matter of weeks at which they did not want a relatively trivial bit of militancy in Swindon to distract from an otherwise very positive annual report and healthy dividend prediction.

But faces needed to be saved. Neither side could be seen to back down so scapegoats had to be found if a satisfactory compromise was to be achieved. The obvious candidate was the Chief Mechanical Engineer, who had exceeded his delegated powers and embarked upon 'this reckless and unauthorised enterprise'. Accordingly, Hartshorne was formally reprimanded, although the Directors were at pains to point out that they unanimously accepted that he had acted with the best of intentions and they reiterated their full confidence in him. He was accordingly given permission to attempt the reintroduction of the Bulldogs, effective retrospectively. The women's claim for higher rates of pay and arrears was agreed to. The dispute was declared resolved.

The Union, for its part, regretted the unhelpful influence of Dr Akaash Ray, the firebrand communist who they felt had prompted the walkout, and formally distanced themselves from his actions. They had, very briefly, thought of allowing Cyn to be criticised for taking precipitate and unsanctioned action, but her father made very clear that immediate and dramatic consequences would follow if any such stance was adopted. The newspapers reported the end of the strike as a victory for common sense and British decency. The right thing had been done. They were easy on Hartshorne, portraying him as a well-meaning if over-promoted mechanic (*Telegraph*), an imaginative engineer unwilling to be trammelled by the excessive bureaucracy that was stopping Britain from winning the war (*Mail*), and a working-class hero who had risen to the top through sheer hard work and application of the type that would build the new, post-war Jerusalem (*Mirror*).

The *Times* and the BBC, once more, said nothing.

The papers were much less circumspect when it came to their coverage of Akaash, who was roundly condemned as a troublemaker, insurgent, revolutionary and all-round bad egg. The *Sketch* front-paged a grainy image of him on the picket line and, never fearful of hyperbole, demanded in the accompanying caption: 'Is this the most dangerous man in England?'

That photograph had been taken when he had been standing near the brazier on a particularly cold morning. His collar was turned up, his shoulders hunched and his hands thrust deep into the pockets of his long coat. The photographer had called out ''Oy! Gunga Din!' and Akaash had turned his head towards the camera just as the picture was taken, which caught him glaring back over his shoulder as though caught in some fiendish plot, the shadows cast over his features by the magnesium glare of the camera flash the very image of evil, an effect heightened by his round glasses reflecting the light, like caricatures of the loathed and much ridiculed Emperor of Japan. He'd actually been delivering a cake Joan had baked for the strikers, which he'd offered to take over to them for her as it was such a miserable day.

When he saw the newspaper, Billy had been illogically put out that it was Akaash, who to his recollection had rarely visited the picket line, that should have been the centre of attention: Billy had been there every day, handing out cigarettes and chocolate – although for reasons less to do with solidarity than an attempt to undermine resistance to a return to work – and had been photographed there many times. Odd, he thought, recalling Dawlish's words about Akaash having bigger problems.

The *Times* ran a feature on Akaash's role in the strike, its tone grave, as though saddened but not surprised by such ingratitude from one blessed with obvious natural gifts that had been nurtured and rewarded by the benevolent hand of the Raj. It listed his education, employment and academic achievements with such precision that their information could only have come from official sources.

It was on the morning of the *Times* article that they came for Akaash. Two constables, one well past active service age, the other looking too young to be in uniform. They met him on his way to the Works and politely asked him to come with them. Billy took a step towards Akaash, asking what was going on, but the younger policeman deftly stepped between them.

'Nothing to get upset about,' he assured Billy, just a hint of a warning in his voice. 'Just a few questions. No one wants any trouble…'

Akaash had been expecting arrest ever since the Union decided to hang him out to dry, as Cyn had furiously put it. He took off his glasses and slipped them into his pocket. He told Billy not to worry and made to hand him his sandwiches and flask.

'I'd bring those with me if I was you, son,' the older of the two officers advised. 'Never know how long these things might take…'

Cyn was lauded by her co-workers, friends and family as the true victor of the campaign but she found little joy in her triumph, for it had come at a cost. Her perhaps naive faith in the virtuous struggle of organised labour had been profoundly shaken by the cynical way the dispute had been resolved, and her treatment in the final few days by her supposed comrades frankly horrified her.

At a personal level she had been hurt that she had been abruptly sidelined by aloof and disengaged officials from headquarters as the dispute escalated. She was even more disappointed in the way she and her constituency of members had been treated – with indifference bordering on disdain. Like foot soldiers to distant generals they were cannon fodder, she reflected sadly, their personal suffering and eventual sacrifice merely a matter of tactics.

Also, as she explained to Billy as Shop B reopened, it just seemed wrong that the eventual granting of what was no more than their due had been bought at the price of Akaash's freedom. Not to mention Mr Hartshorne having to eat humble pie for doing something that he should actually be applauded for. She felt that she'd got everything that she'd wanted, but the liberty of a friend and the good name of someone she admired and respected was too high a price to pay.

Billy, just happy to be getting back to work, was indifferent to whatever Machiavellian manoeuvrings had ended the action and deep down was actually looking forward to Akaash not being around for a while. He recalled a lesson from school about Pyrrhic victories, which he tried to explain to Cyn but got so hopelessly lost that they agreed they'd pop into the Mechanics Institute together after the final hooter and look it up before going to see if they could visit Akaash.

Work resumed in Shop B, but without the cheeriness and sense of something new and exciting happening. The women workers were being paid their due, and with back pay promised for the end of the week, would be well-off – albeit briefly – and able to settle debts incurred, including loans from the tallyman. But the women were treated differently following their return to work. Less patronisingly, certainly, but also less affectionately and less tolerantly. For the men in the Works, rather than siding with their fellow Union members and celebrating their success, now regarded them as interlopers who had quite simply betrayed the Works and the town to London End. And shamed a good man and a great engineer in the process. Something had been lost and it seemed doubtful the spirit of those early days could ever be recaptured.

Work elsewhere on site on the three renovated engines – test running, painting and finishing – continued apace, everyone determined to vindicate Hartshorne's judgement. All GWR requirements met, they merely needed certification from the Ministry of War Transport to pull carriages packed with troops and wagons loaded with armaments. No one gave this requirement too much consideration as, given the GWR's long-established reputation for stringent testing and over-cautious engineering, certificates had been issued with only the minimum of checking.

It therefore came as an unpleasant and wholly unexpected surprise when the ministry refused to issue the necessary certificates and declined to enter into any discussion about why. Hartshorne seemed remarkably indifferent to his ticking off, but was insulted and infuriated by the lack of certification for his engines. The men in the Works also suspected the women of Shop B of being the reason – although no one could come up with a credible explanation of quite why – for the vital certificates being refused.

And as for Akaash, who as everybody knew wasn't a real railwayman at all – however much the Abbots might argue to the contrary – there was really very little concern. Uppity foreigner. Probably got no more than what he deserved, seemed to be the consensus.

'Look out, lads!' cried a delighted Curtis as the two constables escorted Akaash into the station. 'Break out the arms chest and lock up your valuables! The most dangerous man in England has just walked through the door! Book him in and take him through to the interview room.'

Twenty minutes later, Akaash – pockets emptied, tie, belt and shoelaces removed – was joined by Curtis, still irritatingly cheerful, carrying a buff folder.

'I'm ready to make a statement,' said Akaash.

'Oh, don't you trouble your little head about that, young Bish-Bash! Already done for you. Just need you to sign it.' Curtis opened the file and took out a single sheet of paper.

'I'm not signing anything written for me.'

'No?' said Curtis, sounding disappointed. 'That's a shame. I think I captured your whiney, hard-done-by tone rather well.' He slipped the statement back into the file. 'You can refuse on a point of principle, I suppose. Say it was given under duress. Yeah, that would work just as well.'

'And I want a lawyer.'

'Of course you do. No more than you're entitled to. I must say, for such a notorious enemy of the state, you're remarkably popular. We've already had the legal representatives of both the GWR and the NUR on the blower.'

'I'm happy to be represented by either.'

'Your faith in British justice does you credit. Personally, I wouldn't let either of them represent my auntie's cat, and I don't even like the thing. Or my auntie, come to that. I declined both on your behalf.'

'You can't do that!'

'No? Oh dear, oh dear, oh dear! Whatever shall we do? I told them you'd insisted on being represented by one of your own. The Union is currently trawling round London for Indian briefs.'

'Why did you do that?'

'I thought it was a nice touch. Anyway, you're not going to be charged with anything. You're far too useful. This is just a bit of a show for the newspapers. We're going to hold you for a day or two, allow some clever little fucker just like you to come down from the big city and patronise us as country bumpkins for a while. Then we'll let him walk out the door with you to a hero's welcome. He looks good, you look good, your commie credentials are hugely enhanced and your value to me multiplies. Everybody wins. The Railway even wants you back. Can you believe it? Silly buggers. Seems your lady friends know how to pull a few strings, even if they don't seem to be much cop at anything else. Plus the Union, who – if you don't mind me saying – gave you a pretty thorough shafting, now say they're right behind you. Threatening all-out industrial action if you aren't released and reinstated. Funny old world. You peckish?'

'I brought my sandwiches. They took them off me at the desk.'

'What have you got?'

'I don't know. It's usually jam.'

'I've got cheese. Fancy divvying them up? I'll swap you a cheese for a jam?'

'What sort of cheese?'

'Fuck me! Cheddar?'

'OK. Can I have my flask as well?'

'Don't push your luck. You can have station tea like the rest of us and be thankful. Now, are you going to sign this statement or not?'

'May I see it?'

'Of course,' said Curtis, pushing it across the table to him. 'But if you correct my English, I swear to God…'

Akaash had several visitors call to check up on him whilst in custody – Cyn, Phyl and Joan, Vincent and Billy. Sally sent her best, and some shortbread that she'd made. Perhaps the least expected was Ernie, of whom they had seen little since the night of the encounter with the GIs.

He sat across from Akaash in the interview room, in the chair usually occupied by Curtis.

'Looks different,' he said, 'sitting on this side of the table. Feels funny.'

'You've been in here?' asked Akaash, chronically bored and glad of any company.

'Loads of times. I was a naughty boy in my youth. They treating you all right? Anything you need?'

'I'm fine, thanks.'

'Good, good.'

There was a long and uncomfortable silence. Ernie crossed his arms and looked round. 'Doesn't look like this place has seen a lick of paint since I was last here.' Another pause. 'That was quite a night, wasn't it?'

Akaash smiled. 'Yes, it was.'

Ernie nodded. 'Oh, well. Better leave you to it. Let me know if you need anything.'

At midday the following afternoon, Akaash was released. The lawyer, a Gujarati solicitor practising in Walthamstow, had been found by Lockyer, who had been asked by Billy to help. Sensing the possibility of lucrative future cases from the massive Union, he was only too happy to drop everything and take the first train down to Swindon to meet his client. He was both surprised and somewhat deflated when Akaash was freed before he'd even been able to present any of the arguments against his client's continued detention without charge that he'd prepared on the journey. It was, he observed wryly, the briefest brief he'd ever had.

The hero's welcome didn't happen either. There was no one outside the station to greet them. Akaash shook his lawyer's hand, thanked him, declined the offer of a celebratory cup of tea and walked back to the Works.

Billy visited the big house on the hill on the following Sunday afternoon and the Sunday after that. The application of the riding crop diminished as his knowledge of Lady Jessica's preferences and expectations grew and he got better at picking up on cues and warnings – although she insisted on keeping it within reach, just in case. He always approached their lovemaking – which had relocated, after a couple of memorable encounters on the stairs, to a guest bedroom – with some trepidation. Her sheer energy and muscular enthusiasm left him literally drained.

They usually, as she euphemistically put it, 'rode to hounds' first. 'Best to get it out of the way,' she observed, with a hungry smirk. On arrival, with ever fewer preliminaries and only the briefest of greetings, they set to it. After, they would lie side by side, staring at the ceiling. Often, they'd dress, take tea or go for a stroll. Polite, sedate, companionable conversation would follow. She encouraged him to tell her all about his work. When he mentioned the problem with the certification for his engines, she wondered if their mutual acquaintance Roddie Dawlish might be able to put in a word on Billy's behalf. That, she assured him, was how most things got sorted out in her experience. He usually made up the fire before he left.

Billy thought long and hard before making the call. He'd explained to Hartshorne that it might resolve the impasse with the Ministry of War Transport certification and asked if he could make the call from the Chief Mechanical Engineer's office. Hartshorne readily agreed, telling his secretary to put through the call and leaving Billy to it.

Dawlish answered on the third ring. 'Billy! How nice to hear from you? All well, I trust?'

'Progressing well at this end, Roddie,' Billy assured him. 'But we do seem to have a slight problem with some paperwork. The ministry…'

'Won't sign off on your engines,' concluded Dawlish, voice rich with insincere sympathy. 'So I understand.'

'Don't suppose you have any idea why?'

'I know exactly why.'

It was clear he had no intention of making this easy for Billy.

'Can you tell me?'

'I could, but I'm not sure I should.'

'Because?'

'Well, you wouldn't help me when I asked you. Why should I help you?'

'Let me get this straight. You won't tell me because I said I wouldn't spy on Rosario for you?

'Well, one wouldn't want to be a sneak, would one?'

'But if I play ball with you, you'll tell me why?'

'I'll do more than that, Billy. I'll get the certificates issued.'

'You can do that?'

'I can. They only withheld them because I asked them to. Unlike you, they're willing to, how did you put it? Play ball.'

'But these engines are vital!'

'Useful, perhaps, but hardly vital. The GWR has always had an inflated sense of its own importance.'

'You're undermining the war effort…'

'No, you are, by refusing to help me safeguard vital intelligence.'

'And if I refuse?'

'All your hard work will have been in vain. Those engines will sit in the Works until they return to the state you found them in. Such a shame. When this could all be sorted out so easily. It's still not too late.'

'I can't believe you'd do this, Dawlish.'

'Oh, you have no idea what I'd do to keep my country safe, Khan.'

On the fourth Sunday, as they lay together getting their breath back, Billy propped himself up on one elbow and gazed at Lady Jessica as she lay with her eyes closed, arms folded over her stomach, ankles crossed. She'd been wearing a skirt and blouse when he arrived. The former was promptly discarded, the latter merely undone, her bra pushed up over her breasts.

He was struck by how much older she looked in repose and how acute his observation of her was after sex. The skin of her neck was reddened and hung loose. There were bluish bags beneath her eyes and tiny cracked veins in her cheeks. Her breasts spread heavily apart, the nipples elongated by their weight. He could see a faint pattern of blue veins beneath the milky white skin. The result of this dispassionate scrutiny of her was a wave of affection that took him totally unawares, a feeling so strong that his chin trembled, his mouth twisted and tears pricked his eyes.

'What are you staring at?' she asked, eyes still closed.

'You,' he said, leaning over to kiss her between the breasts.

'Well, don't. And don't come here again until I tell you to.'

'Why?' he cried, pulling back from her. 'What's wrong?'

'You know very well what's wrong,' she replied irritably. 'I told you there were rules. Don't let me keep you,' she concluded, eyes still shut.

As he trudged miserably back down the hill towards Swindon, Billy felt very much alone, confused and, not for the first time, sorely used. It started to rain as he walked across Commonhead, the chill and the damp suiting his mood well. What ground rule had he transgressed? He had been, as he'd promised, the soul of discretion. Was it his fault if in this gossipy, nosey dump of a town others took pleasure in talking about them? He'd only ever treated her with respect. He'd allowed her always to be in charge. Where did his fault lay?

Then it dawned on him. Affection. And, God forbid, almost love.

Women!

He tried to put the thoughts of Lady Jessica out of his mind. Now – what the hell was he going to do about Dawlish, Vincent and those bloody certificates?

The first thing he did was to invite Vincent out for a drink. Not at the Queen's Tap, which had become their usual haunt, but to the Goddard Arms hotel, up the hill in the Old Town beyond the Christchurch Alms houses. There they sat in armchairs beside a log fire. Vincent was unsure what this sudden desire for his company presaged, particularly as Billy was tongue-tied and uncertain. He feared it was going to be a confession of some indiscretion or something equally embarrassing and unwelcome.

Billy ordered them both tea. Also not a good sign. He hummed and hawed. On the walk up the hill he'd exhausted topics such as Vincent's work, latest news from home and the progress of the war. He was clearly struggling to get to the point and Vincent had no idea how to help him and little desire to do so in any case.

'Look,' said Billy, edging his chair nearer to Vincent's and leaning forward. 'I have a problem. You remember that official chap who met us at the docks? Dawlish? Well, he says unless I, well, tell him what you're up to, I'll never get my engines certified.'

This, Vincent thought, is getting ridiculous. 'Is that it? Tell him whatever you like. I'm not up to anything. I've got nothing to hide.'

'Really?'

'Yes, really. I don't know why they don't just ask me. There's nothing I have seen or heard or written down that isn't obvious and there for all to see. Poor Lapworth was blackmailed into stealing my notebooks so that the police could check them. If they'd just spoken to me, I'd have shown them the blessed things.'

'Lapworth? Your limp-wristed chum?'

Vincent bristled. 'He's not my "chum" and I have no idea what his wrists are like. He's a good man who was threatened and scared half to death unnecessarily. Now you. Well, spy on me to your heart's content! Better still, I always make a note of where I go and what I do. Why don't I just give you a copy?'

'Still doesn't feel right.'

'Nor does it make any sense. I've come here at their request. I've done my best. If they have a problem, why don't they just send me home?'

'I hate it but I don't suppose I've got much choice,' Billy began.

'Of course you've got a choice! We've all got a choice. If you want to spy on me, do it. I really don't care. But no one's forcing you.'

'Of course they are! Unless I do…'

Vincent held up his hand. 'Shut up for a moment. Just let me think.'

Billy sat back and sipped his tea. He could almost see Vincent's mind working.

'If you really hate the idea,' said Vincent, 'then I think there just might be a way... Where's Akaash?'

The three of them met up in the kitchen of No. 23. Billy repeated his threats from Dawlish and reiterated his unwillingness to act as informer. Akaash listened in silence, reflecting uncomfortably on how easily he'd been turned and how readily he'd agreed to watch Vincent on Curtis's behalf. Of course, the stakes were much bigger for him. Literally life or death back home, not just some chit so a few old engines could run.

They asked him how far he, Joan and Phyl had progressed. Akaash summarised their thinking. Expecting a sneering response from Vincent at least, he was surprised and relieved to see him nodding thoughtfully and even smiling. Billy was clearly barely listening, preoccupied with his own concerns for his engines.

'How much of your plans does Mr Hartshorne know?' Vincent asked.

'The broad outline. No new codes, just a build-up of telegraphic and telephonic traffic, including at first a significant proportion of fake details, indicated by a regularly changing signifier.'

'Billy? Your first batch of engines are ready?'

'Absolutely. Tenders fully coaled with best South Wales anthracite. Just a matter of hours to get them fired up, on line and in steam.'

'And my recommendations are to increase real traffic on critical routes and through key junctions to build up the necessary flow capacity. For which...'

'You need trains!'

'And Akaash's system could be tested and fine-tuned on their journeys. I think the three of us need a meeting with the CME.'

Inevitably Hartshorne's main concern was the lack of certification: an insult to his professionalism and the reputation of the Swindon Works.

'Without ministry certificates, the Bulldogs can't be used to pull trains carrying military personnel or equipment,' Vincent acknowledged. 'But otherwise, no one can tell you what you can and can't run on your own tracks, in your own region.'

'And those engines are as reliable and safe as any motive units around,' added Billy. 'They've met or exceeded all GWR specifications, which, as you know better than me, far exceed current ministry requirements.'

'And if you accept my recommendations, they won't even be shifting people or loads. They'll be running with empty carriages and wagons.'

'It's a risk,' mused Hartshorne. 'And a cost.'

'But a necessary cost,' Vincent observed.

'Actually,' said Akaash, 'initially at least, this doesn't have to add any cost.'

That clearly appealed to Hartshorne, who looked towards him. 'Go on.'

'Well, I know from analysing signals traffic that a lot of trains run empty simply to get carriages and wagons back to where they are needed for the next load. Basically, to Bristol, Newport, Swansea and Cardiff. To get the next shipload of American troops and gear to wherever they're heading.'

'Yes!' cried Vincent, picking up the theme. 'Use them on the Down Line to get empty rolling stock to the docks. Then run them as ghost trains on the Up Line via key junctions on their return journey.'

Hartshorne chewed his bottom lip pensively. There was a long silence, and then he asked, 'How soon could we start on this?'

The three of them looked at one another. 'Tonight?' offered Billy.

Akaash and Vincent nodded.

'All right. Let's give it a go. Send *Tremayne* up to Old Oak Common tonight and if all goes well, let's get her pulling stock back down the following night. Then we'll see what happens next.'

'Can I use your telephone once more?' Billy asked.

'I suppose so. Why?'

'I want to find out if Colonel Dawlish's Hindi runs to *behenchod*.'

Approaching 11 p.m., virtually the whole of Shop B gathered with the three Indians on the Up platform to wave as *Tremayne* steamed through. The first of their engines to run on the main line, at long last. There were eleven repaired and refurbished coaches waiting to be dispatched to the huge stockyard at Old Oak Common just outside the London terminus, and these – as fine and pristine as the engine – made the sight even more glorious. Empty and unlit, but a proper train! The driver sounded her whistle, the fireman took off his cap and waved and the Shop B crew cheered her on her way. As the slit light at the back of the guards van disappeared into the darkness, they shook hands, hugged, laughed and cried.

There were still a few passengers at the station, waiting for the last Down train timetabled for Newport, Cardiff and Swansea. Among them was a clutch of cold and tired-looking young women, huddled together as though for warmth and mutual support, who greeted Vincent cheerily. One in particular caught Billy's eye. She was taller than the others and wearing a headscarf and a thin coat. As he watched, Elsie left Doreen's side and crossed to speak to her.

'Didn't see you earlier, Mary,' Elsie said, her tone as chill as the night.

The girl she had called Mary looked down guiltily. 'Sorry, Mrs Coggins,' she murmured, taking a purse out of her pocket, opening it with hands that trembled from more than just the cold. She took out a note and a few coins and handed them to Elsie.

'Think on, Mary Hughes,' Elsie warned, pocketing the cash. 'You ain't all that, even if you might think you are.'

'I will, Mrs Coggins.'

Elsie took a few paces towards the stairs where Doreen was waiting for her. Clearly having second thoughts, she returned to a frightened Mary Hughes and handed her back some of the coins. 'Get a little something for whatsisname,' she said.

''is name's Georgie, Mrs Coggins,' a surprised Mary replied.

'Well, you get something for little Georgie from his Auntie Elsie.'

'What was that all about?' asked Billy when he'd caught up with Keenan, busy chatting with the old warrior who had escorted Vincent home on the night Ernie and Akaash had faced off with the American GIs.

Keenan looked skyward. 'Don't ask! Waiting for the "Tart's Express". Last train back to Wales. Poor little things! Someone's daughter, every one of them. Someone's mother too, half of them, though they hardly look old enough to be out of school. You got to feel for them.'

Billy took another look at Mary Hughes, now giggling with the other girls and showing them the money Elsie had given her. He certainly felt for her. Just not, he was pretty sure, in quite the way Keenan had meant.

Both Billy and Akaash had volunteered to work on Christmas Day and to be rostered for fire-watching duties on Christmas night. Accordingly, the celebrations at No. 23 were brought forward to the 24th of December. There had been some discussion during the preceding weeks about precisely what was going to happen. Inevitably there were disagreements. Three issues in particular proved fraught: the first had been raised by Billy a couple of weeks earlier.

'They want us to be the three kings,' he announced proudly over breakfast one morning. 'I'm not too sure precisely who they are,' he admitted. 'But it's nice to be involved in these things, isn't it?' he added when there was no response.

'Never heard of them,' said Akaash dismissively. 'Anyway, why do they want us to do it?'

'*We Three Kings…*' sang Vincent. 'No?… *from Orient are*?' he continued. '*Bearing gifts, we traverse afar*?'

'Oh no! Absolutely not.'

'Why not? It's for the Works' kids' party.'

'It's degrading and patronising, that's why not.'

'Is it?' wondered Vincent. 'What about us being proud of where we come from?'

'Strangely I don't expect the Magi traversed all the way from India.'

'Thought you'd never heard of them?'

'I went to a Catholic-run school,' said Akaash. 'Of course I've heard of them.'

'Then you'll know that one was from Arabia, one from Persia and one from India. So there.'

'Except they're make-believe.'

'Well, I'm happy to do it,' said Billy.

'You would be,' sneered Akaash. 'You won't even need to dress up. Just wear that stupid uniform of yours.'

'Mr Hartshorne is going to be Santa Claus,' interjected Vincent before Billy could react.

'Christian theology has clearly moved on since I left school,' said Akaash, starting to enjoy himself. 'Father Christmas and the three kings appeared together on Christmas Eve?'

'Very funny,' said Vincent. 'Fine, don't do it. I heard the Yanks were going to do it anyway. Happy to, in fact. Three of their sergeants will black up. You know, like minstrels? Al Jolson?'

'That sounds truly awful,' said Akaash.

'Apparently they're hilarious. As good as the Three Stooges, they say.'

'Who are they?'

'Who cares?' said Billy. 'You're not going to do it anyway. And a little bit less lip about my uniform if you don't mind.'

Akaash finally put aside yesterday's newspaper. 'Well, I'd sooner we do it than a bunch of blacked-up Yankees. As railwaymen, I mean. I'm sure Mrs A can run us up costumes out of some old curtains or something.'

'I think she's got more than enough to do,' said Vincent, prompting a grin from the other two at the speed with which he had leapt to her defence. 'We're not the children here. We can sort something out. But I heard the Americans are also bringing along gifts for the kiddies.'

'Well, we'll do that instead,' said Akaash airily. 'Or at least, he will,' he concluded with a nod in Billy's direction.

'I'm sure the Durbar will be delighted,' said Billy, still smarting from the crack about his uniform. 'I suppose any show of appreciation from you would be too much to ask for?'

'Well, it's not as if it's really their money, is it?'

Fortuitously, the Works hooter sounded, ending further debate.

The next bone of contention was discussed three days later over beers at the Queen's Tap: Christmas presents at No. 23.

Vincent, without much hope of success, begged Billy not to go over the top. It wasn't fair and it would spoil things for everyone, Mrs A in particular, he insisted. Billy, desperate to end the conversation before Vincent found it necessary to remind him yet again of the debacle of the 'Deluge', assured them both he'd learnt his lesson and restraint would be his star above the stable. Having had only a patchy exposure to Christianity, the details of the Christmas story was pretty much new to him and he took great pleasure in including references to it in conversation wherever possible.

Akaash announced that he would not be buying presents because he didn't believe in celebrating religious festivals and, in any case, he couldn't afford to. However, as a gesture of goodwill, he was happy to announce that after considerable reflection he had decided that he would suspend his hunger strike for the festive period.

Unfortunately he made this declaration just as Billy was finishing his drink, a fair bit of which ended up sprayed over the table as a result of the coughing fit it provoked. 'That's a gesture of goodwill? To us? I'm overwhelmed,' croaked Billy as he wiped his mouth and chin with a handkerchief.

The final issue was midnight Mass, which they discussed as Sally put out their evening meal. Vincent explained that it was a tradition and that he would be going to Christchurch with Sally for the service. Billy said he'd be happy to come along. Akaash shook his head.

'Come on!' urged Billy. 'It's about being part of a community. Isn't that what you communists are meant to believe in?'

'I'm not going into a church.'

'Why not? If you don't believe in God why does it matter? Christmas is a time to be with friends and family.'

Vincent raised a doubting eyebrow.

'It's not the church I have a problem with. It's…the graveyard all around it.' He tried but failed to disguise a shudder of disgust. 'All those corpses, slowly rotting in the ground all around you…'

Sally let out a small sob and left the room.

'You really are a thoughtless prick,' said Billy as the door closed behind her.

'And that is an example of the pot calling the kettle black,' observed Vincent. 'Unusually, however, the pot is right. You are a thoughtless prick.'

'What?'

'Her daughter? Her only child? Buried at Christchurch?'

'Oh, sorry. It didn't occur to me.'

'For an intellectual it's surprising how little seems to occur to you,' said Vincent.

'You should come, if for no other reason, just to make it up to her,' insisted Billy.

'I couldn't. To walk among all those graves… I just don't understand how people can do that.'

'I thought you were an atheist?'

'He is,' sighed Vincent, rising from the table. 'A Hindu atheist. And, as you correctly observed, a prick. Put the kettle on and I'll take Mrs A a cup of tea.'

On Christmas Eve morning they opened their gifts with one another. There was also, much to Sally's surprise, a bottle of wine left on the doorstep from Ernie next door. She had knitted balaclavas for Akaash and Billy – 'For the fire-watching,' she explained – and a scarf for Vincent. Billy seemed to have heeded Vincent's pleas and been uncharacteristically restrained in his present buying – there was a new notebook for Vincent and a pair of socks for Akaash. However, whilst all other gifts were wrapped in brown paper or newsprint and tied up with string, his were packaged in paper decorated with holly and candles – paper which Sally leapt on, smoothed out and folded up carefully as soon as it was stripped from their gifts – bound with red ribbon in bows and neatly labelled. On Vincent's, Billy had written 'Something for the man who checks everything', and on Akaash's, 'Socks always come in handy', which prompted a raised eyebrow from the recipient.

His gift to Sally was a shawl, deep purple with a pattern of flowers and leaves, finely embroidered in gold thread. She was stunned by its lightness, beauty and colour. 'It's really nothing very special,' he assured her, studiously avoiding Vincent's suspicious glare when she thanked him, the shawl wrapped round her shoulders as she turned this way and that to view it from different angles in the mirror over the fireplace. 'I think it's the loveliest thing I've ever seen!' she sighed. 'But I can't accept it. Our Derek…'

'Is fighting for a world where his wife can enjoy nice things,' concluded Vincent. 'It suits you.' With another hard stare at Billy he slid his own gift for her – a scarf from McIlroys on Regent Street that he'd spent hours selecting and which had required a disproportionate number of the clothing points on his ration card – under his chair. 'Now for mine. It's a joint gift. For the two of you. Mrs A, yours will follow...'

He placed a cardboard box before them on the floor. Akaash reached down and opened it. Inside were a range of jars of various shapes and sizes with labels in Hindi. Indian pickles – brinjal, mango and lime. There was a small box of peppercorns, paper bags containing a root of ginger and two garlic bulbs. Finally, there was a masala dabba – a round stainless steel box containing in the six highly polished cups within, coriander seeds, cumin, chilli powder, turmeric, cloves and cardamom.

'Where on earth did you get all this!' cried Billy, inhaling the aromas of home with eyes closed and a deeply satisfied smile.

'Some in Cardiff, most in Bristol. There's quite a few Indians living around the docks in both cities. Some have been there for generations.'

Billy shook his head in wonder. Akaash held the dabba out to Sally, who regarded it with deep suspicion and sniffed warily at the spices within. 'I'm not sure I'd ever have the first idea what to do with that lot!' she warned, wrinkling up her nose. 'I've no clue what any of these are.'

Billy studied the various spices. 'Well, I think this one is, um, haldi,' he ventured. 'Or maybe it's garam masala...anyway, don't you worry your head about it, Mrs A. One of us will just have to learn how to cook.'

'I know how to cook,' said Akaash. 'And that's jeera. Cumin.'

'You never mentioned you can cook!'

Akaash shrugged. 'You never asked. Of course I can cook. We don't all have servants.'

'So we could have been eating desi food all this time? Vincent could have got these ages ago. You could have cooked…'

'No squabbling on Christmas!' interrupted Sally, the shawl still draped over her shoulders. 'Honestly, you're worse than kids! Vincent, come and help me get the dinner ready. You boys lay the table. You need to be at the Mechanics Institute by three. We'll try a drop of Mr Norris's wine with our dinner,' she added unenthusiastically. 'And someone needs to think about what we can give him in return.'

'Not to worry, Mrs A. I'm sure I can find a little something for him,' Billy assured her.

'I'm sure you bloody well can,' muttered Vincent irritably.

'What's that supposed to mean?' Billy asked as Sally left the room.

'You know perfectly well. What did I say about showing off? How much did that shawl cost you?'

Billy shrugged. 'Nothing.'

'It looks bloody expensive to me.'

'I would certainly hope it is. I've got another five of them to hand out as gifts from Gwalior State. Suppose I should have mentioned that. Wouldn't want her getting the wrong idea, would we? And all being well, the delectable Lady Jessica will be getting hers, if you'll excuse the expression, in the New Year.'

'Can I have one to give to Cyn?' asked Akaash hopefully.

'Absolutely not. Anyway, I thought you didn't believe in presents at Christmas.'

'It's paying for them he doesn't believe in,' said Vincent. 'Dare we risk a glass of Ernie's special?' He picked up the brown bottle and looked at the gummed label. 'Dandelion. Isn't that a weed?'

They uncorked the bottle and poured three glasses. Sally came in to join them, declining the wine but agreeing to join them for a pre-lunch toast with a small sherry.

'Well, here's to…' began Vincent.

'Peace,' offered Sally.

'Freedom,' suggested Akaash.

'Not getting dandelion poisoning?' proposed Billy.

'Us,' said Vincent. 'And safe returns.'

Lunch – a rabbit, roast potatoes and veg followed by a heavy, doughy pudding – was concluded in good time for them to make it to the Mechanics Institute with their costumes and bags of small gifts. Despite Vincent's protests, Sally had ended up cutting and stitching costumes for them out of offcuts of seat coverings from the Carriage and Wagon side provided by Cyn's father, supplemented with discarded curtains and end-of-roll stock from McKilroy's. Accordingly, they were swathed in upholstery fabric in GWR colours, floral prints and chintz, wrapped around with threadbare red velvet cummerbunds and topped off with golden turbans. They were in costume well before the audience, or even Father Christmas, arrived. With time on their hands, they decided on a few extra touches: Billy curled up the ends of his moustache and Akaash, who – to his own and others' surprise had got quite into the swing of things – had borrowed a cloak from Joan and had even acquired some wax crayons, suggested they make up their faces with the crayons to heighten the dramatic effect of their appearance on stage.

Their entrance was to be cued by Hartshorne, as Santa, looking into his sack and announcing sadly that Adolf had stolen all the children's presents. As the chorus of enthusiastic booing subsided, they were to slowly march in bearing, if not gold, frankincense and myrrh, a gross of Cadbury's Dairy Milk chocolate bars that Lockyer had acquired and dispatched to Billy a few days earlier. Much cheering. Lots of laughter. Sweeties for all the kids and a subsequent trip, still in costume and character, to the children's ward of the Medical Fund Hospital for a similar routine.

All seemed set for a thoroughly enjoyable afternoon.

Unfortunately, no one had thought to let the US Army know that their Magi was no longer required. The American Balthasar, Melchior and Gaspar duly appeared, accompanied by a dozen soldiers carrying musical instruments, three nurses from the newly constructed US Military Hospital in Bath and a staggering amount of merchandise including – somewhat surprisingly, this being a children's party – several cartons of cigarettes, lipsticks, dozens of pairs of nylon stockings and even a box of Havana cigars.

Billy realised that a difficult conversation was clearly about to happen, which, he thought as he turned to the new arrivals, would have been better engaged upon without them being discovered by the GIs carefully applying make-up to one another's faces.

'Can I help you?' Billy asked in his most disdainful tone.

'Uh, we're da Three Kings?' offered one of the sergeants in a thick Brooklyn accent.

Billy looked around exaggeratedly at Vincent and Akaash. 'Clearly not. *We* are the Three Kings.'

'We're from the US Army?' said the sergeant, slowly, clearly hoping carefully enunciating every word might aid comprehension.

'And we,' chipped in Akaash, 'from the Orient are.'

'Could I just have a word in private with my colleagues?' asked Vincent. 'Have you seen the stuff they've brought with them?' he hissed to the other two as the Americans withdrew.

'So?'

'So, no one's going to be very pleased with us if we stand between them and all that Yankee largesse.'

'Well, they can't just come swanning in here acting like they own the place,' protested Akaash.

'You didn't even want to do this,' Billy reminded him.

'Well, I do now. It's a matter of national pride.'

'What, being dressed up in a pair of curtains and a woman's cloak pretending to be from Persia?'

'You may choose to characterise it so. I see it as presenting a positive image of my country. And I'm Gaspar, by the way. The one from India. A nation that will not be pushed about just because others are bigger and richer.'

'Who appointed you Gaspar?'

'No one. I am a self-proclaimed Gaspar.'

'Why don't we see if there's scope for a compromise?' suggested Vincent, feeling, not for the first time, like the only adult present.

There was – albeit an uncomfortable one reached only after considerable and at times acrimonious debate. The Indians would still be the Magi, but one of the sergeants would accompany each of them on to stage bearing the gifts. After an initial reluctance, the Americans became quite taken by the idea of their changed roles. Indeed, if they did so as slaves, they observed brightly, they could still black up. Seeing lots of comic opportunities ahead, they immediately started improvising strutting cakewalk routines full of 'Lawdy Lawdy, Massa', hand-waving and eye-rolling, perhaps even a chorus of 'Mammy'? Yes, they thought, that might work. After all, the whole 'I'd walk a million miles' shtick would fit real well…

Vincent politely suggested that being viziers to their kings, sans slap and slapstick, would allow them to utilise the costumes they'd brought along and might be somewhat more dignified. The latter part of this argument cut little ice with the three would-be comedians, dignity not being an aspiration of any performance they envisaged. However, when Vincent added that the sing-song they wanted to lead and their subsequent dance routine would be much funnier to a British audience in the characters he had suggested, they were persuaded and began changing into costume. They tried excruciatingly bad comic Indian accents – wholly indifferent to the presence of three real Indians – and insisted on first names and beers later, overall acting as if they were the Indians' new best friends.

'Can I also be a snake charmer?' one asked hopefully.

'If you like,' sighed Vincent.

'If I find a basket, could ya put a green sock on yuh hand and be mah snake?'

'Not in a thousand years.'

The other soldiers who had come with them were a swing band. The nurses were Andrews Sisters impersonators. Together they brought to the event a touch of glitz and glamour that even with the best will in the world would otherwise have been sorely lacking. The three sergeants were indeed funny. Some of the references in their jokes were lost on an audience mainly comprised of children under ten years old but they went down well with the accompanying adults, and everyone enjoyed their final pie-in-the-face routine. The band were more than competent musicians and when the trio of nurses gave a spirited rendition of 'Boogie-woogie Bugle Boy of Company B' everyone was on their feet to cheer and clap. Father Christmas's empty sack was more than replenished with Hershey bars and chewing gum as well as the Gwalior State-funded bars of Cadbury's Dairy Milk. The event ended with Robinson's squash and sticky buns served at trestle tables by the Women's Institute, led by Lady Jessica, who ignored Billy's attempt to catch her eye. The children, slightly overawed, silently tucked into the accompaniment of most of the swing band, who remained in the hall playing carols.

Santa, the three nurses, the Magi, their viziers and two trombonists traversed not very afar around the corner to the

Medical Fund Hospital. Dr Falk, in white coat and party hat, awaited them at the front doors. She led them through to the ward that, reeking of disinfectant, reflected Victorian belief in the health-giving properties of sunlight and fresh air in its wide windows and high ceiling. The spartan, barrack-like space was brightened by paper chains looping from one dangling light to the next. In big metal-framed beds nine youngsters too poorly to be allowed home for Christmas lay, propped up on pillows.

The nurses sat on the children's beds, played I-spy and Simon Says. The trombonists played 'Merrie Melodies' tunes. One of the sergeants performed some sleight-of-hand magic, with disappearing coins magically produced from an amazed child's ear. Another juggled whilst the third quietly handed Dr Falk a package of toiletries and stockings.

'From the colonel,' he confided. 'To say a little thank you for looking after our boys when, you know…'

Dr Falk looked longingly at the box of wonders. Luxuries so long out of the shops that they were almost things of myth. She reached out and touched the nylons. Even the packaging seemed almost decadent in its extravagant use of paper, card and cellophane. She was briefly, sorely tempted. Then she shook her head sadly and withdrew her hand.

'I'm sorry, it's very kind of the colonel, but I was just doing my job. I can't accept this.'

She was aware of a heavy presence at her shoulder. Mrs Richards, the hospital pharmacist sighed theatrically, clearly less than impressed by this display of professional ethics and personal morality.

'No one needs to know…' suggested the American.

Mrs Richards cleared her throat pointedly and muttered something about gift horses.

'I'd know,' said Dr Falk, trying to ignore her.

'The colonel's gonna be real upset.'

Mrs Richards harrumphed.

'What *is* it?' snapped Dr Falk, turning on her.

Wordlessly, the pharmacist handed her a list of items the pharmacy lacked. 'Oh, good thinking, Mrs R!' cried the doctor. 'Could you help us out with some of these?' she asked, glancing at the list and handing it over.

'Consider it done,' said the relieved sergeant.

As the last hour of Christmas Eve ticked away, Vincent and Billy, faces glowing in part from an afternoon well spent but in larger part from the abrasive scrubbing required to remove their wax make-up, accompanied Sally to Christchurch for midnight Mass. It was a dry, cold night and their breath formed clouds as they walked past the old brickworks and began the climb up Cricklade St. Others were heading in the same direction and down from Old Town. In the dark, there was silence. Sally carried a sprig of holly with a small bow of red ribbon from Billy's gift-wrapping tied to it, which she placed on her daughter's grave. The three of them stood in silence for a moment. Then, with a tight little smile, she nodded and they made their way into the dimly lit church.

'Aye, aye,' a voice called out as they entered the church, 'Here come Wilson, Keppel and Betty!'

There were a few suppressed chuckles. Billy grinned, mystified but quite content to be the butt of whatever joke this was. Vincent, presuming an insult, bristled and glanced at Sally. Seeing her blush slightly and laugh, he caught Billy's eye, shrugged and smiled too.

The vicar welcomed the large congregation, promised them something to remember and introduced the first carol, 'Once in Royal David's City'. The old building filled with enthusiastic voices. Off-tune, ill-timed but spirited and, to Vincent, deeply moving. For the first time, anywhere, he had felt a stirring of a kinship and almost a homecoming and this service seemed to encapsulate that feeling of unexpected security. He was secretly deeply moved by the fact that both Billy and Lapworth had decided to confide in him the pressures put upon them to report on him. There was Lapworth, three rows further forward, sharing his hymn book with the man he lived with, who he invariably introduced as his cousin. There was Billy, frowning down at the hymnal and trying unsuccessfully to keep up and in time. Vincent would never have thought that he could feel such a powerful sense of ease, with himself or his surroundings. It was as odd as it was unexpected for him, far from home and community. He was with people who, for all their faults, he was convinced would stand by him, as he would them. He was sharing a hymn book with Sally, both comfortable as only lovers or dancers could be, with bodies in such close proximity that they almost touched, each holding one side of the book even though neither of them needed to glance at it to be able to sing the words.

As the carol ended, there was the usual shuffling of feet, wet coughing and clearing of throats. Sally, standing between Billy and Vincent, noticed a movement to the left and turned to see, easing in to the pew beside Billy, a trembling Akaash, eyes wide and clearly having passed through a dozen nightmares to make it through the graveyard and into the church. Her eyes filled with tears and she reached across in front of Billy to grasp his icy cold hands. 'Thank you,' she mouthed. 'Thank you.'

After two more carols, the vicar climbed into the pulpit, checked his watch and with a huge grin nodded to a church warden, who gave a thumbs up and half ran down the aisle to the tower. Uncertainly at first, ragged and discordant, Christchurch's peal of ten bells sounded across the town. The timing was rough and changes clumsy, but to those in the church it was the most beautiful series of chimes they would ever hear, for it rang out not merely to celebrate the birth of Christ but in confidence of the passing of dread threat. Since war had been declared four long years earlier, the sounding of church bells had been prohibited except to announce the arrival of the Germans. As the bells rang, it was as though the very sound of the word 'invasion' itself was transformed from being redolent with terror to resounding with hope, liberating and triumphant. The gathered worshippers turned to one another and in a very un-British display of emotion, embraced and wept with sheer joy.

'There. That wasn't so hard, was it?' sniffed Billy to Akaash as he blew his nose and wiped back a tear himself.

'Never, ever again,' sighed Akaash, as he shook hands and shared season's greetings with those in the pew in front of them. 'Happy blooming Christmas, bloodsucker.'

Billy laughed and slapped him on the shoulder. 'Happy blooming Christmas, arsehole.'

All three worked – at least on paper – on Christmas Day, and covered fire-watching duties overnight too. The atmosphere in the Works, running at staffing levels just sufficient to keep furnaces burning, equipment maintained and emergencies avoided, was quite different from the noise and activity of a normal working day. Those in spent most of the day smoking and chatting – Management, office staff and foremen being very thin on the ground. In Shop V the few boilermakers and turners present ran a card school most of the afternoon and in Shop T there was a rat-catching competition between a group of apprentice brass finishers with a sweepstake on the side.

Fire-watching was taken a little more seriously. Christmas bombing raids weren't unknown – Manchester had suffered very badly a couple of Christmases earlier, but given the lack of enemy attention Swindon had attracted to date, no one seriously expected the fire-watchers to have to do anything much more than keep each other awake and while away the hours. And so it proved to be.

It was Boxing Day when the long-awaited and eagerly anticipated attempt at Indian food took place. With their meat ration already used up, Sally found them some anonymous white fish that was available on the points system. Akaash proved to be a very competent cook and the fish curry he prepared left them all deeply satisfied.

Sally tried a little out of politeness and said it was lovely, but was clearly deeply suspicious of the range of foreign seeds and powders involved in its preparation and distrustful of any fish that ended up quite that colour. After they'd finished, Sally shooed them out to the pub or the Mechanics Institute and opened all the windows in the house in spite of the cold. She even tried squirting the last of her Lilly of the Valley perfume around, but with little effect.

The next day, *Birkenhead* and *Sir Stafford* joined *Tremayne* in running as ghost trains. As the Shop B teams got back into their stride they were delighted to hear that three more Bulldogs had been located and were on their way. Vincent and Lapworth worked on a list of priority routes to be built up. The suggestions Phyl, Akaash and Joan had put forward for an increase in fake radio traffic were formally accepted and their section promptly wound up. Phyl had not returned after Christmas Day and failed to respond to any messages either from Akaash directly or dispatched via Joan. The remaining two of the team were tasked with introducing and checking the effectiveness of the system that they had proposed.

It looked as though their time in Swindon would soon be coming to an end, and a successful end at that. Vincent could see little need for him to remain but found himself strangely ambivalent about the prospect of returning to the place, to himself at least, he no longer called home. Akaash was happy to stay, for he was earning good money that was desperately needed back home, but he would be perfectly willing to be sent back to India. He was missing Cal, suffering badly from the damp and the dark and very conscious that his role in politics and his academic career were both on hold as long as he remained away.

Billy was determined to stay as long as he could. Whilst he had no doubt that he would at some point be returning to his old role in Gwalior, he was now very aware of how parochial it had been and how unchallenging it would all seem after this experience. Every additional Bulldog found was a cause of celebration as it meant another reason to delay. He was expecting daily to receive an invitation to resume 'riding to hounds' with Lady Jessica and all in all was enjoying the whole experience immensely.

They were all learning a great deal, and it was such a lovely, quiet, easygoing sort of place. Well, except for the occasional flap with visiting Yanks, of course. Otherwise everyone seemed to get on, mind their own business and do their bit.

On the 29th of December, Akaash took a couple of days off to speak at some more meetings in Oxford that Joan had arranged. Whilst there he thought he'd carry on up to London and drop in on Phyl to check if she was all right. He'd got her address from Joan, who had also been surprised and troubled by her sudden absence and complete silence.

It had begun to snow as Billy and Vincent returned to No. 23 after work. There was word that the German battleship *Scharnhorst* had been sunk and they chatted about the implications of the event. They were easier with one another than at any time since their arrival, even sharing a joke about their performance as the three kings. But once they got back to No. 23 it was obvious something was seriously wrong. They tried to use their keys to open the front door, but it was bolted on the inside. They knocked, and when it was finally opened, an angry man in crumpled khaki stood scowling at them.

'Sergeant Atkinson?' Billy asked, offering his hand.

Derek Atkinson thrust his hands deliberately into the pockets of his trousers. He was dangerously, furiously angry, glaring at them as if he wanted them dead. His unshaven face was flushed and they could smell the beer on his breath as he snarled, 'Your bags are packed.' He jerked his head to the left and over his shoulder. Billy could see their suitcases lined up in the hallway. Atkinson turned, grabbed each case one after the other and threw them out of the door at them. 'Now sling your hook.'

Sally came through from the kitchen, her eyes red with crying and an ugly red mark on the side of her face. 'I'm so sorry. It's just that…'

'Shut your mouth!' Derek snapped. 'I told you to stay in the kitchen. Go back inside.'

'What's the problem here?' Vincent asked.

'The problem, you little turd? I'll tell you what the problem is. I won't have your sort in my house, stinking the place out with your filthy foreign food. That's the fucking problem. My mates in the first battalion are out there in your shithole country fighting to keep you all safe, and you know who they're being shot at and killed by? The Japs? Yeah, you'd think that, wouldn't you? 'Sept it's not. It's you lot! Fighting for the Japs! So you clear off out of here, you fucking traitors. If I see you near my house or speaking to my missus ever again, I swear to God I'll swing for you!'

He slammed the door. They could hear him shouting at Sally. She was shouting back. A door slammed. She was sobbing. Silence, then something that sounded horribly like a slap. Vincent pushed past Billy and was about to pound on the door when Billy grabbed his arm. Vincent turned on him. 'You're willing to let that bastard knock her about? Well, I'm not.'

'Just stop and think for a moment,' said Billy. 'Look around.'

Already several people had come into the street, or were standing on their doorsteps watching, silent and concerned. An elderly man walking his dog gave them a hard stare and then hurried on. In several windows in the houses opposite, net curtains were pulled back so that others could catch a glimpse of what was going on. A young mother came out, stared anxiously at them, and then shepherded her two children who had been playing in the street back into their house. With a final, fearful glance over her shoulder, she firmly shut her front door.

'This is his wife, his house, his country,' Billy said sadly. 'We're just visitors. Remember how they turned on Akaash when he got involved in their rows? All we can do right now is make things worse. For her. Let's get out of here and try to work out what to do.'

Ernie Norris was standing at his door, watching them. 'Grab them bags and come in here,' he said gruffly. 'That Derek Atkinson always was a cunt.'

They followed Ernie into his house. In layout it was a mirror image of No. 23 but in detail and atmosphere it could hardly have been more different. It was dingy and had a musty smell. Not unpleasant, but heavy and all-pervasive – as though the whole place needed all the windows thrown open and the curtains pulled back to be flooded with light and fresh air.

'Isn't there anything anyone can do?' asked Vincent desperately.

Ernie shook his head. 'Englishman's home is his castle. Can't interfere in a domestic. No one can. These things are between man and wife.'

They dumped their bags in the hallway and followed Ernie into the front room. Whereas next door it was the pride of the house, kept neat and clean for entertaining visitors, here it was clearly the room Ernie spent most of his time in. Newspapers were spread on the floor and there was a cup and saucer on a small table. They saw two armchairs, one of which showed significant signs of wear and tear. Above the dusty, cluttered mantelpiece hung a cheap copy of *The Hay Wain*. The large window of the room looking out to the street was covered by a dusty net curtain. A row of small terracotta pots were lined up on the windowsill, each containing a seedling carefully marked with the name of the plant neatly printed on a little flat wooden stick. By the window was a folding table and two dining chairs. Ernie told them to sit down and left them there. They could hear the back door opening. Through the wall, they could hear the shouting continue. Vincent sat hunched up, clearly deeply tormented by the sound and their inability to do anything.

Ernie returned with a couple of bottles and three teacups. He placed the bottles on the dining table, uncorked one and poured out the contents. He handed a cup to each of them. 'Happy days,' he said, raising his glass as a loud thump could be heard on the connecting wall with No. 23. Ernie sighed, put down his glass and told them to stay where they were. He went around to the front door of No. 23 and banged his fist on it. 'Atkinson? Keep the fucking noise down or you and I will be having words. You hear me? Or maybe I should just call the law?'

He returned and picked up his glass. Things quietened down next door.

'I thought you said no one can interfere in a domestic matter in this country?' said Billy.

'That's right,' agreed Ernie.

'So why did the threat of the police make him stop?'

'Well, a husband can knock seven bells out of his wife in his own house and no one can do anything about it. But he can't disturb the neighbours. So if he shouts too loudly or she screams too much when he takes his belt to her, the police pop round and tell them to keep it down.'

'That's barbaric.'

'Says the man from the country where they burn widows alive. And if I know Derek Atkinson, he won't be that keen to see the police. I noticed he's lost his sergeant's stripes. I wouldn't be at all surprised if he's gone AWOL again.'

'AWOL?'

'Absent Without Leave. What do you think of the wine? Potato peelings. 1942. Not sure it's totally successful, but after another year or two, who knows?' As they sipped, they heard the back door slam next door and an explosive curse from Derek Atkinson.

Ernie went through to the kitchen and looked out of the window. 'Seems to be pissing on a piece of cloth now…'

'We really can't do anything more?' said Vincent, almost pleading.

'Well, you can think about where you're going to live for starters. You sitting here listening to them going at it next door isn't going to do any of us any good. Why don't you go to the Tap and let things settle down a bit? You can leave your bags here.'

A night of reflective drinking at the Tap did nothing to improve their mood but did at least evince several offers of temporary accommodation. Billy, never short of money and ever willing to spend it, suggested they both take rooms at the Goddard Arms. Vincent nodded, thanked him absently, said he'd meet him there later. Billy hired the station taxi to collect their bags from Ernie's and take them up to the hotel. Vincent went for a walk to clear his mind.

It was well past midnight. The snow hadn't even settled and it had turned into a clear, dry night. Vincent had walked for several hours around a closed-up and blacked-out Swindon. He went up Victoria Hill into Old Town, along Bath Road, down Kingshill and across fields and marshy open land, then back along the side of the single-track railway line from Cricklade to a dark and deserted Old Town station, where he sat awhile on a bench, looking up at the moon and wondering what to do. His normally immaculate clothes were muddied and his hands scratched with brambles. He felt as crumpled and soiled as he probably looked, he reflected. Like a tramp, a homeless, weak and embittered outsider, forever squinting through windows and peeping into doorways. An observer of other lives being played out. A person without worth in the eyes of both society and himself.

Almost without conscious effort on his part, his solitary wanderings took him back to Ashton St and the Atkinsons's front door. He had no idea what he was going to do. He had no idea what was going to happen next. He just knew that there was nowhere else he should, or could, be.

He raised his hand to knock, then changed his mind and tried the door. It was unlocked. He eased himself into a darkened hall that was all too briefly a haven and a home but now once more foreign and alien territory. He could hear sobbing and saw light under the kitchen door. He pushed the door open. Sally sat at the kitchen table, hunched over and curled forward, her arms wrapped around herself like she wanted to roll up into a ball, to make herself insignificant and not the target of any more of her husband's curses and blows. He stood over her, glowering down at her.

Derek Atkinson turned, seemingly unsurprised to see Vincent. 'Well, well, well. Look what the cat's dragged in! Is it right what I hear?' he snarled, his voice slurred with drink and his face flushed with rage. 'You been walking out with my wife?'

'We only went to church, Derek,' Sally pleaded.

Atkinson spun round, reached over and grabbed her chin, forcing her face up to look at him. 'Didn't I tell you to keep it shut? What is wrong with you? You like a good slapping?' With his other hand he reached back, lining up the blow she knew would follow even before she'd opened her mouth to speak.

'Don't,' said Vincent.

'I beg your fucking pardon?' said Derek, with an amazed half-laugh. 'Are you serious?'

'Yes,' said Vincent, even though he was quaking inside, massively intimidated by this brute of a man and with absolutely no idea what he was going to do next.

Derek looked down at his wife, shook his head and loosened the grip on her chin. 'First, I'm gonna sort out your lover boy here. Then I'm going to make you sorry you let him come sniffing around you like the whore you are. Why didn't you just die when the kid did?'

He turned back towards Vincent, rolled his shoulders, flexed the fingers of his hands and tilted his head first to one side, then the other. He sighed. 'Come on, then. Come to daddy. I've always wanted to take one of you lot apart.'

Vincent stood very, very still. A lifetime of slights and insults, of doubts and misgivings seemed to coalesce and then simply evaporate within him. He could almost feel it happening. He was pretty sure he was going to die and yet suddenly there was no fear. Just the absolute certainty that whatever happened now, he wouldn't cringe, he wouldn't cower and he wouldn't beg. And he most certainly wasn't going to run.

Derek took two paces towards Vincent but the calm he now saw gave him pause. As he hesitated, his wife swung a frying pan at the back of his head, sending him stumbling forward. Vincent realised he had only the briefest of moments to make full use of his fleeting advantage. As Derek crouched to avoid a further blow and reached up to feel the back of his skull, Vincent grabbed his head in both hands and brought it crashing down, aiming for the kitchen table. Derek tried to dodge sideways. As a result, the impact was not on the surface of the table as Vincent had intended but the corner, which stove in the right temple of Derek's head. Without a sound, he folded up and fell at Vincent's feet.

Vincent dropped to feel for a pulse. To find any sign of life. He crouched down, muttering a prayer, listened for any breath, feeling desperately for any sign of a pulse. Nothing. 'I've killed him,' he said quietly as he slumped back against the door. 'Sweet Jesus, I've killed him.'

'No,' said Sally, wiping her hand across her face and gulping for breath. 'I've killed him. And I'm glad. Glad he's dead and glad I did it. Get out, Vincent. Go! Get as far away as you can. This is nothing to do with you. I wish I'd done for this… pig years ago.'

Vincent rose and took a step towards her. She held up a hand. 'No! Don't come near me! Don't touch me! Go! This day was always coming. I'm just relieved it's finally here.'

Shuddering, bruised and terrified though she was, Vincent glimpsed a kernel of toughness deep inside. Beneath the surface appearance of a victim there was not just a survivor but, he suspected, a warrior.

'I'm not leaving you to face this alone. Or to take the blame. I did it and it's my responsibility.'

Both jumped at the sound of a knock at the front door. Sally started to push Vincent towards the back door but he took her in his arms and held her for a moment. He could feel her heart beating and the trembling that shook through her body. It reminded him of a time he had picked up a terrified, exhausted bird. 'Stay calm,' he whispered. 'Stay quiet. Wait.'

'Sergeant Atkinson?' the voice outside shouted. 'I don't want any trouble. I'm just looking for my friend Mr Rosario. Is he in there?'

Vincent let out a long sigh. It was Billy. He couldn't help but think that it was typical of the man that in an effort to be helpful he would loudly announce those present at a murder scene to the whole world.

'Go,' said Vincent. 'Let him in. I'm not going anywhere and nor will he, so the sooner we stop him banging and shouting the better.'

He realised he was still holding Sally and released her with an embarrassed shrug. She nodded, sniffed, clearly trying to be brave, and went to open the door. Billy stepped in and surveyed the scene in the kitchen.

'Fuck!' he said, adding an apology for his language to Sally. He glanced up at Vincent. 'Did you…?'

'Yes,' said Vincent.

'No,' said Sally. 'I did.'

'Is he…?'

'Yes, he is. As a doornail.'

'What do we do now?'

'I don't know,' said Vincent, suddenly feeling dizzy. He reached for a chair to steady himself. Billy reached out to give him support but Vincent shook his head. 'I'll call the police,' he said.

Billy slumped into the chair Vincent had grabbed and looked down at the crumpled body. Derek Atkinson looked a lot smaller now than he had standing in the doorway that afternoon. Funny, he thought, how death does that. 'Let's just think for a moment,' Billy said. 'This is serious. This could be murder.' He looked up at them both. 'You could both hang.'

There was a further knock. Vincent rolled his eyes. This was getting ridiculous! 'What is this?' he muttered. 'Paddington station?'

It was Ernie standing at the door, dressed in pyjama bottoms and a string vest, a greatcoat over his shoulders. 'We heard the row. Walls are paper-thin. Where is he?'

'We?'

Ernie jerked his head back. Vincent looked behind him and saw Elsie Coggins, wrapped in a dressing gown and wearing men's bedroom slippers.

'What?' said Ernie defensively.

'Nothing,' sighed Vincent. 'I don't suppose I can persuade you to just go home and forget what you might have heard?'

'Not a chance.'

'I thought not. You'd better come in. It might be better if you came through alone.'

'That's not fucking happening, either,' insisted Elsie, pushing past them both.

Ernie took her arm. 'Let me take a look first, old girl.'

'Who did for him?' Ernie asked after having stared at the body for a moment. Not for the first time Billy and Vincent were struck by his offhand attitude to violence and its aftermath.

'Me,' said both Vincent and Sally in unison.

'Do we have a plan?'

'We should go to the police,' said Vincent, but with somewhat less conviction than before.

'Well, you could do that,' said Ernie, nodding slowly as though considering the merits of the idea. 'But given you're both insisting you topped him, unless you want to swing for him together you might want to consider an alternative plan PDQ.'

'PDQ?' said Billy.

'Pretty Damned Quick.'

'Aaah. Right. Sorry.'

Elsie pushed past and stared at the body with the corners of her mouth turned down. 'The bosh,' she said simply.

Ernie looked thoughtful. 'Ooh! Could do...'

'He won't be the first little embarrassment solved that way,' Elsie added.

'True,' nodded Ernie. 'Solved and dissolved.'

Vincent and Sally looked confused. Billy knew they were talking about the boiling tank of caustic soda in Shop B. They were right: a few hours submerged at high temperature would see flesh and bone lost into a sludge in the bottom of the tank. But could they do it? Should they? He looked over at Sally and Vincent, for both of whom he suddenly felt a huge wave of affection and a strong desire to protect. They hadn't wanted, sought or deserved this. If Ernie and Elsie were willing to take the risk, he was damned if he was going to desert them in their time of greatest need.

'OK,' he said, resolved. 'I'm in. Ernie and I can get the... remains into the Works on his handcart. I've got the key to the side door of the Shop...'

'No,' said Ernie firmly, taking the key from Billy. 'You'll stay here with the women. Organise a complete scrubdown of this room. Me and Vincent here, we'll do the needful.'

'But I'm twice the strength of Vincent,' protested Billy. 'I know my way around the Shop and how to operate the bosh. I'll do it.'

'It's Vincent and me, or it don't happen,' insisted Ernie. 'And I don't need you to guide me around the Works, thank you very much. Cheeky bugger! I know them a hell of a lot better than you do. Especially after dark. Take it or leave it.'

Reluctantly, Billy agreed. Ernie looked at Vincent, who nodded his concurrence.

Ernie turned to Elsie and placed a hand on her upper arm. 'All right, old girl? Good. Now you take young Sal next door. Get a glass of the Sloe gin into her. You need to make sure she holds it together and it's best she don't see what happens now. And fetch a bottle in for us too. We're all gonna need a drink before this night's over.'

Elsie led Sally away, an arm around her shoulders, pulling the kitchen door closed behind them.

'OK, that's better. Now, either of you ever handled a dead 'un before?'

Billy shook his head.

'I'm from Bombay and I work with the Railway. Of course I've had to deal with corpses,' said Vincent, in an unnaturally high and shaky voice.

Ernie studied him, recognising the symptoms of shock. 'Hold it together, pal. Up close, fresh topped and still leaking?'

Vincent looked down and said nothing.

'Well, if he hasn't already, he's gonna shit himself. They usually do. And there may be some odd noises. But that's all to be expected as the body settles and cools. As you're about to find out, there's no bloody dignity in death. And if he's going in the bosh, we'll need every bit of metal off him. If he's got any fillings in his teeth, they're gonna need to come out. Simplest thing to do is strip him down to his underwear before he stiffens up and get to work with a pair of pliers on his mouth. What? Don't look at me like that. I didn't fucking kill him.'

Vincent and Billy gingerly started to undo buttons and unbuckle Derek's belt. Ernie shook his head. 'You two are as much use as a fart in a colander. Leave it. We'll sort it when we get him to the Works. Anyway, the sooner he's out of this house the better. I'll get dressed and bring the cart round the back. Gather up everything he brought with him. Bags. Boots. Any sign of him ever having been here tonight.'

Ernie wheeled the handcart round the block to the rear gate of No. 23 and returned with a sheet of stained tarpaulin, which he used in his back garden for suppressing weeds. Billy and Vincent carried the body out. Derek may have looked smaller in death, Billy reflected, but he felt a great deal heavier than seemed possible. Halfway down the garden they had to put him down so that Vincent could stop to get his breath. They lowered him gently, almost reverently, into the cart, much to the amusement of Ernie. 'Bit late to worry about bruising him now,' he observed. 'We're going to need some bits and pieces to put over him,' he added, nodding to the detritus of Billy's repair jobs on the outhouse cistern. 'Stick that pile of shite on top of him.'

Whilst he and Billy loaded the handcart and tried their best to secure and disguise its load, Ernie sent Vincent back into the house to fetch cigarettes. It didn't even occur to Vincent to question why as he headed off in search of a pack of Billy's Balkan Specials: Ernie was totally in charge, icy calm and clear about what to do, when to do it and how. Both Vincent and Billy felt his confidence holding back the near panic they were sure would otherwise have overwhelmed them.

With a final nod Ernie and Vincent left Billy at the back gate watching them trundle the cart down the alley. They moved along the back of the row of silent houses and out towards the street, wincing at every clatter and rattle. The town was deserted, windows dark and lights out. They saw no one and no one saw them until they reached the gate through which Ernie said it would be safest to enter the Works. There, a bored nightwatchman looked out through a barred opening in the locked gate.

'Ernie Norris! You're up and about early! You coming in?'

'That's right, Two-short. How's the missus?'

'Mustn't grumble. Not that it would make much difference if I did. What you got there? A dead body?'

Vincent almost whimpered in fear. Ernie just chuckled. 'Well done, Two-short. Right first time! Old Himmler came looking for Hess. I caught him having a go at my homemade wine.'

'Well, too much of that would finish anyone off, right enough. Shame it isn't one of those bloody Yanks you had a run-in with. Who's that with you?'

'One of the lads staying next door to me.'

'OK. He the one who helped you sort those Yanks? If he is, I'd like to shake his hand.'

'Nah. This is the one who keeps pissing off those London End twats in Movements.'

'Even better!'

Ernie nudged Vincent, who was feeling as if this conversation had been going on forever, and jerked his head towards the still-locked gate. Vincent was initially confused, but then realized what he meant. He took out a packet of cigarettes, muttering something about helping Ernie out and it being nice to do a real job for a change and offered the pack up to the grille with one cigarette protruding invitingly.

'Don't mind if I do,' said Two-short, taking the offered cigarette. On Vincent's urging, he gratefully pocketed the rest of the pack, and then unlocked the gate and let them in.

'Seriously, Ernie,' he said, lighting up and exhaling with a satisfied sigh, 'What you got there?'

'What do you care? You're meant to be stopping things coming out, not checking things going in.'

'Well, there is a war on. You two might be fifth columnists. Sneaking a bomb in or something,' Two-short reasoned.

Ernie sighed exasperatedly. 'Jesus, Two-short! Do you not think if Adolf wanted to put a bomb in here he might just get the bloody Luftwaffe to do it for him? It's just some odds and sods that have found their way Outside which shouldn't have. Word is there's a stocktaking today. It would just be better for everyone if these things weren't found missing.'

With a challenging smile and a wink at a clearly deeply scared Vincent, he held up a corner of the tarpaulin, adding, 'Want to come and have a look?'

'Nah, I trust you, Ernie. If only everyone was as straight as you, the world would be a better place. You coming out this way?'

'Dunno. Why?'

'Just that I'm off at six. So you might want to be on your way home before then. Thanks for the fags. See you later.'

'His wife suffers badly with her nerves,' said Ernie conversationally as they trundled the handcart up the slope and into the Works, heading towards Shop B.

The Works in the early hours of the morning was a very different place from the hive of activity it was during the day. A place of shadows. Empty, silent, dark and, to Vincent, deeply foreboding. The Shops and Sheds loomed over them, sinister and grim. There was a chill in the air and draughts blew along alleys and eddied around corners, occasionally causing signs to creak and doors to rattle and rasp on dry hinges. A discarded, balled-up sheet of newsprint turned lazily over. Rats scurried around the place. It was not just the cold that caused Vincent to shiver. He wanted this over and he wanted to get out of the Works and out of this town. For the first time since his arrival he felt profoundly homesick for Bombay. But first this had to be done.

'Why's he called Two-short?' he asked, as much to ease the tension as through any real desire for an answer.

'Opinions differ. Some hold it 'cos he's thick as two short planks. Others that it's 'cos he's two cards short of a full deck. Either way, the meaning's the same – he's not the brightest candle on the cake. Good enough bloke but blimey, he really is away with the fairies half the time. I blame the gas.'

Vincent was relieved to find that they'd reached Shop B. Ernie told Vincent to wait with the cart outside whilst he slipped silently in and switched on the heating system for the bosh. He came out, locking the door behind him and with a grunt started to push the cart away from Shop B and towards the Foundry.

'What are we doing?' hissed Vincent. 'I thought we were going to dump him in the caustic soda tank.'

'And as far as everyone else is concerned, that's precisely what we've done. They'll come in tomorrow and find it bubbling nicely away and, wonder of wonders, no sight of dear old Derek. But I've got a better idea. The Foundry! And best to maintain silence from now on. There'll be fire-watchers up on the roofs from here on in.'

Once inside the Foundry, warm and illuminated by the glowing firepits in the furnaces that were never extinguished, they paused as Ernie had a coughing fit. Vincent felt like he had been holding his breath ever since they'd left Shop B. He exhaled, took a deep breath and then another before asking, 'Is this why you wanted me here rather than Billy?'

'Damn right,' croaked Ernie, wiping his eyes. 'How long do you think this is all going to remain a secret? Two-short will have already forgotten seeing us but Captain Toilet Cistern? Nice enough chap but can't keep his mouth shut to save his life. Elsie's no better. Young Sal is near breaking point. I wouldn't put money on any of this staying under wraps.' He looked down at the shrouded body and smiled grimly. 'Under wraps, get it? That's why we're going to have a little insurance policy, you and me. I think you're a man who knows how to keep a secret and sure as shit sticks to a blanket I know I am. That's why it's you and me. And the winner of the bonus prize is...Derek! We're gonna give him the Swindon Works version of a Viking funeral. A lot better than melting away in the Shop B bosh. A lot better than he probably deserves, too. Let's get him prepared for his send-off. I think furnace No. 3 looks most promising...'

As they moved him, Derek let out a low moan. Vincent leapt back in horror. 'Please tell me that was one of those noises you said he'd make?'

'I'm afraid not.' Ernie stared down at the body on the handcart and shook his head slowly. 'Derek, Derek, Derek,' he murmured, sounding like a disappointed teacher. 'You've always been such a useless pillock. You couldn't even manage to get yourself properly murdered.'

'He's still alive!' cried Vincent, eyes wide.

'I noticed that. Well, we can't leave things like this, can we?' He pulled the tarpaulin away from the body, placed one hand on Derek's chin and the other on the back of his head and gave a sharp twist to the right, then to the left. There was a sickening snap and a slow, rattling exhalation from the body. 'Now *that* was one of the sounds I meant.'

Vincent turned away, heaved and vomited. Ernie sighed. 'Go and get a fire bucket and swill that into the drain. And if that made you puke, you'd better not watch this next bit.'

'What could be worse than that?' croaked Vincent, wiping the back of his hand across his mouth.

'This,' said Ernie, taking a razor from his waistcoat pocket and opening it. 'I'm gonna slit him,' he said in a matter-of-fact way. 'We don't want him exploding as he goes in. That would create a mess that would take more than a few buckets of water to wash away.'

'Wait!' cried Vincent as Ernie pulled up Derek's vest and leaned in to cut. 'Listen to me! I think I might have a better idea.'

Ernie paused. 'I'm listening.'

'I've been thinking, ever since the bosh was first mentioned. If he completely disappears, Mrs A will never be free of him. There'll always be someone looking for him.'

Ernie shrugged. 'Do we care? As long as there's no evidence…'

'But what if we could end all the doubts and suspicions and investigations, everything, right now? Tonight? A clean end. For all of us.'

'Still listening.'

'There's a ghost train heading for Newport due through here in the next thirty minutes. Suppose he was to be hit by that train?'

'That could work. We'll need to get him looking like he was out and about.'

'I've seen people after a train strike. Just get his clothes buttoned up and his boots on him.'

They set off to the tracks and laid Derek's body on the Down line. Vincent suggested that rather than placing him across the rails they lay him face down between them so that the body would be less likely to be spotted and impact hardly noticeable to the train crew. With luck the body would be dragged some distance. Ernie nodded appreciatively. 'Now we're talking!' he said as they laid the body on the sleepers.

'We're gonna have to sit here for a while to make sure the job's done properly,' Ernie grunted. 'Should have brought sandwiches… got any fags on you?'

Vincent shook his head. 'Gave them all to Two-short.'

'Well, at least someone got something out of all this. Wonder if Derek's got any.'

'You're kidding?'

'Well, he's not gonna need them, is he?' asked Ernie, as he knelt and went through Derek's pockets. 'Blimey!' he cried. 'Look at this.'

Reluctantly, Vincent joined him and looked down. Ernie held up a thick wad of banknotes. 'Maybe Two-short isn't he only one who's going home a sight better off.'

'Put it back in his pocket,' said Vincent.

'You must be out of your mind! There's a small fortune here that's gonna be spread halfway to Chippenham when that train hits him.'

'Put it back. Please.'

'Look, I'm not saying I want to keep it all. We'll share. Christ, we'll even give some to his missus too. But all this cash…'

'Exactly! All that cash. It's clearly stolen or from the black market or something: leave it on him and it guarantees no one is going to think he's been murdered. Who'd be so stupid as to leave all that money in his pockets?'

Both heard the slightest hiss of the rails. The first hint of the approaching train.

'Aaargh!' cried Ernie in exasperation after a long, agonised pause. 'All right. But I'm gonna regret this for the rest of my natural,' he added, shoving the money back into Derek's shirt pocket and carefully buttoning it up.

They leapt back from the track and crouched low as the ghost train – *Birkenhead*, Vincent automatically registered, running well – thundered past them, a long train of empty wagons rattling behind her. As the rear of the guards van disappeared from view, Ernie returned to the tracks, eager to see what remained. He turned back to Vincent. 'When you said a clean end for all of us, I'm assuming you didn't include Derek?' he said with a grin. 'I'd spare yourself too close a look. Just take my word – job done. Let's go home.'

'You almost seem like you're enjoying this,' said Vincent.

Ernie gave the cart a shove. 'People think I keep myself to myself because of the terrible things I saw in the trenches. How I suffered. That's true of a lot of blokes, but not me. I loved every minute of it! And I was bloody good at it too. Specially the night raids. Live or die, him or me, kill or be killed. I should have stayed in the army, but I had a wife and I thought I had a life back here. But I'd changed, see? I tell you, I've had more fun since you blokes arrived than I've had since the end of the last lot. You certainly do make life more interesting.'

'And Elsie?'

'What can I say? A man has needs.'

As they pushed the now empty handcart back through the Works, Ernie chuckled to himself. Vincent couldn't imagine himself laughing or even smiling ever again. He looked at Ernie in amazement.

'I was just thinking. Imagine if Derek had sat up when we were talking to Two-short! That would have made the poor bugger jump! And you! The man who checks everything! Didn't do a very good job with him, did you?' He brought the cart to a halt and nodded towards a pile of neatly stacked planks. 'I think we'll just have a little of that fine mahogany over there. Seems wrong to wheel an empty cart out of here.'

He looked around for Vincent to help him lift the wood and saw the disapproval on his face. 'What? You've confessed to a botched murder, been an accessory to one done decently, illegally disposed of a body and now you're going to be sniffy about a bit of light – bloody hell, not so light actually – pilfering? Grab hold of the other end. If it's not chained up or nailed down, it isn't theft. Anyway, I'm owed. That was a serious bit of currency you talked me into sacrificing there.'

At twenty past six the next morning, two police officers – a sergeant and a police woman – knocked at No. 23. Shown through to the front room, the policewoman sat beside Sally Atkinson, a hand on hers, whilst the sergeant informed her that it appeared that her husband, his remains identified by the documents found on the body, had been killed in a tragic accident on the railway. They asked if she had anyone she'd like to sit with her. She said she was fine. There was Mr Norris next door. They asked when she'd last seen her husband. Although Ernie had suggested that she deny Derek had ever been to the house, far too many people had seen and heard the arguments to make that a credible story. She explained that Derek had come home, been unhappy with finding the lodgers there and that there'd been 'cross words'. The police officers noticed the bruises on her face but said nothing about them. He'd been drinking, she said, and then had left about midnight. He hadn't said where he was going. That was it.

The police officers said they would probably need to speak to her paying guests. Avoiding eye contact they added there was some uncertainty about a formal identification, given the state of the body. They said they'd get back to her on that. In the meantime, there'd be a post-mortem examination later in the day. Was she sure there wasn't anyone they'd like them to fetch to sit with her?

The post-mortem was carried out that afternoon by a nervous but extremely excited Dr Falk, assisted by a US Army medical orderly – one of the trombonists who had visited the hospital on Christmas Eve and who had taken something of a shine to her. She carefully examined and described everything she saw as he, white-coated and sitting with knees up under his chin at a child's desk in the corner of the operating theatre, typed to her dictation. She listed all the injuries consistent with death as a result of having been struck by a train, noted signs of prolonged heavy drinking and, almost as a footnote, recorded a couple of inconsistencies with the otherwise seemingly obvious cause of death.

Billy and Vincent were sitting at the same table in the Queen's Tap that Akaash and Cyn had shared on the night the Americans had burst in. They were sitting in silence, waiting for Akaash to come off the Down train. They'd decided to remain at the Goddard Arms at least for a day or two, and Akaash needed to be told that he should also make alternative temporary arrangements. They'd been kicked out by Sally's husband, who had subsequently got hit by a train and killed – that was all they intended to tell him. Even as they rehearsed it, however, they were very aware how thin it sounded and how many questions this truncated version of the truth begged. Both were still numbed by what had happened. Untouched half-pint glasses of Arkell's 3Bs and an unopened pack of cards sat on the table beside the empty ashtray as they waited in silence.

Akaash burst in, nodded to various familiar faces and slumped into the empty chair. 'Phyl's pregnant,' he said.

'Really?' said Vincent, raising his glass.

'Which one is she?' asked Billy, reaching for his beer – a drink for which he alone seemed to be developing a taste – deeply relieved to be distracted from having to talk about Derek's death. 'The lanky horse-faced one or the Hindi speaker with the big tits?'

Akaash glared at him. 'The one in charge.'

'Oh, horse-face. Well, well, well. Wonder what poor bugger put that in foal.'

'Me. It's my child.'

They put their drinks down and stared at him. 'How?'

'Well, when a man and a woman really, really like each other…'

'I'm impressed you can still be such an arsehole at a time like this. I meant where? When? I didn't know you two were…'

'We weren't. We aren't. It just…happened.'

'When?'

'The first night we did fire-watching. Now, can we just stop the questions and think about what I'm going to do?'

There was another silence. Then Billy asked if he could be allowed just one more question.

'Oh, for God's sake! What?'

'Were you wearing my coat?'

'When?'

'When you did it.'

'That's your question? Yes. As a matter of fact, your coat caused it.'

'You sure? I would have thought all that man and woman liking each other stuff caused it.'

'I mean, it happened because of the coat. She'd been joking that there was room for two of us in it. She was cold. Shivering. I took off the coat and offered it to her and she suggested we wrap it around us both. Snug as a bug in a rug we'd be, she said. Then, well, one thing led to another and, that was it. Why are you looking at me like that?'

'Nothing. Just remembering a conversation about a sock. You should've used a Johnnie.'

'That's just one of a whole litany of should'ves in my life right now, starting with I should've never come to this bloody country.'

After a pause, he added, 'You know, after we'd, well, done it, she said the strangest thing.'

'Was that it?'

'No! She said "Thank you. You've just saved a life."'

'Wonder what that meant?'

'No idea.'

'What are you going to do?'

'Likewise, no idea.'

Vincent had remained silent to this point. 'Who else knows?' he asked.

'Her parents. Their family doctor. No one else.'

Billy found himself reflecting again on Dawlish's parting comment to him about Akaash but said nothing.

'How far gone is she?' asked Vincent.

'What? I don't know.'

'Shouldn't be that hard to work out, especially for a mathematician. How long ago was that night?'

'Why?'

'Because that impacts on what your options are for...well, what the options are.'

'I would never agree to anything like that. To me, all life is sacred.'

'Says the man who will be going home in a few months. Or in a few days in all probability if her father knows. Maybe the unmarried woman who's going to have to deal with that sacred life for the rest of hers might have other thoughts? Have you asked her what she wants to do?'

'She's not talking to me right now.'

'Shame your conversation wasn't curtailed earlier. Well, you need to discuss things. Can the other one, whatshername, help?'

'Joan? She doesn't know. And Phyl wants it kept quiet.' He slumped forward, his head in his hands. 'What a bloody mess.'

Billy frowned thoughtfully. 'Didn't you tell us once her dad is someone important?'

'Second from the top at the Ministry of War Transport,' mumbled Akaash.

'Should've used a Johnnie,' Billy repeated. 'I think it might not just be her you've well and truly screwed.'

'Thanks. You can always be relied on for a totally unhelpful observation. Anything interesting happen here while I was away?' Billy and Vincent looked at one another, each hoping the other might start. Vincent took a deep breath. 'Well...'

'Forget it,' said Akaash, cutting him off. 'I don't know why I bothered asking. Why is it only me that everything happens to?'

At Derek Atkinson's inquest on 2nd January the coroner was fulsome and somewhat patronising in his praise for Dr Falk's efforts and airily dismissive of her suggestion of evidence of an inconsistent, possibly earlier, blow to the deceased's head. Unspoken, but in the back of his and everyone else's mind, was the realisation that any alternative to a verdict of death by misadventure would inevitably involve some combination of the words 'War Hero', 'Deserter', 'Suicide' or 'Murder', no mix of which was likely to be in anybody's interest. The body was released for burial and a quiet funeral hastily arranged.

Given the ambivalent circumstances – a decorated hero, subsequently demoted, dying in mysterious circumstances whilst absent without leave and with an unexplained wad of cash on him – it was agreed that it would be a private funeral, without military honours but paid for by the Wiltshire Regiment. The regiment's march, 'A Farmer's Boy' was played by the organist as the coffin was borne out to the grave dug for him two rows behind his daughter's. A clutch of neighbours, Derek's mother and sister, Ernie and Elsie, a few wives of fellow soldiers – maybe in total two dozen silent mourners – stood with Sally Atkinson as her husband was laid to rest.

Vincent and Billy watched from a distance, both reliving the events of the past few days and still struggling to come to terms with how quickly and absolutely every single thing in their lives could change forever. Akaash was at the police station as Curtis had sent word that there was something he wanted to discuss with him.

After the funeral, Sally hosted the mourners to tea and biscuits in the front room of No. 23 whilst an unintentional gathering, comprising those who most disliked Derek and those most involved in his demise, congregated at the Queen's Tap. There was little said. At what was now their usual table sat Billy and Vincent. Ernie forsook the bar and sat with them – a first as far as anyone present could remember. Also present were several men who had worked unhappily with Derek prior to his call-up, Cyn's vegetarian brother, into whose mouth Derek had once crammed the remnants of a half-eaten pork pie, and even Two-short, a regular target of Derek's cruelty. All stood or sat, drinking and smoking. There was no gloating over his death, just an unspoken but palpable relief that he was now, once and for all, out of their lives.

The tallyman was also present, it being his usual time to give loans and receive instalments. He sat at his usual table but wasn't drinking. He just squatted there, still in hat and coat, arms crossed, ledger and pencil before him, waiting. Billy noticed Ernie glance across at the tallyman once or twice. He knew what the tallyman did, and also knew that a number of the Shop B women had resorted to him for loans, particularly during the strike, and that despite back pay and their best efforts several still struggled to fund weekly instalments.

Ernie nodded to himself, clearly having made up his mind about something. He got up and limped across to where the tallyman sat, and stood over him, looking down in silence. Both Vincent and Billy marvelled at how such a slightly built, crippled old man could exude such profound menace. How he could go from amiable – if always slightly edgy – company to one capable of engendering dread in others. Around the bar the few desultory conversations faded away into silence. People shuffled uncomfortably.

'Ernie…' warned Harry the landlord.

'How much is owing on Sally Atkinson's account?' Ernie asked quietly.

'That's none of your…' began the tallyman, before his last reserves of bravado evaporated. 'That's private information,

Ernie. I mean Mr Norris,' he corrected himself, removing his hat and mopping sweat from his forehead with a grimy handkerchief.

'Neither of us wants me to have to ask twice,' said Ernie, holding out his hand. The tallyman handed over his book. Ernie squinted as he flicked through the pages until he found what he was looking for. He ripped out the relevant page and handed the book back. Then, with the same smile as when he'd asked Two-short if he wanted to check what was on the trolley, he winked at Vincent and took out a roll of notes. Licking his thumb, he began counting them out. 'Enough?' he asked after a while.

The tallyman nodded.

'Good,' said Ernie, taking two more notes and putting them on the table. 'That's to ensure you never bother Sally Atkinson again. 'Cos if you do, you and I will be having words.'

The tallyman snatched up the money as if afraid Ernie was going to change his mind. 'There are far worse people than me she could have had that money from,' he grumbled.

'I don't doubt it,' said Ernie, nodding at the reasonableness of the observation. 'But there are no worse people than me to cross. Remember what I said.'

As Ernie limped back to Billy and Vincent, there was a communal exhalation of breath around the room and a sudden burst of chatter all around.

'That was a noble thing you did, Mr Norris,' said Billy, clearly impressed. He got his wallet out. 'Let me…'

'Save your money, son,' Ernie said, reaching for his drink. 'That wasn't my cash. Something her old man left me to do for him. A request you might say,' he smiled at Vincent, 'from beyond the grave.'

'Well, at least let me get the next round in,' said Billy, gathering the glasses and heading for the bar.

'That's not possible!' Vincent hissed once he was sure Billy was out of earshot. 'I saw you put that money back. They found it on him!'

'Well, maybe the man who checks everything should've checked that ALL of that gurt big wad of dosh got back into Derek's pocket. Oh, yeah, your mate's gurt big Bulldog made that impossible. Now, do you want to tell young Sal the glad tidings or shall I? Between us we've got two nasty wankers out of her life for her. Oh look! Here comes Captain Toilet Cistern with our drinks. God bless the King and confusion to his enemies!'

Akaash sat in the interview room at the police station, waiting for Curtis. He was becoming quite a regular, greeted with nods and grunts much as he was at the Works, left to find his way to the room unescorted and left to sit there unaccompanied, with the door left unlocked.

Curtis appeared after ten minutes, Akaash's file under his arm. Akaash assumed it was more for show than because Curtis thought he was likely to need to consult anything in it. 'Well, well, well! The geographic spread of people you've pissed off just grows and grows!' he said in greeting. 'You didn't tell me you were heading for the big city: you said you were off to talk to some pacifist twats in Oxford.'

'It was a spur of the moment decision.'

'Was it indeed? Well, let's not have any more of those. From now on you tell me, no, you *ask* me before you leave this lovely little town what we call home.'

'It's that…*that* we call home.'

'Of course it is. I knew that. I also knew you wouldn't be able to resist telling me so. You're becoming depressingly predictable. "What" is more poetic than "that", but then, there's no fucking poetry in your soul, is there? No humour either, come to that. Mind you, I've yet to meet a commie who does have a sense of humour. S'pose if they did they wouldn't be commies in the first place.'

'Was that what you wanted to tell me? Can I go now?'

'Coo! You're in a bad mood! No, it wasn't actually. I want to give you a little bit of advice.'

He leaned back, took out a cigarette and put it in his mouth. 'Don't worry. For later,' he said. 'Now you and me, young Bish-Bash, we're men of the world,' he began. 'Not in that poncy, gentleman-playboy sort of way that people use that expression these days. We're men of the *real* world. Christ, you're young enough to be my son, but you and me, we understand how things really work, 'cos we're politicos. Not politicians, mark you, no – sod that for a game of soldiers! Politicos. Back home, you were a politician. Back then, you lived in the two-dimensional world. Black and white. Right and wrong. Them and us. But now you've joined me in the shadows. A politico, dealing forever in shades of grey. You made that transition when you very sensibly agreed to inform – ooh, probably a poor choice of words there – let's say, keep me abreast, of the goings-on among the comrades. And people like us, we know things aren't always as neat and tidy as most people like to think and our masters like to pretend. Take your Indian mates for example: yes, I know, they're not your mates,' he said cutting off an objection from Akaash. 'Let's call them your two oppos. They think they understand things. They're older, more experienced and, cards on the table here, actually seem a lot more likeable than you are. Sorry, but there it is. Anyway, they know how systems run and machines function, but they're not like us. They're not politicos. We understand how the real world works. And it's full of inconvenient contradictions.'

'Is there a point to all of this coming any time soon?'

'You really are grumpy today! Just as well I'm feeling so mellow or I'd feel obliged to give you a slapping for that. Yes, there is a point, Dr Ray of fucking sunshine, and it's this: if some piece-of-shit deserter got himself killed by an Indian…' He held up his hand as Akaash began to speak. 'No! Keep your mouth shut. This deserter, he gets himself topped by your oppos who step in to stop him smacking his old lady about: got the idea?'

Curtis paused, sighed at the tragic nature of life and shook his head sadly. Then he looked hard at Akaash. 'Does that sound to you like a story anyone wants to hear told in an English court? No. Doesn't much to me either. But if that killing took place then it would have to be looked into, because no matter how damaging to morale and embarrassing to a nation at war, it would have to be investigated and end up before a judge and jury. After all, isn't that what we're fighting for? Truth and justice? But as one politico to another, I'm saying it's best if it never happened, don't you think? Especially after that nice coroner so briskly returned a verdict of death by misadventure. Should be the end of it.

'I'm just telling you all this, so as when you see your oppos back at the grieving widow's house, you might want to tell them that there's not much that gets past nosey neighbours in a place like this. See, lots of people saw Derek Atkinson go into his house, lots of people heard the ruckus he kicked up, but not a one saw him come out. But they did see your two oppos go in after him. And heard that old nutter Norris pushing his cart around in the middle of the night. And that Dr Falk…now there's a bright girl! She keeps scratching away at some wounds on the body that don't quite fit…contradictions.'

Curtis laughed as Akaash's eyes widened in horror as it finally dawned on him why Billy and Vincent had been acting so strangely since his return. The policeman chuckled for a while as he watched him, eventually taking out his handkerchief and wiping a tear of laughter from his eye. 'Oh dear,' he sighed. 'You do make me laugh! You're as easy to read as a book. I'm really gonna miss you when we finally have to hang you.'

He folded away the handkerchief. 'Now, where were we? Oh, yeah. Contradictions. Bloodstains, for example. They can hang around for a surprisingly long time. Little witnesses waiting their moment to betray you one day. And interestingly, Derek Atkinson's army records show he was of a very rare type. So, if my colleagues in uniform felt it was necessary to search No. 23 Ashton St – which I'm not saying they will, but even if they did, I'm pretty confident they won't be doing it for a day or two, today being the funeral and all – *that* would be the kind of thing they would be looking for. Not that they'd find anything, of course, would they? Because none of this ever happened, did it? Especially if the house had been given a very thorough spring cleaning. Got it? Good. Now, tell me all about your trip to London. Or do you have something more important to do right now?'

They had wondered if, and if so, when, they should return to No. 23. It had only been their home for a few months but each missed it. Of course, at least for Billy and Vincent, everything had changed there. It was no longer just their temporary place of residence. It was now a crime scene. And their landlady was no longer a soldier's wife helping to make ends meet by taking in paying guests. She was a widow, a victim and an accomplice.

None of this, however, troubled Akaash, who moved back in the day after the funeral. It hadn't even occurred to him that there would be any issues about doing so, other than perhaps to remember to be a bit more sensitive to their landlady's feelings in the short term. Plus, he wanted to check the house for incriminating evidence: as far as anyone else was concerned, he'd paid his rent in advance so he had every right to be there and that was that. He searched the place thoroughly, wiped down surfaces and handles, even though they all looked perfectly clean already, then reclaimed his bags from the Goddard Arms – where Billy had taken and stored all their luggage – and settled himself back in whilst Sally was out shopping.

She returned to find him sitting at the kitchen table reading. Deeply involved in the book, he hadn't even taken off his hat and coat. Nor did he look up when she arrived or seem to notice when she dumped two string bags full of shopping on the table with a relieved sigh. She took off her headscarf and glanced around. Did the place seem to smell more distinctly of bleach than it had when she'd left? She dismissed the thought and looked at Akaash, still apparently oblivious to her arrival.

'Tea?' she asked.

'Ummm,' he replied. Then he looked up, noting how much she seemed to have aged in the past few days. He knew he really ought to say something. Express his sympathy. What was the word? Oh, yes. Empathise.

'We got any biscuits?' he asked.

On hearing Akaash had moved back in, Billy followed. He'd been a great deal more comfortable and better catered for at the hotel. By comparison with No. 23 the accommodation was palatial and the food gourmet, but it wasn't the same. Plus, he felt he needed to be at Sally's over the coming days. It didn't look as though anyone was very interested in enquiring further into the circumstances of Derek's death, but to stay away might look suspicious and to stay apart might be misconstrued. He and Vincent remained in ignorance of the warning from Curtis as Akaash was acutely conscious that sharing it would invite unwelcome questions about his relationship with the police.

It was Vincent who struggled most over whether to return and when. Unsure how he would face Sally, to whom he'd barely spoken since that terrible night, he didn't know what the right thing was to do. Further, he didn't want to have to face what they – no, he – had done. He couldn't see how he could be in that house, sit at that table, without always thinking of Derek's temple crashing into the corner of it, with his hands on the back of his head, driving it down…

Billy insisted it was time. Vincent said he needed to talk with Sally alone first. Billy promised to ensure that both he and Akaash would be out when Vincent first returned.

They sat in the front room, Sally with hands clenched on her lap, looking down. Vincent noticed her fingers never quite stayed still, as though troubled at being unoccupied. He hadn't been aware of that before.

'How are you?' he asked, knowing how inadequate that sounded but unable to think of anything else to say.

'Better some days than others.'

'How are you managing with Akaash and Billy being back?'

'Good. Fine. They're a comfort,' she said, sniffing back tears. 'It's almost like nothing happened, with them being back and all. Like old times. Well, not such old times, I suppose. But you know what I mean.'

Vincent nodded. Sally looked up and attempted a brave smile. 'Except you're not here. I miss you. They do too.'

Vincent smiled back. 'I very seriously doubt that.'

'Well, anyway, I do.'

There was a silence. Not uncomfortable but not companionable either. 'Is it right they call you the "Bof"? Elsie Coggins says they do.'

'Apparently. Short for "boffin". Silly, really. If anyone should be called that you'd think it would be Akaash.'

'There are worse things to be called,' she reflected.

'Ernie tell you about…'

'The money? Yes, he did.' She paused, then continued, 'It was Derek's, you know.'

'I know.'

'The debt, I mean.'

'Oh, I see. Right.'

Another silence, easier this time.

'I only married him because I was…you know.'

'With your daughter?'

She shook her head. 'There was another child. Miscarried. Didn't even need to get hitched as it turned out.'

'Can I move back in?' he asked.

'Of course. Whenever you want to.'

'I'd like there to be some changes,' he said. 'From now on, I'd like to sleep down here. You have your room back.' He smiled. 'And if it makes you feel better, you can charge me less rent.'

Life moves on. Although it would have seemed impossible when they'd stared down at Derek on the kitchen floor, with each passing day the gap separating them from that night widened and the horror was progressively rationalised by self-assurances of the inevitability of it all. None of them forgot a single grim minute of it – they were probably years away from being able to do so – but that detail was inexorably absorbed into a new view of reality which progressively historicised and then embraced it.

By an unspoken agreement, no mention of what had occurred passed between them. Inevitably, anything that had involved or been witnessed by Elsie would – in the strictest confidence, mind – be widely confided. But amid all the other salacious tales that circulated about Derek Atkinson and speculation on his final hours, that odd thread of truth, stretched in the telling, disappeared amid the warp and the weft.

It was late January. The days were perceptively getting longer and the sky seemed bigger. Snowdrops – tiny white helmets trembling in the icy wind on wire-thin stems – bloomed among tufts of frosted grass. Buds swelled, silently asserting life on otherwise seemingly dead branches. Predawn mist formed in ditches and over marshy ground. Billy, ever the optimist, assumed on waking each morning that this would be the day he received his invitation to return to the big house on the hill. Each evening he would end the day saddened that it remained awaited. Surely it couldn't be that his brief, vigorous encounters with Lady Jessica were over? If so, he still had absolutely no idea why things had ended as they had.

At least his work assuaged some of his growing frustration. Shop B hummed with activity. More engines were rumoured to be on their way. The sight of one of their Bulldogs rattling past hauling empty rolling stock barely turned a head now. There was a general atmosphere of quiet professionalism and occasional examples of really quite superb craftsmanship that Keenan and Billy both felt warranted the Chief Mechanical Engineer's personal inspection and commendation. This was no longer a Shop full of amateurs of varying levels of enthusiasm: these were now proud teams of progressively improving mechanics and engineers. Elsie, regarding Billy as her co-conspirator in dark but necessary out-of-hours deeds, treated him with a new respect at work that mystified those not party to the whispered secret. Those in the know spotted how Billy glanced warily at the bosh whenever he walked anywhere near it, as though he was wondering about Elsie's reference to its use in the past for making inconvenient objects disappear.

Vincent and Lapworth pressed for ever-shorter signalling intervals between trains, fighting for every second and celebrating every little victory over their deeply conservative – but no longer quite so hostile – colleagues in Movements. But for the receding shadow of that one terrible night, Vincent would have said that this was one of the most satisfying and enjoyable periods of his working life.

On 28 January, Akaash and Joan began the pilot-testing of their fake signal system. The first messages were exchanged between Cheltenham Spa and Bristol Temple Meads and the bogus information was successfully differentiated from the real, thereafter respectively designated 'chaff' and 'wheat'. Arrangements for the build-up and roll-out of the system across the region began. Now that Phyl was no longer with them, Joan was determined to speak only in Bengali to keep her linguistic skills honed. With little work now to do, they spent many amiable hours in the office making and comparing translations of Tagore.

On alternate Thursday evenings, Akaash attended the meetings of what was now designated the Communist Workers' Movement at the Glue Pot. Until then, though the name of the gathering regularly changed, its progress tended to be tediously predictable, with earnest, determined speeches, impassioned declarations of support and motions of censure, and resolutions proposed, debated and passed. But on one occasion, the first Thursday in February, things were very different. It was obvious as soon as Akaash entered the room. There was a conspiratorial, tense atmosphere, as though a new, big and scary kid had suddenly appeared in their playground.

And one had – a heavily built man with a pockmarked face, dressed in a shapeless beige suit and large flat cap, who chain-smoked and glanced around warily with small, darting eyes. He stood up when Akaash entered, came over to him and placed a huge hand on his shoulder muttering something about brothers in the struggle against British imperialism in such a thick Ulster accent that Akaash could only make out every other word. Everyone else in the room treated this new arrival with respect verging on awe –

laughing a little bit too loudly and too quickly at anything he said with a cynical grin and nodding far too earnestly to thoughts expressed with a frown.

No name was mentioned in his introduction once they were all seated. Several references to the 'Boys' and the Easter Martyrs ensured that Akaash and everyone else worked out that their speaker was from the proscribed IRA. He spoke of taking the real war to the true enemy – hitting the English ruling classes where it hurt and when it mattered. Akaash may have been cripplingly inadequate at picking up on people's feelings at an individual level but he was finely attuned to the mood of a political gathering. Looking around, he sensed the discomfort among a large number of those present, for whom class loyalty and socialist solidarity were clearly in conflict with patriotism and/or pacifism.

But for a few, there were no dilemmas, and their eyes glowed with fervour as they nodded to affirm his every pronouncement. This man put into words what had long been in their hearts and minds – that the true enemy wasn't over the Channel, out there, to be defeated when some fabled invasion finally took place. No! He was right here, lurking in their midst and needed to be rooted out, right now! And the real war, the battles that mattered, would not be a hard slog through France and into Germany, with every mile paid for with the lives of their brothers and sons, their fellow workers in uniform. The real war would be fought in the factories and mills of Britain, in towns like theirs by men like them, rising up against their exploiters! Forget Germany; let our Soviet brothers claim their blood debt. Churchill and all his kind were the real foe. Remember Tonypandy.: it wasn't Hitler who unleashed troops on striking miners, it was Churchill! And, he added with a steady look at Akaash, think of the millions starving to death in Bengal thanks to the actions and inactions of this evil old man. Workers everywhere must take up arms, as they had in Russia, as they had in Ireland, to free themselves from the yoke of the capitalist elite, he roared to a mix of polite and rapturous applause.

Akaash clapped with the rest. He was among the first to stand and the last to sit when the chairman finally waved them back to their chairs. He agreed with everything this man said and had used many of the same words himself. And at last someone was actually talking about the famine!

Yet something just didn't ring true.

That impression grew in the subsequent discussion. The Irishman seemed particularly keen to hear Akaash's views. Flattering and not unexpected, except that he wasn't asking about events back home. That would have made sense. That was what Akaash had been hoping for. Instead he was quizzed about how things stood in the Works: the mood of the workers, his opinion of the opportunities for further industrial action, possibilities of promoting social unrest in the town. Whenever Akaash tried to raise the situation in Bengal, the Irishman seemed to tune out until he could work the conversation round to more local matters: were there, he wondered, other groups Akaash knew to whom he could speak? Would he be at all interested in helping to build up a stockpile of weapons for the great day…

As always, Akaash agonised over what and how much to tell Curtis about the meeting. He had begun to feel physically ill as he approached the police station, a sensation that seemed to be getting worse since he'd learnt of Phyl's pregnancy. He reminded himself that he wasn't the only source the policeman had among those who attended the meeting. He found great comfort in the thought that his reports usually served merely to confirm what Curtis already knew – a salve to his troubled conscience. But he was still filled with self-loathing as the appointed time approached.

When he visited the police station the next day – still on the pretext of meeting the requirements of his temporary paperwork –

Curtis was not his usual cheery self. Akaash had never seen him so annoyed.

'Well?' he snapped.

'There was an IRA man at last night's meeting...' Akaash began.

'IRA, my auntie's cat!' fumed Curtis. 'Just tell me the names of the idiots who fell for it.'

'Why? What are you going to do to them?'

'Suggest their comrades give them a few lessons in not being so bloody gullible. We're meant to be the ones to make the Micks look like thickos, not the other way around.'

'So he *was* one of yours!'

'How dare you! He was most certainly not! I'm not in the business of entrapment. It's against the law.'

'But he was a...'

'Agent provocateur is the expression you're groping for. Not like you to struggle with our language. And don't tell me that isn't a term you've heard back home.'

'I knew it!' cried Akaash triumphantly.

'Really? You were cheering him as loudly as the best of them, I hear,' said Curtis.

'Yes, but I knew there was something wrong with him.'

'Funny way of showing it. Well, if you did, you were right. On the payroll of some cloak-and-dagger bunch up in London. MI something or other. Posh boys playing "smoke out the cloth-capped commissars".'

'Did you know?'

'Of course not! They don't tell people like me what they're up to. Oh no! We just get a call after the event to tell us who to arrest and what to charge them with.'

'But you're on the same side.'

'For a supposedly bright lad you can be breathtakingly dense! Have I taught you nothing? Of course we're not on the same side.'

There was a long silence. Curtis seemed lost in unhappy thoughts. Then he glanced across at Akaash. 'This is all your fault, you know.'

'Mine? How can this be my fault?'

'The strike. All that "Most Dangerous Man" bollocks in the newspapers. Got yourself too noticed. Got us all noticed.'

'Really? That would explain why he was so interested in what I thought. About the level of militancy in the Works, things like that.'

'Did he ask if you could introduce him to your Oxford set?'

Akaash nodded.

'So bloody obvious! What did you say?'

'I said I'd see what I could do.'

'Make any arrangements to see him again?'

'No. He said he'd be in touch.'

'As soon as he contacts you, just let me know.'

'Why? What are you going to do?'

'I'm going to arrest the bugger. They want to swan in here and mess with my town? Well, not on my tic, son, and not on my fucking tab.'

The first hints of spring seemed to cause Billy's thoughts to turn not to love but to an uncharacteristic introspection, an abiding melancholy that even the sight of another Bulldog leaving Shop B couldn't lift. Both Akaash – who had his own demons to grapple with – and Vincent – who, apart from a recurring nightmare about Derek, Ernie and furnaces, didn't – tried to ignore the sighing. Sally urged them to get Billy 'out of himself' and pumped various homemade 'pick-me-ups' into him, but nothing seemed to have an impact on the general malaise and frequent muttered wondering about what was the point of anything.

Eventually, it was Vincent who brought it up at the end of their meal one evening. True, the Toad in the Hole Sally had served up was hardly likely to lift any spirits, even if it had actually contained meat. Akaash observed that it should have simply been called 'Hole'. Vincent responded – instinctively defending Sally – that the potatoes were warm and filling, and the way she had attempted to substitute carrots for sausages to accommodate Akaash's vegetarianism was a kind thought, even if they had emerged from the oven as charred pulp. He also pointed out that he'd replenished their jars of pickles during a recent visit to Cardiff Docks and Tiger Bay, although even that seemed to do little to cheer Billy up.

'It wouldn't do some people any harm,' Vincent concluded with a significant look in Billy's direction, 'to acknowledge the kindnesses of others rather than mope around like death warmed up.'

'Your own phrase?' Billy couldn't resist asking.

'Lapworth's. He has a nice turn of phrase. A wet weekend would do equally well apparently.'

'Two pennyworth of Gawd help us?' offered Akaash. 'Something Cyn said about…well, never mind.'

'What *is* wrong with you?' Vincent asked Billy.

'I think I lack character,' Billy sighed. 'That's why women get fed up with me so quickly.'

'That's nonsense. Everybody has a character,' Vincent said.

'Actors have lots of them,' pointed out Akaash unhelpfully.

Billy shook his head. 'I don't mean like that. I know who I am and I'm usually happy with the identity I've got…although I wish Shop B wouldn't keep calling me "His Highness"…anyway, I don't mean that. I mean moral fibre.'

Vincent tried not to laugh. 'Well, you have clear views on things, don't you?' he offered.

'Only on engineering. Even then, I'm easily persuaded. Show me a better way and I'll follow it. I'm not like you two. You, Akaash, you believe in ideas and causes, and there are all sorts of things you're perfectly clear you will and won't do. Lines you won't cross. You're willing to suffer for what you think is right, no matter how misguided you are. I respect that.'

Akaash shifted uncomfortably but said nothing.

'And you, Vincent, you're so obsessed with what's right and what's wrong you don't care how many enemies you make, how many people you hurt, as long as you do the correct thing by your estimation. Now *that's* character. By the way, I meant that as a compliment but it sort of came out wrong.'

'Never mind. I get your drift.'

'But me? I just do whatever seems like a good idea right now. I don't think I've ever been put in a situation where I have to make a hard decision. Where I have had to jeopardise my own well-being for a higher purpose or someone else's benefit. Women can detect that sort of thing in a man.'

Vincent tried to hide a smile. 'This isn't like you! You're normally so annoyingly full of yourself, bursting with confidence. Look, you're a decent enough man doing the best he can to meet the expectations of others. What's brought this on?'

'A serious lack of female company. I think maybe I haven't suffered enough in life. By the way, that's the nicest thing you've ever said to me.'

'Well, let's be fair. You were quite upset when you found out you couldn't get any more of your fancy cigarettes from Bombay.'

'Oh, didn't I tell you? Lockyer managed to get a few gross shipped over. The man's an absolute wonder. Arriving next Thursday with any luck. Anyway, where was I?'

'Suffering insufficiently?'

'Exactly. Look at Akaash here. Always bashing on about his starving family back in Bengal. Do you know – I'm ashamed to admit it – but until I came to this country, I'd never actually gone to bed hungry? Not once. Even in Ramadan, fasting was never real hunger to us because you knew there was a gurt feast waiting at sunset and you'd stagger off to bed well-stuffed.' Dewy-eyed, he took out his wallet and handed a five-pound note to Akaash. 'Here,' he said with a loud sniff. 'Add this to the money you're sending home. And I'm sorry I've been so hard on you.'

Akaash took the note, folded it carefully and slipped it into his breast pocket, reflecting that he too had rarely, if ever, slept on an empty stomach back home. Not that that made his outrage for those starving any less valid, just that he had perhaps based his authority to champion their rights too readily on the unchallenged assumptions of others that he had shared their suffering. Was it his fault if people assumed he was some sort of peasant child prodigy? True, he regularly mentioned that his family lived in a village, he just failed to add that they moved there only when the city got too oppressive. Or that they owned their home as well as a fair amount of the surrounding land. Eech! Billy's glum reverie was getting him down too. It was all so much easier when this fellow could just be dismissed as a doomed aristo.

Vincent too was finding this new mawkish Billy somewhat wearing. 'Oh, for God's sake!' he cried. 'We're all faced with difficult choices between unsatisfactory options. If I was so absolute about right and wrong that night would have ended differently, and a great deal worse for everyone.'

'What night?' Akaash asked.

'You know, when…' Billy began. Vincent cleared his throat pointedly. 'Oh, come on! If we can't trust one another, who can we rely on in this world?'

Billy proceeded to tell Akaash all about the night of Derek Atkinson's death. Or at least the part that he knew. Vincent felt profoundly grateful he'd not shared what had actually happened inside the Works. As far as Billy and Sally were concerned, what had happened was that, much to Vincent and Ernie's surprise, Derek had suddenly regained consciousness, leapt from the cart and raced off, tragically ending up on the tracks just at the wrong time. Nothing to do with them. Everybody's hands were clean. Akaash did his poor best to pretend he was surprised. All three left the table burdened with new, mutual suspicions.

'Out of sorts,' Sally murmured to herself as she cleared the table. 'What those boys need is a good dose of salts.'

It might have been Billy's glum mood, or it might just have been the weather having again turned, as though determined to remind the town that winter wasn't that far behind them after all, but the following afternoon, on his early return from the Works, Akaash too found himself unusually reflective. It was as though his skin had been peeled away and suddenly he could feel every brush and breeze. He was also uncertain about a range of issues that he'd previously regarded as unambiguous. He was struggling to comprehend what Billy and Vincent had seen and done the night Derek died. How had they managed to keep it to themselves for as long as they had? He'd blurted out the news about Phyl and the baby the moment he saw them.

He sat at the kitchen table, staring blankly ahead.

Phyl and the baby. Phyl and his baby. Those words kept swirling around in his brain. So much uncertainty. So much doubt. What had Curtis said? Contradictions. He wondered if this was how others felt all the time. If so, he was glad he wasn't like them because he really didn't like it at all.

And at the heart of all this, ever since he'd first told Curtis about what went on at the Glue Pot meetings, was the fact that whenever he looked in the mirror, he saw staring back the face of a traitor.

But treachery, he quickly reasoned, was like any other wrong. Its gravity was the sum of two variables: intent and impact. He hadn't meant to betray anyone. He didn't set out to do this. He wasn't accepting any money for it. He'd been trapped into this situation. In fact, looked at logically, he was more victim than wrongdoer.

So much for intent.

But what about impact? Surely, he reasoned, there was a massive difference between betraying your own people and betraying members of the race that had looted and oppressed your own kind for the best part of two centuries? And then, even among your oppressors, a distinction could be drawn between selling out strangers as opposed to those you knew, cared about and who in turn cared about you.

He had earlier rationalised away any lurking doubts that he might have retained about betraying the cause: that was a concept so grandiose and all-embracing that it lacked any real meaning. After all, he was a man who dealt in precision: if you couldn't measure it, it didn't exist. Yes, he might have slightly muddied his militant credentials but let's face it, that was the one characteristic every successful revolutionary in history shared. The uncompromising died at the first barricade. Only martyrs could afford simple principles, and then, only post-mortem. They'd paid the price, but all save a few had cashed in their chips for very little. Of the many heroes who perished in the struggle, most rotted forgotten in nameless graves or were reduced to combined ashes on mass pyres. For every Spartacus, a thousand died anonymous, mere statistics if even that. No, if anything worthwhile was to be achieved, compromise was inevitable and survival the prime requirement.

So, what mattered, and what didn't? That was the essential decision every true revolutionary must make. The people mattered – yes, of course. But again, like the cause, it was too broad a concept. Who exactly were the people? Experience was rapidly teaching him that only direction distinguished the masses from the mob.

Cyn mattered. Of course she did. So did her father. Her brothers too. Good people. Workers who had reached out to him.

Offered him help and a welcome. The revolution must take such decent people into its sheltering embrace in return. Otherwise, who was he betraying? Just unimportant white exploiters. That may not have been what they wanted to be, they may not even realise that's what they were, but empty villages and raped indigenous industries bore eloquently silent witness to the truth of the fact.

Joan? Someone who had learnt Hindi and Bengali? Someone who'd not only read Tagore but translated him? Had even read his own papers in the original – or at least tried to – and helped him connect with others in Oxford who shared their common political beliefs? Unimportant?

And Phyl? Mother of his as yet unborn child: how could she be an enemy? Could anyone a true revolutionary like him had taken as a lover, albeit so unintentionally and briefly, be condemned? In fact, the more he thought of it, their unplanned grapple on the Pattern Store roof seemed his most truly revolutionary act. Intercourse across class boundaries at its most essential – not nuanced, truly honest. An angry, radical passion. He had, literally, fucked the ruling class. On his part, he had subsequently rationalised the act as an urgent, authentic desire to possess all from which he was unjustly excluded by birth and race. On hers, he assumed, it was the hollow, sad cry of an empty, doomed existence. He didn't love her and was perfectly content to acknowledge that she had only negative feelings for him. They were class enemies and at all other times she treated him with disdain. An ethnic enemy, too. An imperialist doyenne but... much as he hated the thought, inside that elitist womb now grew a significant bit of him. Indeed, if he were to die here and now, all of him that would remain. Horrific though the thought was, that tiny life growing inside her might end up being the only thing that distinguished him from those nameless, lost millions.

Was that really his only chance at value? As someone potentially important's accidental father?

Whether that was true or not, Phyl needed to be spared, too.

This betrayal stuff was hard to parse!

The comrades who met at the Glue Pot? The revolution was hardly likely to stumble in its inexorable march towards the new dawn if they fell. Enthusiastic though their speeches may be, resoundingly though their declarations might echo, they were depressingly bourgeois in their hopes and hates. Likeable enough, but they were not going to set the world on fire, individually or en masse, by accident or design. And what did betrayal of these worthies really mean? Think of impact, Akaash reminded himself: no appointment with the gallows or the guillotine would await these sadly tepid radicals. No firing squads would line up at dawn for them. Suspended sentences, docked pay and conditional discharges would be the worse consequences of selling these men out to the powers that be. Compared to ensuring food for people back home – brothers and sisters, even if not biologically his own brothers and sisters? A small cost indeed. Minimal impact. A bargain.

It seemed a very long time since he'd briefly considered making up some tale about Vincent being a Nazi agent to get Special Branch off his back. Amazingly, they actually now seemed to think Vincent might indeed be a Nazi and would presumably be grateful to anyone who corroborated that suspicion. And Billy had blurted out all about the death of Derek Atkinson. How things change in a few months! He now had a receptive audience and an actual crime to report, yet it would now do him little good. Curtis would not thank him for doing anything to help London, whilst the policeman listened to descriptions of the goings-on at the Glue Pot with world-weary amusement, he was far from sanguine about outside interest in 'his' town. Hadn't he actually advised Akaash to ensure that whatever happened in the kitchen of No. 23 was properly covered up?

He realised with a start that he was relieved not to even have to think of compromising his relationship with his fellow boarders, whatever it was. He was still sure it wasn't friendship and it certainly wasn't fraternalism or solidarity, but there was some bond between them, no matter how unlikely, ill-defined and unwelcome.

So it was simple, really. The same formula he'd applied from the outset remained the optimal solution: tell Curtis the truth about the Glue Pot meetings. Lie to anyone who asked about the Oxford gatherings. Make sure the Abbots were not implicated in anything. Say nothing to harm his – what had Curtis called them – his oppos. Well, for now that would do.

But would it be enough to stop this niggling voice in his head whispering guilt?

And what about his child? What should he do about that? It? What could he do? Phyl had made it clear that she never wanted to see him or hear from him again. Her father had backed that up with threats of police action if he ever came near their house again. But he had spoken to her long enough to know that an illegal abortion was out of the question, as was her keeping the child. It was likely to be sent to an orphanage somewhere far from London. That's what she'd told him they proposed to do, with the scant chance of a possible adoption at some point in the future the best that could be hoped for.

Unexpectedly, tears welled up and he found himself sobbing uncontrollably. He knew he should be feeling for that unloved child facing a cruel future. For Phyl, whose whole life was changed forever by their one fumbled coupling. But actually, it was himself he felt most sorry for. He'd been tricked and trapped and only ever wanted to do his best and everything had gone wrong. He folded his arms on the kitchen table, slumped forward and wailed his misery.

That was how Sally found him. He'd assumed he had the house to himself when he'd come in but she'd been in her newly reclaimed front bedroom, enjoying the space and privacy it allowed her. She heard Akaash arrive and knew it was him.

Each of her three lodgers sounded quite different on return from work. She'd intended to spend just a little longer on her own but his clear distress brought her running into the kitchen.

She put a hand on his shoulder, and he turned. She put her arms around him, making comforting, motherly sounds. Still seated, he wrapped his arms around her waist and buried his face into her chest. Her embrace – the warmth, the comforting softness and the familiar, wholesome soap smell – was the very thing he needed at that moment.

After a minute or two, he quietened, and both felt suddenly uncomfortable. Sally stepped away, smoothed out her blouse and tugged her skirt straight. He sniffed loudly, twice, and wiped his eyes with the palms of his hands.

'What on earth was that all about?' she chided, handing him a tiny scrap of a handkerchief she kept tucked up her sleeve. 'Honestly! You big ninny! Whatever it is, it can't be worth all that fuss.'

'I've made a mess of everything,' he said, swallowing back more tears.

'Well, you're in the right house for that. Let me put the kettle on. Then why don't you tell your Aunty Sally all about it?'

53

No. 23 Ashton St became a place where conversations were only warily embarked upon. With several secrets now partially shared, everyone wondered how much each knew about a spreading range of issues. A carapace of normality – or if not normality, familiarity – formed, which superficially hid this new unease with one another.

Of the patterns wordlessly re-established, the most significant was Sally and Vincent returning to their sharing

Saturday evenings dancing to the big bands on the Home Service in the front room. If anything, they were even more formal than they had been, carefully avoiding looking at one another whilst waiting for the next tune to begin. Yet whilst their bodies maintained a rigorously guarded distance as they danced, they seemed more instinctively in tune, moving with greater sympathy with each other.

On one such evening, as the programme neared its conclusion, Sally moved a little closer to Vincent. 'What are we going to do?' she asked.

Ever since Derek's death, Vincent had been feeling that some sort of conversation like this was inevitable. He'd rehearsed what he would say and was ready for it, not even nervous. But he felt a deep sadness, knowing that with his reply, everything would change. He had desperately wanted to preserve at least these close moments. He opened his mouth to reply but she gently put a finger to his lips.

'Don't say anything. Not just yet,' she whispered. She stepped in closer, resting her head on his shoulder. He bowed his head forward, resting his cheek on the crown of her head.

'I know…you're not like other men. Not interested in… you know.'

He pulled back slightly.

'No!' she said urgently. 'That's OK, really. Believe me, I've had enough of all that. But I'm so, so lonely. I've been lonely ever since I got married. And we're such good friends. I've never ever felt at home with anyone in my life. Sometimes it's like, for all the terrible things that have happened, we're meant to be together.'

'Can I speak now?'

She smiled and nodded.

'These times, when we dance, these are the best moments of my life. But they can't be enough.'

'But it's not just these times, is it?' she countered, stepping away from him and turning off the wireless. 'When we go to church. Here at home. Even when we're doing the washing up. Just being together. It feels so right.'

'We both know I have to go back home. I'm almost done here.'

'To your folks?' she asked as she glanced at the family photographs he'd now moved into the front room. There was something in her tone that jarred with him.

'Yes,' he said shortly. 'To my folks.'

'But in the meantime?'

'I'm here. We're here. Together.'

When Vincent arrived at Swindon station from a late afternoon visit to Gloucester two days later he was surprised to find Billy waiting for him. It was clear something was wrong and his first thought was that it was about Sally. The next was that it concerned the police. Billy assured him that everything was fine at No. 23 but seemed to be having difficulty saying quite what was bothering him.

'You know Lockyer? The Maharajah's man in London?'

'Of course. Your source of chocolates, fancy cigarettes and ludicrously expensive toilet cisterns.'

Billy winced. 'That's him.'

'Well, what about him?'

'He came to see me today. About some news from home.'

'Oh. Everything all right, I hope?'

'No, I'm afraid it isn't. He says there's been a huge explosion in Bombay. In the docks.'

Vincent frowned. 'There's been nothing in the newspapers about any explosion. Or on the radio.'

'I know. Lockyer thinks there's a news blackout about it, to keep up morale. But he says it's pretty serious. I'm sorry.'

'I need to get back there.'

'That's what I thought. I've asked him to make some enquiries for you. Tried to hold a berth.'

'That's good of you. I'll pay you back whatever it cost.'

'Well, this is where it gets odd.'

'Odd?'

'Yes. When Lockyer started ringing around to try to find the next sailing, he got a call from that blighter Dawlish. He told him you can't leave the country.'

'But that's crazy! I've done everything they wanted. More! Why on earth can't I go home now?'

'They say you know too much.'

'This is ridiculous!' fumed Vincent, 'I'll speak to the CME first thing tomorrow… Are you coming home?'

Billy had paused and now lagged a few paces behind. He had spotted Mary among the girls waiting for the last Down train and was clearly torn. 'No,' he called, 'you carry on. I'll see you back at No. 23.'

Mary Hughes had been bemoaning the continued absence of American soldiers in Swindon. Yes, there was regular trade along Manchester Road, she said, reliable enough on a Friday after wages had been paid out. And there was always the possibility of some squaddies home on leave, but a Yank? That was the real prize…

Billy approached and introduced himself. 'You a pal of the Bof?' the girl to whom Mary had been speaking asked him in such a strong Welsh accent that Billy had no idea what she'd said.

'Absolutely,' he ventured. 'Cold evening.'

'Lovely man, the Bof,' she continued. 'Such a gent!' She looked Billy up and down. 'What d'you want then, handsome?'

'Er, your friend. Mary, isn't it? I was wondering if we could have a word?'

She tutted. 'It's always bleedin' Mary they want! I'm off to the Ladies. Powder my nose. Anyone coming?'

A couple of the other girls joined her. Billy offered Mary a cigarette. She shrugged and took one. She automatically rested her hand gently on the back of his as he held his lighter up, and then looked at him warily as she took a long drag and blew out a fine stream of smoke. 'There's no trade on railway premises,' she warned.

'No, no. Of course not,' agreed Billy hastily. 'God forbid. I was just wondering if I could invite you to join me for a drink sometime?'

'Won't do you no good. Drink or no drink. I don't do darkies.'

'I beg your pardon?'

'Nothing personal,' she added, with a quick, sympathetic smile. 'It's the Yanks, see? They find out you've done it with a darkie, they don't like it.'

'Don't they indeed?'

'No! They take against that.'

'Well, I won't tell them if you don't,' offered Billy.

'No, but someone might, see?' reasoned Mary gravely. 'One of them bitches,' she said, tossing her head towards the ladies' toilet.

'Hmm. I see. You have a lot of…um, trade from the Yanks, do you?'

'No, that's the problem. There's no bloody Yanks in this dump.'

'Well, we've had one or two. Shame you missed them. I could have introduced you.'

'I know!' agreed Mary, eyes wide. 'I heard about that night. Can you believe it? On the one night I've missed for months! My little one was poorly, see? Wouldn't settle with me mam. Easy money too, the girls said. Paid up front and too drunk to do anything!' She gave a heartfelt sigh at the unfairness of it all. 'Loads of 'em in Bath. Bristol too.'

'Why don't you work there, then?'

'Won't even let us off the train! Local girls got it all stitched up. They hate us lot there. Prejudiced, see?'

'People can be very unkind, can't they?'

'Can't they just?' She cocked her head to one side and treated him to an affectionate beam. 'Aaaah! Very understanding you are! Lovely man. Shame you're, well, you know.'

'Yes, isn't it? Pay well, do they? These Yanks.'

'So everyone says.'

'Well, suppose I said I'd pay you twice what you'd get from any American?'

She shook her head. 'Sweet of you to offer, luv. Really it is. Don't think I don't appreciate it. Flattering. Just what a girl needs to hear at the end of a long day. But it's not worth it, see? Not in the long run.'

'I don't understand. You don't have any American clients. There's none here. I'll pay over the going Yankee rate. What's the problem?'

She laughed delightedly, suddenly sounding disturbingly young. '*Clients*! Makes me sound right la-di-da!' She looked around, then leaned in towards him confidingly. 'See, the thing with Yanks is, they might marry you and take you back over there with 'em!' Her eyes shone with hope. 'I seen it on the newsreel. War brides, they call 'em! Half of 'em ugly as sin too! That's why I can't risk it.' She looked up and down the platform once more, then stood on tiptoe and kissed him on the cheek. 'Thanks for the fag. No hard feelings?'

Billy shook his head. But he was lying. Because he did have hard feelings. Because he was, once more, in love.

Vincent got little joy from his urgent appeal to Hartshorne the next morning. The Chief Mechanical Engineer explained that all of this was nothing to do with him. Was Vincent sure about this? How did he know? There'd been nothing about it on the BBC news. Hartshorne said he'd be loath to see him go but Vincent had done them a great service already and if he really had to return home then of course the company couldn't stop him.

Others, however, could. Billy still had Dawlish's card and suggested Vincent ring him. He did the next day after Lockyer advised him that all telegrams sent to Bombay were still going unanswered.

'Nice to hear from you, Mr Rosario. Is there something I can do for you?'

'I want to return to Bombay.'

'Do you indeed. Well, sadly, few of us get what we want in life. Why this sudden desire to go home?'

'I think you know the answer to that very well. This explosion.'

'I know nothing of any explosion. All I know is that you are in possession of a great deal of sensitive information that cannot be allowed to fall into enemy hands. There is no question of you going anywhere for some time to come.'

'But I'm needed back there,' Vincent pleaded.

'No, you're not.' Dawlish assured him. 'We had you replaced before Christmas. There's now three people doing your old job. Very flattering, I'd have thought. Draw some comfort from that. If you need me to try to contact anyone on your behalf, or check on the well-being of relations, *if* something has happened, I'll be happy to try my best. But don't even think of attempting to leave these shores. That will only be permitted to happen when all you now know poses no threat to our interests.'

'You're keeping me a prisoner!'

'Oh, for goodness' sake, man! You people are always so overdramatic. You're in a well-paid job, doing excellent work according to the GWR, and from what I hear getting on famously with your recently widowed landlady. You're free to carry on making your immensely valuable contribution to the war effort. You're just subject to travel restrictions in the interests of national security, as are thousands of others.'

'Who can I appeal to? Where do I apply to have this changed?'

'No one, Mr Rosario. Nowhere. There is a war on.'

'But I have to make sure my family are OK.'

'We both know that's not true, Mr Rosario.'

'I don't know what you mean. I have to get back. Isn't there anything I can do?'

'No. You have no idea how much it disappoints me to say it, but I really don't think there is. Sadly, you have absolutely nothing I want.'

Sally felt for Vincent's situation, but it came a poor second to her concern for Akaash's unborn child. She just couldn't stop thinking about it. It seemed to her that she had to do something, and the more she turned it over in her mind, the clearer the best course of action seemed. The fact that Vincent was now trapped in Swindon, possibly for the duration of the war, may be hard for him but it offered her a wonderful opportunity.

She put her proposal to Vincent one evening whilst they were washing up.

'I can't bear to think of that baby, Akaash's child, ending up in an orphanage. What's its life going to be like, being half-Indian, looking different, being singled out with no one to stick up for it? No one to love it?'

'I know what that's like.'

'I'm sorry, Vincent, but I don't think you do. Oh, I know you say people like you are outsiders in your own country but where you grew up there were lots of others like you. People who you could look to. Your kind. You had a family. Who will this poor little thing have?'

'Well, maybe. But this isn't your problem, Sally. It's not your responsibility.'

'It could be. I keep thinking that he or she will look like a child you and I might have had.'

There was a long pause. 'Listen, Sally…' Vincent began.

'No. Please Vincent, you listen. They're not going to let you leave the country until after the invasion, right?'

He nodded.

'That could be months away. A year. That baby will be born long before that.'

'So?'

The words came out in a rush, tumbling over and running into one another. 'If you married me, I could adopt her.'

'Her?'

She shook her head impatiently. 'Him. Her. It. That child faces a lonely, cruel life. I have nothing. No one. I could make a future with it. And for it.'

'If I marry you.'

'Yes. That's all I ask. You marry me so that I can adopt Akaash's child. After, you can go back home, divorce me, whatever you want. I won't ask for anything more from you. Ever. Oh, Vincent, I'd love it if I thought we could have a future together, I really would. The two of us, the three of us. But I know you'll go as soon as you're allowed to. That's OK. I won't hold you back.'

'Have you spoken to Akaash about this? What does he say?'

'I haven't asked him. Not that it's got that much to do with him really, if you think about it. I wanted to see what you thought about this first. Am I being crazy?'

She looked so desperate. He smiled and reached out to touch her hand. 'Yes, you are. Absolutely crazy. How could this even work?'

Sally looked at him intently. 'We agree with this poor girl that we adopt her child. We get married and once the baby arrives, we sort out the paperwork and it's ours. Well, mine, anyway. It'll have a name…'

'My name.'

'Yes. So will I. I suppose I'll have to get used to that. But more important, in all this horrible war, one little soul will find a home and a life and all the love I can give it. What do you think?'

'Well, the timing couldn't be much worse, could it? You've only been widowed for a few weeks, and in suspicious circumstances. If you and I get married now there'll be talk.'

'This is Swindon. There's always talk. Yesterday it was all about Derek's death. Today it's Billy mooning around after some little Welsh hussy. Tomorrow it'll be something else. Yes, there'll be raised eyebrows and people gossiping behind our backs. But let them. It'll pass. There's far too much happening for anyone to give a damn in six months' time.'

'And the expectant mother?'

'Why wouldn't she jump at this chance? She can't keep it. Or doesn't want to. This would give it a home. A decent, loving home.'

Vincent was silent for some time. Sally stared at him, willing him to speak. 'Give me twenty-four hours. Let me think. And let me speak to Akaash.'

'Is that a yes?'

'It's a maybe,' he said. He tried to speak firmly, but his voice and his heart were too full of affection and compassion. 'But it's a definite maybe. In the meantime, let's stop calling it "it".'

'Agreed. What should we call…him or her?'

Just at that moment, there was a hard slam against the party wall with No. 21 and a muffled stream of curses on the other side. Vincent smiled. 'How about we just call it Little Ern for the time being?'

'Agreed.'

55

'It's part of my culture,' Billy insisted. They were sitting at their usual table at the Tap. It was a Tuesday. Billy kept glancing out of the window to see if he could spot Mary, causing Akaash to smirk and Vincent to glance heavenward and shake his head.

'Welsh prostitutes?' Vincent asked. 'You learn something new every day.'

'No, stupid. *Mujra* girls. Beautiful courtesans, pampered odalisques, kept in a life of luxury for the pleasure of a nobleman.'

'Pampered odalisques? That has to be a phrase you've just learnt?'

'It is indeed. Read it in a racy novel I borrowed off Dr Falk. For such a serious professional she has a surprisingly fruity taste in reading matter. There're hidden depths there.'

'I think I saw something like all this in a film once,' said Akaash. 'Set in Oudh, I think. It didn't end well. Opium featured quite a lot.'

'Bit hard to translate the palaces and pleasure houses of Lucknow to a Saturday afternoon shag in Swindon,' Vincent observed.

'Shag?' Akaash repeated, looking at Billy.

'Don't bother,' Billy said. 'Known that one for ages.'

'The opium might help,' Akaash suggested.

'True,' Vincent agreed. 'Where were you thinking of installing this houri of yours? Above the bar at the Glue Pot?'

'He'd have to avoid every other Thursday. Unless he wants her working-class consciousness awoken,' Akaash pointed out.

'Very funny. But yes, I was thinking of renting rooms for her somewhere.'

'And then what?'

'Well, I'd pop in and spend the evening with her now and again.'

'And what's she meant to be doing the rest of the time?'

'I don't know. Read, so that she could engage in improving conversation with me. Learn to sing and play a musical instrument to entertain me.'

'Have you been working with solvents lately?' asked Vincent.

'Can't see what the problem is,' Billy replied huffily.

'It's just wrong, that's what the problem is.'

'I agree,' said Akaash. 'Totally exploitative. Taking advantage of this girl's poverty, ignorance and desperation. Typical of your class and type.'

'I'd have thought that I'm accepting the responsibilities of my class and type. *Noblesse oblige.* Improving her life chances, and all at my own expense. It's not like I'm corrupting some innocent little convent girl. I'm rescuing her from a future of ten-bob knee-tremblers up against a wall in Manchester Road.'

'I'm guessing you've just learnt that expression, too?'

'I have! A corker, isn't it? Evocative. An Elsie-ism. Anyway, I want to give her the opportunity to go up in the world.'

'Well, it's not really a gift, is it?' asked Vincent. 'What about her child?'

'She has a child?'

'A son. You didn't know?'

'Why would I know that? More to the point, how do you?'

'Yeah, how do you?' wondered Akaash.

'I speak to all sorts of people. And, unlike either of you, I listen to what they tell me.'

'You've spoken to her?'

'To all the girls who get that last train. Lots of times. I've learnt a lot from them.'

'I bet!' chortled Billy.

'A true education!' sneered Akaash.

Vincent pointed his cigarette at Akaash. 'You – don't be pathetic.' Then, turning to Billy he said, 'You – don't be even more disgusting than usual. I talk to them about the punctuality of late night Down trains. One of them even notes delays on the journey back to Cardiff for me.'

'I don't think it's him who's being pathetic,' replied Billy shaking his head. 'A gaggle of lovelies like that and all you want them to take down is train times? That is called odd.'

'No, it's called being an adult. I ask again: what about her son?'

'Well, she can bring him with her. Perfectly usual for *mujra* girls back home. He'll be company for her. In fact, the more I think about it, the better I like the idea. It'll be two lives that I'm enhancing.'

'What does she say about this wonderful opportunity?' asked Akaash.

'She says no.'

'Incredible! Why?'

'She don't do darkies, apparently,' said Billy sadly as he gathered up their glasses and headed to the bar to replenish them.

'I think that man gets more ridiculous every day,' sighed Vincent. He looked at Akaash and thought this moment of shared disapproval of Billy might be the right time to raise Sally's plan. 'Look,' he said, leaning forward and dropping his voice, 'don't ask questions and don't interrupt me, I've got something I want to talk to you about...'

Quickly, he outlined Sally's idea, concluding with, 'I'm not saying I agree with this or even if I did that it would work, but I need to know what you think. '

As Vincent had requested, Akaash had listened in silence, remaining infuriatingly quiet for a while after Vincent had finished. Fortunately, Ernie had limped into the Tap and Billy waited at the bar to stand him a Guinness.

'Well?' cried Vincent impatiently.

'You'd be my child's father?'

'Jesus! Yes, I suppose so. At least on paper. I'm not promising to stick around to bring it up, but then nor are you. And before you say another word, just remember, your child will be Anglo-Indian.'

'That wasn't what I was thinking about.'

'What then?'

'I can't believe you'd do this for me.'

'I'm not doing it for you. I'm doing it for Sally and the child.'

'Well, I think you and Mrs A would make wonderful parents.'

Vincent searched for the barb that he was sure must lurk within that statement but couldn't find it. 'Are you trying to do that British "saying the opposite of what you mean" thing?'

'No. How do we make this happen?'

'Well, I suppose we first need to speak to the mother.'

'Good luck with that. She won't speak to me. She probably won't speak to you either. Why don't we ask Billy's friend Lockyer to broach the issue with them? These *goras* find it easier to discuss sensitive matters among themselves rather than with one of us.'

'That's a remarkably perceptive bit of thinking for you.'

'I know. Parenting does that to a man. You'll probably find that out for yourself.'

'Let's not get ahead of ourselves,' said Vincent. 'No time like the present,' he added as he saw Billy heading back towards them with their drinks.

Mary's complete disinterest in him was a powerful aphrodisiac for Billy. So much so that Akaash had taken to hiding his socks. Her indifference was also totally mystifying to a man who by charm, largesse or contacts had always got pretty much everything he'd ever desired in life. True, he wasn't obscenely rich like his cousin brother, the Sardar. He didn't inhabit a suite of opulent rooms in the family mansion, but he'd done all right, thank you very much. Maybe his wants and tastes were limited but, as he liked to boast, as there was nothing he desired which, by one means or another, he couldn't obtain, that must surely make him one of the richest men in the world.

To be so comprehensively dismissed by an ill-educated girl, who was not even bothering to pretend to be dazzled by his exoticism as Mollie had, who had none of the breeding and class that Lady Jessica possessed? It made no sense. What did he need to do to impress and possess her? It was maddening, especially as he was tormented by the thought that all that glorious pulchritude denied to him was sold for shillings in rushed and sordid couplings during which neither participant probably even bothered to extinguish their cigarettes.

It was just plain wrong.

To meet up with Mary at the station late every evening as she waited for the last train was both torture and delight. He convinced himself that he was steadily reaching the soul beneath the caked face powder and smudged homemade mascara. He told himself he was a balm after the indifferent handling she'd received all evening.

She accepted his cigarettes and was quite happy to chat to him rather than listen to the other girls sharing stories of odd requests and sad companions. But his attempts to capture her heart failed. All his charm left her deeply unimpressed.

But she quite liked the way he smelt. Expensive. And could he talk? Never shut up! On and on. But she liked that too. He even brought her tea in a flask, love 'im! On one occasion, after freezing all evening on the corner of Manchester Road and Corporation St and not earning a penny, she'd lost her temper with him. 'Why don't you go with that Nicky Williams? She'll do anything with anyone, that one! Right little slut!' But he'd looked so crushed she'd immediately relented. Feeling terrible, she accepted two of his cigarettes to make it up to him.

Yes, he was welcome to sit with her in the waiting room or out on the platform. But as trains came and went, she was determined that he never forgot the one golden rule: 'A Yank steps off that train and anyone asks, mind you tell them you're with that cow, Daphne Harrison.'

A Yank did step off the train. Several, in fact. It was a miserable night and most of the girls were smoking and chatting in the ladies' toilet to escape the cold and the rain. Billy and Mary were sitting side by side in the waiting room. She was getting over a chill, her nose red and her voice still croaky. Billy had offered to pay her a few nights' earnings to stay at home but she'd refused. She had her pride, she said. She'd been struggling to keep her eyes open for some time. Now she was dozing with her head on his shoulder. He'd promised to wake her for her train, but at the first hint of an American uniform, like a carnivore scenting prey, she was awake, alert and utterly focused. Billy felt sick.

'Right! Off you go. Keep your fingers crossed for me!' she said, quickly tidying her hair. 'How's my make-up? How do I look?'

'It's fine,' sighed Billy. 'You look lovely.'

Billy looked at the earnest, eager glint in her eye. He was torn apart with a desire to see her happy and a yearning to defend her from these bloody Americans. She seemed to sense his torment.

'Why don't you go on home?' she said sympathetically. 'No point you sticking around here.'

'No, I don't suppose there is. Good night, Mary. Good luck.'

Heart near breaking, he turned away and headed towards the steps down from the platform. He kept his head lowered, unable even to look at the crowd of soldiers, the first of whom had sensed working girls on the platform and was opening up a line of light-hearted banter. The girls in the toilet came out in an excited rush to join Mary, who glared possessively at them, the first lioness at the kill. Billy, shoulders hunched and hands thrust deep into his coat pockets, resolved that this ridiculous infatuation had to come to an end. It had been stupid and he had made a fool of himself. Again. Everyone was laughing at him. Again. He really should...

'Hey, don't I know you?'

Billy kept walking but a hand on his arm held him back.

'I'm talking to you.'

Billy smiled grimly. Nothing would give him greater pleasure at that moment than to punch one of these over-entitled white bastards. He turned to face the soldier. He didn't recognise him but assumed he'd been one of the drunken gang who'd invaded the Tap. He took his hands out of his pockets, stood with feet apart, straightened up and met the American's stare.

'You have something you want to say to me?' he asked, with a quiet menace that Ernie would have been proud of. Go on, he silently prayed. Call me names. Insult me. Threaten me. It will be the last thing you'll do for a very long time. Because right at that moment he desperately needed to punch an American face really hard and go on hitting it until he was dragged off. And then have a crack at a few others too.

'Yuh, I got something to say to you,' replied the American. 'That night…'

'Yeeees?' said Billy slowly, in a superior tone he hoped would piss off the soldier as much as it would him if he were on the receiving end of it. 'What would you like to say to me about that night?'

'I'm sorry.'

'You're *what*?' cried Billy, totally confused.

'I'm sorry. We behaved like a bunch of jerks. You see your friend, tell him sorry too.'

Billy shook his head. What was wrong with these bloody people? You want to enjoy a quiet drink and they want to beat you to death. You want to fight them, they want to be your friend. He turned and began to walk away. He heard Mary's false laugh echo along the platform. Then another younger soldier with a broken nose suddenly stepped in front of him and thrust a blade into his stomach. There was no sharp pain, only a massive, winding ache like he'd been struck in the midriff with a sledgehammer. As he curled forward and sank to his knees, he heard the GI he'd spoken with shout out in horror, 'What the fuck, Woody? Jesus, what have you done?'

Billy awoke in the Medical Fund Hospital with an anxious Dr Falk peering down at him.

'YBE?' he groaned.

She smiled, gently brushing his hair back from his forehead with a gloriously cool hand. 'For you, Mr Khan? Always. Now just rest.'

The next thing he was aware of was Akaash, sitting beside his bed, reading. On hearing Billy mumble, he stood up, leaned over and frowned down at him, and then hurried off. Billy tried to lift his head to look around but the pain even that movement generated was so great he gave up with a moan and closed his eyes again.

When he opened them again, he detected a familiar, cheap perfume mixed with the hospital reek of polish and disinfectant. Very gently, he turned his head. An exhausted-looking Mary now sat where Akaash had been. Billy, struggling to distinguish between reality and fevered dreams, assumed that she was part of the latter. He faded away again.

When he awoke five hours later, Mary was indeed there, holding his hand. She was asleep but felt him stir and called for a nurse. She dipped some gauze into a tumbler half full of water and dabbed the soaked material to his parched and cracked lips. He tried to suck at it, desperately thirsty.

'Steady, steady,' she murmured. 'Doctor says you mustn't drink anything just yet.'

'What happened?' he croaked.

'Some bloody silly Yank stabbed you, that's what.'

'Big hamper.'

'What?'

'Why does my head hurt so much?'

'You banged it when you went down. On the platform.'

'How long…you been here?'

'Don't worry about that. You just get better, all right?'

'She hasn't left your bedside for the last two days,' said Dr Falk, smiling approvingly at Mary. 'Now, what are we going to do with you?'

The first part of that question was to work out how to manage the succession of well-wishers. This shouldn't even have been a problem. Visiting hours were clearly signed and normally strictly policed: 2.30 to 3.45 in the afternoon, 6.15 to 7.45 in the evening. No more than two visitors by the bedside at any given time. Unfortunately, that system collapsed under the weight of concern for Billy Khan.

Hartshorne, probably as he was chairman of the Medical Fund Management Committee, considered himself entitled to wander in and out whenever it suited him. Cyn claimed similar rights on behalf of the Union. Her father found a regulation which allowed next of kin to visit outside normal times and Billy suddenly found himself with no fewer than four claimants vying to be so designated: Rosario, V.; Atkinson, S. (Mrs); Ray, A. (Dr); and, why or how no one knew, Coggins, E. (Mrs). Only Keenan studiously followed the rules, turning up every evening on the dot of 6.15 to report on progress in Shop B.

Mary had been allowed to stay by special dispensation of Dr Falk, who had also arranged a change of underwear for her as well as a regular supply of tea and sandwiches. After three days, with Billy past the worst, Dr Falk ordered her back to Cardiff to get a proper night's sleep and to sort out arrangements for her son to be looked after.

Finally, Ernie, to whom no rules in Swindon ever seemed to apply, popped in last thing each night.

The hospital was also inundated with gifts. Flowers and a fruit basket from Lady Jessica. An evening Guinness every night from Harry, the landlord of the Tap. A range of sworn-by country remedies and natural unguents from his colleagues in Shop B, all of which the pharmacist, Mrs Richards, binned after a single disapproving sniff at each. A pair of huge pink bed socks knitted by Doreen – most useful, as his feet had felt like blocks of ice ever since he'd woken up. On Ernie's second visit he had left Billy a bottle of his wine, which Mrs Richards poured into the toilet and flushed away before the front doors had closed behind him.

The second, and more important, part of Dr Falk's question was where to care for Billy. The Medical Fund Hospital had dealt with more than its share of crushed limbs and broken bones trolleyed over from the Works over the years. In normal circumstances a wound like his should have been well within its competence. But these were not normal circumstances. Supplies and expertise to deal with serious trauma had for months been diverted to military hospitals preparing for potentially thousands of wounded being shipped back from invasion beachheads. As a consequence, cottage hospitals in industrial towns struggled to deal with anything other than minor injuries whilst ward after ward in military hospitals stood empty and silent, their bored staff aching for something useful to do.

One such hospital was the vast US Army facility built on a hill overlooking Bath, from which the Andrews Sisters-impersonating nurses had come. The American authorities were desperate to do, and be seen to do, everything in their not-inconsiderable power to minimise the repercussions of their young soldier's mad act. Whilst the perpetrator himself sat in Shepton Mallet Prison awaiting return to the States for full psychiatric assessment, a range of ever more senior medical officers called to urge Billy's transfer to their care the moment he was deemed fit to travel. They had an ambulance standing by and some of the most highly trained and best-equipped medics in the world. He just had to give the word…

On learning of this, the word Billy gave was a very firm 'no'. He had, he said, been on the receiving end of quite enough Yankee attention for one lifetime, thank you very much. Instead, he told

Vincent to contact Lockyer and ask him to sort something out. Lockyer had proven extremely helpful to Vincent in finding out about contacts in Bombay once communications had resumed and the fact that a ship had indeed been blown up was officially acknowledged. He had also agreed to broach Sally's idea about the baby with Phyl on his behalf. Billy was pretty confident that the resourceful Lockyer would find an appropriate, expensive clinic to transfer him to, or a Harley St specialist who could be dispatched to Swindon to oversee his care. Never one to disappoint, he found both.

Billy had another reason for so adamantly refusing the proposed move to Bath – a conviction that Mary would loyally accompany him. And the last thing he intended to do was to allow his injuries – which had, albeit at the cost of quite excruciating pain and a worrying amount of blood, now won him her undivided attention – to be the reason she ended up being surrounded by healthy, eligible Yanks.

'Colonel Dawlish?'

'Inspector Curtis. I've been expecting you to call. Presumably you're ringing to tell me poor old Billy Khan has had an accident?'

'It wasn't an accident.'

'No? I think you'll find it is.'

'Stabbed deliberately in an unprovoked attack? By one of the GIs he'd had a run-in with before Christmas? I'd call that a criminal assault at the very least. GBH or attempted murder, more likely.'

'Well, we'll see. I suspect this will all blow over. How is he?'

'Khan? Awake. The next forty-eight hours are critical to see if there's any infection.'

'Well, thank you for keeping me informed.'

'You're welcome. But that's not why I'm ringing.'

'No? Then to what do I owe this pleasure?'

'To my asking you to tell your fake Irish rebel not to come back.'

'I have no idea what you're talking about.'

'Of course you don't. But just share the word with the people who do. If I get wind of anyone attempting to wind up and entrap my people, I'll have him in front of the Beak and named in the papers before you've got time to stop me.'

'That would be an extremely dangerous thing to do.'

'Wouldn't it? So let's both do our best to ensure that it won't be necessary.'

The day after Vincent called him, Lockyer swept into Swindon in a large car with a doctor and nurse in tow and the address of an exclusive sanatorium in Buckinghamshire in his pocket. Sally and Vincent were sitting with Billy. Sally was knitting, Vincent glancing through a newspaper, Billy dozing. All three had long run out of things to talk about. Mary had yet to return from Cardiff but had told one of the other girls to look in, check how he was doing and give him her love.

The doctor, a heavyset, muddy-faced man in his early fifties with small eyes behind half-moon glasses, listened with barely disguised impatience to Dr Falk's summation of Billy's injuries and current state. He glanced through her case notes, reading them aloud with exaggerated slowness, grunting occasionally. He then checked Billy over and declared him fit to travel. The nurse, similarly disdainful, supervised his move into a wheelchair, wrapped him in a large tartan blanket and wheeled him out to Lockyer's waiting Hispano-Suiza. Once she'd got him settled in, Billy asked for a moment with Dr Falk. The nurse sighed and pointedly looked at her watch but Billy insisted. Dr Falk came out and slipped into the back seat of the car next to him.

'Well, this is all very grand,' she said, looking around the leather-and-walnut interior of the car.

'I'm not sure I want to go,' Billy said. He had been surprised how weak he was. How much just being moved from the ward into the car had exhausted him.

'Nonsense,' said Dr Falk briskly. 'We can't do any more for you here. Anyway, you're taking up valuable bed space. Glad to see the back of you. Now we can hopefully get back to normal without all your visitors cluttering up the place. Poor Mrs R is near to a breakdown!'

'I'll never forget all you've done for me.'

She gave him a matronly pat on the knee. 'Well, just get better and come back to us soon. Shop B won't be the same without you.'

Sally replaced Dr Falk in the back seat beside Billy as the doctor headed back into the hospital. She dabbed away a tear and gave him a kiss on the cheek. He smiled, feeling tearful himself. She tucked the blanket more carefully around his knees. 'There,' she said, 'that's better. Can't have you turning up there looking like something the cat's dragged in.'

As Billy was taking his extended farewells, Lockyer beckoned Vincent aside. Together they stepped a few paces along the pavement and lit cigarettes. Lockyer took out a card. 'The address and phone number of the sanatorium that I'm taking him to. So you can keep up to speed with his progress.'

Vincent thanked him, tucking the address into his top pocket.

'And on that other matter,' said Lockyer. 'They're willing to talk. They propose neutral ground. My office is at your disposal if you'd like.'

'That's extremely kind of you,' Vincent said, excitement fluttering in his stomach. He couldn't wait to tell Sally. He looked back at the car, saw her fussing over Billy and felt a surge of affection.

'It's always nice to see problems solved,' Lockyer assured him. 'Shall we say next Tuesday, midday? My address is on the other side of that card. Right, better get our wounded hero on his way. There'll be hell to pay back in Gwalior if he gets a chill because I'm standing chatting to you instead of rushing him off.'

Together they walked back to the car. Vincent leaned in, wished Billy godspeed and promised to keep an eye on things for him. Sally and Lockyer assumed he meant the Bulldogs in Shop B but Billy knew he was referring to Mary and nodded his appreciation. Billy looked terrible. A greasy sweat covered his face even though he was shivering. His eyelids fluttered and he appeared about to pass out. The nurse checked his pulse, looked meaningfully at the doctor and said they needed to be on their way.

Lockyer and the doctor bundled into the car and they set off. Sally, Vincent, Dr Falk and three nurses watched them until they turned onto Emlyn Square, heading for Oxford Road. For all except Vincent, there was a deep melancholy.

'What are you smiling about?' Sally asked, frowning at Vincent. 'You look like the cat that got the cream.'

'Phase one of Operation Little Ern is complete!' he chuckled, reaching for her hand, before remembering that they were on the street, in the middle of a busy morning. A queue of housewives outside a bakery across the street were watching them, only too glad to stare at anything that would help pass the ages they'd be standing there. He followed Sally's glance across at them and automatically raised his hat. Several turned away, but more nodded their greetings and one or two waved back. 'Next Tuesday we meet the expectant mother.'

As it turned out, Vincent and Sally didn't meet Phyl. By this stage she had been packed off to stay with a deeply disapproving aunt outside Chester. Her parents, Sir John and Lady Grigg, were already in Lockyer's office just off Russell Square sipping sherry when they arrived. For Vincent, taking the train up to Paddington and going on into the city by Underground was, literally, all in a day's work. For Sally, it was a huge new challenge and her Swindonian distrust of 'London End' was compounded by the sudden renewal of German bombing raids in what was rapidly becoming known, ironically enough, as the 'Baby Blitz'.

Sir John was a large man with thinning brown hair combed over to try, unsuccessfully, to disguise a bald pate. He had bags under his eyes and a small scar on his chin. His mouth was turned down and his bottom lip thrust out, looking deeply unhappy. His wife was immaculately dressed in a deep blue suit. Her silver hair was swept back and carefully pinned up. She had finely chiselled features and parchment-like skin. Sally noticed Lady Grigg's hands. They were so finely manicured and well cared for, with elegantly shaped nails. She glanced down at her own hands, reddened and coarsened by too much hard work, and her blunt, chipped nails. She was already feeling deeply anxious about this meeting and the clear difference between the couples at that moment screamed out at her. Even dressed in her 'kept for best' weddings-and-funeral outfit, she knew she looked horribly dowdy and parochial.

Sir John pushed himself up out of his chair as Lockyer's secretary showed them through, shook hands with them both and asked after their journey. He'd met Vincent twice before and greeted him now like an old acquaintance. He'd been impressed by the rigour of the research Vincent had done and his efforts to shake up the GWR. Something long overdue, in Sir John's opinion. He also greatly admired the way that the deployment of the Bulldogs had so neatly circumvented the difficulties over their certification that Dawlish had insisted he create. Sir John did not like being told what to do by the likes of Dawlish, especially when they refused to give any justification other than some nonsense about the 'exigencies of Total War'. He had been secretly pleased that Dawlish's schemes, whatever they might have been about, had been frustrated at least as far as those old engines went.

'Just been hearing about poor Mr Khan,' Sir John said as Sally and Vincent took off their coats. 'So glad he seems to be on the mend. Disgraceful state of affairs!'

Lady Grigg sniffed. She had acknowledged their arrival with a slight shift of her head but had said nothing. Lockyer offered sherry. Sally asked for a cup of tea. There was small talk about the war. Comments about spring seeming to be not too far way now. Then an uncomfortable silence.

Sally mentioned that she'd never actually been to London before, prompting a raised eyebrow from Lady Grigg. A further silence. Then Lockyer announced he needed to be elsewhere and left the four of them. The strained silence returned.

Sir John asked after the progress of Vincent's work, but before he'd finished, Lady Grigg cut across him. 'Oh, for goodness' sake! That fellow Lockyer says you want to take Phyllida's... the bastard.'

'Yes,' said Sally, suddenly very calm and determined. 'I recently lost my husband. A few years ago my little girl died. We can give the child a home with people who will love it.'

'And look like it,' Vincent added.

'As I understand it, you aren't married?'

'Not yet,' Vincent admitted. 'But if your daughter agrees to this adoption, we'll marry by special licence.'

Sir John looked troubled. Sally glanced desperately at Vincent. Clearly something was not right.

'There will not be an adoption,' Lady Grigg said, speaking very carefully. 'If this is to happen, the child will be handed over to you immediately and you will register the birth, with the two of you recorded as its parents. There can be no question of Phyllida's name appearing on any official documentation relating to this matter.'

Vincent opened his mouth to object but Sally placed a restraining hand on his arm. 'Agreed,' she said.

'I see that we understand one another, Mrs Atkinson,' acknowledged Lady Grigg, allowing herself a slight, frosty smile. 'There are now two separate conversations that need to take place. Mr Rosario and my husband can deal with the financial side. You and I, Mrs Atkinson, need to agree on the practicalities.'

'There's no need…' Vincent began. Again, Sally stopped him.

'Go and speak with…Miss Grigg's dad,' she whispered. She couldn't quite bring herself to call him 'Sir John', but knew 'Mr Grigg' wouldn't be acceptable. 'Sort things out.' Then, turning back to the Griggs she asked, 'This is what your daughter wants to happen?'

'Absolutely!' Sir John assured her. 'One hundred per cent. You have my word.'

'And you?' Lady Grigg asked Sally after the men had left, her mouth twisted and her voice bitter. 'Is this really what you want? This...lavender shotgun wedding?'

'I don't know what you mean.'

'I think you do. You may not be carrying this baby, but you're rushing up the aisle before the brat appears, which is the defining characteristic of a shotgun wedding, isn't it? And your intended… I assume he's going along with this to camouflage what he is. So don't tell me you don't know what a lavender wedding is. He is one of them, isn't he?'

'Whatever he is, whatever kind of wedding this is,' snapped back Sally, 'it will be you, your husband, your daughter and your grandchild who will benefit from this the most.'

'And will no doubt be made to pay dearly for the privilege. Well, we can afford it. I hope for your sake that you know what you're doing.'

The plan they agreed on was simple. They would marry as soon as possible. Sally would go and stay in a bed-and-breakfast in Cheshire as Phyl's date of confinement approached, remain there until the delivery and then register the child as hers and Vincent's. Sir John, who before being called out of retirement to serve in his present position had been Deputy Chairman of the London, Midland and Scottish Railway and a long-term resident of Cheshire, assured them there'd be no difficult questions asked at that end.

Sally intended to claim the baby had been born prematurely, to be able to say that it was conceived on their wedding night. Whatever anyone thought, they would have a marriage certificate and the baby a birth certificate. That was all that really mattered. And once the proper paperwork was done, whether Vincent stayed or went, whatever anyone else said or thought, no one would ever be able to take the baby away from her.

The Griggs would arrange Sally's accommodation and transport, meet all costs and help arrange the special licence for their rushed wedding. Once the details were agreed, they were very keen to make the whole process as easy as possible for everyone involved. It was clear that they regarded Akaash as the author of all their woes and dearly wished to see some retribution visited on him. Such was their fury at him, Sir John had even rung the despised Dawlish to demand that Akaash be immediately arrested and interned – something he now regretted, as it could potentially compromise their plan. Their daughter they spoke of as a sweet but incredibly unsophisticated bluestocking. They'd sheltered her far too much from the realities of life outside a devout Catholic home. She was an innocent – determined to put her remarkable intelligence to work in the war effort – and must have been an easy target for an exotic foreigner keen to take advantage of her naivety, they concluded.

As they left Lockyer's office, Sir John assured Sally and Vincent that he was determined to do everything in his not-inconsiderable power to make this work. He also secretly resolved to ensure that the GWR Bulldogs got their certificates, and to hell with that bloody man Dawlish.

Billy spent two weeks at the sanatorium west of High Wycombe. He was well cared for and made good progress. He was surprised at how enervated he had been by the attack, how distrustful he now felt and how urgently he wanted to leave. Everyone who looked after him was professional and courteous and yet he felt desperately friendless, suddenly very much the foreigner far from home in an alien place. His healthy young man's assumption of immortality and invulnerability had been ripped from him and he was, for the first time since his arrival, frightened by his surroundings. However, it was not Gwalior to which he ached to return, but No. 23 Ashton St, Swindon. He knew this made no sense, but it just was how he felt. He begged Lockyer to arrange for his discharge, but the Maharajah's agent, who visited him every few days, categorically refused until the doctor confirmed that he was well enough. To Lockyer's deep discomfort and his own horror, Billy burst into tears. A sympathetic nurse assured them both that it was shock, and only to be expected. Nothing to be embarrassed about.

A small delegation from Shop B came to visit, travelling on tickets issued by Hartshorne specifically for that purpose – Elsie, Cyn, Doreen and Keenan. They brought cards, gifts and assurances that he was sorely missed. Although work was progressing perfectly well in his absence, they'd concocted a series of imaginary problems on the journey, to reassure him of his value. He played along but knew that they were just trying to be kind. At the end of the visit, Elsie held back as the others headed into the corridor. She looked around conspiratorially, then slipped him a pink envelope from inside her handbag. 'From Mary,' she whispered. 'She's no use to man nor boy these days. Lovestruck. Daft little cow.'

Billy wasn't sure how he felt about that, other than unutterably sad. He thanked her, again becoming somewhat weepy.

'And you need to pull yourself together and all,' Elsie unsympathetically advised. 'You big girl.'

It was only the visit of Sally and Vincent – who had come to share the news of their impending wedding and to ask him to be best man – that finally broke his malaise and started to improve his spirits. He said he'd be delighted, and couldn't think of a finer couple. Sally patted his hand – he'd noticed lots of people had been doing that lately, time to put a stop to that – and told him the reason for their rushed plans, and he was even happier. They'd fixed the date for just a few days later. Billy assured them he'd already decided that it was time to get back to Swindon.

'We're not getting married in Swindon,' Vincent explained. 'It'll be at a registry office in London. There'll just be the four of us. You and Akaash will be our witnesses.'

'Do you think you're up to it?' asked Sally, patting his hand again.

'Just try to stop me being there,' Billy replied, withdrawing his hand. He was already wondering how much he could get away with spending on gifts without Vincent getting angry. One thing was for sure: among the purchases would be a new frying pan. Since that night with Derek the old one had been regarded with deep foreboding…and Billy had a craving for bacon.

Lockyer was immediately suspicious when he received the invitation from Dawlish to afternoon tea at his club just off St James. He knew that this was no social courtesy. Men like Dawlish tended to sneer at men like Lockyer. As he walked up Park Place to the imposing building at its end, he felt like a particularly ill-prepared fly approaching an exceptionally elegant web.

He paused at the doorway to allow an elderly dowager to enter before him. He raised his hat politely and received a haughty nod of acknowledgement. Leaving hat and coat with the porter, he was directed through to the Buttery. A couple of retired colonial administrators sat chatting loudly over cucumber sandwiches. Two officers of an Indian regiment, Rajputs if he wasn't mistaken, were smoking cigarettes and reading newspapers. Then he spotted Dawlish sitting alone at a table silhouetted against a high window looking out onto the garden and Green Park beyond.

Dawlish rose and offered his hand. 'Good of you to come. You know this place?'

'I think I probably still have membership,' Lockyer replied, settling himself into the chair opposite Dawlish. 'A few years ago the Maharajah of Gwalior funded the renovation and decoration of the dining room downstairs. I was in and out of here all the time then.'

'Really? Tea? Or something stronger?'

'Tea will be splendid, thank you.'

They ordered, and Dawlish asked about affairs in Gwalior. Innocuous, trivial questions about old acquaintances, sport and the weather. To each question, Lockyer responded warily.

'Tell me, how long have you chaps been the Scindia's agents?' Dawlish wondered.

'I'm the third generation.'

'Must give you an interesting insight into things.'

'Not at all. Mainly pretty routine stuff.'

'Seen some changes though...'

'Indeed. But whatever changes occur, the Scindias know they can always rely on our probity and discretion.'

Dawlish smiled. 'Warning shot across the bows duly noted. Shall we talk about our visitors in Swindon instead.'

'I'm afraid that all depends. I'd regard anything to do with Mr Khan as covered by my duty to the Palace.'

'But you have no such relationship with the other two.'

'Absolutely not.'

'Then tell me, what reason did Vincent Rosario and his landlady have for their recent visit to your office?'

'It was a private matter I was...helping out with.'

Dawlish sat very still, studying Lockyer, barely blinking, seemingly not even breathing. Lockyer couldn't hold that stare and glanced uncomfortably away. He was profoundly grateful when the tea arrived.

Wordlessly, Dawlish poured the tea. He was clearly content to let the weight of his silence work on Lockyer. It did.

'It was purely personal,' Lockyer blurted out. 'Nothing to do with his work, or India, or the war. A domestic matter.'

'Who else was there?'

'I don't think…'

'I'll ask again. Who else was there?'

Lockyer pushed his cup and saucer away and began to stand. 'I'm sorry, colonel, but I think this conversation is over.'

'It's over when I say it is. Sit down.'

Lockyer sat.

'Listen to me. Carefully. I know Gwalior thinks itself the centre of the world but just at this moment I have no interest in Gwalior State. Horror of horrors! So before you get too precious about what you'll tell me and what you won't, just bear in mind that the next few years are likely to be difficult ones for all of us, most especially for people like you and those you represent. A friend or two could be extremely valuable. A favour or two owed might turn out to be the difference between success and ruin. It's your duty to your country and to those you serve to answer my questions. Who else was there?'

'Sir John and Lady Grigg,' Lockyer said miserably, not lifting his gaze from his teacup.

'And what could those four have to talk about?'

'The Griggs's daughter is carrying the child of the Bengali, Ray.'

'I already know that. What has any of this to do with Rosario?'

'He and the landlady are going to take it.'

'Is that why he's applying for a special licence to marry? In order that they can adopt it?'

'Yes. Except there won't be a formal adoption. The child will be handed over and registered as theirs from the outset.'

Dawlish slumped back in his chair. 'Well! Congratulations, Mr Lockyer. You've managed to do something that I'd thought impossible. You've actually taken me by surprise.'

'Can I ask something?'

'I think I owe you that. Go on.'

'Why are you so interested in Vincent Rosario?'

'Him being in possession of an embarrassing amount of sensitive information not being reason enough? Because there's something not right about him.' He smiled, seemingly in an expansive mood. 'Doesn't it seem to you odd that after all the fuss he made over getting back to Bombay, he now seems happy to stay and get married?'

'I understood you'd imposed travel restrictions on him.'

'True. But they won't last forever. And how about that list of people he asked you to check up on after the explosion?'

'What about it?'

'Didn't strike you as odd that none of them were called Rosario? Not a one. He's got photos of parents, brother, sisters, aunts and uncles, nieces and nephews in his room in Swindon.

Yet the people he wants to know are safe are either employees of the BBCI or attendees at a dance hall. Not one relative.'

'Well, at least you know there's nothing sinister about his meeting in my office,' said Lockyer, glancing at his watch.

'A fraudulent registration of a birth? I must check but I think that falls under the 1911 Perjury Act. A criminal conspiracy, involving the Deputy Head of the Ministry of War Transport, aided and abetted by you. Dear me, Mr Lockyer. What would the Maharajah say? Your reputation for probity looks like it now depends on my reputation for discretion.'

EXHIBIT

A monochrome photographic image, 8″ x 10″, bearing the name of the photographer, 'Jellicoe', in the right-hand bottom corner.

Image appears to have been taken on the steps of an office building, the windows of which are cross-taped and the entrance sandbagged.

Image shows four figures, posed, standing side by side. Three male, one female. All four are formally dressed. The men in suits and overcoats, holding hats. The woman in a hat and coat with what appears to be a paisley patterned scarf or shawl around her shoulders. She is holding a small bunch of flowers.

The two figures in the centre of the image, a man and woman of similar height and age, stand with linked arms. To their left is a smaller figure. He is younger and has a noticeably darker complexion than the others. He is wearing glasses. To their right, a taller, bearded man is leaning on a walking stick. He is more expensively dressed than the others and wears a flower in his lapel. He stands awkwardly, as though in discomfort.

All four are smiling.

In the foreground, the shadow of the photographer can be discerned.

Another partial shadow to the left suggests at least one other observer.

On the reverse of the image is the word 'Marylebone' and a date: 8 March 1944.

Billy's return to Swindon was greeted with obvious pleasure and, as he had predicted, an exceptionally large hamper of humility, the contents of which he asked Keenan to share-out in Shop B. However, news of his return was quickly swamped in the flurry of gossip and speculation surrounding the news of Sally and Vincent having secretly married. Ernie shook his head in wonder and produced the inevitable bottle of wine. The term 'unseemly haste' was mentioned with many a knowing expression.

Lots of people offered bemused congratulations, several wondered what was going on and one or two – such as Elsie – couldn't resist asking why. After all, many thought Vincent was, well, you know. A bit like that Oscar Wilde. Plus, Sally Atkinson, sorry Rosario, was a good-looking woman with whom several men had planned to try their luck as soon as a suitable period after Derek's death had elapsed. Who'd have thought that the Bof would pip them all to the post? Foreigners, eh? No respect. In the Tap and in the Works he was regarded with a new esteem. He was, as Ernie observed and all agreed, a bloody dark horse.

Billy returned to the care of Dr Falk and after a few days began to make brief visits to Shop B, but it was obvious to him that he needed longer to convalesce. Shop B hummed with purposeful activity and, much as it pained him to admit it, Keenan seemed to be doing a perfectly good job running things in his absence. Work, he was assured, would wait, and sadly it looked as though for him at least, it could.

What couldn't, though, was what to do about Mary.

Elsie, untypically circumspect, had called her lovestruck: others used less polite terms but all acknowledged and mocked her obvious and all-absorbing devotion to Billy. The only problem was – now that he finally had her all to himself and she had spent long hours sitting with him – he had begun to notice a number of traits that he'd either overlooked or had regarded as endearing before. She sniffed noisily. She had an irritating way of simpering to people in authority and, truth to tell, in harsh daylight or under bright hospital lighting, she wasn't actually as pretty as he'd always thought. Her legs had looked good in high-heeled shoes but padding around in a pair of slippers on loan from the fearsome Mrs R, her calves struck him as heavy and her ankles somewhat thick.

He felt bad about this transformation in his feelings. He knew how much she'd given up to care for him, and he would make sure that she wouldn't be out of pocket. He'd see the manager at Lloyds Bank and draw on his allowance from the State. He'd buy her some decent clothes. Give her money for her son. Give her enough that she could leave the streets for good. But one way or another, he was determined to get rid of her. Where once the mere thought of her had made him dizzy with desire, she now annoyed and embarrassed him. In hospital, she mothered him like a sick child, lovingly combing his hair. She read to him and hummed to him as he fell asleep. It was awful, and it had stamped all desire for her in him stone-dead.

To be fair to her, she'd never once said anything about the future. Never presumed that they even had one together. But she showed up whenever she could, which was depressingly frequently, and now when she did, the atmosphere in No. 23 was pretty tense. Sally made it very clear that she wasn't happy having a woman of her sort, no better than she should be, under her roof. Mary was used to being sneered at, spurned or ignored by respectable women like Sally and she tried very hard to behave impeccably in her disapproving presence. Billy found it best to race to the front door on hearing her knock, grab her arm, turn her around and quickly lead her away, insisting that the doctor had told him that he needed a good, long walk. Hopefully, he usually prayed, one during which they might avoid both the smirks and sneers of his colleagues and the cheery hellos of some of her more brash customers – most of whom she seemed happy to see, usually sighing, 'Ah! Lovely man,' as she returned their greetings.

Billy prepared himself for a difficult conversation, one for which he felt desperately ill-equipped. He realised that he'd never actually broken off a relationship. In the past, his experiences were confined to brief flings or longer romances in which he'd been the one to receive their marching orders. What on earth was he going to say? All he could think of was something about star-crossed lovers or ships that pass in the night, which was as unhelpful as it was trite. Maybe he could just send her a cheque in a 'Thank you and Goodbye' card and tell Sally not to answer the door the next time she came?

No, he supposed he had to do the decent thing.

On their return to Swindon immediately after their wedding, Vincent and Sally also had some uncomfortable conversations to have. The idea of their marriage, seen solely as a mechanism to allow Sally to adopt, had been fine. They'd both committed to it and had worked together well to make it happen. But now, back in No. 23, they needed to consider the practicalities of living as man and wife. And the first, most obvious issue, was sleeping arrangements.

Billy and Akaash had temporarily moved out to allow the newly-weds some privacy. Strangely, even the thought of dancing together seemed wrong now. They were unusually ill at ease in one another's company, struggled to find things to say, and wished the two tenants hadn't been so considerate. Two...? Vincent realised with a start that he wasn't actually a paying guest any more and appreciated, perhaps for the first time, the magnitude of the step he'd taken.

'What are you doing?' asked Sally as Vincent went into the front room to make up his bed on the sofa as usual.

Vincent paused, turned and looked at her.

'We're husband and wife,' Sally pointed out.

'On paper. For the baby,' Vincent quietly replied.

'Husbands and wives sleep in the same bed.'

'Sally, I...'

She reached out and took his hand. 'I know,' she assured him. 'Nothing will happen.' She gave him a huge smile and patted his cheek. 'Don't worry. Your honour's safe with me! But we're sleeping in the same room, ideally in the same bed. If we're doing this, we're doing it properly. We're going to look married and act married. And that's that. I'll go up first and change. You go and have a smoke. I'll be tucked up tight in bed with the light out by the time you come up. I won't say a word to you until tomorrow morning. Good night, husband.'

As the Rosarios went uncomfortably to bed, Billy had a flash of inspiration. The US Army was desperate to keep all word of his stabbing quiet, and the British authorities seemed only too willing to collude in keeping it out of the news. The appearance of total Allied harmony must be preserved at all costs: Britain welcoming its cousins from across the pond, the Yanks only too happy to be here to help out. To be fair, the Americans' concern for Billy wasn't entirely cynical. They seemed genuinely keen to do whatever was in their power to show their regret and sympathy.

Billy had been reflecting on the wisdom of his decision to so abruptly reject their offer of a transfer to the US Army hospital in Bath. Perhaps if he had, Mary wouldn't now be a problem. Then it occurred to him: maybe it still wasn't too late? What if he, with

Mary of course in tow, asked them for a second – well, third – opinion on his injuries and treatment? Could Mary be gently encouraged to rekindle her initial ambition of catching a Yank? After all, despite the hours – the days – that she'd spent with Billy, she still hadn't yet actually done it with a…well, with him.

Mind you, she'd be encountering medical professionals, on duty and sober. Better potential husband material perhaps but not at all the class of men she was used to dealing with. She'd need to be smartened up a bit and sadly, even if he gave her the money and got her the clothing coupons, Billy didn't think he could rely on her choosing something appropriate. Her tastes were a bit… cheap. Lockyer would probably consider kitting her out beneath his dignity. Anyway, the old fossil would be hopelessly ill-equipped to do so: probably would end up dressing her like Queen Mary. Sally wouldn't do it. Wasn't even worth asking her. Who'd have imagined that she'd be such a snob? He smiled. She'd fit into Anglo-Indian society very well, he thought. Dr Falk had taken a shine to Mary: maybe he could ask her to help? Say it was a thank you for all Mary's kindness to him whilst he'd been laid up? No, he concluded glumly, that probably wouldn't work either.

Well, well, well!' cried Curtis as he flung Akaash's file on the table in the interview room and sat down opposite its subject. 'Your oppo Rosario: who'd have guessed. Talk about still waters! Got to hand it to him though. You lot ought to be called the Three Bears!'

'What?'

'"Who's been sleeping in my bed?" Didn't think it would be him.'

Akaash glared across the table. 'I don't think you should talk like that.'

Curtis regarded him suspiciously. 'What's got into you all of a sudden? I thought you didn't like him?'

'I think Mr and Mrs Rosario both have the right to be spoken about with respect, that's all.'

Curtis shook his head. 'I don't think I'll ever understand you. No sign of our three-bob Paddy?'

Akaash was momentarily confused. 'Who? Oh, the Irishman. No. Not as far as I'm aware.'

'Which, as we both know, tends not to be very far. Anything interesting happening?'

'Not really. There's still a lot of anger that Billy Khan's stabbing is being covered up.'

'I should bloody well hope so. And…?'

'There's talk of contacting the *Daily Worker*. Getting them to write something on it.'

'Waste of time! Since the Soviets changed sides they're more gung-ho than the *Telegraph*. Better off trying the *Mirror*. At least they're getting steamed up about the black lads the Yanks keep hanging at Shepton Mallet.'

Akaash looked confused. 'I thought you people wanted it all hushed up.'

'You're doing it again, young Bish-Bash. Confusing me with them. You get cross when anyone says you and your oppos are all the same. We are not all alike. I, for example, don't like foreigners coming into my town and cutting up rough, then being told they'll sort it all out between themselves. This isn't Italy. I don't expect to see a man knifed here and to be told that it's nothing to do with the law of the land. That's not the way it works, however London may see it. You do whatever you want. Good luck to you.'

'Do you know what happened to the soldier who did it?'

'Shipped home. Dishonourable discharge. Off to an asylum. Or so they say. One of the ones you and that old twat Norris had a run-in with, apparently.'

Akaash's eyes widened. 'Not the young one?'

'How the fuck do I know? Anyway, who cares? It shouldn't have happened and when it did, it should have been handled properly. Anything else? No? Well, I've got something for you.'

Curtis opened the file and took out a sheet of foolscap paper, folded in half. He carefully unfolded it and spread it out on the table. 'Go on. Look at it.'

Akaash picked it up. It was a list of money transfers in rupees, confirmed as received as per his instructions in Calcutta and recorded as collected from the General Post Office. The dates looked right but there was something wrong with the figures. Starting from mid-January, there was a sharp increase to a level that was then maintained in all later payments. He didn't need to run the maths in his head to recognise that even at the most generous exchange rates, this was significantly more than he had been forwarding. A mistake? He very much doubted it. He looked at Curtis, who met his stare with a complacent smile.

'You've done well by them. Especially since the turn of the year. Probably more money than mum and dad would see in a month of Sundays if you were still at home. Now, what does a bright lad like you notice about those sums? Nothing? You disappoint me. As usual. Well, we both know that they're getting more than you're sending.'

'You want me to say thank you?'

Curtis raised his eyebrows. 'You think I'm adding to the Ray family's dinner money? Thanks for the compliment but I'm not in the habit of paying for something I'm already getting for free, as the bishop probably said to the actress. No, I want you to explain to me where that extra money is coming from.'

'I have no idea.'

'Who else are you working for?'

'No one. Honestly, I don't know what's going on.'

'As per usual.' Curtis stared hard at Akaash. 'Really?'

'Really.'

'Well, for once, I hope you're lying. 'Cos if you're telling the truth, there's a day of reckoning coming your way. And on that day, I really wouldn't want to be you. Because I've got a nasty feeling I know who your fairy godmother just might be.'

The whole idea of Lent, of forty days of Christian self-denial prior to Easter, had a particularly hollow ring after so many months of ever-shrinking rations. A couple of years earlier, people used to joke that it would be nice to actually have something to resist. But by the fourth Lent of the war, that wisecrack had itself become the only thing most people could afford to give up.

Blossom was beginning to burst forth on fruit trees. Tulips were opening as daffodil heads shrivelled. Celandines and dandelion glowed bright yellow among thickening grass in the spring sun. Sticky weed rampaged up embankments and through hedges. The sky seemed larger and lighter and there was a first hint of warmth in the sun. Seed trays were prepared and laid out under glass for salads and summer greens. In Farringdon Park, the lawns not yet dug up for allotments or heavily clinker-coated for the parking of military vehicles had their first spring cut and the air filled with the heady scent of the newly mown sward: a promise of better days.

In back gardens, beds were dug over and clay clods broken up. Ernie planted out onion sets and early potatoes, top-dressing the latter with fresh horse manure – the collection, delivery and selling of which was ensuring that he and his handcart were in and out of the Works several times a day. Next door, Vincent enjoyed the feeling of the sun on his back as he bent to thrust a peg with string knotted to it into the freshly raked back garden. He carefully paced backward, unrolling the rest of the cord and then, closing one eye to select the ideal line, pushed the second peg into the ground.

He straightened, surveying his first baby steps as a gardener with deep satisfaction. He had assiduously raked and hoed the prepared bed until the tilth was free of both stones and weeds. Hearing a quiet chuckle, he glanced across to see Ernie on the other side of the fence, urinating on a pile of last year's vegetation rotting down in a corner of his garden.

'It's not the Chelsea Flower Show, mate,' Ernie observed. He stepped back, crouched slightly and buttoned up his flies. 'Look at you, laying out that bed with military precision.'

Vincent smiled. There was a time when he would have instantly taken offence at Ernie's crack. Now he simply took out his cigarettes and offered one across the fence. 'Dare I ask what you were doing?'

'Fixing nitrogen in my compost heap,' Ernie replied, as though it were the most obvious thing in the world. 'It's what real gardeners do. I wouldn't worry. You're years away from being mistaken for that.'

'You think so? Let's just see whose onions do best.'

'Bloody hell! Are you serious? Five minutes ago you didn't know a trowel from a tree and now you're challenging me? And on onions? Who got you the bloody things? Cheeky bugger. I think it's about time you went home.'

It was. Past time. For whilst each of the men at No. 23 had plenty else to think about, their work was pretty much completed. The 'Wheat/Chaff' system devised by Phyl, Joan and Akaash was rolled out across the region and seemed to be working well. Vincent and Lapworth were increasingly marginalised as the Movements team adopted the new timetabling arrangements – daily more convinced that it had all been their idea anyway – and the continuing influx of American troops at Cardiff and Newport docks presented lesser challenges. As new records of numbers of disembarking GIs handled and speed of dispatch achieved were regularly set and as regularly broken, ghost trains were reduced and the Shop B Bulldogs entered full service, their Ministry of War Transport certification issued as unexpectedly as their initial rejection had been declared.

The only thing that kept them was an unwillingness of the powers that be to allow them to go. Not that they were being singled out for such treatment: towards the end of April, an absolute ban was announced on all foreign travel. Citizens, visitors and even diplomats from Allied powers were subject to indefinite restrictions whilst hundreds of thousands of ordinary people living along the south coast of England were forcibly relocated further inland.

It was thus a strange hiatus for them, a lacuna. It was the same for many others, but they alone seemed so out of kilter with the mood of the times. Whilst everyone else felt part of a nation – a family of nations – building up to the big push, preparing for the great throw of the dice, readying themselves yet again to do their bit, for the three Indian gentlemen, their bit seemed comprehensively done. They had met the challenges set for them, made their contribution and exceeded expectations. A range of personal matters still cried for resolution but, as far as their reason for being here was concerned, they were just marking time until they were permitted to return home.

The first stage of Billy's plan to rid himself of Mary's irksome presence succeeded so far beyond expectations that he was sorely tempted to abandon the rest of the enterprise. Expensively turned out in a red knee-length A-line skirt and a candy-stripe blouse with puffed sleeves, matching shoes and handbag, gloves and the hat that she'd finally settled on, she really did look stunning. She'd had her hair professionally cut for the first time in her life. As Billy was now providing her with funds, she was eating regularly and sleeping well. Her skin, no longer heavily made-up, glowed with youth and health and when she gave him that smile she only ever bestowed on him, she really was quite beautiful. If only she would stop mothering him, talk a little less and a bit more quietly – in fact a lot more quietly – and stop that infuriating sniffing, he might have reconsidered the necessity of his plans for her.

In the end, unable to find anyone else willing to do it, he had taken her out for her transformation himself. They'd visited haberdashers, milliners, shoe shops and a hair parlour, and spent hours searching through the latest stock in Anstis and McIlroys, the department stores that dominated Regent St. While shopping, Billy was discreetly advised that if he'd care to step into the gents' outfitters, the store now had official approval to reintroduce pockets on men's suit jackets and turn-up cuffs on trousers. He'd declined politely, expressing his pleasure in the news, not realising that they'd ever been forbidden. Mary, excited as a child on Christmas morning, had wanted to try on everything, dashing in and out of changing rooms, mixing and matching accessories, striding out, swirling and striking a fashion-model pose with a movie-star pout. She asked his opinion on each costume change, wondered if this one was cut right 'up top', or that one hung wrong at the hips. He was surprised to find that he too was actually enjoying the whole experience – her joy, the intimacy. He decided that they'd make an additional call at Mr Isles, the jewellers on Market St, to select a necklace. Perhaps a bracelet too. But not, God forbid, a ring.

'Scrub up well, don't I?' she said happily, turning to admire herself in the full-length mirror on the changing room door. Then she looked at him, playfully suspicious and decidedly arch. 'Why you getting me all dolled-up like this? Got something in mind?'

'It's just a little thank you for looking after me,' Billy assured her uncomfortably. Fun though this bit might be, he really wished that this whole thing was over. 'I have an appointment at the American hospital in Bath the day after tomorrow,' he continued, trying to sound nonchalant. 'Just a checkup. But I thought you might like to come. We could make a day of it. Maybe have tea at the Pump Rooms…'

'Surprised you'll let me near all them Yanks dressed up to the nines like this…' she laughed, then her smile froze and faded as realisation dawned. 'Oh, I see,' she sighed, suddenly looking much older as she slowly unpinned the hat and took off the gloves.

'Mary, I…'

Her eyes were bright with tears and her face contorted as she fought to hold them back. 'You just had to say. That's all.' She sniffed. 'I wasn't the one doing the chasing.'

'I just want you to be happy,' Billy pleaded inadequately.

'No. You just want shot of me. You just had to say,' she repeated.

'Mary, I'm so sorry. I never intended to hurt you.'

'Men like you never do, do they? Yet somehow that's how it always turns out. You can have all this clobber back tomorrow. You know where I'll be.'

In preparation for the story they had thought of to explain the arrival of the child, Sally had started wearing loose-fitting clothes that hid her figure. Several people already wondered if it might disguise a baby bump. She desperately wished there was something, anything, more practical that she could think of to do. For her too this was a somewhat lost period of inactivity, awaiting the outcome of events over which she had no control, for Phyl wasn't due to give birth until mid-June. With hindsight, they'd probably rushed headlong into the wedding unnecessarily. They could have afforded to wait a couple more months, but she had been haunted by the thought that some other arrangement for the child might have been made, or that Vincent would leave or change his mind. No, she concluded, she'd done the right thing.

Of course, most folk ascribed their hasty wedding to the fact that they'd been 'carrying on' behind Derek's back and that she was already, as they variously surmised, in the family way, up the duff, with a bun in the oven or one up the spout. Derek's mother had screamed as much to her face, calling her a filthy whore who'd dishonoured her wedding vows, which Sally thought was pretty rich coming from a woman whose own past was nothing much to write home about. Others too disapproved. The tallyman was unusually loquacious about the matter, announcing in the Tap to anyone who'd listen that for two pins he'd go round there and teach them both a lesson they wouldn't forget in a hurry – until reminded by Harry that Ernie lived next door, at which he sank back into sullen grumbling. But by and large, disapproval was muted.

The idea of some filthy foreigner bedding the little woman back home whilst hubbie was off bravely fighting for King and Country was a regular theme of German propaganda and an abiding worry for those responsible for keeping up morale among the troops. The reality was inevitably much more nuanced. It went on, everybody knew. Especially with the Yanks. And as long as it wasn't flaunted, so long as no one made too much of a song and dance about it, most people seemed to feel that it was all just best ignored. Turn a blind eye, mind one's own business and carry on as though nothing's happened.

Sally remained bemused by Vincent's monk-like celibacy, his seeming dislike of most physical contact yet his obvious enjoyment of dance. She wondered if something had happened to him as a child. After all, she reasoned, you heard stories like that, confided in whispers. Funny uncles, most often. Drunken fathers. Dodgy priests. The more she thought about it, the more likely it seemed. Maybe even one of the people in his family pictures? He'd done her a massive kindness in marrying her. She owed him something and if her body was of no interest to him, perhaps she could bring him comfort in some other way.

Sally gathered up the half-dozen group photos that Vincent had brought with him. He had kept them in simple frames, stood on the mantelpiece when the front room was his bedroom. Since moving back upstairs to share their chaste marital bed, he'd stacked them carefully, each wrapped in a folded sheet of newspaper, and put them away. Odd, she'd thought, even as she'd watched him do it. OK, their marriage was hardly typical or likely to be of long duration, but she'd sort of felt that he ought to introduce her to his kith and kin, if not in the flesh, then at least through a review of those photos.

She lay the pictures out and studied them. The old couple were presumably his parents. A studio shot. The woman sitting, the man standing behind and slightly to one side of her, both dressed in Western clothes in a style long out of date. They looked deeply uncomfortable, and held themselves abnormally stiffly, as though apprehensive at being photographed. She held up the picture and examined it closely, looking at their faces for any resemblance to Vincent. But there was none that she could immediately see. Perhaps the woman's nose?

Next, a gathering in a garden. Sharp contrasts, long shadows. Five couples, standing around a table with a cloth on it, laid out for a picnic. A couple of children, holding their mothers' hands. One of the men had a cigarette in his mouth. Another held a cup and saucer. Impossible to make out much more. On to the next.

A wedding. Again, formally posed. Again, Western clothes. Again anonymous.

Vincent entered as she moved on to the fourth. He stood watching her, saying nothing.

'Why don't you put the kettle on, and then come tell me who's who?' asked Sally, feeling suddenly guilty, as though she'd crossed a line, invaded his privacy. Silly really, given that she'd seen these photos virtually every day before their wedding.

He lifted the kettle, shook it, decided there was enough water in it and lit the gas ring. 'I don't know,' he said very quietly.

'What do you mean you don't know. They're your family, aren't they?'

Vincent sat down across the table from her. 'Where would you like to start?'

Sally picked up the first image she'd looked at: the couple she'd assumed were his parents.

'I found that in a pile of old photographs that were being dumped. The photographer had gone out of business. They were in a box in the street outside his studio in Colaba. So was this one,' he said, reaching across and picking up another photograph. 'That one too,' he added, pointing to another. 'Next?'

She offered him the picnic scene. 'That's the first one I acquired. It's a group of people from the church I attended. I know one or two of them. They worked with the Railway too. See the man on the far right? The one with the cigarette? Died in the explosion, Mr Lockyer thinks.'

'I thought they were your family.'

'You were meant to. Everyone was meant to. That's the point.'

'So who are these people?'

'Just people. I like the idea of them.'

Sally struggled to understand quite what he was saying. 'Why would anyone make up a family?'

Vincent shrugged. 'Why would anyone be so willing to help you give Akaash's child a home?'

She reached out and placed her hand on top of his. 'Oh, Vincent. I'm so sorry. When you said you had an idea of what the poor little thing's life would be…'

He gently eased his hand from beneath hers. 'I don't want sympathy. Yours or anyone else's. I have no family. I grew up in an orphanage. That wasn't my choice nor my fault. I survived.

But I wouldn't wish it on another and I don't want it to define me. So I invented a family. And I agreed to help you so that Akaash's kid has a real one.'

'You've got one now as well, Vincent. If you want one. Right here. What have you got to go back home to? Nothing. No job. No one.'

'It's my home.'

'So is this. You're a railwayman in a railway town. The GWR would be glad to have you, I'm sure, and so would I. We can make a family. For you. For me. For…'

'Little Ern?'

'Yes. And that kettle's going to boil itself dry.'

Akaash and Joan prepared extensive notes on the 'Wheat/Chaff' system and, now that the pressure was off, came up with several workable coding processes that they also wrote up with a view to publishing once the war ended. For them both, one day seemed much the same as the next, until one morning when Akaash noticed a sudden flurry of unexplained activity in the Works. Joan, more finely attuned to mood, noted a change in the atmosphere. Together, they watched and listened and wondered as their concerns grew day by day.

A number of senior staff had failed to appear, and when Akaash or Joan asked why the answers were inconsistent and evasive: family reasons, outstanding holiday entitlement needing to be taken by salaried staff before the end of the leave year, hospital appointments, upcoming professional examinations for which the company allocated paid study time. The Movements team, less Lapworth and Vincent who were designated to remain, were dispatched to York at short notice to meet with their opposite numbers on the London and North Eastern Railway. All secret work in Shop X came to a halt and a number of mysterious, bulky shapes draped in tarpaulin were loaded on wagons, shunted on to the main line and added to a long train heading west. Engines nearing completion of their routine maintenance were in steam and on the move before the paperwork was finalised. Others were dispatched to marshalling yards around the region. Several engines a day normally arrived at the Works but this too seemed to have come to a halt. Fire-watchers were on roofs during the day as well as at night.

'A flap,' Joan concluded ominously, 'is clearly on.'

But about what? London was receiving its heaviest bombing raids since the dark days of the Blitz three years earlier. Perhaps that's what this was all about? At the turn of the year it had seemed pretty clear that the Germans were on the back foot. Italy was out of the war. The Soviets were remorselessly pushing forward on the Eastern Front. Cities across Germany were being nightly pulverised by thousand plane RAF and USAAF raids. The once-invincible *Scharnhorst* had joined the *Bismarck* at the bottom of the sea. By air, land and sea terrific blows were daily being dealt to the enemy. Surely it could only be a matter of time before they threw in the towel? But now, as the death toll in London mounted, such confidence seemed seriously overoptimistic – a premature blossom, touched with frost. Could this reassessment be sufficient to explain the scale and rapidity of the changes going on around them?

Joan thought not, and decided to pop along the corridor and ask Hartshorne's secretary to see what she could find out. Her desk too was vacant. Hearing her enter, the Chief Mechanical Engineer called out from his office, the connecting door to which was ajar.

'Can I help you, Miss Fraser?'

'Sorry to disturb. I was just looking for Miss Jennings.'

'On leave.'

'As a lot of other people seem to be.'

'Always the way, this time of year. Come on through. What did you want her for?'

Joan pushed the door open wider and entered somewhat warily. She found the Chief Mechanical Engineer an austere and forbidding presence at the best of times. Hartshorne looked like he hadn't slept in a week or changed his clothes for days and was carrying all the world's worries on his shoulders. 'Is everything all right, Mr Hartshorne?'

'Apart from the war, you mean? And the inability of anyone other than Miss Jennings to make a decent cup of tea? Yes, everything's fine. Now go and find something to do.'

'"Either you have work, or you have not. When you say, 'Let us find something to do,' the mischief then begins."' Joan recited, prompted by nerves more than thought.

'I beg your pardon?'

'It's, um, poetry. From India. Tagore. Well, my translation of him, anyway.'

'Is it?' he asked, with a wintry smile. 'Say it again.'

Joan repeated the couplet.

'A very wise man. You and Dr Ray really don't have work now, do you? And we don't want any mischief. Take the next few days off.'

'Well, we still do need to…'

'Starting now.'

Akaash had been thinking for a while that a drink with Cyn and her father might be timely. He had been avoiding them, in large part because he'd been preoccupied with his personal problems since Christmas, but also because he'd decided that the less he saw of and spoke with the Abbots the better he could avoid having to make any mention of them in his reports to Curtis. Now, there seemed little alternative.

He waited for them until they emerged from the Works among the mass that flooded out after the 4.30 hooter that announced the end of the working day, and invited them to join him for a post-work beer at the Tap. Joan, lost for something to do and with a massive admiration bordering on hero worship of Cyn's authentic yet refreshingly unintellectual struggle for equality, tagged along uninvited.

Cyn too had noticed the unusual steps being taken but had similarly been assured that they were no more than a combination of last-minute leave-taking and sensible precautions given the ongoing 'Baby Blitz'. Her father was not convinced.

'I've been Inside twenty-five years. Never known it like this before. People take leave this time of year, but everyone knows that, so all education and training, any off-site working, it's all postponed. Always. This year more people than ever are on leave and yet dozens more are being sent out for various reasons. Don't make sense.'

'It does if they know there's going to be an attack on the Works,' said Akaash. 'I think Management are making sure that all their key people will be well out of the way when it does.'

'Keep your voice down,' warned Abbot, glancing around.

'Well, I suppose they have to take reasonable precautions?' Cyn said, voice lowered and glancing around as her father had. 'Just in case. You never know.'

'No, I believe it's much more than that,' said Akaash. 'I think they do know. And its going to be soon.'

'How could they?' Joan wondered, thrilled at being in a genuine working-class pub among real Trade Unionists at last and keen to make a contribution.

'Because they've been told.'

'That's crazy! The Works are critical to the war effort,' Joan protested. 'If the powers that be knew it was going to be hit, they'd stop it. Say what you like about Churchill – Tonypandy and Bengal and all that, the man's a swine, we all agree – but Mr Bevin is a friend of the workers, surely? He'd never allow anything to happen to somewhere like this. It must be just a precaution, as Cyn says,' she concluded with a comradely smile at her.

'But one that only applies to the bosses,' said Akaash. 'Not to the working man.'

'Or woman,' added Cyn automatically.

Abbot Senior, whose regard for Akaash's intelligence and left-wing credentials was matched by his profound distrust of the prime minister and all those in power, did not share Joan's conviction. 'I knew Ernie Bevin before the war, Miss,' he told her. 'He's a Union man all right and was a good party man – then. But he's a minister in a national government now. One of them. Not one of us.' He took a sip of his beer, then looked at Akaash. 'What do you think we should do?'

'Call everyone out,' Akaash replied. 'Empty the place. What Management has done for their people, we should do for ours.'

'Hang on,' Cyn said, holding up her hands as though she could physically halt a discussion which seemed to her to be rapidly running out of control. 'You're asking our dad to declare an unofficial strike? Weeks, days, before the invasion?'

'It's all right, Cynthia,' her father began, but she cut him off, for the first time in her life.

'No, dad. Sorry, but it isn't! I respect Akaash as much as you do, but he's not the one who's going to be getting it in the neck this time. It'll be you. Remember how they treated him when all he did was support Shop B coming out? How they treated me? Christ, I was spat at in the street! Now, we're talking about the whole of the Works, not just one Shop. There'll be in a right two and eight, and you know it! Look how they cracked down on the striking miners in Kent and Scotland – arrests, fines, prison. They'll crucify you, dad.'

Joan took a deep breath and was about to launch into a speech in support of Akaash, but Cyn turned on her. 'This is between me and our dad, love. Why don't you and Akaash piss off and talk foreign to one another for a while?'

'No call to be rude to a guest, Cynthia, and no call for blasphemy, either. What would mum think if she could hear you? Anyway, all I can do is call out Carriage and Wagon. It'd be up to the other convenors…'

Cyn sighed. 'You know they'll follow you, dad. They always do. 'Cos everyone trusts and respects you.'

Her father smiled and patted her hand. 'You're a good girl, Cynthia. I'm proud of you.'

'Proud of you too, dad,' Cyn murmured in reply. Then she glanced across at Joan and Akaash who, having stepped away as she'd asked and were now standing in pointed – and in Joan's case, piqued – silence a few feet away. 'I don't want your reputation destroyed if this isn't right.'

'Why would he lie?' her father asked, following her gaze.

'I'm not saying he's lying. And I know he's as clever as a wagonload of monkeys. But he could still be wrong.'

The tallyman, sitting in his usual corner, smiled to himself. Finishing his drink, he slunk out of the bar and scurried off towards the police station. At least he could get one of these bloody foreigners banged up. And that self-righteous prig Abbot too with any luck. He knew defeatist propaganda when he heard it. Curtis could have this one for free.

Thirty minutes later, the tallyman's written statement in front of him, Curtis rang Dawlish.

'It's Dr Ray. The Bengali?'

Dawlish sighed. 'I do know which one he is.'

'Well, he's agitating for a strike.'

'What a troublesome little fellow. What's he got a bee in his bonnet about now?'

'He thinks there's going to be a raid on Swindon.'

'What on earth makes him think that?'

'Apparently he can read the signs.'

'Goodness, the Eastern Mystic now, is he?'

'No. The signs he's talking about are twenty-four-hour fire-watches, key staff sent off and all War Office work closed down and shipped out.'

There was a long silence. 'Let me call you back. Stay by the blower.'

It was always a bad sign when people like Dawlish decided to try and speak like everyone else, Curtis thought. He was right. Within twenty minutes, Dawlish was back on the line.

'Arrest him. Right now.'

'For what?'

'Good God, man! You are Special Branch, aren't you? Make something up. I'm on my way,' he snapped and slammed down the phone.

Curtis held the phone away from his ear and shook his head. 'Duty sergeant!' he shouted. 'Who's around? We have an arrest to make.'

Vincent retuned to No. 23 after a long afternoon with Lapworth in the otherwise deserted Movements office to find a car parked outside the house. The front door to the house was open. Inside, a stranger, whom he assumed was the driver of the vehicle outside, sat at the kitchen table sipping tea and reading a newspaper.

'Lady of the house is upstairs,' the man said, not lifting his gaze from his *Daily Mirror*.

Vincent ran upstairs to find Sally desperately throwing clothes into a suitcase – one of Billy's, he noticed – the usual contents of which had been upended onto the floor. 'What's wrong?' he cried.

'Oh, Vincent, thank God you're here!' She threw herself at him and held him tightly. 'It's Miss Grigg. She's gone into labour! Weeks premature. Oh, why didn't I have a bag ready?'

'You're going? Right now?'

'As soon as I've got this stuff packed. That's their car outside. I've made the driver a cup of tea. He's come all the way from London! As soon as I've sorted myself out, he's driving me up to Cheshire. Says it'll take hours. Can you make sandwiches?'

'Of course I can. Shall I come too?'

'Travel ban?'

'Yes, yes. Of course! Sorry. Just…this isn't how we thought this would go, is it? I wish we could be together. I really feel…'

Sally stopped tossing underwear and shoes into the suitcase and looked at him.

'Sandwiches?' she reminded him sternly.

'Of course,' said Vincent, rapidly retreating to the landing. 'Jam or cheese? I think we might still have a tin of that Spam from Billy's hamper…'

'Really?'

'OK. Not the time. Sorry. I'll just decide for myself, shall I?' He realised he was rambling. There was so much he desperately wanted to say to her, yet she was so totally focused, so single-minded that he knew he was little more than an aggravation. 'OK. I'm on it.'

'Good. And a flask. Tea.'

The arrest took place as Akaash was escorting a somewhat hurt Joan from the Tap to the station for her train back to Oxford. This was not as chivalrous as it might sound given that it simply involved crossing from one side of Station Road to the other, but she was glad he'd opted to accompany her rather than stay with the Abbots. She had been full of questions, deductions and hypotheses that she expressed in the rapid amalgam of Bengali and English that had become their lingua franca.

When the two police officers approached them, she was excited, frightened and determined, all in equal measure. Her active involvement in radical politics at university, in the rarefied atmosphere of Oxford, had involved little risk of a confrontation with the forces of the law. Convinced now that together they had uncovered a plot, and having drunk real beer with true workers and an Indian nationalist to boot, she felt ready to take on the world.

Had both the officers been male, or the arrest taken place earlier in their shift, it might probably have ended better. But one was a policewoman, fed up with rubbish jobs and hours of patronising comments and pitiful innuendo. She was desperate to prove herself on the streets and to date had had precious little chance. A mouthy Trotskyite with a posh voice was the answer to a uniformed maiden's prayer.

'Excuse me, officer? Perhaps you'd care to explain on what authority…'

That was as far as Joan got before a harsh slap across the face silenced her. Utterly stunned, she staggered back, wide-eyed and gasping for expression. Akaash took a step forward and the male officer placed a restraining hand on his arm. 'Easy…' he warned.

'That station, home and a nice, warm bed,' snarled the policewoman, indicating the building behind her with a thumb over her shoulder, 'or our station, strip search and a night in the cells. Two choices, dearie. One chance to get it right. You decide. Now.'

Joan, stifling a sob, headed meekly to Platform 1 and the 18.45, bitterly aware that in doing so she was not only betraying Akaash and the cause but all her better angels. Her cheeks burnt from more than that painful and degrading slap.

She did not look back. She was not to know that she would never speak to Akaash Ray again. In any language.

'Feeling all right?' the young policeman asked his female colleague as they walked along Station Road, one on either side of Akaash.

'Yes, I am actually. Why?'

'You don't think that was a little…heavy-handed?'

'No, I don't. Stuck-up bitches like that really get on my… nerves. Acting like they own the bloody world. *"Excuse me, officer…"*,' she mimicked, catching Joan's excessively precise pronunciation so well her colleague couldn't help but grin. 'Who does she think she is? Cow.'

'Can't say fairer than that. Quick drink when we get off?'

'Oh, all right. But just the one. And no hanky-panky, mind, Percy Evans, or you'll get what I gave her.'

'I wouldn't dare.'

They suddenly realised that they had fallen a pace or two behind Akaash, who, knowing his way to the police station all too well, had strode on ahead. They tried not to be too obvious and, as briskly as dignity would allow, increased their pace to catch up with him.

Billy was feeling wretched. He'd kept his appointment in Bath alone. The Americans outdid themselves. Attentive and professional, shifting him briskly from trauma specialist to chief surgeon to muscle damage consultant to physiotherapist. It was not just because they were determined to do their part to make up for the unprovoked attack on him that he received such attention – it was also that they had absolutely nothing else to do except repetitive practice with dummies to perfect their readiness to receive the anticipated large numbers of invasion casualties. A sentient being to interact with was for all involved an absolute delight.

Although they made a huge fuss over him, even getting two of the three Andrews Sisters impersonators who'd joined the Christmas party in Swindon to come along and say hi, there was little of practical value that they could do to aid his recovery. The care that he had already been receiving had been exemplary. He was young, well-nourished and strongly built. Risk of infection was long past. His wound had scarred over nicely and he was healing well. They provided him with a course of medication unavailable in Britain, recommended an exercise regime based on the 'Dynamic Tension' principles popularised by Charles Atlas and cautioned him against becoming reliant on the walking stick he still constantly used. Then they offered him coffee and doughnuts, loaded him up with supplies plus a card from the medical orderly who'd assisted at Derek's post-mortem for Dr Falk and, with the promise of more medicines to follow and an invitation to return any time, drove him to Bath Spa station for his return journey to Swindon.

Billy wasn't sure if he was hoping or fearing that he might see Mary at the station. He was thoroughly ashamed of himself. He had behaved, he told himself over and over, like a complete shit. Unforgivable. He checked the medicines in at the station luggage counter and mooched aimlessly around Bath for a while, deciding a later train might be best.

He was also a little thrilled at the prospect of delivering all those donated medicines, as that would mean an opportunity to see Dr Falk.

Vincent saw Sally off, kissing her on the cheek and murmuring his best wishes, promising to pray for the mother and child and urging her to ring the Movements office whenever she could. She was so preoccupied that she barely acknowledged his presence as she dived into the car beside the driver and urged him to go.

'Might be a bit more comfortable in the back, missus,' the driver suggested.

'Just go,' she cried.

The driver turned to face her. 'Not until you're in the back,' he said firmly.

She leapt out swearing and Vincent rushed to open the rear door for her.

'Get out of my way,' she screamed at him. 'Satisfied now?' she snapped at the driver.

'Absolutely,' he said as they pulled away.

Vincent stood silently watching as the car headed towards the end of the street. Then it pulled to a halt, Sally got out and ran back to him. 'I'm so sorry, Vincent,' she cried. 'I've been horrible, I know.'

'Just go,' he urged. 'Go on. And bring Little Ern back home. I'll be waiting.'

For some reason, she glanced at the house. Their home. Then she smiled at him, kissed him quickly on the cheek, ran back up to the car and left.

She would never see No. 23 Ashton St again.

It wasn't Curtis to whom the two officers handed Akaash over when they arrived at the police station. It was to a man Akaash had last seen when he'd first arrived at Southampton harbour.

'I have to hand it to you, Dr Ray. You're a very smart young chap,' Dawlish observed, lighting a cigarette. 'Possibly a tad too smart for your own, and everyone else's, good.'

Akaash sat in the interview room in his usual seat, determined not to speak. Or cough. Dawlish paced back and forth behind him like a caged tiger.

'You were overheard speculating to all and sundry that His Majesty's Government knows that the Works are about to be targeted by German bombers?'

'I don't deny it.'

'That makes life a little simpler. Let's just suppose for a minute that you were right.'

'I knew it! I knew…'

'Calm down. This is one of those theoretical exercises that you academics so enjoy. I said suppose. Suppose we did know that a raid is coming with sufficient certainty to adopt all the measures you say we have taken. How? How could we possibly know?'

Akaash paused. Not because he struggled to find an answer – he had already worked out the implications of all he suspected – but because he knew that he needed to choose his words carefully. Yet he couldn't resist what might be his final chance to demonstrate the quality of his mind and the clarity of his thought.

'There are only two explanations,' he said. 'One, you have spies in Germany who are telling you these things. Two, you're intercepting and reading their communications.'

Dawlish sighed. 'As I said. Too clever for your own good. Now, this is neither a yes nor a no to either of those suppositions, but let's hypothesise a little further: if either were true, if by one or other of those means we knew in advance that a critical facility like the Works was going to be bombed, why wouldn't we have cleared the site ourselves?'

Their eyes met. Dawlish smiled and nodded.

'You're wise not to say anything. A strategy I'm sure we all wish you'd adopted earlier. But as this is just between us, I'll say it for you. Because if we did learn in advance about a raid, it would be absolutely vital that the enemy never found out that we know. That means that sometimes, we have to take the hit, even if we know it's coming. A terrible responsibility for whoever has to decide when to act on what we know and when to let events take their course. I thank the Lord it isn't me. We were willing to sacrifice hundreds of thousands of your people to deny the Japanese resources if they invaded Bengal. We stand equally ready to sacrifice a factory, a town, and a few hundred of our own when we must. Total War means Total War.'

He crushed the stub of his cigarette into the tin ashtray screwed to the table in front of Akaash and immediately lit another. 'Now you have created something of a problem, for us and for yourself. We have to assume Jerry has agents here too. What happens when they report that the Works very conveniently came out on strike just before they decide to bomb it? Our source is threatened with exposure. Just when every bit of our secret intel will be vital to the success of the invasion. All because of you. We can't allow that to happen. The strike has to be stopped before it starts. And you need to be silenced.'

'What are you going to do?'

'What indeed? If we were the Germans, or the Russians – goodness, probably even the Americans – this would all be so easy. They know just how to deal with people like you. A quick show trial if we really felt it necessary, down to a cellar with a bag over your head if not. Either way, bang! Problem solved. Unfortunately, we're too bloody decent for all that.'

'You're going to kill me.'

'Do try to pay attention. I just told you, we don't do that kind of thing. Au contraire, we'll be letting you go in an hour or two. Unfortunately, an Irishman of your acquaintance is at this moment in somewhere rather quaintly called the Glue Pot. He's busy sharing evidence of the payments we've been making in your name in Calcutta and telling everyone you've been acting on our orders all along. Then he's going to suggest to the more hot-headed of your comrades that you, a traitor to the cause exposed to be on the government payroll, are a risk that ought to be, how shall we put it, neutralised. If all goes to plan, they'll be waiting for you when you're released.'

'You're going to kill me,' Akaash repeated.

'Not me. Not us. I told you, we don't do that sort of thing.'

He stood directly behind Akaash, leaned forward and spoke quietly into his ear. 'Unless of course you could be persuaded to do the decent thing? Save everyone a lot of unpleasantness? I think a glass of whisky and a loaded revolver is the traditional offering, but there is a war on.' He placed one hand on Akaash's shoulder and with the other, took a length of strong bailing twine from his own pocket and slipped it into Akaash's. 'Oh, and sorry to be the bearer of sad – or happy, depending on your outlook – news. But just in case it helps you make up your mind, Phyllida Grigg suffered a miscarriage yesterday. A huge relief to all concerned, I imagine. Except the Rosarios! Poor things. All that trouble for nothing. Now, I need to be off. Wouldn't do to be here when…well, when what we know is going to happen, actually does.'

Vincent was at a loss for quite what to do. He washed up the cup and saucer the driver had left on the table, made a cup of tea for himself, folded up and stacked the pile of Billy's clothes Sally had dumped on the floor, then tried to read the driver's discarded newspaper but simply couldn't focus. He realised that he only had the vaguest idea what the implications of Phyl going into labour weeks before her due date might be. He knew it couldn't be good, but as to what the chances of the child surviving were, he had no clue. Even if it did, what were the possible consequences longer term? Again, no idea.

He was not comfortable being so ignorant about something so crucial. He threw the newspaper aside, snatched up his coat and strode off to the Mechanics Institute reading rooms to find out all he could about premature births.

Curtis stood at the door to his office, jacket off, arms crossed, leaning against the doorframe as Dawlish emerged from the interview room. 'All done?' he asked conversationally.

'Yes. Seems I overreacted. Sorry to have caused so much inconvenience.'

'No inconvenience to me. What do you want us to do with him now?'

'Hold him for another two hours, then let him go.'

Still leaning against the doorframe, Curtis watched Dawlish leave. Then he pushed himself upright and sauntered into the interview room. 'He's a bit of a prick, isn't he?' he said amiably to Akaash, who was coughing into his hand. He sniffed the air. 'Smoking in here too, when I specifically told him about your bad chest. I don't know. Here, take my handkerchief and come on through to my office.'

'What's happening outside?' Akaash asked, his voice croaking and hoarse, once they'd settled in Curtis's cluttered office.

'Nothing much. Arthur Abbot is working himself up into a lather about us arresting you. There's an extraordinary meeting called for tonight at eight in the Glue Pot. You tell me what's going on, young Bish-Bash.'

'There's going to be a raid…'

'Yeah, I know all about your ability to predict the future. I meant with Sonny Jim from London?'

Akaash said nothing. He put his hand into his pocket, felt the ball of twine and was about to tell all when the desk sergeant knocked and asked for a word with Curtis.

When Curtis returned, he looked profoundly sad. 'This was handed in at the desk for you,' he said, tossing a small, heavy bag onto the table. The bag fell open and a number of small silver coins spread out.

Akaash looked mystified. 'What is it?'

'Tanners. Sixpenny bits. At a guess, fifteen bob's worth.' Curtis paused. 'No? Thirty pieces of silver? The Judas price? I'm surprised they're willing to stump up so much for a cheap – well, not so cheap – gesture. They must be in funds. Unless it was given to them.'

'Who left it?'

'Who do we know who believes in the cause and knows her Bible?'

'Cynthia Abbot?'

'Afraid so. Sorry, son. There's this too.'

Curtis handed over a beer mat. On it, in capital letters, was scrawled 'BENCHAT'. Akaash tossed it onto the table beside the coins.

'Any idea what it means?' Curtis asked.

'No, no idea.'

'OK. Well, I'm told we can let you go around nine but I think we'll hang on to you for a while longer, if that's all right with you.'

Akaash looked at the money, which seemed to glow with the contempt in which he knew he must now be held. By Cyn and all the rest of his erstwhile comrades. He looked down again at Cyn's enraged attempt to recall and transcribe on the beer mat Billy's Hindi insult from the time when Shop B came out on strike. Then, she'd stood with her hand on his shoulder. He felt the dead weight of his oh-so-trivial betrayals crush down on him. The shame of ruining Phyl's life and the tragedy of the death of a child he never wanted but now, knowing it was gone, he truly mourned. He wrapped his hand around the suddenly comforting rough twine in his pocket.

'Fine by me.'

The meeting in the Glue Pot was, even for the yet again renamed Working Men's Collectivist Movement, unusually fractious. The Irishman had done his work well. Almost everyone present was convinced that Akaash had from the outset been an MI5 agent placed in the Works to infiltrate the Union and undermine the wider socialist cause. Demands and resolutions proposed ranged from motions of censure, sending him to Coventry to dismissing him from the Union with ignominy. A quiet hardcore group said little but resolved to visit far more extreme retribution on the traitor.

There was an uncharacteristic and intensely painful difference of perception between Abbot father and daughter. Cyn felt the sting of Akaash's betrayal far more intensely than anyone else present. For her, this was profoundly personal. She had invited and inducted him into their Union, embraced his as a comrade, invited him into her home, eaten with him, drank with him, listened to him, trusted and respected him. Christ! She had even stood shoulder to shoulder with him against the drunken Yanks in the Tap. And all along, she now realised, he must have been laughing at her. She could visualise him smirking as he shared tales of her gullibility with his political masters.

The thirty pieces of silver had come from her own money. Her dad had invariably fished a sixpenny bit out of his pay packet on a

Friday for her when she was little before handing the rest over to Mrs Abbot and receiving his beer money in return. She'd assiduously saved the coins for the annual school outing and trip, keeping them safe from the depredations of her brothers by hiding them, wrapped in the bag she'd handed in at the police station, at the back of her knickers drawer. She kept up the habit of putting away a sixpenny bit a week once she started Inside. It was because she wanted to both hurt Akaash and punish herself for being so bloody naive that throwing the most emotionally precious of her possessions in his face seemed so fitting. She'd tried her damnedest to remember what it was that Billy had called Akaash and wrote the best approximation to it on a beer mat snatched from the bar downstairs. She was furiously, scorchingly angry.

Her father on the other hand was far more phlegmatic about the so-called revelations that the Irishman had confided. He wasn't totally convinced of either the credibility of the messenger or the message. He'd wondered how such conveniently packaged evidence had come to be in the hands of a supposedly dangerous republican terrorist at just such an opportune time. Seemed all far too pat to him, but no one else seemed to want to pause and wonder with him.

Abbot Senior may only ever have been out of Swindon for the annual trip to the seaside, but he had been around long enough to know that things were never quite as straightforward as everyone else would like them to be. And he'd always prided himself on his ability to spot a wrong 'un, which he was pretty sure was precisely what this Irishman was. Just as, despite all the hullabaloo going on around him, he felt in his water that Akaash was all right. He was also becoming convinced by all this argy-bargy that Akaash's suspicions were more valid, not less. Now, its proposer so thoroughly discredited, calling the strike would be almost impossible. But he still believed it to be the right thing to do.

He looked across at his daughter, her face set in anger. He tried to catch her eye, but she was wholly absorbed in the raging debate about Akaash. Quietly, he eased himself out of the meeting, nodding towards the gents when anyone looked around questioningly to see why he was on his feet and heading for the door. Once outside, he walked alone into the silent Works and to the Chief Mechanical Engineer's office, where he was not at all surprised to discover Hartshorne dozing in an armchair in the otherwise deserted building.

He knocked and waited in the outer office as Hartshorne woke and gathered himself together. The Chief Mechanical Engineer hadn't shaved for two days and his clothes were crumpled. His collar had detached itself from its stud but without a mirror in the office and no one to point it out to him, it had gone long unnoticed.

'Abbot? What are you doing here?'

'Want to consult, Mr H,' Arthur Abbot replied gruffly. He respected and admired the Chief Mechanical Engineer as much as any man, but decades in the Union had inculcated in him only one way to speak to Management – tersely.

Hartshorne was clearly glad to have any company. 'Well, come on in, man!' he cried. 'How are you?'

'Mustn't grumble.'

'Why change the habit of a lifetime? Only joking! Sit yourself down. Family well? Your Cynthia is a credit to you. As of course are your boys…'

Arthur Abbot frowned. 'What are *you* doing here, Mr H?'

Hartshorne looked around his office. Realising that it would be impossible to deny he'd eaten and slept there for several days, he just smiled. 'You know how it is this time of year. So many people on leave. So much to do, what with the war and all. Just easier than going home. Anyway, what did you want to consult me about?'

'You've sent most of Management away and stopped new engines and rolling stock coming in. You're sitting here like a captain preparing to go down with his ship. Dr Ray thinks the Hun is about to blitz this place. Is he right?'

'I'm really sorry, Abbot, more than you can ever know – but I can't tell you. We all have obligations. Duties. London End says we carry on as normal. That's what I must do.'

'But what should I do, Mr H? Call my lads out like Dr Ray thinks?'

'I can't tell you what to do. Other than to do your duty to those who put you in your place, as I have to do mine.' He paused, scratched his chin and wished, not for the first time, that he'd brought a razor with him. He looked at Arthur Abbot, a man he'd known since they were boys. Different schools, him being Roman Catholic, and never exactly friends, but on the same Scout Troop and of course, together every year on the schools trip. He'd attended one of the Abbot children's christenings – couldn't recall just at that moment which one. The first time he'd ever been in a Catholic church. Old man Abbot's funeral was the second. Nasty business. Should never have happened. If the Banksman…he jerked his head up as he realised with a start his eyelids were drooping and he was drifting into sleep. Reverie, or slipping into dotage? He cleared his throat and sat up straight.

'As you're here, Abbot, did I mention I'm thinking of an across-the-board cut in pay of ten per cent?'

Arthur Abbot grinned. 'Really?'

'Well, I might be tempted to. Unless of course I saw an immediate and emphatic demonstration of your members' unwillingness to accept such a move. What could be more normal than that? London End knows only too well what a troublesome lot you are. Good night, Abbot.'

'G'night, Mr H,' Arthur Abbot replied, getting up to leave. 'Don't suppose I can persuade you to come along with me?'

'I'm afraid not, Abbot. Like I said, we all have our duty.'

'Anything I can get sent in for you?'

'A razor wouldn't go amiss. And if you see your sister-in-law, a flask of her special tea would be very welcome. Two would be even better.'

Vincent felt uncharacteristically in need of company. He wished that he hadn't read quite as much as he did about premature births. He returned to Ashton St but No. 23 seemed horribly empty. Desolate and soulless without Sally in it. He went around to Ernie's and knocked, but there was no answer. Probably was at the Tap, Vincent realised, but he didn't want to go there. He should perhaps go to Christchurch, to pray for the child's few chances of a safe delivery and later well-being, but that didn't feel right either. For the first time he actually craved the company of Billy or Akaash, preferably both. He walked aimlessly towards the Milton Road Baths and then recalled that Lapworth lived a short distance away, on Deacon St. He walked on in darkness towards Commercial Road, past a hardware shop and a builder's merchant, until he came to the junction with Deacon St. He climbed steadily until he neared the north-eastern side of the huge Radnor St Cemetery at the top. He found Lapworth's house, knocked and, breathless from the climb, mopped perspiration from his brow. He was relieved to see Lapworth's surprised smile greet him as the door was opened.

He was shown through to the front room, offered tea with the stock apology of the lack of anything stronger being available, although Vincent knew Lapworth was teetotal. Vincent could hear someone else in the house, clearing away dishes in the kitchen. He assumed it was the man Lapworth shared the house with, the fair-haired man whom he always introduced as his cousin.

'Anything I can help you with?' Lapworth asked after the usual pleasantries about the weather and shared musings on the oddity of the current state of affairs in the Works.

Lapworth was, Vincent noted, a very different man in his own home. He seemed physically larger and much more confident. The hesitation in his speech hardly noticeable.

'Not really. I just felt the need for company,' Vincent admitted. 'Just for a chat,' he added quickly, recalling their earlier misunderstanding.

Lapworth smiled. 'Of course. What would you like to chat about?'

It was the stench of excrement that first alerted Curtis to something being seriously wrong. He flicked open the cover on the peephole in the cell door and saw to his horror Akaash hanging from a noose of bailer twine secured to the bars on the window. Cursing to himself, he fumbled for the key to the door, threw it open and raced in. He took out a pocket knife and cut through the rope, catching Akaash in his arms as he slumped forward and lowered him gently to the floor. Curtis could detect no sign of breathing, although as he stripped away the twine from Akaash's neck and felt for a pulse he thought he detected a very faint beat.

'Shit! Duty sergeant! Duty sergeant!' he bellowed at the top of his voice as he massaged Akaash's neck, hoping that might help get blood and oxygen up to the brain. 'I will not let you die!' he roared. 'You hear me? You do not get to do this in my station! Come on!' He put two fingers into Akaash's mouth to ensure the tongue had not blocked the airway, then turned him onto his side and into the recovery position. Deciding that might not be the best course of action, he flopped him back over again and began to give mouth-to-mouth resuscitation, taking deep breaths and forcing air into Akaash's mouth, inflating then depressing the chest, taking another deep breath and repeating the process, over and over. He took a break to check the pulse again and pleaded, 'Come on, son! Don't go like this. Not like this.' There was no reaction. He wasn't even sure he could detect a pulse any more. His own heart was beating so rapidly he realised that he was probably incapable of feeling anything else. He looked at Akaash's face, grey and bloated, then slapped him hard, jerking his head first to the left, then to the right. 'Come on, you little cunt!' He shouted for the duty sergeant again. Where was the bastard? He pumped the heart with both hands. 'Come on, come on! Don't you dare bloody die!'

There was a cough – weak and faltering, but it was at last some kind of reaction. 'Yes! Oh, you little beauty! You little bobby dazzler, you! Come on!' Finally, the duty sergeant appeared, bleary-eyed, uniform jacket undone, clearly roused from sleep. 'Where the fuck have you been?' snapped Curtis. 'Smelling salts and hot water. Brandy. Blankets. Now! Move! And get the duty doctor.'

Akaash gave a vast gasp, a series of croaking breaths and a desperate, heartbroken whimper. Curtis rolled from bending over him to lying beside him, gasping for breath almost as desperately. He stared up at the ceiling, shaking his head. 'You stupid…what d'you think this would have done to your parents? Made them proud? Was this helpful to anybody? I can't believe you could be so bloody daft. I thought you were meant to be smart. Fuck!'

'You sentenced me to death,' Akaash croaked. 'The day you made me a traitor.'

Curtis turned onto his side, propping himself up on one elbow to stare down at Akaash. 'Grow up! All I've ever done is teach you what real life is like. And it was a free lesson: you gave me nothing in return. You haven't once told me anything that I didn't already know, not once. Even if you had, would it really be worth all this?'

'You've made me everything I despise. In my own eyes. In the eyes of my comrades.'

'For the love of God! Half your bloody comrades are on my payroll. And every single one of them is much better value than you've ever been. And if you're thinking about those toffee-nosed pricks in Oxford you've been meeting up with, you can forget about them too. A bunch of spoilt brats playing at being commies to upset mater and pater. They won't be giving a fuck about you and your lot in ten years' time. They'll be fat and rich and happy, take it from me. They won't even remember your name in six months' time, and you'll forget all about this when you get home.'

'How can I ever go home, go anywhere, with everyone knowing what I am?'

'I'm disappointed in you. I thought you were a great deal smarter, I really did. But you win. I give up.'

In a formal voice he continued, 'Akaash Ray, I arrest you for treason in that you did within the United Kingdom invent, devise, I forget the next bit, something about intent…to deprive or depose his Majesty the King Emperor from whatever, whatever, his Majesty's dominions, etc., etc., in contravention of Section 3 of the Treason Felony Act, 1848. You are not obliged to say anything, but anything you do say will be taken down as evidence and may be used against you in court. There. I've just made you a fucking hero of the cause. Happy now?'

Akaash sobbed. 'Thank you,' he croaked.

'Twat!' sighed Curtis. 'Now where's that duty doctor?'

72

Once he started talking, Vincent couldn't stop. He told Lapworth the real reason for his hasty wedding. Shared his deep concerns about the next few hours and days. Even told him about having made up a family back home. About how he was desperately scared of committing to Sally yet even more frightened of a life without her. He had no idea what he truly wanted because he realised, for the first time that evening, that if he wasn't the fiction he'd created, he was not at all sure that he knew who he really was.

Suddenly conscious of how much he'd said, Vincent smiled uncomfortably. 'I ought to be going,' he said, embarrassed by his own candour. 'Thank you for listening to me. I hope...'

'Not a word,' Lapworth assured him, getting up to see Vincent out. 'You're welcome here any time. I hope you know you have a friend. If you want one.'

'Thank you. I do know that.'

They shook hands. Lapworth was joined at the door by the man he called his cousin and together they watched Vincent as he walked off down the hill.

'Were you earwigging?' Lapworth asked.

'Is the Pope a Catholic?'

'What do you think? Ginger?'

'As a nine-bob note,' the other man concluded. 'Without a doubt. You?'

'As a coot. Poor dear.'

Dr Falk examined Akaash in the cell and immediately insisted on his removal to the hospital. He needed to be under medical supervision for the next twenty-four hours at a minimum, she insisted. She glanced across at Curtis, who suddenly looked horribly pale and sweaty. She took his wrist and checked his pulse.

'You're not here to bother about me...' he protested feebly. Bright lights were bursting in front of his eyes and he felt decidedly woozy.

'Shhh. You need at sit down for a while. Loosen your collar and tie. Sweet tea. You'll move Dr Ray to the hospital?'

'Must we? I'd sooner keep him here.'

'I will not be responsible for his care unless we move him straight away. Anyway, what are you worried about? Look at him: he can hardly breathe. Doesn't look like much of an escape risk to me.'

'You do your job. I'll do mine. Anyway, it's not what *he*'ll do that I'm worried about.'

'He'll be quite safe in my care.'

'Yes, he will. Because he'll have an armed police officer at his side twenty-four hours a day.'

'Is that really necessary?'

'Let's hope not.'

An hour later, Dawlish stormed into Curtis's office, slammed the door behind him and glared down at the policeman impassively lighting up a cigarette. He was white with fury.

'What the hell do you think you're playing at?'

'The proverbial bad penny. I thought we'd seen the back of you,' said Curtis. He was feeling much better, having gulped down the brandy and water finally brought for Akaash rather than the prescribed sweet tea.

'Fortunately for us all I decided to visit a friend at Liddington. I say again: What are you playing at?'

Curtis said nothing. Just drew on the cigarette and let out a long breath of smoke.

'You cut Ray down?'

'Yes, I did. Wonder what made the daft little blighter try to top himself? Wonder where he found the rope, too.'

'Then you charged him with treason?'

'I did. He'll appear before the bench tomorrow morning. Quite an event for us, all this. We've never done a treason summons before. We're still looking up the right form of words.'

'Are you quite mad?'

'No. I'm not,' said Curtis, getting heavily to his feet and facing Dawlish across his desk. 'But I think you might be.'

'Where is he now?'

'In the hospital.' He saw a sudden glimmer of hope in Dawlish's eyes. 'Under armed police guard,' he added. The light in Dawlish's eyes quickly went out.

'They trust you country bumpkins with weapons?'

'They do indeed. They also trust us not to be so fucking stupid as to allow someone like you to use our interview room without making sure one of us was listening at the door. Walls have ears, or in this case, corridors do. And you don't get to use my town to commit your crimes and sucker my people into being your killers. You want to see this lad strung up, that's up to you, but you'll do it legal and proper. Through the courts. There'll be no lynch mobs here. Not in my town. Not on my tic. Not on my tab.'

'There's a bigger picture…'

'There always is. It's what your type always use to excuse all sorts of bollocks. And please, don't bother lecturing me about Total War either. That lad is under the protection of the State now, in the form of the Wiltshire Constabulary – specifically, me. And if any harm should befall him, I'll know where to come looking. And I will come looking. That's a promise.'

Dawlish looked as though he were about to threaten, curse and list the dire consequences of Curtis's actions, but then he suddenly changed tack. He smiled, and for the first time, Curtis felt troubled. 'We always win,' he purred, almost sympathetically. 'You know that, don't you? We just can't help ourselves. That's not even a promise. It's a statement of fact.'

He turned towards the door, still smiling. 'Goodbye Inspector. We won't meet again. But trust me, I shall follow your future career with interest.'

At 11 p.m. those on the night shift in the Works were instructed by their Shop Stewards to down tools and walk out. Within thirty minutes the site was left to those exempted by local agreement from industrial action: fire-watchers, the emergency maintenance team, the fire brigade and the skeleton gang needed to keep the furnaces from cooling and cracking. Dozens of men and women thus remained but were spread so thin over the vast estate that the place seemed deserted.

Hartshorne took a torch and a tin hat and wandered around his cavernous empire, reflecting on how much of his life he'd spent Inside. Without conscious intent, his steps led him to where it had all started so many years ago – Shop B. He pushed the doors open and shone his torch around.

If this was all about to be destroyed, he wanted to say a last farewell to a Bulldog.

Another torch beam was dancing around the empty shed. 'Who's there?' Hartshorne called. He was not at all surprised at seeing the person who stepped out of the shadows. 'What are you doing here, Mr Keenan?'

'Same as you, I reckon, Fred.'

'You should be at home. With our Edie.'

'Sent her off to Nana G's in Bassett. Told her to take the dog too. They'll be safe enough there.'

'Hope so. How is she?'

'Good, thanks.' Keenan took out a hip flask from his breast pocket. 'Fancy a nip? I've been saving it for the final victory, but tonight seems as good a time as any. And this as good a place.'

Hartshorne shook his head. 'Suit yourself,' said Keenan and took a swig. 'Whew!' he gasped. 'Bites back when you've lost the habit. A ten per cent pay cut, Fred?'

Hartshorne remained stony-faced. 'Just an initial consideration of the matter.'

'Well, it seems to have cleared out the night shift PDQ. Almost like that was what you wanted.'

'I'd take a dim view of anyone suggesting such a thing. What engine is that?' he asked, indicating a huge shape almost lost in the deep shadows towards the back of the shed.

'3414 *Albert Brassey*. Came in just before the ban.'

'*Albert Brassey*! I had no idea! Where on earth did they find her? When was she rolled out? 1903?'

'End of '02. Came off the line with *Edward VII*,' Keenan replied as they walked together towards the latest arrival. He began to chuckle. 'You remember young Jerry Wittington? How he got all upset when he thought he wouldn't get to sound her whistle? Burst into tears. Nearly wet himself.'

'Only because you were being so mean to him. Teasing him like that.'

'It was just a bit of fun.'

'He didn't think so. Whatever happened to him?'

'Vimy Ridge. Never found the body.'

'Of course. Stupid of me. Well, this old lady has survived. She'll probably survive us all. Much need doing?'

'Not much. In pretty good nick, all things considered. Hey, you remember Spooner?'

'What, Sammy Spooner?'

'Yeah…'

And in such reminiscences, they spent their final hour before the sirens sounded.

73

The plaintive, undulating wail of the air-raid warning began forty-two minutes after midnight. It was hardly unexpected. The town had prepared for just this eventuality in practice after practice, drill upon drill over the preceding years. The population were as ready as they could be and, thanks to

Akaash, Arthur Abbot and Fred Hartshorne, much more alert and widely dispersed than they would otherwise have been.

Those who had a role assigned snatched up gas masks, helmets, armbands and equipment and rushed to their designated positions. First-aid posts were set up in church halls and public buildings. Trestle tables were folded out and stacked with bandages, cotton wool padding and dark bottles of iodine. Camp beds were set up in rows with grey blankets folded at their foot. Shelters were readied in cellars and underground stores to accommodate those without an Anderson shelter at the bottom of the garden or a Morrison indoors. The Air Raid Precautions teams, the Home Guard, the Women's Institute and the Salvation Army all braced themselves for action. Police, ambulance and fire services followed well-understood protocols.

For the police, this included – rather unnecessarily given the continuously sounding siren – several officers cycling around their designated patches with boards hung from their shoulders emblazoned with the words 'TAKE SHELTER' at both front and back. Among those cycling was Percy Evans – one of the two police officers who had arrested Akaash – for whom it was turning out to be quite a day and night. The promise of a drink with his female colleague was now postponed, but he had been trusted with a weapon for the first time, and had stood guard over Akaash at the Medical Fund Hospital until a properly trained firearms officer was found to relieve him. Sadly, he'd had to abandon both post and weapon in favour of bike and signboard. There was, after all, a war on, and he was finally doing his bit, that too during an air raid.

Billy had opted for the last Up train, knowing it was scheduled to arrive shortly after the final Down of the night which would be taking Mary home to Cardiff. In fact, if both ran on time, they'd pass one another just west of Chippenham. Not that timetables meant that much when all military traffic was given priority. Inevitably delayed, it was just as the sirens began that they arrived in Swindon. The platforms were deserted and disembarking passengers were brusquely urged to hurry up so that the train could be on its way. Billy was now very much aware of the weight of the bag of medicines he was carrying. If this raid warning was the real thing, these needed to be taken to the hospital. He discarded his stick and hurried off.

Vincent was alone in No. 23 when he heard the sirens. He quickly dressed, threw on a coat and ran out into the street. A Warden shouted at him to head for the shelter and pointed the way. He went to knock on Ernie's door but the Warden shouted again, telling him that No. 21 was already cleared.

'Sure?' Vincent asked.

'Positive,' the Warden replied. 'Now go!'

Without looking back, Vincent followed his neighbours to the shelter.

In the hospital, all patients who could safely be moved were walked, or their beds pushed, to their allocated secure area. Wards were prepared to receive the casualties that would be sent on from first-aid posts. Patients who could not be moved – of whom there were only three, including Akaash – were left in the care of a junior nurse whilst her more experienced and senior colleagues readied themselves for the arrival of the seriously injured.

The first wave of bombers could be heard approaching from the southeast at 1.07 a.m. The first stick of bombs fell on Drove Road, the second in the Brick and Tile Works and the third around Holy Rood Church on Groundwell Road. All were incendiary bombs and did little damage, most burning away harmlessly on waste ground, in back gardens and on roads. A few fell on buildings but of these the majority failed to penetrate tiled roofs. Four houses and a storeroom were set ablaze. Casualties were few and injuries minor.

Searchlights picked out the bombers, and they were identified as Dornier Do 217s. 'Pom-Pom' anti-aircraft guns on the hill above Wroughton and out at the Supermarine factory in Stratton opened up. Fighter squadrons from 10 Group were scrambled.

Curtis, with no specific role to play in the event of a raid, manned the station so that his uniformed colleagues could be about their duties. After it was all over, he'd have lead responsibility for the proper identification of the dead and for dealing with looters, but at that point, as he heard the bombs fall and the guns fire, he was frustratingly unoccupied. He saw Percy Evans dash in, deposit his signboards and race out again. Curtis called after him, wondering what the hell was going on – he was meant to be guarding Akaash at the hospital – but there was far too much going on for the young Evans to hear him.

The second stick of bombs were high-explosive and did far more damage. Falling on Farnsby St and Exeter St, they demolished several houses and killed a family of four as a result of a direct hit on their shelter. Numerous injuries were sustained, several serious.

There was a pause in the bombing for four or five minutes. It was during this lull that the Irishman slipped into the hospital and made his way to the tiny isolation ward where Akaash lay, sedated. He paused, absorbing the detail, then grinned as his eyes fell on the discarded pistol. Next to it lay a scrap of paper torn from a police notebook on which was scrawled 'Police Property. Do Not Touch.' Savouring the delicious irony of faking a successful suicide attempt with a police-issued revolver, he carefully draped a clean handkerchief over his upturned hand, then picked up the weapon, placed the muzzle under Akaash's chin and, leaning back and turning away to avoid too much blood spatter, pulled the trigger. Nothing. Again. And again. Nothing. Cursing, he broke open the gun. Every chamber empty. He closed the revolver and carefully placed it back where he had found it and then, returning to his original plan, eased the pillow gently from below Akaash's head.

The lull ended with more incendiaries raining down into the Carriage and Wagon side of the Works. Fire-watchers threw themselves at the bombs, getting water and sand over them before they could ignite. The Works' fire brigade extinguished several small fires that broke out where inaccessible bombs had ignited, but they were unable to save the Carriage Stock and Varnishing Shop which roared into flames and would blaze furiously for many hours. Much damage was done but no casualties were sustained.

Billy arrived at the hospital to be greeted by the terrified junior nurse left in charge of Akaash. Billy had got to know her well during his own stay. Wide-eyed, she ran to him. 'Thank God you're here. Dr Ray…' She told him about the Irishman who had pushed past her, and pointed down the corridor even as the building shuddered from the blasts of high-explosive bombs. Billy ran in the direction indicated by her and threw himself through the door. He leapt on the man bent over the bed, dragged him away, threw him against the wall and punched him over and over.

He couldn't believe how good it felt finally to be hitting someone. The Irishman, recovering from the shock of the furious onslaught, fought back. A lucky blow to Billy's wounded stomach sent him staggering back, roaring in pain and half falling as he stumbled into the bed. He pushed himself upright and readied himself for another attack.

'Yer belly troubling you there, so?' smirked the Irishman, spitting out blood and similarly squaring up for a fistfight. 'There's a pity.'

He feigned two quick jabs at Billy's head and as Billy pulled back, launched a kick at his stomach. Billy retreated further.

'You're the one who got himself knifed, I'm guessing? I got no beef with you, pal. Let me do what I have to, you can walk away.'

Curtis rushed in, swinging his left foot to take the Irishman's feet from under him. 'You're. Fucking. Nicked.' he snarled, punctuating each word with a kick to the prone man. Adding a final 'Cunt,' with an accompanying shoeing for good measure.

'Me?' gasped Billy, holding himself up against the wall.

'No, not you, idiot. Jesus!' said Curtis, dropping to his knees, rolling the groaning Irishman onto his stomach, sticking a knee into his kidneys and deftly snapping handcuffs onto his wrists behind his back.

'You need a hand with him?'

'Do I look like I do?'

'I don't suppose I could just carry on punching him, could I?'

'Absolutely not! He's in my custody.'

The Irishman spat out a stream of threats, demands and obscenities, ordering Curtis to take a card from his wallet and call the number written on it immediately.

'Mind you, I haven't properly cautioned him yet, so technically… OK, I'll look the other way while you kick him. But only once, mind. So I suggest you make it a good 'un.'

'Thanks,' said Billy, swinging his foot back. But then, as the Irishman resignedly curled himself up into a ball in readiness to receive the blow, he lost his appetite for it. Instead, he walked over to Akaash and satisfied himself that he was still breathing. 'What the hell happened?' he asked.

'Now's not the time,' Curtis replied. 'Just make sure he keeps living.' He picked up the revolver on the bedside table and looked down at the man on the floor.

'An empty weapon?' the Irishman cried incredulously. 'You guard your man with an unloaded gun? And a guard who runs away? What kind of fucking amateurs are you?'

Curtis chuckled. 'The kind that wouldn't trust a willing but not terribly bright lad like Percy Evans out with a loaded firearm. The kind that's going to charge you with attempted murder.'

Before the Irishman could respond, Curtis dived for the floor as four bombs fell in quick succession on Shops U and J. Billy sheltered Akaash with his body. Dust fell from the ceiling and the lights flickered, went out and then came back on.

Curtis got to his feet. 'He all right?' he asked, indicating the still unconscious Akaash.

'You tell me. He seems to be still with us.'

'For the moment. I need to get this piece of shit into a cell. You ever handled a gun?'

'Since I was twelve.'

'Good,' said Curtis, feeling in his pocket for the cartridges he'd brought with him. He picked up the pistol, loaded the brass shells into the chambers and then offered the weapon to Billy. 'I'm appointing you Special Constable. Raise your right hand.'

Billy, confused, did as Curtis told him.

'Repeat after me: I do solemnly and sincerely declare and affirm that I will well and truly serve Our Sovereign Lord the King in the office of constable, without fear or affection, malice or…'

The pattern of explosions was moving further away from the hospital, upending the 1902 balanced turntable between the Pattern Store and the Stripping Shop. Curtis and Billy both ducked. 'OK,' said Curtis. 'Let's just agree you're duly sworn. Stay with young Bish-Bash. I'll be back as soon as I can. On your feet, Paddy…'

Two more bombs fell, rupturing the Down line eighty yards east of Rodbourne Road.

In the Works, Hartshorne strode out of Shop B, spread his arms and glared up into the night sky. He raised his right arm, as though in a Nazi salute, then turned his palm, bent his elbow and made the 'V' sign up at the bombers. 'My Works? My Works, damn you? Damn you to hell!'

Keenan ran crouching out into the yard, one arm protectively over his head and grabbed Hartshorne. 'Bloody hell, Fred, you mad old sod!' he shouted as he hauled the resisting Chief Mechanical Engineer back towards Shop B. 'Get back in here!' More bombs fell further away, taking down the corner of Shop A.

After a while, it seemed like the worst might be over. But one final bomb fell on the alleyway behind Ashton St.

The raid ended at 1.31 a.m. Whilst fires were tackled and the wounded cared for, all remained on maximum alert, ready for the next wave. It never came. After another hour, and a phone call from RAF Middle Wallop, the All Clear was sounded.

By the time Vincent was let out of the shelter and reached Ashton St, the Air Raid Precaution wardens and a group of tin-hatted volunteers were already there. The bomb that had fallen in the alleyway behind the odd-numbered houses had severely damaged Nos. 19 to 25. All still stood, just, but their roofs had collapsed in and their walls were cracked and bulging, leaning out precariously in several places. All the other houses on the street had shattered windows. Those on the opposite side of the road had their roof tiles completely stripped from their eaves.

Ashton St itself was a mess of bricks, shattered tiles, shards of glass, broken furniture and ripped timber. The fire engine couldn't get through, nor could the ambulance. Both, in any case were fully occupied elsewhere. Water spurted out of shattered mains and there was a strong smell of gas. Smoke and dust hung over the ruins, but as yet, there was no fire. There was the odd creaking, the occasional sound of falling masonry and a tinkle of shattered glass, but otherwise a strange silence pervaded. Vincent ran towards the remnants of No. 23 but was ordered back by the single police officer present.

'That's my home,' cried Vincent. 'I don't know where…'

'It's OK. Calm down,' Percy Evans said, trying to sound in charge. He was ridiculously young, Vincent thought, looking more like a Boy Scout in a uniform several sizes too large for him. 'Everyone's accounted for except, um, Mr Norris in No. 21. Whereabouts currently unknown.'

'He's in there! Why won't anyone listen to me? I'm telling you he's in there!' He turned to see Elsie, dust-covered like everyone else. She looked like she'd powdered her face and hair with flour, through which tears had cut streaks down her cheeks. Beside herself with worry and anger, she was shouting to everyone and no one. 'You gotta go in and get him,' she insisted. 'He's in there!'

'Ernie's inside?' asked Vincent. 'Under that lot?'

She seemed to find comfort and strength from seeing Vincent. 'Yeah, silly bugger,' she sniffed. 'Went in there to get a bottle of his bloody wine. He's in there. I know it.'

The Chief ARP Warden walked over, looking grim. He shook his head sadly.

'Can I go in?' Vincent asked him urgently. 'Can I try and find him?'

'Well, I'm not authorising entry until the gas is shut off. That lot can go at any time. But I can't stop you. I can only tell you it's a bad idea. A very bad idea. And I'm not sending anyone in to get you out if you get yourself into trouble. I've got a responsibility to my lads.'

'I understand. Can someone give me a torch?'

They handed him a torch as well as a first-aid kit, a tin helmet and a canteen of water. 'You sure you want to do this? Very well. Put a wet cloth over your mouth and nose. Stay low, move slow and make sure you keep your exit route clear. If you feel yourself getting light-headed, come straight back out,' instructed the Chief Warden. 'And good luck.'

Cautiously, Vincent approached the wrecked hallway. The front door was hanging on one hinge and he eased it aside. 'Stay low!' the Chief Warden shouted. Vincent raised a hand in acknowledgement of the reminder, dropped down on to his hands and knees and edged his way carefully towards the kitchen. 'Ernie?' he called out. 'Ernie? Can you hear me?'

He thought he heard a low moan, but it was immediately drowned out by a rending sound above and a series of agonised creaks and groans as the weight of the collapsed roof on the floor above stretched the tolerance of the timbers above his head near to their limit. Vincent realised that the warning and reservations of the Chief Warden made sense. The entire building could come down on him at any moment. The air was so thick with dust that he could hardly breathe and the torch beam didn't penetrate far.

He took out his handkerchief, poured some water from the canteen over it and then tied it round his mouth and nose, wishing he'd paid more attention to the advice he'd been given and done this outside. It provided a little relief but his mouth and nose still felt full of gritty brick dust. He blinked and he could feel it like sand in his eyes. He was painfully aware of broken glass and shattered china under his hands and knees.

'Ernie?' he called out again, and this time he was sure he heard a response ahead of him in what remained of the kitchen. He crawled on along the hallway, easing himself under a wardrobe which had dropped through from the floor above and come to rest tilted at an angle with its doors half open and a mass of clothes hanging out of it. The kitchen door lay flat and he crawled over it to see into the ruins of the room. He could hear water gurgling out of pipework and smell the sulphurous reek of coal gas.

The torchlight picked out Ernie trapped beneath the sink and draining board – which had been blown from the wall – and a Welsh dresser from beneath which just his head and one shoulder and arm protruded. Vincent's first feeling was one of relief. He felt pretty sure that he'd be able to shift the wreckage sufficiently to get Ernie out, and even if he couldn't, he hoped he could persuade some of those outside to come round and enter the house from the back to help him. But as he raised himself into a crouch and got nearer, he saw the blood – a dark, congealing pool that spread from beneath the wreckage that trapped Ernie.

Their eyes met and he could see resignation in Ernie's eyes, which seemed abnormally bright and large in a pallid face slicked with sweat and coated with dust, dry blood caking around his mouth and nose.

Ernie turned his head slowly and painfully. 'Blimey,' he croaked. 'Look what the cat's dragged in.'

'That's what Derek Atkinson said,' Vincent whispered, his voice hoarse from the dust.

'Well, this is probably gonna end the same way. You'd best piss off out of it, while you can.'

'I can get them to come in the back and get you.'

Ernie groaned, and turned away. 'Not happening. I'm skewered. On fuck knows what, but I've seen enough blokes gut-stuck to know this only ends one way. Good of you to try, but you need to bugger off now.'

'Do you want some water?' asked Vincent, offering him the canteen.

'No, I don't want any fucking water, thank you very much! Don't suppose you got anything stronger? No? Didn't think so.'

He tried to raise his head but the effort seemed too much.

'There was a bottle of the 1937 Elderflower and Blackberry under the sink. That's what I came back in to get. I suppose Jerry got that too?'

Vincent shone the torch around, but amid so much shattered glassware it was impossible to work out which was the remains of the bottle that Ernie had come looking for. 'Looks like it.'

'Bastards! How could they miss the bloody Works and hit my house? Worse than the Yanks.'

'Actually, they hit the alleyway behind our houses.'

'That's meant to make me feel better?'

'No, of course not. Sorry. Guess we'll never know whose onions would have done best.'

'Bollocks. We both know it would have been mine. Your oppos OK?'

'I think so. I heard say at the shelter that Akaash is back in custody.'

Ernie tried to laugh but the pain was clearly too much. 'That boy's spending longer as a guest of the King than I did at his age. Captain Toilet Cistern?'

'Still in Bath, as far as I know.'

'Young Sal?'

'She's safe.'

'She's a good girl. Just made some bad choices. Make sure you're not another one. Treat her decent.'

'I will.'

'Till you head home?'

'Yes. Until I head home. Elsie's outside.'

'Christ, that's all we need! Right, now you really have to get out of here. This lot's coming down any minute, and I'm feeling very cold, and it's getting dark. And I think I know what that means.'

Very slowly, Ernie raised his right hand. 'That was quite a night. In the Works. With Derek.'

'Not one I'm likely to forget,' Vincent assured him, taking Ernie's hand in his. Ernie chuckled, which brought on a coughing fit. After it had passed, he seemed noticeably weaker. 'Shame we couldn't give him his Viking funeral, eh? Leave me a cigarette and some matches.'

'Ernie, the gas…'

Ernie treated him to a long stare. 'I choose my time, and I choose my way. Don't make me ask twice.' Vincent handed over the packet but Ernie told him to just take out one. 'That's all I'll need,' he assured him. 'Put it in my mouth. Now off you go, my old mucker. And remember what I said about young Sal.'

As Vincent carefully made his way back out, he heard Ernie start to sing. Quietly and quavering at first, and then with greater strength. It wasn't a song he recognised.

'The sun had set beyond yon hills,
Across yon dreary moor…'

Once outside Vincent was surrounded by people asking about Ernie. He just shook his head and looked over at Elsie. 'I'm sorry,' he said quietly. 'He's not coming out. He wouldn't make it. He said, well, he sends his love.'

But she wasn't listening to him. She heard the singing and her bottom lip quivered with pride. It was clear that others too knew the song. Some paused and looked up. Some shook their heads and smiled in sad wonder. Vincent was suddenly desperately tired and taken with a violent shivering. A blanket was thrown over his shoulders and he was led away. Someone washed his face with cold water and started picking shards of glass and splinters from his ruined hands, which Vincent was dully surprised to see were dripping blood.

Elsie, with tears streaming down her face, got as close as they would let her to the door, and then fell to her knees and sang.

'Weary and lame, a boy there came,
Up to a farmer's door.'

Two or three of the volunteers clearing rubble also paused and began singing too. Before long there were six, seven, then ten voices joined in chorus.

'Can you tell me if any there be
That will give me employ…'

Vincent felt a lump of emotion, a deep comradeship and an all-engulfing wave of belonging at the sound of these rough voices that sang so tunelessly yet so beautifully. He wished he could join in.

'To plough and sow, and reap and mow,
And be a Farmer's Boy?'

The Chief ARP Warden held up his hand and the voices trailed away.

'Vincent? Elsie?' Ernie shouted. 'Can anyone hear me?'

'I can hear you, love,' Elsie cried out, and had to be restrained from trying to get into the house.

'Elsie, you got a copper out there?'

Percy Evans made his way forward as two ARPs dragged a struggling Elsie back.

'No. 716, PC Evans. I'm here.'

'Young Percy?'

The policeman looked round, clearly uncomfortable, and then said, 'That's right, Uncle Ernie. It's me.'

'Right, listen careful, Perce. You gotta get everyone well back, 'cos this lot is going to blow in a minute.'

Percy looked round, clearly bewildered and unsure quite what to say or do. No one would meet his eye.

'Get them back, Percy. Tell 'em, Vincent. I've chosen my way.'

Vincent leapt up and shouted, 'Get back! Everyone, back!'

Years of practice in so-called 'feigned raids' for just such a night as this had sharpened reactions. The warning cry was echoed and repeated as they all ran back into the road. An ARP Warden threw his arms around Elsie and stumbling, half dragging her, shielded her with his body. Vincent dragged Percy Evans to the ground.

'Right, I'm lighting this fag. God bless the King and…'

'Down, everyone! Get down!' the Chief ARP Warden bellowed as he dropped to a crouch and wrapped his arms over his bent head.

There was a dull boom, and the remains of No. 21 seemed to lift and expand slightly, as though it too was taking a final breath, before collapsing in on itself with a deafening rumble, clatter and crash, dragging down a large part of No. 23 with it. Clouds of dust and smoke rose. There was a final tinkling and a shiver of a sound, like hailstones falling on tin, and then deep silence broken only by the sound of Elsie sobbing.

'Jesus Christ! Ernie Norris, you always were a mad bastard!' muttered the Chief ARP Warden as he stood up and dusted himself off. 'Anyone hurt?'

'Not me,' someone called out.

'All good,' another voice added.

'Cuts and grazes,' shouted a third. 'Nothing serious over here.'

'For Christ's sake, will someone get that bloody gas turned off?' The Warden looked across at the stunned Percy, sitting where Vincent had pulled him down, and fixed him with a flinty stare. 'You all right?' he called.

'I...I don't know,' gulped Percy.

The Chief Warden walked across to him, offered his hand and pulled him up on to his feet. 'Get a hold of yourself, son,' he whispered, gently. 'Remember the uniform you're wearing. Right?'

Percy nodded.

'Good man.' He looked across at Vincent. 'OK, you. There's nothing more you can do here. You're just in the way. Oh, and you might want to take this with you,' he added, taking a photograph from the breast pocket of his overalls. 'One of the lads found it in the street outside No. 23. Thought it might be yours.'

The Chief Warden shone his torch on the image. It was the one of the older couple everyone had assumed to be Vincent's parents. Vincent glanced down at it, then shook his head. 'Not mine,' he said.

'No? Oh, well. Get yourself off to the first-aid post, and for God's sake take her with you,' the Chief Warden said, indicating the prostrate Elsie.

'That song...' Vincent said as he helped Elsie to her feet.

'Regimental song of The Splashers,' she said, through sobs.

'S'right,' the Chief Warden said, folding the photograph carefully and putting it back in his pocket. 'Most of us served with Norris in the last lot. He was a bloody lunatic even then. You got her?' he asked, nodding at Elsie.

'I've got her.'

'Off you go, then.'

Vincent arrived at the hospital shortly before 5 a.m. He'd left Elsie at the first-aid post, where his hands and knees – and a graze on the side of his face of which he'd been totally unaware and had no idea how he'd received – were cleaned up and temporarily dressed. One particularly vicious wound to his left hand would require stitching, so he was referred on to the hospital for non-urgent attention.

He arrived to find a line of walking wounded ahead of him and learned from the same nurse who'd directed Billy to Akaash's rescue that his oppos were there. He left the tired and dusty queue and walked to Akaash's room.

'What in God's name…'

Billy yawned. 'Arsehole tried to kill himself, then I had to drag some demented Irishman off him and now I'm a Special Constable. You?' he asked, nodding at Vincent's bandaged hands.

'Ernie's gone. Our home too.'

Billy shook his head sadly. Vincent leaned his aching back against the wall behind him and slid slowly and painfully down until he was sitting on the floor with his wrists resting lightly on his grazed knees. He started laughing, a sour, humourless chuckle. 'This isn't how this was meant to end, was it?'

Billy grunted his agreement.

Vincent nodded at the weapon. 'You know what you're doing with that?'

'Why does everyone assume I don't know how to handle a gun? Of course I do.'

'Better than you know how to fix a toilet cistern?'

'Very funny. Is, er, Mrs R OK?'

'Sally? She's safe. Or at least I think she is. Gone to be with…' He glanced at Akaash and lowered his voice, 'The baby's come early.'

'There's no baby,' Akaash croaked. 'The baby's dead. Gone.'

Vincent tried but failed to get back up. 'What? How do you know?'

'They told me. The man. From the docks.'

'Dawlish?' frowned Billy.

'Yes. I'm so sorry,' Akaash sobbed painfully.

'He really needs to pull himself together and all,' Billy muttered, recalling Elsie's advice to him. 'The big girl.'

Shortly before 7.30, after two hours of trying and failing to sleep, Curtis called in at the hospital to check on Akaash's condition. Behind him marched a burly policeman carrying a Lee-Enfield rifle and looking like he would love the opportunity to show that he knew how to use it. The wards were full of injured people, the corridors blocked up with their relatives. Later, he would go to the mortuary at the Victoria Hospital up on the hill with Dr Falk in her dual capacity as police surgeon and de facto town pathologist. Together they would check that the dead had been properly identified, sort out arrangements for any post-mortem examinations deemed necessary and, with the agreement of the coroner, subsequent burials.

But before that, there were three things he was determined to get done. The first was ensuring that Akaash was safe.

He found Billy sitting on the foot of the bed with the revolver in his hand. Vincent was dozing in the chair.

'Halt! Who goes there?' Billy demanded, leaping up.

'Very funny. Never point a weapon at another officer.'

'Don't worry. The safety's on.'

'The last words many a man has heard. How's young Bish-Bash?'

'Who? Oh, Akaash? Rallying, Monica says.'

'Monica?'

'Dr Falk. He came to, briefly. Said...well, that Colonel Dawlish had spoken to him.'

'I know,' Curtis said. 'And Rosario?'

'Exhausted.'

'Looks it. The hero of the hour, from what I hear. Went in to try to get Norris out when no one else would. OK. You're relieved, Special Constable Khan,' he added, holding out his hand for the gun. 'Point the bloody thing at the floor and hand it over grip first! Blimey! Constable Orr will take it from here. You eaten?' he asked, once the revolver was securely in his hands. 'No? OK, get along to the police station and tell them I said you're to have breakfast in the canteen. Then get your head down for a couple of hours. I recommend one of the cells. The section house has been turned over for temporary accommodation and it's full of screaming kids...'

He paused as the Works hooter sounded for the first time that day.

'Sounds like I need to get to work,' said Billy.

'You'll be better at the station,' Curtis said. 'The cells are empty. Except for one profoundly pissed-off Mick.'

'This is the BBC. Here is the news, and this is Alvar Lidell reading it. Last night the Wiltshire town of Swindon suffered its heaviest bombing of the war to date. Substantial damage has been done to its historic Railway Works, considerable parts of which are likely to be out of action for some time. The main line between London, Bristol and Cardiff has been severed. There is no information as yet on casualties sustained. The government has announced an immediate

ban on all rail travel west of Didcot. This ban will remain in place until further notice.

Few of the attacking aircraft made it back to Germany. An undisclosed number were destroyed by Spitfires and Hurricanes scrambled from across the west of England.

In other news…'

Hartshorne turned off the radio as the hooter blasted out its second wailing summons across the town. He looked out of the window at the workers starting to return. The strike had been promptly called off on assurances that talk of a pay cut had all been a misunderstanding. More than a few muttered about some jiggery-pokery but no one complained. Turning back, he surveyed a dusty, bandaged Vincent standing in his office beside a slightly less-dirty but equally exhausted-looking Keenan and a pristine, fresh-faced Miss Jennings.

'Sounds a lot worse on the wireless than it looks out of that window eh, Chief?' Keenan observed. 'Bloody London! No idea what they're talking about. As per.'

'I think that's the plan,' Miss Jennings concluded. Keenan looked confused.

'That broadcast's not for us,' Vincent explained. 'We want the Germans to think that they've done more damage than they really have.'

'Might not do any harm to make it look that way,' mused Hartshorne. 'Let's not be in too much of a hurry to repair the damaged shops. Shift work around the site as necessary. Pile up all condemned material that will burn around the place and get some fires going. You'll see it done, Mr Keenan? Good. Any word on the Down line?'

'Permanent way have possession. Reckon they'll be ready for testing and hopefully slow running by tomorrow evening.'

'Well, I'm sure they can do a great deal better than that. Whatever they need…'

'You heard about poor old Ernie Norris?' Keenan asked.

Miss Jennings nodded. 'Such a shame.'

'Mind you, we'll probably see a significant drop in losses to pilfering now,' Hartshorne observed dryly. 'I apologise,' he added hastily, feeling the sting of a severely disapproving glance from his secretary. 'That was unworthy. And you've lost your house too, Mr Rosario? I'm so sorry.'

At that moment, the loss of No. 23 was not Vincent's primary concern.

'I need to get to Cheshire,' he said. 'Straight away.'

'I'm afraid you're not going anywhere,' Hartshorne replied. 'You and Mr Lapworth are currently our entire Movements office. You need to start rerouting across the region immediately. We've got God knows how many Americans sitting at Newport and Cardiff in trains that should have been on the move hours ago.'

'Give me twenty-four hours,' pleaded Vincent. 'It's my wife. I think...she's lost our baby.'

'I'm deeply sorry to hear it, but I don't have twenty-four hours to give you. There's a...'

'Yes, I know,' sighed Vincent, resigned. 'A war on. Can I at least use your telephone?'

'Happily, if it was working. The lines are down. You want to call your good lady in Cheshire?'

'Yes. I must know what's happening.'

'Of course. You have an address for her?'

Vincent shook his head. In the rush of Sally's departure, neither had thought it necessary. Vincent wasn't even sure that she knew where she'd be putting up.

'I just know she's in Cheshire. Sir John Grigg arranged it all.'

'Grigg? Well, well, well. It will mean asking a favour or two of the LMS, but we must all make sacrifices. Dictate the message for your wife to Miss Jennings and I'll make sure it reaches her.

You have my word. Now, for goodness' sake, man, get to work! If ever we needed your special skills, it's now. And where's Mr Khan? We need engines! We have a schedule to keep, a railway to run and a war to win! YBE, Mr Rosario! YBE.'

The second of Curtis's tasks took him to the Abbot's front door. Arthur Abbot answered.

'Ah, the Papist Prole,' said the policeman amiably. 'Not going in today?'

'About to.'

'Our Dr Ray was right about the bombing. Bright lad, that.'

'There's more than a few seeing today who wouldn't have been but for him. Where is he now?'

'In hospital. Tried to kill himself. Any idea why?'

'No. What's going to happen to him?'

'Well, I've charged him with treason, so if he survives, we'll probably end up hanging him. But in the meantime, I'm going to make sure that he's kept out of harm's way. Any of the comrades still intent on doing him any harm, advise them to think again. From me.'

'Anything else?'

'Yeah. I've also charged an Irish friend of yours. With attempted murder of said Dr Ray. I'm disappointed in you, Abbot. Thought you were a great deal smarter. Oh, and give this back to your daughter,' Curtis added, pulling out from his pocket the bag of coins Cyn had left at the station. 'That was a mean thing she did to him last night. You put her up to it?'

'Not as mean as all you done to him, from what I hear. Can I see him?'

Curtis shook his head.

'Then we're done. Never come to my door again. You and I have a need to speak in the future, send a man in uniform.'

Inside, Cyn heard the door slam. She looked up as her father walked in and, tight-lipped, dropped the little bag of sixpences into her lap. She burst into tears.

'That was small, Cynthia. Petty and, like that swine said, mean. That's not you. That's not my little girl.'

'I'm so sorry, dad!' she sobbed. 'I feel terrible. I'm so ashamed. I drove him to it! He was all alone and all he'd tried to do was protect us, and I…'

'That's enough,' her father growled. 'We need to get to work. I'll walk you in. But for the first – and I hope the last – time, I won't be proud to do it.'

Curtis's final task of the morning more than made up for the unpleasantness of the first two.

He picked up the telephone and asked to be connected to the number on the card the Irishman had told him to take out of his wallet. He wasn't the least surprised to be advised that no such number existed. He asked for the one Dawlish had given him. The same response. He put down the phone with a smile. The rest of the day would be grim, but the prospect of telling the Irishman that his 'Get Out of Jail Free' card – as he'd smirkingly referred to it – mysteriously seemed to have expired was a real joy. He intended to savour it to the full.

77

The next three days in the Works were lost in a fury of urgent repairs, fake damage creation and attempts to get the rest of the place back to something like normal. Hartshorne was everywhere, full of energy. Encouraging, chiding, disapproving, urging everyone to ever greater efforts. He seemed ten years younger than he had before the bombing. Permanent way had the Down line working ahead of schedule. He could start running trains through the town again. His beloved Works had survived and so had he and woe betide anyone, on orders from Berlin or London or anywhere else, who ever attempted to interfere with either again.

Billy returned to oversee work in Shop B and Keenan was dispatched to supervise discreet repairs to Shop A whilst maintaining an outward appearance of disaster. Elsie, deep in mourning and unusually subdued, was temporarily promoted to replace him as Shop B Supervisor. Vincent and Lapworth, everyone agreed, had worked wonders whilst the Down line was out and the Up line subject to severe speed restrictions, rapidly diverting troop trains and munitions shipments with an inventiveness, dash and flair that would enter local legend, to be retold years later with the same awe as the fabled 1892 conversion from broad gauge.

Homeless now, Vincent lodged temporarily with Lapworth and his cousin. Billy moved into the rooms in the Goddard Hotel that he'd retained ever since Derek's return, where a significant part of his luggage had long been stored. He devoted the next few evenings to searching for and asking after Mary, but she seemed to have disappeared off the face of the earth. No one seemed to have the first idea of what had become of her. To his frustration, he discovered that the working girls routinely dissembled among themselves about home addresses. He couldn't even find out where she lived.

Akaash remained in hospital under police guard, gradually gaining strength. He was the indirect recipient of so much goodwill, gifts and gratitude that Dr Falk pined for the calmer days when Billy had occupied that room. Curtis took a perverse delight in letting slip at regular intervals his intention of adding further charges against Akaash, stoking the flames of righteous indignation in the Bengali's favour ever higher.

Vincent received a brief acknowledgement from Sally, assuring him that she was well and would be heading home soon. On the third day after the raid, he received an urgent summons to the Chief Mechanical Engineer's office. On arrival, Miss Jennings beamed at him and ushered him through. Billy was there and on seeing Vincent, raced to him and gave him a huge hug.

'Mr Rosario!' cried Hartshorne. 'You need to get to the station. You're to meet the 14.42 from Cheltenham Spa. Well, what are you waiting for, man? Go!'

Vincent reached Platform 1 just as the 14.42 pulled in. There was confusion, noise, clouds of steam and a platform full of people mostly in uniform, who seemed to have no idea where they were or what was going on. A whistle sounded two sharp blasts and almost everyone reboarded the train. It jerked forward, slowly gathering speed.

The only person remaining on the platform was a woman.

Holding a baby.

Vincent stared down at the child an exhausted-looking Sally held in her arms. It was well wrapped, all bundled up in an excess of pink knitwear and a crochet blanket. Just its tiny face – eyes tightly shut – a wisp of dark curly hair and a minute, perfect hand were exposed. Vincent placed his forefinger under the palm of that hand and felt a totally unanticipated jolt of pure love surge through him at the instinctive and surprisingly strong grip.

'The birth certificate wasn't a problem?'

'No. She's ours in the eyes of the law. Yours and mine. What's happened to you?'

Vincent glanced down at his hands, now much more lightly dressed. 'There's lots to tell you. You heard about the house? Ernie?'

Sally nodded.

'You know, this doesn't look much like any premature baby I've ever seen,' Vincent said, bending forward to kiss the little hand. 'Not that I've seen that many,' he added, quickly.

'She is a very good weight and head circumference,' Sally agreed. 'The midwife said she seems remarkably mature for a thirty-six-week delivery.'

'Do you think she looks a bit like Mr Churchill?'

'All newborn babies do.'

'Really? He was premature, you know? Napoleon too.'

'Been checking, have we?'

'Had to do something while you were gone. It's not as though much has been happening in your absence. Look at these perfect little fingernails. How in God's name do we cut them?'

'We'll manage.'

'She's got Akaash's colouring though, hasn't she?'

'More of it than Akaash has himself. What do you think of the name Erin?'

'I love it. Hello, Little Erin. We're your mum and your dad. Welcome to Swindon. Unusual hair.'

'I thought that. But they say that's just something called lunago – foetal hair. No indicator of what her real colouring will be.'

'Back home they shave that off.'

'Might be wise.'

They stood in silence for a while, looking at their child.

'What are you thinking?' Sally asked gently.

'Well, how can I put it,' Vincent began. 'She's, um, rather more coffee than tea, isn't she?'

They looked at each other and began to laugh. 'Poor Akaash! This country has hardly been kind to him, has it?'

'No. Looks like Miss Grigg's life hasn't been quite as sheltered as her mum and dad thought either.'

Then, still chuckling, Vincent leaned across his tiny daughter and kissed his wife.

'How on earth are we going to explain this?' he asked.

'I haven't the foggiest. What do you want to do?'

'Take our little girl home. If we had one.'

It was several months before the overseas travel ban was lifted. It was another few weeks after that before Swindon's Indian gentlemen were allowed to leave Britain and berths could be reserved on a boat sailing for Bombay. By then, D-Day was long past and the Allies, despite occasional setbacks, were embarked upon their inexorable advance towards Germany. The GWR had more than played its part in the greatest invasion in history, and its three Indian gentlemen had more than done their bit.

Charges against Akaash were first reduced, then dropped altogether following an agreement that he would never speak or write about his activities on the night of the bombing, or how he'd concluded such an attack was likely. Just to be on the safe side, Curtis decided to keep Akaash in custody to ensure that he would be under police protection until he was safely, and silently, back in India.

On a warm late August afternoon, they waited at Swindon station for the train that would take them back to Southampton Docks. It was hard to believe that only a year had passed since their arrival. There was a large gathering – or more accurately, several small gatherings – of people to see them off. Keenan, Elsie, Doreen and almost all of Shop B were there to say farewell to Billy. Officials of the NUR, senior members of the British Communist Party and a delegation of Indian students from Oxford and London universities held banners declaring their support for Akaash and protesting his continued detention and now gagged deportation. Joan, with Arthur and Cyn Abbot, stood at the front of this earnest group. The formal farewell committee comprised the Mayor, the Chief Constable, Lady Jessica, Lapworth (now Head of Movements), Dr Falk and, at their centre, preparing to read a short valedictory speech,

Hartshorne. Local and national newspapers had photographers and reporters present.

Vincent stood with his wife. Their daughter, Erin, lay sleeping in a pram, gently being pushed to and fro. A young woman came to stand silently and uncomfortably beside Vincent.

She glanced down into the pram. 'Yours, Bof?' she asked quietly. Vincent nodded.

'Aaah! Sweet little thing!' she cooed. 'Don't look much like you, though,' she observed.

Vincent caught Cyn's eye as she gave him a sympathetic and supportive grin. 'Funny, no one's ever said that before,' he said, with a nod back at her. 'Oh yes, I remember now. Loads have.'

Elsie came over to join them. 'Well, well. Look what the cat's dragged in.'

Why did people always say that, Vincent wondered. What did it even mean?

'You got something to say about my godchild, Mary Hughes?' Elsie continued, an Ernie-esque threat in her tone.

Mary shrugged. 'Just saying…'

'Well, don't. She's Swindon. You ain't. So you just button it and think on. You ain't all that, young lady.'

What on earth did any of that mean, Vincent wondered. He may have been confused but Mary clearly understood.

'I will, Mrs Coggins. Sorry,' she said.

'Where have you been?' Vincent asked Mary, as Elsie, with a final glare in her direction, returned to the Shop B women, muttering something deeply unpleasant under her breath. 'Billy searched high and low for you.'

'I know. Didn't want to be found. Not by 'im.'

Billy glanced across towards them and his eyes widened. He quickly made his apologies to the reporter he'd been speaking to and dashed across. He reached out to take her hands. 'Mary! Where in God's name…'

'Come to see you off,' she said, taking a step back.

Billy dropped his hands. 'I'm sorry, Mary. I'm so sorry.'

'Forget it. Just come to say goodbye.'

There was a buzz and a roar of support as Akaash arrived, handcuffed to Percy Evans and accompanied by Curtis.

'Oh, damn and blast! I have to go. Can I write to you?' asked Billy.

Mary shrugged. 'S'pose so. If you want.'

Billy leaned forward quickly and kissed her cheek. Surprised, she put her hand up, touching where his lips had been. He gave her a big smile, and then strode quickly to where Curtis was unlocking Akaash's handcuffs. 'I'm entrusting him to your custody, Special Constable Khan. He's to speak to no one other than you and the ship's officers. There'll be someone waiting for him at Bombay. Until then, he's all yours.'

Billy saluted and Curtis shook his head.

'You're sure I can't have a gun?' Billy asked hopefully.

'Absolutely bloody certain,' Curtis assured him as he looked with a wave of affection at his erstwhile informer, who stood rubbing his recently freed wrist. 'Well, young Bish-Bash, I told you I'd send you home a hero: look around. Swindon thinks you're a great man, and your lot back home do too, so I'm told. The brave young patriot, buggered about and generally abused by perfidious Albion.'

Akaash turned to nod to Billy and wave to the Rosarios, then returned his gaze to Curtis, unsure quite what he truly felt, or should feel, for this man who'd used him, doomed him forever, saved him more than once, and now...what? Seemingly secured for him a tenuous redemption in these last few ghastly months?

He took a long look around. Saw the faces of his erstwhile comrades – people who'd embraced him, turned on him, then shamefacedly and belatedly hailed him their saviour. The librarian from the Mechanics Institute. The official farewell delegation. The Shop B women. The demonstrations in his support organised by the Union and the Communist Party. He saw Joan and Cyn waving, desperate to catch his eye. Arthur Abbot giving a thumbs up and calling for three cheers. Sally and Vincent and the pram containing the child once was supposed to be his.

'I hate this place,' he said simply, as the hurrahs died away.

Curtis sighed. 'You're a funny bugger, young Bish-Bash. Remember me when they make you president. In the meantime, try to keep your mouth shut and your nose clean. And for your own sake, don't let Khan persuade anyone to trust him with a gun.'

Leaving Erin – with some apprehension on Sally's part – in Mary's care, the Rosarios walked over to say their final farewells. Billy briefly returned Akaash to Percy Evans's custody and reached out to take Sally's hands in his. His eyes were full of tears.

'"I came to your shore as a stranger, I lived in your house as a guest, I leave your door as a friend",' he recited.

Sally grinned, her heart full of affection for this big, silly, wonderful man. 'That's lovely, Billy,' she sighed.

'Did you just make that up?' Vincent asked suspiciously.

'Good Lord, no! That chap Tagore Akaash is always wittering on about. My new friend Joan taught it to me.'

'Well, you just look after our Akaash,' Sally said, looking past him to smile and nod encouragingly to Akaash as Vincent glanced doubtfully at Joan.

'Don't worry about him. I'm pretty confident the little bugger's going to abscond as soon as we land in Bombay. Can't trust these Bengalis as far as…'

'And promise you'll come back and see us. They reckon we'll have a prefab out Pinehurst way by the end of the year. Come. And stay.'

'Absolutely. And Mary…'

Sally looked away, but Vincent said, 'Of course. I'll keep an eye on her.'

'Until you head home,' Sally murmured automatically.

Vincent smiled. 'Until I head home,' he agreed.

'Not too close an eye, I hope,' Sally said, brightening. She beamed at Billy. 'Off you go. Give this to Akaash,' she added, thrusting a brown paper package of sandwiches towards him. 'And send us a postcard.'

'Thank you. Both. This is for our little angel,' he added, taking the food and quickly squeezing a tightly rolled fifty-pound note into Sally's hand before returning to the reporter he had been speaking to.

Vincent sighed. 'He just can't help himself, can he?'

As the farewells were being made, a gaunt figure watched from the curtained window of an otherwise empty first-class compartment towards the London end of the platform.

Major Usborne, formally known as Colonel Dawlish, marked, noted and inwardly digested a number of important scores yet unsettled.

It was, he reflected with a smile as he lit a Balkan cigarette from an Armenian tobacconist, a very long way to Bombay.

EXHIBIT

Newspaper cutting: *Evening Advertiser*, 27 March 1986

A large crowd gathered at Christchurch yesterday for the funeral of the popular retired railwayman, VINCENT ROSARIO, who passed away peacefully earlier this month, aged eighty-five.

Mr Rosario was one of the 'Indian Gentlemen' seconded to the GWR in the darkest days of World War II and who played a critical part in the run-up to D-Day. Many will know of Mr Rosario's role following the so-called 'Turntable' raid of April 1944. He married a Swindon girl and settled in the town, one of the first from the subcontinent to do so. He joined the Railway on a permanent basis at the end of his secondment and remained with the GWR up to nationalisation. Thereafter he continued to serve the Western Region of British Rail in various capacities, retiring in 1965. He was also known as an accomplished dancer, three times winning the Works' 'Light-foot' Trophy with his regular partner in dance and life, Sally. In later years, he was frequently invited to judge competitions around Britain. He was also well known as a highly successful gardener, his onions regularly winning prizes in the Fruit and Flower Show. He was a long-standing and active member of the congregation at Christchurch.

A funeral oration was given by Sir Gordon Lapworth, with whom Mr Rosario had worked during the war. The 23rd Psalm was read by the recently retired Chief Constable of Wiltshire Constabulary, Percival Evans, CBE, QPM, a long-time family friend.

Among the many floral tributes was one with a card from India. It read simply, 'Heading home'.

As Mr Rosario was laid to rest, the Swindon Works hooter sounded for the last time, after nearly 120 years of service – a fitting tribute to a true railwayman.

Mr Rosario is survived by his widow, Sally, to whom he was married for forty-two years, their only daughter, Mrs Erin Abbot, and three grandchildren, Ernest, William and Cynthia.

A FEW FINAL WORDS

I hope you've enjoyed *Mrs A's Indian Gentlemen*. This is, first and foremost, a work of fiction. Not everything in the story happened as described. I have invented one or two things, conflated some, separated others and changed dates and details when it helped to tell the tale I wanted to tell. I have, however, tried to capture the flavour of the times and be true to the spirit of the town and the voices of the people. As a result, I've used some expressions which, although I've always known what they meant, I have no real idea how they originated. 'A right two and eight' for example I assume is Cockney rhyming slang for an emotional 'state', although I don't know why two shillings and eightpence should be the particular sum used. I guess it just sounds better than 'three and eight'. I don't know and haven't found the origins of 'sod that for a game of soldiers', but know very well it translates into BBC English as 'I have profound doubts about the wisdom or efficacy of the course of action under consideration and am unwilling to commit myself further to it.' But, come on! Which would you rather say?

It was only when researching this story I really appreciated just how different a place Britain was before the significant immigration, sexual liberation or increased social mobility of the decades after the war. Before supermarkets, television, credit cards, antibiotics, plastic bags, mobile phones and the world wide web. Before Swinging London, James Bond, The Beatles, Monty Python, Cool Britannia and Harry Potter. Before the Profumo Affair, the Suez debacle and the uncovering of the Cambridge spy ring. Before balti meals and chicken tikka masala. The past really is a foreign country. They do indeed do things differently there.

Past Britain was a country in which, if you were born into a working-class family, you left school at 14, most likely to work in the same trade, factory or farm as your parents. There, unless you lived in a large city or a seaport, you were unlikely to ever encounter anyone from a culture all that much different from your own. It was a rigidly stratified society in which your interactions with anyone outside your class were limited to terse exchanges about work or the weather. Here, before the widespread availability of contraception and changes in the law and attitudes, children born 'out of wedlock' suffered massive and enduring social stigma, their mother far worse. Here, gay men lived a shadow existence of fake relationships and stern denial under the ever-present threat of arrest, prosecution and public shaming. This generated a language of euphemism and veiled references which appear in the text – limp-wristed: effeminate; a cottager: a man who solicits gay sex in public toilets. The exchange between Lapworth and his 'cousin', as they contemplate Vincent's sexuality hopefully catches this. Is he ginger? Ginger beer: queer. Queer as a coot? Bent as a nine-bob note?

There are also several references in the story to contemporary radio and music hall performers. Most are self-explanatory, but some may be a bit obscure. Akaash on fire-watching duties is mockingly compared to Bud Flanagan (one half of the highly popular double act, Flanagan and Allen) who often donned a huge coat on stage. Vincent, Billy and Sally are teasingly called Wilson, Keppel and Betty on arrival at church. Wilson and Keppel, and a succession of Bettys managed to make a decent living for decades with a simple and still funny routine where the two scantily clad skinny men, dressed in vaguely Egyptian costume, danced po-faced whilst Betty carried out a kind of dance of the seven veils.

Britain began the Second World War as arguably the world's only superpower, pretty convinced it was a force for good in the world. Children were taught that the sun never set on the British Empire as a statement of geography, if not a prediction of the future. Britain ended the war victorious but exhausted. Battered and bankrupt, its leaders uncomfortably aware that its power had been eclipsed by that of the USA and the USSR. Buildings that had stood for centuries lay in ruins and the old certainties no longer seemed so certain: knowing one's place and respecting one's betters simply wouldn't cut it any more.

It is on the cusp of monumental change this story is set.

Given how different that world was I thought there may be some aspects of the story that might benefit from a little context or additional explanation. I've also noted the books I drew on in my research.

Race

There are many excellent books and articles written about attitudes to race in Britain. Stereotypes of 'the other', reflected in humour and song at the time this tale is set focused mostly on fellow Brits. Jocks – the Scots – were either loutish, violent drunks or sanctimonious skinflints. Paddies or Micks – the Irish – were also violent drunks, but mad or stupid too. The Welsh, well, at primary school we were taught a nursery rhyme that went, 'Taffy was a Welshman, Taffy was a thief. Taffy came to my house and stole a leg of beef...' You get the idea. The English were characterised in return by those others as condescending hypocrites who would steal your land and depose your leaders whilst wittering on about English liberty. Oh yes, and then squander your young men's lives in pursuit of their imperial ambitions. Hard to imagine why anyone would think that of the English, but there you are. Whether this was all just good-natured banter among a family of nations or something much less appealing depends on the ear of the receiver. The rest of the world was dismissed in a range of epithets ranging from the affectionate to the patronising to the downright offensive. Some of these terms appear in the text:

Yanks were Americans, Eyeties were Italians and Jerries, Germans. The one thing they all shared was that they were all, poor things primarily, but also irredeemably foreign.

The English reserved their most withering contempt for those of mixed race, as the discussion between Billy Khan and Dawlish about Vincent when they first meet attempts to capture: the smug superiority with which they debate whether he is first- or second-generation Anglo-Indian ('Semi or Demi?'), and Dawlish's repetition of the myth that no matter what the colour of the skin, the mixing of the races reveals itself in blue gums. Elsie Coggins is alert to this attitude to those of mixed race and is ultra-protective of her godchild for that reason: family, community and class, thank goodness, trump race.

The first big wave of foreign immigration, particularly into the west of England, was of American troops – GIs. However offensive British attitudes to race may have been, the visceral loathing with which white GIs regarded their black comrades-in-arms and the elaborate arrangements required to keep them apart came as quite a surprise.

Class

Due to the lack of social mobility, places like the Swindon Works were full of people of all sorts of intellect and talent working side by side, effectively trapped by their class. For some, given the GWR's obsession with promoting from within, the Works was actually one of the few places where a bright youngster could rise (as the Chief Mechanical Engineer had) to the very top. For the majority, frustrated abilities were channelled into breathtaking craftsmanship or found fulfilment in a range of hobbies and interests, many of which the Mechanics' Institute enabled and supported. Among their number was Alfred Williams (1877–1930) 'The Hammerman Poet,' a student of Sanskrit and author of numerous volumes of poetry and prose. The most famous, *Life in a Railway Factory*, was a stark account of working conditions which could hardly have endeared him to the GWR management.

All regarded those of a higher social status with a sort of sullen deference, summarised in the half sneering, half envious reference to Phyl and Joan as 'debs' – short for debutantes, the unmarried daughters of aristocratic families of an age to 'come out' into society in the London social season. In the 1940s, the middle classes – the bank manager, the solicitor, the vicar and the doctor – inhabited a different world to their working-class compatriots. Indeed, in Swindon, they literally lived in a different town: the 'Old Town' up on the hill, whilst the workers occupied the 'New Town' down below.

For those with political ambitions, the National Union of Railwaymen (NUR) offered a way for such workers to influence events through elected office as Shop Stewards or higher-ranking convenors. The Trade Unionist views on history differ markedly from received wisdom. They also have long memories. Even today, Winston Churchill's decision, when Home Secretary, to deploy troops against striking miners in Tonypandy in 1910 is neither forgotten nor forgiven. Such men and women were among those swept to power in the Labour Party's landslide election victory at the end of the war. They were the ones who set about creating the welfare state, including a national insurance scheme modelled on that of the GWR Medical Fund. Mine and subsequent generations owe them a huge debt of gratitude. Without their visionary reforms, someone from my background would never have had the opportunity to go to university. Many would not have survived beyond childhood.

War

It would be hard to exaggerate the impact of the two great conflagrations on the whole of the 20th century in Britain. The cost in soldiers' lives in the First World War (1914–18) was formidable and whilst subsequent accounts of 'a lost generation' were probably exaggerated, the statistics remain truly horrific. The great battles entered the culture as epic tales of heroism and doomed youth: the retreat from Mons; the Somme (the first day of which the British side alone suffered nearly 20,000 dead and a further 38,000 wounded); Ypres; Vimy Ridge. The thousands of memorials erected in village churchyards, towns halls and city parks across the country listing their fallen warriors had barely weathered before, just 20 years after the end of that 'war to end all wars' the country was at war again.

The death toll, at least for British troops in the Second World War (1939–45) was less than half that of the First, but by modern standards it was still profound. Plus, for the first time, extensive bombing destroyed significant amounts of infrastructure and resulted in large numbers of civilian casualties on what was called 'the Home Front'.

For a working-class lad with a sense of adventure, or a pressing need to get out of town, taking the King's shilling (volunteering for military service) has long offered escape. Since the 1880s, the British 'line' regiments were organised primarily on a county basis, of which the Wiltshire Regiment is a perfect example. In this story, not only does Ernie Norris have their regimental badge tattooed on his arm, he sings the regimental march, 'A Farmer's Boy', after the bombing. Reference is then made to their nickname, 'The Splashers'. During the Seven Years War (1756–63), having run out of ammunition, the regiment was forced to melt down their buttons to make musket balls. Thereafter, their buttons bore a special mark, a 'splash' to commemorate the event.

As Vincent observes, among the many impacts of this age of global conflicts, one was of several generations of men tempered in war: men used to handling weapons, inflicting violence and seeing friends and neighbours hurt and killed; men who thought very differently from those of us who have been spared such an experience.

Pubs

At the time this story is set, indeed for centuries before and enduring still, public houses ('the pub' or 'the local') were the hub of working-class social life. For a traditionally reserved and understated bunch, the English certainly go to town when it comes to naming pubs, and nowhere more so than in Swindon, which boasts among its many pubs 'The Roaring Donkey', the 'Moonrakers', the 'Beehive' (which gained national fame back in the 1980s as being the only pub in Britain to employ an academic to philosophise at the bar) and, of course, the 'Glue Pot' and the 'Queen's Tap.' All, I'm pleased to say, still exist, as does Arkells, the local brewery mentioned in the story.

Mid-20th century pubs had two distinct drinking areas: the public bar, or saloon, and the lounge. The former was very much a male reserve, usually sparsely furnished with a bare wood floor, sometimes spread with sawdust to soak up spilt beer. The lounge was more refined, usually carpeted and furnished with tables and chairs. Female customers were more welcome here, although it was a brave woman who entered unaccompanied by a man.

In the saloon bar various games were played. Card games and dominoes were common, as were those involving flipping beer mats, arranging matchsticks or, one of my favourites, placing the palm of your hand on your shoulder, balancing a pile of coins on your elbow them flicking your arm forward and snatching them out of the air. This becomes a great deal more amusing after a few drinks.

Most pubs had a dartboard on the wall in the public bar and a line, the oche (hockey, without the 'h'), painted on the floor precisely 7 ft 9¼ in. away from behind which the thrower must stand. Country pubs might also have a skittles alley and on occasions would hold a 'splat the rat' competition, which I'm afraid was exactly what it sounds like. It remains a popular sideshow event at village fetes to this day, albeit with stuffed and weighted lumps of fake fur dropped through a drainpipe substituting live rodents.

Strict laws licensing the sale of alcohol imposed fixed opening and closing times. There was a set routine as closing time approached. Ten minutes before, the landlord would announce, 'Last orders' and a surge of final purchases would be made. After he had called, 'Time, gentlemen, please!' there was an allowance of a further 10 minutes drinking up time at the end of which the remaining customers were encouraged towards the door with cheery farewells such as, 'On your way. I have a home to go to even if you don't.'

The Railway

Here, I enter dangerous territory. The railway holds a hallowed place in local history. It is a brave/foolhardy author who writes with anything short of awe if he lives in Swindon and is describing the Great Western Railway, but here goes.

The railway was the mid-19th century equivalent of the Internet. An enabling technology which attracted a frenzy of initial investments, empowered previously unimagined communications and forced new ways of thinking about law and society. Railway building was enthusiastic, ill-disciplined and totally uncoordinated, a fact that impacts rail travel in the UK to this day. One of the results of this was that tracks were laid on completely different gauges, which made changing from one railway company's network to another a tortuous affair. More on that later.

By the end of the 19th century, there were well over 200 separate railway companies. The majority of these were amalgamated on a regional basis in the 1920s by an act of parliament into what became known as 'The Big Four', all of which get a mention in the story. The London Midland and Scottish (LMS), the London and North Eastern (LNER), the

Southern Railway (SR) and of course, the most mythologised and romanticised, the only one to retain its former name and impose it on all those which were grouped with it, the GWR: the Great Western, or God's Wonderful Railway.

The railways had their own language: engines were motive power; carriages and wagons, rolling stock; the tracks on which they ran, permanent way; their timetabling, movements. Swindon, as a railway town, used and extended this terminology. Those employed in the Works, worked 'Inside'. From 1880 through to the 1960s, the Works closed down for a week in early July for 'Trip', when special trains took workers and their families to the seaside for a welcome (albeit until 1938, unpaid) holiday. During Trip week Swindon became a ghost town. Pubs, shops and cinemas closed their doors for lack of customers.

Trip only features in this story as a memory as it was cancelled for the duration of the war.

The Great Western Railway was a Victorian employer in the best and worst senses. Sternly paternalistic, socially encompassing, forward thinking in its attitude to workers' well-being and education outside of work, deeply conservative and penny-pinching in its employment practices. As Vincent observes, it grew too fast, absorbed too many other companies, failed to integrate them into itself and maintained anachronistic ways of working long after others had modernised. But for all that, it achieved some remarkable things. Mention of two is made in the story.

Vincent reminds his new colleagues at their first meeting that on 6 June 1932, the *Cheltenham Flyer*, a train hauled by a Castle Class engine designed by the GWR's Chief Mechanical Engineer and built in the Swindon Works, set a new world speed record with a time of 56 minutes 47 seconds at an average speed of 81.6 miles per hour (131.3 km per hour) between London and Swindon.

The other great moment, to which Vincent's later achievements are favourably compared, is the conversion of the last of the GWR 7 ft 'broad' gauge track to the 'standard' width of 4 ft 8 ½ in. At 10.15 a.m. on Friday, 20 May 1892 the final broad gauge train, *The Cornishman*, left Paddington station. On Monday the 23rd, the first standard gauge *Cornishman* travelled the same route at the same time. During the intervening weekend, all remaining broad gauge track had been lifted and relaid. The statistics still have the power to impress: 13 miles of special sidings built in Swindon to receive the remaining 195 engines, 748 carriages and 3,400 wagons designed for broad gauge. 3,500 workers. 171 miles of track. One weekend.

Not long after the war ended, the GWR was absorbed into the newly nationalised British Railways as its Western Region.

Sources which informed my description of life in 1940s Swindon include:

Alfred Williams, *Life in a Railway Factory*. London: Duckworth, 1915.

Molly Lefebure, *Evidence for the Crown: Experiences of a Pathologist's Secretary*. London: W. Heinemann, 1955. Also published as *Murder on the Home Front: The Unique Wartime Memoirs of a Pathologist's Secretary*, London etc.: Grafton Books, 1990.

Graham Smith, *When Jim Crow met John Bull: Black American Soldiers in World War II Britain*. New York: St. Martin's Press, 1988.

Mike Brown and Carol Harris, *The Wartime House: Home Life in Wartime Britain 1939–45*. Stroud: Sutton Publishing, 2001.

Katherine Knight, *Spuds, Spam and Eating for Victory: Rationing in the Second World War*. Cheltenham: The History Press, 2011.

Mike Brown, *Christmas on the Home Front*. Cheltenham: The History Press, 2013.

Susan Major, *Female Railway Workers in World War II*. Barnsley: Pen and Sword Books, 2018.

ACKNOWLEDGEMENTS

A few final thanks.

To the highly professional team at Hachette India who have made the process of converting my scrappy manuscript into this fine-looking book a joy to be part of. To my editor, Ansila Thomas, to copyeditor Tapojoy Mandal, cover designer Mónica Reyes and everyone else involved, many, many thanks. Also to John Wilson for his initial review of the manuscript, suggestions for improvements and for bringing his awesome knowledge of the GWR to bear.

To the Local Studies team at Swindon Central Library for advice and help in accessing their impressive collection of resources on the town and the Works.

To Prita Maitra for her constant encouragement and support, for persuading me to write this at all and for reading and advising on early drafts.

To my business partner 'Sundance' for always supporting my writing, even when its pursuit was to the detriment of our business.

And to my partner in life, Kauser. Writers often say theirs is a lonely occupation but in truth, it's a self-centred business that can only be pursued with the backing, or at the expense, of others. I am remarkably blessed to live with someone who has always offered unstinting encouragement, honest feedback and generous support.

Thanks to you all.

MRS A'S INDIAN GENTLEMEN

Neil McCallum, who writes as Dawood Ali McCallum, has been travelling extensively in India for more than 40 years and has researched, written about and lectured on historical aspects of several of the Maratha princely states. He is the author of four previous novels, *The Final Charge* (2014), *The Peacock in the Chicken Run* (2009), *Taz* (2007) and *The Lords of Alijah* (1997). He lives in Swindon with his wife and two children. Find out more at www.dawoodalimccallum.com.